Behind the Rainbow

K. J. Jones

AuthorHouse™ UK Ltd.
500 Avebury Boulevard
Central Milton Keynes, MK9 2BE
www.authorhouse.co.uk
Phone: 08001974150

© 2011 K. J. Jones. All rights reserved.

No part of this book may be reproduced, stored in a retrieval system, or transmitted by any means without the written permission of the author.

First published by AuthorHouse   5/24/2011.

ISBN: 978-1-4567-7457-8 (sc)
ISBN: 978-1-4567-7458-5 (dj)
ISBN: 978-1-4567-7459-2 (e)

Any people depicted in stock imagery provided by Thinkstock are models, and such images are being used for illustrative purposes only. Certain stock imagery © Thinkstock.

This book is printed on acid-free paper.

Because of the dynamic nature of the Internet, any web addresses or links contained in this book may have changed since publication and may no longer be valid. The views expressed in this work are solely those of the author and do not necessarily reflect the views of the publisher, and the publisher hereby disclaims any responsibility for them.

Acknowledgements

I would like to thank my wife, Jo, for insisting that this novel be finished. Her most telling comment was that, "I have ready many books worse than yours, and they were still printed," how can you deny such logic.

Linda Ann Mills who took on the job of retyping the manuscript and placing it on file such that I could complete the book. Without her help, this could not have happened.

Warwick Smith, who had the unenviable duty to edit the book, and spent many hours reading the manuscript, his input was invaluable.

Geoff Fish for the flying sequences when a Cessna is pitted against a Mig. I took a little too much licence with his advice.

To my friends that read the book and encouraged me to finish I thank them all.

Chapter 1

The herd moved slowly across the plain, basking in the early morning sun following the cold winter night. Dropping their football sized dung and leaving the pungent smell of their urine on the slight breeze. There were thirty-two elephant in the herd, only three bulls, nineteen cows and ten calves, ranging in age from two to ten years.

The matriarch leading the herd was a single tusker and belligerent. She had lost her tusk at adolescence, tackling a tree that was too strong for her young tusks. She was disadvantaged and had to intimidate the other elephants, at times, to get the succulent leaves on the upper branches of the trees.

This had made her the natural leader. She was well past breeding age and wizened like a witch, with deep cracks in her grey skin, but she alone held absolute domination over the herd. She had been the matriarch through twenty-seven seasons. The animals fed slowly, lingering over the tasty morsels from the tops of the trees.

The old bull some fifty years old had travelled throughout Africa and survived several attempts upon his life. His senses, though dulled with age, were still more acute than the rest of the herd, as they had never felt the horror of the hunted. He felt uncomfortable but could not determine why. He had found this paradise set in a crater in Tanzania. He had been chased across Africa from Angola, Zimbabwe, Mozambique and Zambia. He had seen numerous wars that had devastated the lands, and had felt the bullets of the small people with their rifles. This thought made a previous wound itch, and he stopped to scratch himself against an ancient Baobab.

The uneasiness would not leave him, and he raised his trunk to test the wind but discovered nothing. His tusks were weighing heavy on him, and he felt his age. Each tusk was perfectly formed and weighed close on two hundred pounds. He stood seven feet at the shoulder and though now past his prime, was still a magnificent specimen of the African Elephant.

The scars of old wounds and conflicts were visible on his flanks, as also were signs of age. Deep cracks on his skin caused by the scorching African sun, and there were pockmarks where poorly designed bullets or shot had marked his skin. Though old and scarred, he had not lost his dignity or royal carriage. He walked with the natural nobility of the elephant.

He had not been hunted now for ten seasons, since finding this paradise. The local people, though seldom seen, had not been threatening, but he still had an inherent distrust of all men. Their noisy flying things had only disturbed them twice in the last ten seasons, and he had never heard the sound of a rifle since he had been in this crater. The crater that had been created millions of years ago by volcanic activity and left as a consequence a land so rich that growth occurred at a phenomenal speed. The shallow terrain was dotted with acacia and tall Mopani. Ancient Baobab's, three times the diameter of an elephant, pointed their fingered branches skywards.

The plains had lush grass that rippled like cornfields in the wind, changing colour as cloud and light alternately reflected on the edge of the wave created by the wind. Water trapped, in small pans, glistened and sparkled. Towering reed beds and dense bush followed the path of the rivers, giving perfect cover to the Buffalo and Reedbuck. The flora existed in perfect harmony with the species grazing at different levels, such that little was wasted in the crater. Nature had the best design for this paradise.

Two younger askari bulls always accompanied the old bull. They were with him now, feeding some fifty yards away. They had never been hunted in their lives, and though they sensed the old bull's uneasiness, they could not understand the reason why. The old bull himself could not place a meaning to his uneasiness, but had learned through his experience, to take heed of his senses. This had saved his life on several occasions.

Although his eyesight was failing him, he stared intently across the savannah they were traversing. The area abounded with the game; as far as the eye could see, there were Thompson's gazelle, wildebeest, zebra and many other species. Many Giraffes were lazily feeding on the edge of the bush, and the whole area was tranquil and calm. This had been the Africa of two centuries past, before the continent was discovered and colonised by Europeans.

He stood motionless and again tested the wind, but could find nothing. His senses told him all was not well, but he could not discover any reason, yet the sense of dread would not leave him. The herd was moving away from the three bulls, and although feeding greedily, they were putting distance between them. He felt he needed the protection of the herd and trumpeted to his companions to follow him. He moved quickly to rejoin the herd. His companions could not understand his distress and did not desire to leave the area where they were feeding.

They snorted back at him, and refused to leave. He moved across to them, nudged the nearest bull that then reluctantly left his feed, and joined the old bull, as he moved towards the herd.

Captain Petrus Khumalo stared intently at the old bull, as he moved off to join the herd. He had not seen such a magnificent bull since Toshenkwani, in the Kruger National Park, in South Africa. He was disappointed that he could not shoot the bull, but managed to control his frustration. He had with him two members of his unit, Sergeant Obed Khubeki and Corporal Meshack Mnini. They were all members of the now defunct anti terrorist unit, a crack South African military unit, which had been based in Natal.

Captain Khumalo watched with interest as the old bull moved, and wondered why he had shown concern, as he was confident that they had not been winded. He opened his bag filled with dust and poured some dust from the mouth of the pouch. The dust fell almost vertically, indicating that what little wind there was, was moving towards them and away from the old bull. Their cover was abundant and he knew he could not be seen or smelt.

The young bull was still feeding on the roots of an acacia it had pushed over. Captain Khumalo raised his rifle and placed the cross hairs just behind the shoulder, as if aiming for the heart. He moved the telescopic sights back to the tusks and studied the animal intently. The tusks were small and would weigh thirty-five pounds at most. The opportunity was not worth taking, as they would have only two chances at most before they would have to run for the border and the waiting helicopter. He decided it was not worth risking the shot. He moved his hand to indicate silent withdrawal.

The team moved away silently in single file, into the surrounding bush, ensuring that they never broke cover. Corporal Mnini covered their tracks by erasing their footprints with a branch that had been broken off a tree by the Elephants.

They could not afford to be traced or tracked. When they were out of earshot, Corporal Mnini asked.

"Why did the old bull move off; he surely could not have known we were there?"

Captain Khumalo responded, "He is an old bull with heavy tusks; he has not survived so long without using his experience to the full. We have been tracking this herd for seven days; he is probably aware of our presence, even though he has not seen or got wind of us" he added. "He will not be an easy target," he concluded. "We will return to base and try again tomorrow," he ordered.

They moved out silently, each knowing that the need to speak was not necessary. They had been in many actions together and trusted their combined skills fully. Captain Khumalo was the marksman, with an extraordinary ability with a rifle, which was not common amongst the black, armed forces, in South Africa. Sergeant Khubeki was the tracker and Corporal Mnini the radio operator.

They all had cross skills and could cover for each other in the event of an emergency. Captain Khumalo was the natural leader and received total obedience from his subordinates. They had been on many anti terrorist missions in South Africa and were accustomed to laying up for days in slit trenches. They would not move from their trenches even to defecate, and they left no trace of their presence once the mission was completed.

They had accounted for many terrorists entering South Africa from the Swaziland border. They always worked as a team of three, never trusting other members of their platoon, when on dangerous missions. Only Captain Khumalo knew the reason for their presence in Tanzania and Sergeant Khubeki nor Corporal Mnini knew why they were there. Nor did they care, as they had missed the excitement of the hunt since independence in South Africa. There had been brief skirmishes in Natal when they were fighting the ANC members, but nothing to compare with their anti terrorist operations. They had become bored and disillusioned, with little respect for the new regime.

They were a disciplined and deadly unit that reported to no government recognised agency.

They had been discharged from the defence force, mainly for their own safety, as their reputations were well known. The new regime did not like the anti terrorist squads amongst them, as they had accounted for many of their members of Umkhonto weSezwi, commonly known as the MK. There were also tribal differences, as these men were Zulu's.

They reached their base camp, which was gaunt and unrecognisable as any kind of camp at all. They could not light fires as this would leave evidence of their presence; all food was from their backpack rations. The tins and packets were crushed and replaced in their packs. Though they knew that their presence was not known, they lay in hiding 100 meters from the camp for one hour, before even contemplating entry into the camp.

They circled the camp and then, when assured of no adverse reception, they came out of the bush into the base camp. They appeared a dishevelled group, as they had not washed or shaved for seven days. They were indeed camouflaged similar to the wildlife around them. The base camp was set in the bush beneath an old fig tree, whose branches stretched 35 meters in circumference. The ground was bare under the tree, and any evidence of entry would be clearly seen. There was no spoor to be concerned about. Captain Khumalo posted Corporal Mnini as sentry, to ensure no surprises.

They both knew that this was unlikely, but they would never risk such a situation developing. Corporal Mnini moved off into the bush some one hundred and fifty meters from the base camp, to a ridge, which had a panoramic view of the surrounding countryside. It would be difficult to approach the camp without being seen. They rested the day there and took four-hour stints on lookout, each sharing the task without rancour or privilege of rank. They all knew those days were behind them.

At sunset, they set out again to locate the herd with the old bull. Sergeant Khubeki found the tracks where they had missed their first opportunity and followed them until midnight. Sergeant Khubeki estimated that the herd was no more than two kilometres away and settled for the evening.

They would rise at 4 am and be in place at sunrise. As usual when on a mission, they slept fitfully and were constantly aware of their surroundings. At four am they arose and moved off into the bush, clearing all traces of their stay in the overnight camp. They moved in single file down the game track, towards the herd, following Sergeant Khubeki. Sergeant Khubeki signalled to stop with the palm of his hand facing back.

This was their signal for close contact, and immediately care was taken not to step on loose twigs or brush hanging branches. Sergeant Khubeki moved forward slowly and continually tested the wind from his dust bag. He saw that the wind was only slightly in their favour and changed approach to ensure the wind was not blowing towards their target. Captain Khumalo felt the tingle of fear and anticipation when approaching his target. The adrenaline was pumping in the men.

They approached the herd stealthily and sighted the first elephant at six hundred meters. Captain Khumalo checked his rifle to ensure it was loaded and felt for other rounds clipped to his bush jacket. All was in order, and he gripped the rifle tightly in excitement.

The old bull woke from his reverie and again the strange sense of fear overcame him. The young bulls felt nothing of the danger and were perplexed with the old bull's behaviour. They moved closer to him in an effort to comfort him but he would not settle. He raised his trunk to test the air and detected nothing; he scrutinised the bush at considerable length but could see no danger. Yet the sense of uncertainty would not leave him.

The old bull moved into thicker bush and decided to circle to test the wind from all directions. The young bulls followed the old bull into the bush. They moved in a wide circle, and the old bull at regular intervals, tested the wind. He circled like this for an hour, testing the wind, but never breaking cover from the dense bush. He circled again and then suddenly reversed the circling, moving at a fast trot in the opposite direction.

He tested the wind repeatedly, and the dreaded fearful scent of human inhabitants touched his senses momentarily. He screamed with rage and headed for deeper cover in a tangle of brush and acacia. The young bulls now sensed the old bulls fear and anxiety, and followed him headlong into the bush.

The herd heard his cry of rage and looked about them apprehensively, unsure of what to do. The matriarch moved to a position between the herd and the place where the old bull screamed and tested the wind continually. She was an old cow of forty-nine years and had some experience of humans, when culling had been performed. She had seen the horror and shock written on the faces of survivors. She had seen the long-term tension created by these events, and she had seen elephants forced out of the herds due to the unnerving influence of the survivors of a culling operation.

She had sensed it in the old bull when he had joined the herd. It had taken four seasons before he would settle down and not run at the slightest disturbance. The other cows joined her at either side, whilst ensuring the young elephants were protected within the flanks of the herd. The entire herd was now concentrating on the bush from which the cry came. They stood with their trunks raised, and ears extended, a phalanx of elephants waiting to determine from which direction the danger would come as they now knew it certainly would; unsure of how to respond to the danger.

The game on the plain sensed the danger, and as one, stopped feeding and stared intently at the elephants. All eyes were focused on the bush where the apparent danger lay; the tension was electric with fear and trepidation. All the animals tensed, positioned to run at the first sign of danger and attack.

The matriarch moved out ahead of the herd, ready to face the danger. She was angry and afraid, but would not let the herd be threatened. She stamped the ground and trumpeted in rage but could not see or smell the danger ahead of her. She watched the bush closely for any movement, her pig like eyes red with rage. She felt the wind change and immediately collected the scent of humans; she knew instinctively that the herd was in danger and charged with astonishing speed towards that hated smell that brought fear to her species throughout Africa.

The old bull heard her cry of rage and came hurtling out of the thicket in which he was hidden, to see the old cow bearing down on the bush opposite him. He also felt an uncontrollable rage and trumpeted loudly and headed for the same piece of bush.

His ears were flat and his trunk between his front legs. He was 90 metres behind the old cow, and they presented a formidable sight when in full charge.

"Shit!" Captain Khumalo said, "The old bull has got wind of us."

At the first sign of movement, by the old bull they had traversed around and away from him, to ensure the wind was again in their favour. They had not anticipated him doubling back. Now caution was thrown to the wind and survival was uppermost in their minds. They had heard the old bull scream and saw him enter the cover of the thicket. They started to move in that direction when they saw that the old cow was now taking a serious interest in the proceedings. They did not want to lose the old bull, but neither did they want to tangle with the old cow.

Sergeant Khubeki and Corporal Mnini looked for guidance from Captain Khumalo. He signalled for them to split into the search mode, some five metres apart. They moved slowly and then Captain Khumalo signalled for them to take cover. They lost track of the wind direction in the excitement and Captain Khumalo instinctively felt the wind change.

He now knew that a confrontation was imminent, and he relaxed to face the danger he knew would be upon them shortly. He looked at his colleagues and saw for the first time, real fear on their faces.

He said in sotto voice, "When she charges, make for a tall tree and climb it."

He checked his rifle, a 450 double-barrelled Rigby; the two round heads of the cartridges shone bright and were comforting. He snapped the rifle shut, removed the scope and drew another cartridge ready and placed it between the fingers of his left hand. He stood up, as there was now no need to hide.

The ground shook with the force of the charge from the old cow. She made no other sound. Behind her, but catching up fast, was the old bull. The herd was frozen, perplexed by all this activity, and unsure of what to do next.

Captain Khumalo held his ground and resisted the urge to run. The old cow was now sixty metres away, and the urge to shoot was almost overwhelming. The old bull was now fifty metres behind the cow; the two of them had the soldiers clearly fixed in their sights. He planned to shoot the old cow at thirty metres, taking a frontal shot to the brain, even if he missed a clean kill, the shock of the bullet would either turn the cow or knock her unconscious. The bull would be taken over the fallen body of the old cow. The cow was now large in his sights. He could clearly see her bloodshot eyes and the long eyelashes above and below them. The noise of the approaching elephants was deafening and the earth was trembling with their combined weight bearing down on him.

He felt cool and calm, which surprised him. When the shot came, it was almost a surprise to him, and the old cow tumbled over like a fallen rabbit. She made no sound as she went down, other than the crash of the body striking the ground, flattening two small acacia bushes. The old bull heard the dreaded sound of the rifle and veered to his left.

Captain Khumalo, now fired up with adrenaline coursing through his veins, fired at the old bull, taking him behind the shoulder. The old bull stumbled, then regained his balance and turned into the bush, away from Captain Khumalo. Captain Khumalo immediately broke the gun and ejected the used cartridges and replaced them with the spares in his left hand. He had a fleeting shot at the old bull through the bush and heard the bullet smack into the back of the old bull.

The old bull screamed with pain and rage. He felt the agony coursing through his body and headed away from the killing ground into heavy bush. He knew he was mortally injured, but he wanted to escape to exact revenge later. The herd stampeded away at the first shot, and were further hastened on their way, with the second and third shot. The whole incident was over in seconds, but had seemed like a lifetime to Captain Khumalo. Sergeant Khubeki and Corporal Mnini had not run away during the charge, as instructed, due to being mesmerised by the scene unfolding before them. They had never experienced such nerve-racking excitement like this before, and they were as pumped up as their Captain.

Sergeant Khubeki said, "Shit! Shit! Shit!" Corporal Mnini stood speechless and trembling. Captain Khumalo recovered first and brought his men to order. "Check the old cow Corporal", he said. "Sergeant, check the direction of the old bull, we cannot let him get away now."

The men moved as directed. Corporal Mnini moved nervously towards the old cow and The old cow was quite dead with a perfect shot to the brain evidenced by the small entrance hole three inches above the eyes.

Sergeant Khubeki found the tracks and the heavy blood trail of the old bull. "The old cow is dead Captain," said Corporal Mnini.

Sergeant Khubeki returned and said, "The old bull is well hit, and there is a blood trail even old Konko could follow," referring to a blind man back in their home village.

"Cover the old cow with brushwood," Captain Khumalo said.

Corporal Mnini started the task, and Sergeant Khubeki assisted. The old cow's one tusk was blackened with age and valueless. They had no intention of cutting it out.

"What do we do about the old bull?" Sergeant Khubeki asked.

"We wait until the wounds stiffen his limbs and then follow him. We will have to wait about an hour and, with a bit of luck, he will be dead by then," said Captain Khumalo. Inwardly he hoped it would be dead by then, as it was no mean task following a wounded elephant in deep bush. "Make the area as secure as possible," commanded Captain Khumalo. "Corporal, stay behind and ensure no follow up, then track us, as we follow up on the old bull."

The old bull ran for well over an hour with the muscles now stiffening. The blood had stopped flowing and the wound covered over, but he knew he would not see another season. A tear formed in his right eye, and was quickly followed by another in his left eye. He knew he was going to die. He had hatred in his heart, and he had to stay alive if he was to exact revenge.

He was now looking for cover to ambush his tormentors. He knew that they would come, and that now he could not escape. He found the perfect place for an ambush; a thicket that would give him perfect cover, but was close to the trail they would follow. He ambled a further 300 metres down the trail, leaving firm spoor on the game trail. The old bull then reversed back down the track, walking backwards using the exact spoor when moving up the track. He backed into the bush, leaving no trace of the movement off the game trail. He stood perfectly still and would wait with the patience of the injured animal, totally focused on his hatred, and would not move until his quarry was in site. The hunter had now become the hunted.

Captain Khumalo followed the blood spoor, which was clearly evident on the game trail. He could see the blood trail for a full fifty metres ahead. He knew he could not be ambushed from this distance. The stories of elephants waiting, and hiding in the bush were legion; but he did not believe the stories, as he doubted the animal had that much intelligence.

The game trail wound through the bush, and they moved cautiously, whenever the game trail took an acute bend. They followed the trail for well over an hour, with the blood spoor slowly but surely diminishing. The foot spoor was not difficult to follow, as the elephant was protecting his right side, and thus walking heavily on his left front leg.

Captain Khumalo walked with the gun loaded, and at the ready; he was not going to be taken by surprise. He felt real fear, and his mouth was dry; it had never been this bad whilst tracking the terrorists. He stopped at regular intervals, to listen to the bush around him, but heard nothing. It was as if the world had stopped turning and breathing. There was an incredible tension created by the total silence.

He felt extremely nervous, and jumped backwards, with a cry, as a francolin exploded from the bush adjacent to him.

The old bull heard the cry, and prepared himself for his last charge.

Corporal Mnini waited the customary hour, and could see that there was no follow up by rangers to indicate that the shot had been heard, and an anti poaching unit was in the area. He cleaned the area as best he could, but with a dead elephant laying there it was impossible to hide their presence at the scene.

He moved off at a steady jog, which would eat up the kilometres, to catch up with his colleagues. Their jogging speed is deceptive, and their unit had often covered fifty kilometres at a time, without a break. It took less than an hour to catch up to his colleagues. He had not even broken out in a sweat, even though the midday temperature was now 35 degrees, such was his fitness.

On closing with his colleagues, he gave the low whistle to indicate his presence. They were aware that he was coming, and had taken cover in the adjacent bush.

The old bull had seen the men coming down the game trail, and stood motionless in his hiding place. They stopped twenty metres from him, and disappeared in the bush. His anger was now acute, and the need for revenge paramount, but he stood and waited.

He heard the low whistle, and saw the men reappear from the bush; they relaxed their guard for a fraction of a second, and that was all the old bull needed. He burst from his hiding place, screaming with rage, and caught the man with the rifle, and flung him deep into the bush. The second man he gored with his tusk, and pinioned him to a tree, between his tusks; he felt the bones crack and collapse. The third man ran into the bush, and he followed him with a focus born of revenge, and caught him with his trunk and tried to pull him down, to crush him with his feet. The third man was lucky, as the old bull, due to his injuries, overran him and did not complete the killing blow.

The Bull's internal wounds were so severe that his trunk was full of blood; he was too weak to continue, and he fell on to his knees. He tried to trumpet defiance, but all he did was spray blood on the surrounding bush. He rolled his head from side to side, to try to remove the blood from his trunk, but he only succeeded in forcing more blood into the portion cleared. He felt himself close to death, and his mind wondered to better times. He laid down his noble head, which rested on his immense tusks. The pain now racked his body as he contorted in the last throes of death. He wanted to move and follow his instincts to die near water. He growled in frustration as he felt the blackness approach, and tried to stand; his once powerful legs would not support him. He died, and finally rested from his tormentors, knowing that he had exacted some revenge.

Captain Khumalo was unconscious, Corporal Mnini was dead, and Sergeant Khubeki, though scratched and bruised, was not severely injured. He knew he was lucky, and he had watched this magnificent animal die. There was no compassion in the man. He had killed many times, he had seen his companion killed by the elephant, and anger overtook him. He ran to the elephant, and slashed at it with the axe they had carried to cut out the tusks. He did this until his arms ached, and the elephant's head was a bloody mess.

Captain Khumalo groaned, and slowly raised himself to his feet, still groggy from the attack. The cold panic came back to him, and he looked fearfully about him for the elephant that had accomplished what no terrorist could ever have done.

He searched for the rifle and found it with the stock broken and the barrels damaged beyond repair. He thought of the force required to do this to a rifle and realised he was truly lucky to be alive.

He moved cautiously back to the point of the attack and found Corporal Mnini's body. He cursed out loud at the thing that was impaled and crushed on the tree. It was a mangled and bloody semblance of his colleague. He could not even determine which of his comrades had died. He gave a low whistle and was relieved to hear a response from Sergeant Khubeki.

Sergeant Khubeki emerged from the bush, saw Corporal Mnini's body and groaned. He had seen death many times, and was accustomed to bloody and blown apart bodies. He had never seen anything like the body that confronted him now.

"We had better clean up," Captain Khumalo said, with no apparent emotion.

Sergeant Khubeki looked at him askance, but said nothing.

They could not cover up the devastation created by the old bull around the game trail. An acacia as thick as a man's thigh had been broken like a twig.

"We have to leave no identification on the body", Captain Khumalo said.

"Who could identify this mess?" Sergeant Khubeki asked.

"They can trace us from his clothes."

"How do we remove them then?"

"We have to burn everything," responded Captain Khumalo. "We must also take the tusks," he added.

"They must weight 100 kilo's each!" exclaimed Sergeant Khubeki.

"We will manage," replied Captain Khumalo, "we are not going to leave them now."

"We will have trouble meeting the deadline for pick up, carrying these tusks," he complained. "Look, we have no radio anyway," as they both realised that the radio was smashed into fragments, as it was strapped to the dead man's back.

"How will we cover our tracks carrying these tusks and our back-packs?"

Captain Khumalo realised now that with only the two of them they would undoubtedly leave tracks. The original plan had been two people to carry the tusks and one to erase their tracks as they moved. They would also move slower without the additional manpower to carry the tusks.

He sat and thought about it, and then decided on the most practical solution.

He took out his map, and searched for a location where they could manage to carry the tusks to, and still be on time for their rendezvous. He saw what he looked for on the map and said, "We will carry the tusks to this point." He pointed on the map to a small contour that indicated a Kopje, some one hundred and fifty kilometres from the crater, towards their rendezvous point.

"To get there will take five days," he said. "If we push hard, we could make it in maybe four and a half days. Now let's clean up this mess as best we can."

Sergeant Khubeki saw the compromise and nodded agreement. They both moved to the old bull, to chop out the tusks.

Chapter 2

Don Scales was sat in his office contemplating the next game count in the crater. He had not been to this part of the reserve for well over eighteen months. Administration duties and the plethora of paperwork had kept him away from this section of the reserve.

Don Scales, a Scotsman from Dundee, was a respected environmentalist, and had worked in numerous remote countries. He was thirty eight years old, recently divorced, and was recently appointed as the Head Warden of the biggest game reserve in Tanzania, East Africa.

He had applied for the position, hardly expecting to receive a response because of his lack of experience with African game. Unbeknown to him, at that stage, was the fact that he was the only applicant with any kind of degree. This was due to the civil unrest, which was rampant in Tanzania, when the advertisement appeared. He was appointed following an interview with Dr Julius Ngama, the Minister of the Environment.

In his favour was the fact that he had a pilot's licence, and over two thousand hours flying time. He had been a member of the Flying Club of Dundee, and had flown single and twin-engine light aircraft.

When he arrived at the capital, Dar es Salaam, he was surprised at the efficiency that had been displayed at clearing customs, and transporting him to Government House. He had been transported in a new Mercedes with escorts either side of the diplomatic car. He had been received by one of Dr Ngama's aides, and whisked through to his office.

He saw no sign of the unrest that had been reported in the media.

The interview was brief, but specific. He had limited experience and would be taken on a trial period of six months. He had agreed to the trial period and accepted the position. He left Dundee, and was in Dodoma within ten days, having spent five days in the capital familiarising himself with the procedures, and regulations.

He had taken to the job with gusto, and had shown a remarkable speed in acquiring the necessary knowledge to control a reserve of over one and a half million hectares. What was blatantly obvious was that the staffing levels, to patrol effectively, were totally inadequate for such a large area. All his requests for more staff had fallen upon deaf ears.

His budget was small and inadequate, but his efforts were bearing fruit in that increased tourism was taking place. Tanzania had reached a level of stability due to the severe action taken to prevent crime and insurrection. Poaching, however, was still a serious headache for him, and despite numerous requests for assistance from the armed forces or increased staff, nothing had been done to assist him.

Scales was an organised man, and utilised his staff effectively. He had two assistant wardens, Jonathan Ndama and Toby Terblanche. Jonathan, Scales had promoted; he was intense, dedicated, and had an affinity for the game he managed. Toby, on the other hand, resented Scales, as he thought he should have been promoted to the Head Warden post.

He was at times taciturn and obstructive, but always performed just sufficient to prevent serious discipline. Scales had tried to resolve his difficulties, but could never get close to the man, or be able to motivate him.

He inwardly believed that Toby, if not plotting his downfall, was certainly not ensuring his success. The man was frustrating his every move to make changes within his department. He would not delegate any responsibility to his subordinates, and trusted only himself to complete a task successfully. This created a noncommittal approach by his team of scouts.

Toby had been born in Kenya, and his family had suffered at the hands of the Mau Mau. He would never trust a black man again. They were no better than animals in his eyes. The area, the Deputy Wardens, patrolled was enormous and required total dedication to managing it effectively. It was more than obvious that Toby Terblanche was not covering his area of responsibility with required gusto or commitment. Game counts were invariably late, and poaching was highest in Toby's region. They had recently lost three black rhino in this region, and the carcasses were some six weeks old before detection. Don Scales pointed this out to Toby, but the only comment was of under staffing; which Don could not deny.

To manage, successfully, such vast areas, patrols of up to ten days, were necessary. This still did not cover the areas as well as Don would like. The problem with Toby was that he lacked either the desire or commitment to vary his patrol direction. This resulted in the poachers knowing the exact movement of the scouts, and they were easily avoided.

Jonathan, on the other hand, was dedicated and varied his patrols constantly. His trackers followed up the spoor of the poachers with considerable success, and in the short time he had been his Deputy Warden, he already had achieved two convictions for poaching.

The two deputies sat outside Don Scales's office, while he was musing about their respective abilities. Toby was certainly well qualified, having obtained his degree at Wits University in Johannesburg, South Africa, in environmental sciences. Jonathan had only achieved a moderate education at Dar es Salaam, with no real environmental studies. Jonathan had been brought up in the bush and understood the game and their behaviour patterns from practical experience. It was fortunate for Don that he had chosen to protect game rather than hunt it, as he would have been an excellent poacher.

Constance brought in his morning tea. He motioned to Toby and Jonathan to join him.

"Thank you Constance," he said. 'Would you like some tea or coffee?' he asked Toby and Jonathan.

"Coffee for me," Toby said.

"Tea for me, white with three sugars," Jonathan said.

"Always trying to be the Englishman," Toby said sarcastically.

Jonathan gave him a pained look, but said nothing.

Don Scales gave Toby a withering look, and motioned for them both to sit down.

"I want to review the patrolling, and game counts in both regions," Don said.

'Toby, go first please."

Toby began his report, covering the game counts and the distribution of the game throughout his section. He discussed the migration of the wildebeest, and the following lion population.

He was thorough and comprehensive about the counts, and the levels of predators. In his opinion, the elephant population was getting close to the maximum that the reserve could sustain, without damage to the environs. Don listened to the report and realised that although belligerent and uncooperative, he was at least professional in his reporting and investigations.

"The poaching is still a problem," he concluded.

"Since losing the three rhino you already know of, we have discovered two more carcasses, at least three weeks old, in the northern region. They where found near Msombu water hole and obviously the horns had been removed. This brings the total count in my section to nineteen. This is well organised poaching by professionals," he concluded.

"Do we have a fix at all in which gang is responsible," Don asked.

"We know that, in this region, it is Moosa's outfit that is doing the poaching, but we still have no hard evidence."

Moosa was an Indian trader that operated in Dar es Salaam, and was known to be involved in smuggling of rhino horn out of the country. He had a network of poaching gangs, which could never be traced back to him. He paid these gangs via intermediaries, and never directly. The intermediaries also did not know with whom they were dealing. They delivered the rhino horn to a drop off point, which was never the same. Communications to the gangs and the intermediaries was always by word of mouth from Moosa's subordinates. He never gave instructions in person.

The police were well paid for their silence, and invariably, looked the other way when information came to light. Moosa had a network of paid police officers, which kept him well informed. He paid by the kilogram for the horn, that was poached, and at a fraction of the global market price. The gangs used were always employed from small villages, either in the reserve or bordering the reserve. They rarely had any other income.

The gangs were equipped with primitive firearms, which were almost as dangerous to the user as to the prey. A number of poachers had lost fingers or a hand, due to the guns exploding on firing. Their prey had killed some of the poachers, but these setbacks did not prevent other potential poachers. The people in their village saw them as the local heroes.
This gave them a Robin Hood like character, and the other villagers would never give any information to the scouts or the police.

The cash for the horn was always left at the dedicated drop off point, and only once was money taken without depositing the horn. The gang concerned was brutally murdered, and the theft was never repeated.

The murders were never solved by the police, and were eventually ascribed to gang warfare or tribal murders. No further investigations were embarked upon. Violent death was commonplace in Tanzania. It was an effective system of need and fear. When captured, the poachers would take their punishment, and never inform on their fellow poachers.

It was an impossible situation for Don Scales, and he suspected that the payoff for looking the other way went well up into Government circles. Yet tourism was the single largest industry in Tanzania, creating jobs for well over a million people. There had to be some leverage to be gained from that. However, most Tanzanians were bitterly poor, and there was easy money to be had from poaching. It was a disturbing, complex dichotomy.

'Damn Moosa and his cronies,' said Don in exasperation. He knew the situation only too well.

"Jonathan, what are your thoughts on this?"

Jonathan thought for a couple of seconds and then said, 'the only way you can catch Moosa is by planting someone in his network.'

Toby laughed and said, "Who would be mad enough to take on such an assignment. It would be certain death if caught, and they would probably murder the family to boot!"

"There are always people who will take risks for the right money," Jonathan retorted.

"Do you know of anyone?" Don asked.

"No," said Jonathan, "but I could put the word out."

"Put the word out," scoffed Toby, "Moosa would be the first to hear about it.

"What do you recommend?" Don asked.

"I don't know Don, I doubt that a local would do it," Jonathan responded.

Don saw the futility of discussing this further and asked Jonathan for his report.

Jonathan went through the game count, and the patrolling of his area. It was evident that the poaching in the southern region had been severely curtailed due to his efforts. Don was pleased with his report and it clearly showed.

"Aren't we the clever boy," Toby said, with undue emphasis on boy.

"What is your problem?"

Toby did not answer, but sat looking sullenly at Don. Don felt his anger rising, but kept control of his temper.

"I am planning a trip into the crater to count the game and check up on the elephant population," Don said. "It is curious that poaching does not take place in the crater; do you know why" he asked them both.

"Yes," said Jonathan, "It dates back to ancient times when the Sangoma's, (African witch doctor), lived there. All the locals believe the place has evil spirits and will not go into the crater."

"Does this include you?" Don asked.

Jonathan looked uncomfortable; he saw himself, as the new generation in Africa but the old traditions and beliefs were never that far below the surface.

"I will go if asked."

"I would like you to come with me," Don said. "Toby cannot be spared at the moment because his district is a hot bed of poacher activity at present."

Jonathan looked uncomfortable again, and Toby laughed.

"You can take the native out of the bush, but you cannot take the bush out of the native," he quipped.

"If you have nothing else to contribute, then please be quiet."

Toby smiled knowing he had broken through the veneer of Scales again. Bloody Scotsman, who thinks he understands these people after being here for five minutes, he thought. When will they ever learn that these people are barely civilised. He scowled at Don but remained silent. You will receive your comeuppance he thought and sooner than you think! He would soon take control, and he would sort out these bloody Kaffirs the only way they would understand.

"When do we go?" Jonathan asked.

"Tomorrow, at dawn."

Chapter 3

Captain Khumalo was ushered into General Mkondo's office; he was not looking forward to the interview. The General was strongly affiliated with the Zulu nation in South Africa, though he kept his allegiance quiet. He would never have risen to this position of power in the South African military if the ANC knew where his true commitment lay.

"Sit down Captain."

"We are none too pleased with your mission."

"It was difficult, to say the least, sir," Captain Khumalo said.

"We used you for your reported skills, and success rate; perhaps you should tell me all about it."

"General, the mission went well until the old cow charged," he started in defence.

The General listened to the story, and did not entirely believe the part about the bull waiting in hiding for them. He also did not credit the elephant with that much intelligence. He looked at Khumalo closely, but could see nothing in the man's eyes that would indicate that he was lying. He had been recommended to him as one of the best officers in the anti terrorist brigade. His source was impeccable.

Captain Khumalo held the stare as long as was necessary, and then said, "Sir, I am telling you the truth."

"Captain, do you realise how important your mission was?"

"Yes sir."

"Let me tell you why."

"A rich American who will pay two million Rand for a pair of elephant tusks the size you are talking about. This money would help finance the struggle against the ANC. The ANC are gathering funds from all over the world, as countries compete to support them. We are not being funded by any of these countries, and are losing out in the propaganda stakes. We need income not only for propaganda, but for the continued battle against the ANC in Natal."

"Yes sir, I understand the reasoning, and also understand the sensitivity of our situation. We can still retrieve the tusks, as we have hidden them in a safe place."

"Elections are scheduled in six months time, and much has to be done before that. How long will it take to retrieve the tusks?" he asked.

"We will need at least three weeks."

"Will you need a replacement for Corporal Mnini?" he asked.

"I would rather not, as you do not know who you can trust nowadays," retorted Captain Khumalo. "But it will take longer than planned without the extra person."

"As you wish Captain, but if you are caught, we do not know you; understand."

"Yes sir, I understand perfectly."

"You may leave Captain."

Captain Khumalo stood and saluted, then left the office. The General sat for a few minutes thinking about Khumalo.

He was correct; whom could you trust nowadays. Everyone was jostling for positions of power in the new government, and that meant old friendships were worthless. Babanango was the last bastion of the Natal Freedom Party, and what future there was for the Zulu nation. He mused that the Zulu's had already fragmented with a large number of Zulu's voting for the ANC. This would have been unthinkable ten years ago.

He wondered if his office was bugged, then decided probably not, as the sophistication of ANC spies would not come up to that level. We know them all anyway, or at least thought we did. Khumalo was right, better trust no one unnecessarily. He rose from his desk as the meeting was schedules for fifteen hundred, and that was five minutes away. He wondered how they would respond to his failure.

The Deputy Chief Minister of Natal, Isaiah Madluso, chaired the meeting. Also at the meeting was Andries Schoeman, Chief of the Natal Police, General Pretorious, Director of Intelligence, General Mtuli, Chief of Armed Forces, Samuel Khubeki, Minister of Finance David Mbeki and Daniel Similani, Minister for Internal Affairs. All people in high positions of power and all people who had a burning desire to remove the ANC from the helm. They were strange bedfellows, and many had been enemies during the Apartheid era. But the ANC stranglehold had forged new partnerships, and now white Afrikaners and black Zulu's were bonded together.

Isaiah Madluso opened the meeting by welcoming them all. He circulated the agenda only at the meeting, and collected the numbered copies after the meeting. Afterwards, he would personally shred all evidence of the meeting.

The room had been checked for bugs and found to be clear.

"Gentlemen, there will be no notes taken at this meeting, nor will there be any written reference to it ever having been held, is that clearly understood by all parties."

The group of people nodded assent.

"Mr. Schoeman, would you please give us your report on the current situation in Natal," he asked.

"Mr. Chairman, the current position is not good. We are being attacked in the south, particularly in Hammersdale. ANC groups are infiltrating NFP villages and townships, and undermining the organisation. Any opposition to the ANC advances is quickly dealt with, and there have been twenty-four political murders of NFP members this month alone," he reported.

"What action are you taking?" The Chairman asked.

"We have identified a number of the insurgents, and have used our special branch to deal with them. The problem is that as fast as we take them out, another bunch turns up. There appears to be an endless flow of them."

"From where do they emanate?" The Chairman asked.

"They are coming from Durban and Pietermaritzburg, Mr. Chairman."

"What are you doing to help General Mtuli?" he asked.

"We have a problem of finance Mr. Chairman; we cannot afford to pay for the required armed force, we are grossly undermanned."

"I did not ask for a dissertation, what are you doing to help," he asked testily.

"Mr Chairman, I was merely pointing out that resources are already stretched. As we move to one problem area, the one we vacate becomes a problem again. They appear to know our every move, and troop disposition."

"What do you need in funding?" The Chairman asked.

"We require a further two thousand troops, which will cost fifty Rand per person a day to keep, and one million Rand for equipment. This is the minimum requirement to maintain the status quo, let alone move us further ahead."

"To move us further ahead, what is the minimum requirement as you see it?" asked the Chairman.

"We will need at least three times that amount."

"Let me see, that would be close on thirty six million Rand a year. A small price to pay for maintaining power I think."

"Minister of Finance, where can we raise the money required?"

"We cannot raise any further funds through taxation or VAT, as any further siphoning of the funds would draw attention from the ANC. There are no remaining assets that can be disposed of; we are in a negative growth position. The violence in Natal is undermining industry with considerable days lost due to strikes orchestrated by the ANC. This fiscal year alone, tax revenue has dropped some fifteen percent, and the outlook is very gloomy indeed," he responded.

"'So what are we to do?" he asked the meeting.

"I have a solution," General Mkondo said.

All eyes moved to the General, it was a brave man who made such a statement in these times. "Please enlighten us General."

"I have put in place an operation which could generate the funds required. It is a covert operation, the details of which you do not need to know unless you wish to," he replied.

"It is not related to drugs I hope?" Schoeman said.

"Not at all," General Mkondo responded.

"I assume it is an illegal operation?" Schoeman further questioned.

"It is, but not in the boundaries of this country and the beauty of it is if they are caught, it is not Natal that takes the blame, but South Africa."

The Chairman raised his eyebrows and looked hard at the General. "How is this possible?" he asked.

"For me to be able to tell you that, you would need to know the full details of the operation. Do you wish to know?" he asked.

The Chairman weighed up his need of wishing to know everything that went on in his government within a government, and his natural caution for clandestine operations, which he did not want to know more than necessary about. Yet they were between a rock, and a hard place, and it was critical these funds were obtained, and fast.

"Alright general, please elaborate for us all."

"It is quite simple; we are already actively obtaining game trophies of the big five for overseas clients. These trophies are obtained from neighbouring countries, and those countries are assuming that poaching by local gangs is responsible. We are about to sell a pair of elephant tusks for two million Rand, to an American big game hunter, for his trophy room. We have our best men on this operation, and they are entirely untraceable to us."

"I do not believe it!" The Chairman said.

"Is there really any money in this kind of thing?"

"There is, and lots more in rhino horn."

"Can you raise thirty six million Rand from this operation?" The Minister of Finance asked in disbelief.

"We believe so."

The members of the meeting looked at each other and decided that they had sufficient information.

"Let's move on," The Chairman said.

"Mr. Chairman, I have a suggestion," Minister Daniel Similani said. All eyes moved to the new speaker. "We are always talking in the defensive mode; I suggest that we attack the opposition."

"And how would you do that?" The Chairman asked.

"I propose that we take the fight into the stronghold of the ANC in Gauteng Province. We would do this by employing our own insurgents, and creating the same problems for them, which they are creating for us. We have a number of tactical personnel trained and briefed in local terrorism, and insurgency. If we bring these people in to play, then we can pin down ANC troops in Gauteng which were destined for Natal," he responded.

There was a silence for a minute while the members of the meeting digested the proposal.

"Your proposal has merit," the Chairman said. "Who would run such an operation?"

"I would," responded the Minister for Internal Affairs.

"Would you need funding?" The Minister of Finance asked.

"No," was the response.

"How far would you go? There has to be some boundaries," Schoeman said.

"I will report my proposals and methods to the next meeting. In the interim, I will set up the units required and put them in place. I will initially disrupt industry by wildcat strike action, and then create conflict in the townships." He waited a minute then asked, "Do we all agree with the proposal?" All the members nodded their approval.

Chapter 4

Don Scales went through the usual safety checks on his aircraft, whilst Jonathan sat inside looking pensive. He was not only concerned about entering the crater, but also terrified of flying. Don looked at Jonathan, and realised the man's terror of flying, and his real fear of going into the crater. This made him respect him more, especially if he was prepared to face both these fears.

Don always enjoyed his flights over the bush, and was never bored seeing all the game below him. They flew at five thousand feet and had a little turbulence, but nothing significant. Within an hour, they flew over the ridge of the crater, and began scouting for elephants below.

The crater had always fascinated Don, it was one hundred and twenty kilometres long, and eighty-five kilometres wide. The old volcano had obviously been inactive, for thousands of years, and the native flora and fauna had taken over entirely. He was also fascinated how the game fit so well together, with all levels of the bush and savannah being grazed at different levels by the various species. It was a perfectly balanced, Eco system.

The crater had an abundance of water, through the streams that crossed the crater at several points. Shallow pans existed in many places, and natural salts are leached from the ground and accessible to the game. The elephants had never been controlled in this part of the reserve, and the evidence of their presence was obvious. Trees had been uprooted, and in some places, destroyed. Don wondered how long this could carry on for, without seriously impairing the ecology of the area. He would hate to have to have to cull the herds.

He suddenly sighted the first herd, at the sound of the aircraft; they started to mill around, showing their fear. The old cows were on the extreme of the herd with trunks raised, testing the air. They moved away from the engine sound with their shuffling gait, appearing slow, but covering the ground with astonishing speed. Don noticed that they seemed more agitated by the aircraft presence than was usual. He looked at Jonathan.

"Jonathan, do they appear more nervous than we should expect?"

"Yes they do, I wonder why?"

Don's gut feeling told him that the crater was no longer the haven of the past.

"I bet Moosa's bastards have been in here."

"I doubt it; remember the local's fear of the crater."

"We must put the plane down, and check the area."

Don landed the small plane on a stretch of a flat, salt bed, on the edge of the savannah. The elephants had moved off and stood and watched them from a distance. They appeared unsure what to do, and milled around aimlessly. There was now no natural leader, and a new matriarch had not been found since the hasty departure of the South African poachers.

Don put his binoculars to his eyes and studied the herd. He could see that they were moving around disturbed, and their enormous ears were flapping wildly. It was a sure sign of distress. The elephants should have held no fear or distrust of people, in their remote location where the locals feared to tread. Don was certain that poachers must have been in the locale.

"I think we should move back out of sight," Don said. "We may induce a charge otherwise."

They moved off into cover and watched the elephants, which had not moved off and were intently watching the bushes where they now lay hidden. Suddenly and without any apparent cause, the herd stampeded away, with the young bulls bringing up the rear. They moved off at a fast pace, and were soon out of sight of the Wardens.

"We must look around and find the reason for their fear," Jonathan suggested.

"I agree, but where do we start?"

"The elephants are still nervous, and they must have been frightened within the last couple of days. We will find the evidence around here I am sure. It is difficult to hide the carcass of a full grown elephant, we will find the signs."

Don looked at Jonathan, and realised that he was essentially dependent upon this person to find the signs. He also realised that the carcass would probably be largely eaten by now which would make it more difficult to find. I do not know where I can start to look in such a large area, he thought. Perhaps it would be quicker to fly up and down the crater to locate the dead elephant. He was convinced that this would be what they would find. He was about to suggest this when Jonathan remarked.

"Look, there are vultures in the trees to our left."

"Where?" Don asked, as he could not see any evidence whatsoever of vultures.

Jonathan pointed in the direction, and Don looked through the binoculars, and saw the vultures clearly. He marvelled at the eyesight of Jonathan.

"Let's go."

"Hold on, there could be lion laid up there." Jonathon warned.

Don looked at the rifle they had brought for protection, and checked that it was loaded. It was an old Holland & Holland side-by-side 400. It had enough stopping power for any game or circumstance. They moved off at a slow jog in the direction Jonathan indicated. They stopped some distance from the vultures, and Jonathan observed them for some time through the binoculars.

"They are certainly intent on something on the ground, as they all appear to be watching the ground to their left. They are aware of our presence, as the birds are not feeding. It has to be lion they are observing. If it were hyena or jackal, they would be feeding with them."

He searched the area for an additional five minutes but added nothing more.

"Do you see any lion?" Don asked.

"Not yet."

The grass was long, up to a man's waist. Lion have a remarkable ability to hide behind the smallest amount of bush or grass. Jonathan stared intently at the bush surrounding the vultures. Don checked the rifle, safety off, cartridges in, and spare cartridges in his left hand. He tapped Jonathan on the shoulder, and handed him two more spare cartridges.

"If trouble starts, stay close." Jonathan nodded.

"Look, if we go marching in there, we will give the lion no time to retreat. I suggest we move to the old Baobab, and climb out of harm's way."

Don saw the wisdom of this, and once again thought how well this person applied his knowledge. They stalked up to the tree with the vultures watching them intensely.

They reached the tree without incident, and climbed until they were well out of reach.

"What now?"

"We talk loudly," Jonathan said.

Jonathan started to speak loudly, and explained to Don that there were animals throughout Africa, which could easily kill a man. He further explained that unless they are wounded, threatened or protecting their young, they invariably avoided humans. They do not just attack. There was a low growl some hundred meters away, and the first lioness stood up; her tail was erect, and she was testing the wind to detect the presence of the men. Suddenly there were five more lionesses, and then, two enormous males with black manes. They growled amongst themselves, and looked around them continually.

"Go away," Jonathan shouted.

The large male growled, and then charged towards the sound. He looked a formidable sight, and Don felt his stomach churn. He sought support from the rifle, and held it tightly. A lioness spotted them in the tree, and bounded towards them. She stopped at the bottom of the tree and roared defiance that shook the earth. This was not the sound of a caged lion in a zoo; this was primeval, and there was hatred in the roar.

The lioness stepped away from the tree, and then tried to jump into the lower branches; intent on deadly damage to the occupants of that tree. She slipped away, and then roared again. The biggest male joined the lioness at the base of the tree; he also roared at the men. The pair was a terrifying sight, and Don thanked God that he had listened to Jonathan, and heeded his cautious approach. Don looked down at the two lions, and pointed the rifle at the most determined lion, which was the largest. He was not an expert shot but, from this range, he could not miss. His fear was that he might only wound the lion, and what the lion would do afterwards. Don would not be able to leave a wounded lion prowling the area.

The lioness again tried to climb the tree, and managed a foothold some ten feet below them. The situation was now getting extremely serious, and he looked across at Jonathan for guidance. To Don's amazement Jonathan smiled.

"Bugger off," Jonathan shouted.

This broke the spell, and the lioness leaped to the ground and was gone in a flash. The second lion followed after a cursory glance in their direction.

"Are you mad?" Don asked.

"They wanted their moment of glory; once they had frightened you they were quite happy to leave."

"Their pride has been restored, and there was no further need to demonstrate."

"How the hell do you know that?"

"It is simple. They have eaten their fill, they have no need to feed, and we merely disturbed them. They just wanted to let you know that they were not happy with us."

Don chuckled and again thanked God that Jonathon was knowledgeable enough to prevent an incident. Jonathan started to climb down the tree, and Don stopped him, and asked if it is safe yet. Jonathan just smiled and proceeded to climb down. Don was not yet convinced and kept a close watch on the area.

The lions had moved away and were observing their descent of the tree.

"Bugger off," Jonathan yelled at them. The lion growled but made off.

"You are quite insane," Don said.

They moved off towards the vultures, which had taken advantage of the lion moving away and were tearing frantically at an elephant carcass. They were fighting and leaping over the carcass to gain access to the meat. There must have been fifty or more birds frantically feeding, and taking their opportunity. As Don and Jonathan neared the carcass the birds jumped, and flew off into the surrounding trees. They made no sound other than the sound of their wings. The Wardens then looked at the carcass, which had been well fed upon; it was a gruesome sight.

The abdomen had been opened up, and the intestines strewn across the ground. Most of the hindquarters had been eaten, and the smell was horrendous. Jonathan seemed unperturbed by the smell, and proceeded to look for the cause of the animal's death. Poachers normally kill an animal of this size with many shots, as the aim is to slaughter or stop the animal quickly. Shots are typically found in the backsides and sometimes in the head. The animal suffers terribly, whilst this mayhem takes place, as three or more poachers, are shooting at the animal. There is no mercy, just opportunity. The animals rarely die quickly, and few, if any, escape. Jonathan could see no immediate cause for the death of the elephant, and began to think that it was due to natural causes. He also noted that the single tusk was still intact, and could clearly see the broken tusk. Poachers remove the tusks regardless of their size.

He looked intently at the head, and then saw the neat hole, just above where the eyes had been. The skin had shrunk back, and partially covered the entrance hole. He dug out his knife and cut away the skin.

"Look at this Don." Don saw the hole and could see it was the killing shot. "This is a professional job, not Moosa's men."

Don looked again and agreed by nodding his head. He had also seen the effects of poachers, and the myriad shots in the carcass. An immense sadness came over him, as he also knew it would be difficult to catch a true professional. Now they had found this paradise, they would almost certainly be back.

"Why kill the old cow though?" Don asked.

"I would guess that they did not want to shoot the old cow, but she must have charged them, forcing them to shoot her."

"I remember this old cow, and the huge bull that was with the herd. I did not see him today," he continued. "They must have been hunting the old bull and this one got in the way."

"The shot is professional, and they probably got the old bull, as well. Have a look round will you."

Don took out his notebook, and wrote down his observations. Jonathan moved off, and started to explore the bush. He was gone five minutes then he called for Don to join him.

"They did shoot the old bull I think as there is an old blood trail here. You can also see the broken branches where he ran through the bush."

Don looked at the blood trail and even with his poor tracking ability, he could clearly see the spoor. He checked his watch, it was fourteen thirty-five; they had been out here for over four hours.

He knew he would have to fly back and return the next day to follow the trail.

"We will have to come back tomorrow with Samuel,' Don said, referring to their tracker.

Jonathan nodded agreement.

Don Scales checked his aircraft prior to take off, to return to his base in Dodoma. They would fly back to the crater with the tracker Samuel the next day.

Early the next morning they returned to the crater. The flight was uneventful, and they touched down without incident. Both Samuel and Jonathan were nervous about being in the crater, with Jonathan controlling his fear and Samuel shivering as if he had a fever.

"OK let's move out," Don said.

They passed the dead Cow, which they had found the previous day. The vultures and scavengers of the bush veldt had been busy, and very little remained of the carcass.

"Let's find the bull, lead on Samuel," he ordered.

The spoor was not hard to follow, and they moved at a fast pace down the game trail. Samuel had no trouble following the spoor; long after the blood trail had dried up. Don could only marvel at the ability of these trackers. As they went further down the game track, he could no longer see any spoor at all, yet Samuel never decreased his speed. Within 2 hours, they arrived at the killing ground. The gruesome sight they encountered where the scattered remnants of a person. The body of Corporal Mnini was all but consumed, including his clothing. The hyena's had made sure that he would never be recognised. Samuel cast around and called the others over when he finally found the dead bull.

The bull had only been partially eaten by scavengers, and the bullet entrance holes were easily spotted.

The bull's tusks had been chopped out, but the bull had killed at least one of them, Scales was pleased to note. He wondered if they would find any more bodies around the site, and instructed Samuel to search a radius of fifty meters. After some thirty minutes had elapsed, Samuel returned, and through Jonathan advised that there were no more bodies, but a clear trail from the poachers, heading South East.

"Jonathan, can Samuel read the signs here and tell us what happened, and how long as the elephant been dead." Don asked.

Jonathan spoke to Samuel, who then did a thorough search of the area and spoor. He reported back to Jonathan.

"Don, it appears that the bull went past this spot, and then reversed down his own spoor, and sideways into the bush. He waited there until his opportunity came. He appears to have thrown one into the bush. The one poacher was obviously charged, and trapped against that tree. He thinks that the bull has been dead for at least ten days."

"What do you suggest Don?"

"To be honest I am not sure what to do. They are probably over the border by now."

"Why don't we leave now, and let Samuel follow their tracks and determine in which direction they have gone."

"Isn't that a bit risky?" Don asked. "What if they are still in the area?"

"You don't know Samuel. We often use him to follow up while we go for reinforcements. Sometimes these gangs can consist of twenty or more poachers."

"Jonathan, ask Samuel to follow up, but how will we contact him to rejoin forces?"

"Don, he will leave signs on the trail, which we can see from the air. There are also villages where he can leave messages. Do not worry, he will either find or contact us."

Don saw the wisdom in this proposal and agreed that this was the proper course of action. They turned, and made off the way they came back towards the aircraft. Samuel just disappeared into the bush. Scales did not even know that he had gone.

"Jonathan, what happens if the poachers have someone like Samuel in their group, surely this will put him at risk?"

"I doubt this very much; Samuel is the best, and is unlikely to get caught. He is far too good for the poachers."

They woke before dawn and were ready to fly at first light. Jonathan still looked uneasy at flying back, and Don smiled and said, "I would have thought you would have been used to flying by now."

"Sorry Don, but I don't think I ever will."

They arrived at the base just after six in the morning and were in their office by six thirty. It was too early to call Dr Ngama's office, so Don called a meeting with Jonathan and Toby. They discussed the recent developments and filled Toby in on the details.

"Any thoughts on where they could be heading?" Don asked Jonathan and Toby.

Toby stood up and walked over to the map on Don's wall and pointed to the area where they had seen the poacher's tracks disappearing into the Bush.

"They will almost certainly have crossed the Ruvuma River into Mozambique. You have already guessed that they are not local poachers and are a professional outfit. What makes you think they are from Mozambique and not from Tanzania or Uganda?" asked Don.

"The direction they have taken from the crater. If they were from Uganda, or resident in Tanzania, they would not be heading towards Mozambique. If they were from Uganda, then they would have headed north, not south. No, they were clearly from across the border and undeniably south of the border. One other thing bothers me. You said the killing shot on the old cow was a frontal brain shot. The old cow must have charged them, and there was no other shot in the body. This was a high-calibre rifle, which as you know, is not used in Tanzania. Poachers use any kind of rifle they can get and use at least a dozen shots to kill or bring down the elephant. This was an extraordinarily good shot, by a marksman of some skill and courage. It is not easy to face down a charging elephant. I would also surmise that the old bull was following on behind, and this marksman shot the first at close range and then shot the second animal, which was also charging. That can only be the work of a pro. The local guys would never have succeeded."

Don sat and thought about this and said, "I think you are absolutely right. The use of the high-calibre rifle also convinces me that they are pro's. But why did they then get caught by the old bull?"

"Stories of wounded elephants stalking and killing hunters abound in Africa. The graveyards of Kenya are full of white hunters killed by so-called dead elephants. They must have gotten careless when they followed up the spoor of the wounded bull, or maybe they were over confident. Do you think they are white?" Jonathan asked.

"I think so, where would the blacks get hold of a high-calibre rifle, and how many blacks do you know who can handle a rifle that good," Toby said.

"Whites were not the only professional hunters in the past you know," responded Jonathan. "What about Kambula, who shot the big five throughout Kenya and Tanzania," he said proudly.

"He was one in how many; and how many have there been since?"

"Ok, less of the bickering. Let's figure out how we are going to catch these guys. I will give Dr Ngama a call and see if we can get some help," Don said.

"You must be joking." Toby said. "You will get no help from that quarter."

Don ignored this comment and called Dr Ngama's office, only to find that he was away on a seminar on tourism. He asked for and received the telephone number of the centre where the seminar was being held. He got through quite quickly.

"Dr Ngama, I need help tracking some professional poachers, who we believe are trying to cross the border to Mozambique," Don said, having gone through the pleasantries of hello, how are you etc.

"Scales, how many poachers are there that you need to apprehend?" Dr Ngama asked.

"There are at least two."

"Scales, did you say two? Are you mad that you would ring me for assistance to apprehend two poachers? Do you really think it was necessary to call me from my seat in the centre to discuss the urgent need to apprehend two poachers," he said angrily. "Scales do not ever bother me again with such nonsense."

He slammed down the phone.

Toby stood there grinning and wanting to say I told you so; he wisely did not.

Don felt and looked rather foolish and said, "We must handle this ourselves; our esteemed Minister of the Environment sees this little episode as below him."

Chapter 5

Captain Khumalo entered Tanzania west of Gomba in Mozambique. They had no trouble reaching the kopje, and had avoided any contact with the local populace. They had travelled mostly at night and arrived on schedule. Against their better judgement, they had brought a third member, namely Moses Khumalo, a cousin of the Captain. They had needed a third person to erase the tracks, and cover their rear from any surprise attack. They all carried AK47's, the ubiquitous rifle of Africa. They were not hunting game; they were only recovering property. They were well armed, but did not want an incident, as this would make it even more difficult for the future operations in Tanzania. They were armed solely for protection as a last resort.

They had arrived at the Kopje just before dawn, and decided to lie up in the surrounding bush. They needed to see if their cache had been discovered. There was no movement on or around the Kopje, but they bided their time to be certain. At noon, they went up the Kopje and retrieved the tusks. They had planned to leave right away, but Moses was too tired and unaccustomed to such hardship, thereby needing to rest. No amount of threatening or coaxing would make him move. It was impossible for Sergeant Khubeki and Captain Khumalo to carry out the task alone. They reluctantly agreed to leave that night.

They observed the tracker from their vantage point long before he came close to the Kopje. Moses wanted to run for it and discard the tusks. Captain Khumalo threatened him with his life if he even moved.

Sergeant Khubeki slipped away and had a close look at the tracker and reported back to Captain Khumalo, that he was alone. It was obvious that the tracker did not anticipate any contact with poachers, and was not prepared for such an eventuality.

Captain Khumalo sent Sergeant Khubeki in a wide circle to ensure that he was the only person following their spoor. He returned after a while and reported no other parties searching. He also reported that the tracker was outstanding and had clearly followed their original spoor, regardless of their attempts of erasure. He would also very likely find their new tracks they had made on their second venture into Tanzania. Yet, thankfully, he was still focused on their old tracks and did not seem to be aware that they had returned to the area.

. Captain Khumalo gave Moses a long, penetrating look, which Moses could not hold. He automatically checked his weapons and ammunition. Sergeant Khubeki did the same. They both looked at Moses and silently agreed to take his weapon away from him, as he was an unknown quantity under pressure. They did not want to shoot their way out. Moses attempted to keep his weapon, but Sergeant Khubeki changed his mind with a long knife held at his throat. This seemed to do the trick, and Moses was subdued.

It would be only a matter of time before the tracker picked up the new tracks they had made. They could delay no longer. They would have to get moving, and assume that the tracker would find and follow the new trail.

He smiled to himself and looked forward to the sport ahead. They must capture the tracker as soon as possible.

It was almost dark when they set out with the tusks. Sergeant Khubeki and Moses taking the first march with the tusks. Captain Khumalo was erasing their spoor and covering their rear; they were heading for Masuguru. They marched for four hours and then changed over with Captain Khumalo relieving Sergeant Khubeki. The Sergeant took over the duties of erasing their spoor. They knew that the tracker would be proficient enough to follow them. Yet, if they did not attempt to cover their tracks, the tracker would become suspicious and would be much more difficult to capture.

This went on all through the night, and no attempt was made to capture the tracker. At four thirty in the morning, they stopped for a break, and Captain Khumalo gave the nod to Sergeant Khubeki.

Samuel had easily followed the spoor and observed all the changes in carrying the tusks. At times, he thought that he was perhaps too close, but still believed that they had no idea he was following them. He decided to play it cautious and stayed two kilometres behind them. They were leaving a spoor a boy could follow. There was no way that they could lose him. They had marched with commendable speed, considering the load they were carrying, and they had shown exemplary discipline at the changeovers and rear protection. He thought that these guys looked like military and not typical poachers. They appeared far too disciplined, and they had a distinct leader that determined when they should change, and in which direction they should travel. His directions or commands were never disputed. This was not at all like the unruly poachers he generally followed. This should have warned him, but he had followed many poaching outfits for Jonathan, and had never been detected.

He watched them stop and eat and noticed that there was one missing and assumed that he had gone to relieve himself. He never heard Sergeant Khubeki, and only became aware of his presence when he was caught from behind, and a knife placed at his throat. He was professionally frisked, and it was determined that he was unarmed.

Sergeant Khubeki brought Samuel into the camp where he was tied up and interrogated.

"Do you speak English," Khumalo asked.

There was no response from Samuel. Khumalo tried Zulu and Portuguese. Still there was no response. He was not sure whether the tracker could understand him, and was almost certain that he could only speak his native tongue. They could not speak Swahili or any of the other dialects.

"What do we do with him?" Khubeki asked.

"We let him go again," Captain Khumalo said.

"Are you mad?" Moses asked.

"He will go straight to the authorities and identify us."

"Whom will he identify, we will be long gone, and how could they find us. We must not mention the name of our country in front of him. Do you understand Moses?"

There was no need to remind Sergeant Khubeki, as he had been in this situation many times before.

He looked at Samuel, and knew that this would lead to trouble, and the appropriate course of action would be to kill him. However, he could not accept this decision and racked his brain for a solution. Moses had a point, in that they would, and could be recognised in the future. He knew that some time in the future, he would be sent back to Tanzania. He would make his decision whilst on the march. He always thought well when he was active.

"We must move on," Captain Khumalo said.

Moses groaned and looked pleadingly at Captain Khumalo; but he knew better than to argue. Sergeant Khubeki just shrugged and made ready to set off.

"There is no point in covering our tracks. We must move as fast as possible to Mozambique. Keep all talking to a minimum and only speak English. We must give nothing away to their tracker," Captain Khumalo said.

"We have to get rid of the tracker." Moses said.

"We are not murderers," Khumalo said.

"Tell that to the ANC," Moses retorted.

In a moment, sergeant Khubeka had Moses on the floor with a knife at his throat.

"You stupid idiot," he cried, as he pressed the knife into the side of Moses neck.

Moses squirmed and tried to get himself free, but was locked in a grip he knew he could not escape from. He felt real fear, as he knew that Khubeki would kill him at an instant, if instructed to do so. He decided not to struggle any further and lay limp awaiting his fate. He knew that, without him, they would not make the border in time, and gave Captain Khumalo a desperate look.

"Let him up," Captain Khumalo ordered, "we still need him."

Captain Khumalo studied his map; he realised that his problems had just begun. There was little bush for cover over the next seventy kilometres. How could they cover this distance without detection? The problem appeared insoluble, and it worried him, as he also knew that the search would be on for them. He guessed that he had at most a twenty-four hour lead on the anti-poaching unit. And if the Wardens did not hear from their tracker soon they would realise something was amiss. He must use all his skills to prevent detection. He signalled Sergeant Khubeki to join him. No names would be used. When out of earshot of Samuel, Captain Khumalo indicated to Sergeant Khubeki to sit down.

"We have a problem. There is a lot of open country between here and where we cross the border into Mozambique. We have our rendezvous with the agent for the tusks in ten days time and cannot afford to be late. This tracker creates a problem and will surely slow us down."

Sergeant Khubeki started to talk, and Captain Khumalo stopped him by holding up his hand, and saying, "wait until I have finished. If we force march for twelve to fourteen hours a day, we can make the border in say five days; our problem is to find somewhere to rest and hide during the day. We can only assume that there will be quite a search party looking for us. We have to make at least fifty kilometres a day in difficult terrain and loaded with the tusks. If we leave the tusks, then we cannot go home again,' he concluded. "Do you have any ideas?"

Khubeki sat and thought about their plight and said, "If we cannot kill the tracker, we must ditch him as soon as possible. He will slow us down, that is for sure. Finding hiding places will not be too difficult, as long as we stay away from villages, as I am sure that they do not have air support."

"You give me an idea. We can feed him false information and drop him off at the nearest village later tonight. If we do this in the early hours of the morning, we can be long gone before they find him. If we set off towards Lindi, they would think we are heading to the coast."

He opened the map and showed Khubeki the way they would take. They both studied the map at length and plotted the direction they would take.

"To make it look realistic, we will have to take this course for at least the first night. We can move towards Lindi but quartering towards Masuguru. The problem is how we accidentally inform the tracker of our intentions without being obvious."

"We can use Moses," Sergeant Khubeki said.

"How?" Captain Khumalo asked.

"If we discuss the extra distance we have to cover he is bound to complain and ask why. We tell him it is a change of plan, and that we are heading for the coast at Lindi."

"It might work," Khumalo said. "Let's give it a try."

They went back to the camp, and Captain Khubeki called over Moses.

"We have a change of plan, and we are now heading towards Lindi, which will be further hundred kilometres," he said.

"What," exclaimed Moses? "Are you serious, an extra hundred kilometres, and why to Lindi for God's sake?"

Captain Khumalo slapped Moses across the face and told him to be quiet. He looked towards the tracker. Samuel appeared to hear nothing. Moses reeled back from the slap and went for his knife. He did not get halfway before Sergeant Khubeki had got hold of him and pinned him to the floor.

"Don't even think about it," he snarled.

"Ok, Ok," Moses said, he moved his hands away from the knife at his belt. "I don't like being hit by anybody."

Captain Khumalo stood up, and cocked his rifle, and pointed it directly as Moses. "Any more problems from you and you will not see tomorrow. Now stand up and give me your knife."

Moses stood up and handed his knife over to Captain Khumalo. He looked belligerent, and Khumalo thought it would be easier to move out, and keep him occupied, to drain his energy. He sensed that Moses was going to be trouble and would have to watch him carefully over the march to Mozambique. He wished that Corporal Mnini had survived, as he certainly needed him now.

He looked across the valley, which they had to cross. There were low sloping hills as far as the eye could see. There were scattered patches of bush, mainly acacia, some elephant grass and long tracts of savannah. There were little pockets of the game, which covered the plain like spots on a Dalmatian. There was not a village in sight. He knew that there was a village some twenty kilometres due east, on the way to Lindi, which was ideal for the turn to Masuguru.

He checked his watch; it was eleven in the morning, and the need for rest was paramount. He knew he could not trust Moses to keep watch and the sentry duty was to be shared between himself and Khubeki.

Chapter 6

The six men dressed in black were virtually invisible in the dark of the night. It was three in the morning; the time when the senses were at the lowest, and if it was your time to slip this mortal coil, this would be the most likely time.

The NFP men moved silently towards their target, a medium sized house in the heart of Alexandra Township. Their intelligence had informed them that the local ANC Director of Internal Affairs was visiting his sister, and her husband. Their target was the director, but it did not matter if they were all killed, as they wanted maximum impact.

Each was armed with an AK47 that was set on fully automatic. Each member of the team was allocated a role, and they had practised many times, having researched the inside of the house in some detail, when the mission was sanctioned by their superiors. All of them had been in the anti terrorist squads before the ANC came to power and had accounted for many terrorists in their time. They were ruthless men, well trained and considered that the Shangaan was no more than dogs. With one exception, these men were all Zulu, and from an ancient fighting heritage. They had seen their people slaughtered in Natal, and the local newspapers had shown little interest in their plight. Richmond had been a killing ground that accounted for two hundred Zulu's, massacred by the ANC terrorist groups, before, and during, the elections of the so-called Government of National Unity.

The killing was still going many years after the elections. The local government elections were imminent, and the ANC was particularly active in the region, making assurances of the Promised Land, if the people voted for them. Where they met resistance they responded in the time-honoured way of Africa; they terrorised murdered and caused mayhem. Each member of this team had lost relatives and loved ones during this period. They were prepared to exact revenge in any way possible. The night was still and totally dark; they had planned the action to coincide with the waning of the moon. Also, they were lucky in that the cloud base was low and further increased the darkness.

They moved silently and dreadfully efficiently towards their target. The house was in complete darkness and total stillness. The surrounding houses were also in darkness; there was no movement other than the hit squad moving towards their target.

On reaching the house, they split into two groups, three men going to the back of the house and the other three to the front. Their signal to enter was a thirty-second time lapse on their watches, set as they parted. The two groups reached the front and back doors simultaneously and waited for the alarm to sound. The thirty seconds seemed a lifetime as they waited. The alarm rang incongruously in the total stillness of the night. The leader started at the sound. They broke down the doors and entered the rooms of the house. The first group entered through the kitchen, and moved as planned, swiftly to the master bedroom. The second group moved through the small hallway towards the second bedroom.

The house was small and boxlike, recently built as part of the low cost housing programme. The leader kicked in the door of the second bedroom and found the occupants. They were woken by the sound of the intrusion but incapable of putting up any resistance. They started their deadly work without command, and the night air was shattered by the sound of gunfire. The Director of Internal Affairs was gunned down before he could move, and his lady friend followed. Their bodies were riddled with bullets and blood was splattered all over the room.

In the master bedroom, the Director's sister and her husband were shot so many times in the head and throat, that the bullets decapitated them. A third bedroom housed the children, and they were butchered without ceremony. The whole action had taken less than a minute. Lives had been shattered and broken in such a short time. The group met in the small lounge, having completed their deadly work and the leader gave the command to leave. They exited on the run, through the front door. They only made twenty yards before they were bathed in bright lights, and each one of them was cut down by automatic fire. There were no survivors.

The incident was reported on the third page of the Metropolitan, a local Johannesburg newspaper. Few other newspapers bothered with the report. The journalist that reported for the Metropolitan thought the story deserved full front-page coverage; her editor did not agree. He was far more interested in the rumour of a Korean conglomerate, building a new plant, in Durban. The Director was not a prominent politician, and his family was not well known. That this was just another partisan murder, amongst so many, was more than evident.

Angela Murchin, the journalist concerned, was not convinced, and she was curious as to why the police had arrived, at just the right time, to catch the hit squad leaving. The locals said that they heard only the gunfire from the police and no command to drop their weapons. How could the police get there in time to set up their ambush but not in time to stop the assault? This worried her, and she could not ignore the incident.

Angela Murchin was an uncommonly talented investigative reporter. Her only downside was that she was a stunning redhead, and not many of her male colleagues would take her seriously.

She knew that she was beautiful and had the ability to use it to get her way without making the ultimate sacrifice. She had been involved with two short affairs, but at twenty-seven, was still single. All her friends were married and most with children. She had lost a couple of friends due to their husbands taking a more than passing fancy to her.

The slaying in Alexandra was still uppermost in her mind and the extremely fast retribution that took place. She could not believe that it was a coincidence that a patrol happened to be on the spot at the time. She had the list of names of both the terrorists and the occupants of the house. She knew that this was no ordinary faction killing as the manner of the slaughter was intended to arouse fear and anger. She read through the names of the terrorists again and again to try and derive a clue as to why they would commit such an atrocity. She read them out loud to herself, 'Tobias Mkohnde, Gabriel Masheko, David Masheko, Daniel Mtamni, Johannes Khubeka, and Jeromiah Dlamini.'

A passing black journalist stopped in his tracks and asked.

"What name did you say?"

Angela looked up and saw Thomas Msibi and said, "I beg your pardon, I was thinking out loud."

"What name did you say?"

Angela started again from the beginning.

"No, the last one," he interrupted.

"Jeromiah Dlamini."

"That's the one," he exclaimed.

"Why do you ask?"

"Jeromiah Dlamini was with the anti terrorist unit in Natal. I know the name well because I came across him often in my research for a story I wrote on black soldiers activities for the Apartheid government. It was never published though. I know he is a citizen of Swaziland, but he was drafted into the unit. He infiltrated the carriers in Swaziland and accounted for many of the MK coming over the border into South Africa. He was lucky to survive after independence."

"Not anymore, he was shot and killed in Alex last week, following an attack on the local ANC bigwig."

"Are you sure it was him, there is a lot of Dlamini's living in South Africa," she concluded.

"I cannot be sure obviously, but if it is him then you could be onto something; let me see the description."

He read the description and the other names on the list; he did not recognise any other name.

"I still cannot be sure that it is the same man, but the description of him appears to fit that of the Special Forces man I researched, you should check it out," he said.

"I could always go to the records of the army based in Natal," she replied.

"No way, they destroyed all the records of the special operatives prior to independence; you will never find the solution there."

"You must go to see the next of kin, find out who claimed the bodies, and search for the answer from there."

"You could interview the next of kin easier than I, as you speak the language; we could work on this together."

Thomas Msibi looked at her long and hard, he knew, and she knew, that he was a result of affirmative action, and had never actually been given any assignment of merit. He was always given the small stories, the occasional mugging or robbery. He yet had to have any feature printed and was used more as the office boy.

"Are you sure that you want to use me?"

"I think you would be ideal for this assignment, but I think we need to keep it confidential, don't you?"

He gave her another long and hard look. She could read his mind and quickly allayed his fears.

"If we find anything of note and we write a story, it will be in both our names, OK."

He beamed back at her, "OK", he said.

"How will we discuss anything I find out?" he asked.

"We will meet and discuss it in the Keg," she said.

The Keg was a pub and restaurant round the corner from the paper.

"I will start right away," he said.

"Excellent, please advise me when you have found any material we can use."

Thomas Msibi walked away with a sense of purpose and pride; perhaps he could make a difference after all. Angela went back to studying the names of both the victims and the aggressors. She wondered what possible connection an ex terrorist hunter had with the murder of a local ANC officer. She doodled with her pen and allowed her mind to wander.

She was brought back to earth when the assistant editor tapped her on the shoulder.

"Angela, forget the faction fighting. I want you to research the company that is rumoured to be building a plant in Durban. Tim Wells will be doing the main story, but he needs background information. The company name is Soong Industries."

"Why would they come to South Africa when the car manufacturing industry is just about at maximum penetration?" She asked.

"Darling," he said sarcastically, "that is why you are an investigative reporter, didn't you know. Now put those good looks and tit's to good use and find out."

Angela was about to express her anger, but decided to let it go with a simple, "OK."

It was pointless trying to take on a boss with obvious problems with female staff. She had seen too many of her female colleagues leave the paper because of this Neanderthal. She gave him her sweetest smile and thought, fuck off you prick.

The editor saw the smile and misinterpreted it as acquiescence; he felt his loins tense and briefly thought what it would be like to screw the arse off the bitch. Maybe he would find out. Angela saw the emotion in his eyes and thought, but did not show it; you have no chance.

"OK girl, move that fine arse of yours and start investigating." She gave him another beautiful smile, packed her briefcase and stood up to leave.

"Leave that other shit behind," he thundered.

She ignored him and walked out of the building to her car. The office staff had stopped working to listen to the interchange between them, and until she stood up and left, the editor had not noticed. He turned and scowled, all heads returned to the computer screens and everyone tried desperately hard to look busy.

The assistant editor returned to his office, and sat looking out of his window, seeing nothing, thinking extremely hard. He looked at the phone and made his mind up, dialling a number in Natal.

Chapter 7

Don Scales was now getting concerned about Samuel, as there had been no contact for two days. He decided to radio Jonathan.
Jonathan came on the line almost immediately.
"Have you heard from Samuel?" Don asked.
"Not yet," he replied.
"Is this usual?" Don asked.
"He sometimes does not contact for two to three days."
"I am getting worried about him. I am going to pick you up, and we will fly back to the area where we last got a message from him, to try and find him."
"I will be ready," Jonathan said.
Don made Jonathan's base in good time and landed three hundred yards from Jonathan. Jonathan covered the ground quickly and got into the plane gingerly. He hated flying at the best of times, but low level flying was even worse, and he knew that was what was called for now. At least at altitude you did not get the feel of hi speed, at a lower level, it would seem as if you are racing across the ground.
Don turned back up the runway and was airborne quickly, performing a tight right hand turn, which glued Jonathan to the passenger window. Don straightened up and climbed to a thousand feet and headed out towards the remote village.
They reached their destination in just over an hour and a half and circled to try to find any evidence left by Samuel.
"What kind of sign does he leave?" Don asked.
"Normally an arrow indicating his direction," Jonathan said.
"Really, that simple?"
"Yes, he sometimes leaves stones to indicate how many days at that mark. One stone for one day, two stones for two days and so on."
"How big are the marks?"

"That depends on the terrain, sometimes as big as five feet but normally one to two feet."

"That's like finding a needle in a haystack."

"We normally know in which direction he is travelling, that makes it much easier to find him. He will leave marks every two or three kilometres."

"OK, lets head on a straight line towards the river and see if we can find a marker."

They flew silently, both searching intently on the ground at two hundred feet below them. They estimated that Samuel would not be more than fifty kilometres from his last location. It was unlikely that he would travel more than twenty-five kilometres a day. They flew for twenty minutes with no sign.

Don reversed his compass bearing and turned back towards the village, moving a kilometre west. They flew back towards the village; still no sign. They flew in this search pattern for two hours and still no sign. A sense of dread came over Don, and he could see by Jonathan's face that he was also fearful. Don checked his fuel; he had enough fuel for one more pass before he would have to return to base to refuel. They were both extremely concerned by this stage. They made their final search but found nothing; they returned to base in total silence.

Samuel had recovered from his shock at being captured and his unexpected release by the poachers. Then he heard the plane. It was too far away for him to either signal or even recognise the plane. The plane moved on, and he continued his search.

Samuel was stubborn, and his pride had been dented from his easy capture. So instead of running for help, which the poachers had anticipated, he had doggedly begun to track the poachers again, this time with greater caution. On his fifth circling movement, he found a stone out of place. He studied the ground intently for many minutes and then deduced the direction that they had taken.

They had turned towards the river. He smiled; they had tried to fool him. He had outwitted them, and he could now track them with relative ease.

He thought about the plane again, and wondered, if it was the boss looking for him. They had always come in a vehicle before, it would not be them he concluded and moved on following the spoor of the poachers.

He found some open ground and started to make a mark. He was about to make a small mark, but realised that there were plenty of stones, so he made a mark some five feet long, and placed two stones at the base of the arrow.

He found a small stream and drank little; to drink too much now would induce thirst later. He had no method of carrying water, and did not have food. He had found the wild berries sufficient to keep his appetite at bay. He searched the bush for tracks of small game and found a lizard; he pounced on it gleefully and quickly broke its neck. He would dine well on the lizard. He collected small brush wood and started his fire to cook the lizard.

Don Scales refuelled and set off again to search for Samuel. His search pattern was the same but on a different line. He knew it was a hopeless task, but could not sit and not know what had happened to Samuel.

Jonathan spotted the fire first and shouted to Don.

"Look down there, is that smoke?"

Don could not see anything, and asked Jonathan to point towards the smoke. Jonathan pointed, and Don made a smooth turn, and headed in the direction indicated. They both saw the marker stones at the same time, and a flood of relief came over Don.

"See, I knew they would not catch him," Jonathan said.

Don flew over the site, and they both could see Samuel looking up at them, with surprise written all over his face. The nearest place to land was some two kilometres away, and Don set the plane down and quickly killed the engines. They both set off after Samuel.

Reluctantly, Samuel left the lizard that he had cooked, and trotted towards the plane. He knew it was the big bosses' plane by the markings. They had always fascinated him, as he could neither read or write.

Jonathan reached Samuel first, hugged the tracker, and said in their language, "I thought we had lost you Samuel."

Samuel just smiled, and then poured out his story. Don stood in frustration as Samuel went on and on, and he could not understand a word of it. He could wait no longer.

"Jonathan, please explain to me, what is he saying?" He demanded.

Jonathan stopped Samuel's outpouring with a raised hand, and turned to Don.

"They did catch him, but they let him go unharmed," he said in bewilderment.

"They were all blacks and very disciplined, except one who appeared to cause trouble all the time. He also said that they are very clever, and he did not know that they knew he was following them, until one of them caught him. He said, he did not see him coming. They all spoke in your language, and that is as far as we got before you interrupted."

Jonathan returned to Samuel and urged him to go on. Samuel then told his story without further interruption. At one stage, Jonathan whistled, and Don heard the word Zulu. He could barely restrain himself.

Jonathan turned to Don.

"Samuel thinks they are military, they spoke Zulu, and they mentioned the ANC. The man that caught him beat the one that mentioned the ANC. The leader they referred to as Captain and the other was a Sergeant, the third man was not military, and was not as disciplined as the others, he was not treated with any respect. They made him believe that they were heading for the coast, and they were very professional in covering their tracks. He has just found their spoor, that clearly indicated, that they are actually, headed for the river, to cross over into Mozambique."

Don looked shocked.

"You are telling me that a South African military unit is poaching in Tanzania; it is not possible, they would not dare. I just cannot believe it!"

"Let's get back to base," Don said.

They moved back to the aircraft, and were anticipating having a problem getting Samuel on board. They both laughed, when Samuel could not wait to get on board, and was trying to get into the pilot's seat. They sent him aft and took off.

"Jonathan, are you sure he said military from South Africa?"

"They could be ex military, operating freelance," Jonathan said.

"The logistics of getting here without support is too incredible to contemplate. They must have assistance to penetrate this far and why Tanzania?"

"Tanzania is still remote without adequate communication. The game in the crater is or was undisturbed, and patrols are few. How they came by this information God only knows," Jonathan said.

"I have an idea where it could have come from. Remember that we had that international conference on listed game and whether the sale of ivory should be allowed again. There was quite a strong delegation from South Africa; in fact, they were the prime movers for a change to the rules."

"Are you suggesting that they would shoot an elephant in Tanzania, and sell the ivory to South Africa?" Don asked.

"Why not, who would know where the animal was shot, and many trophy hunters would pay good money to have the set of tusks that they took from the old bull," Jonathan said.

"A hundred thousand dollars would not be excessive for such tusks, maybe more. Imagine what some people would do for that kind of money," he concluded.

"Then why did they let Samuel go?" Don asked.

"That I do not understand. He was very lucky indeed."

"It is quite a puzzle, they catch Samuel with ease and he is one of your best trackers. They give him disinformation and let him go. They obviously hoped that we would fall for it and head for the coast."

They both sat and thought about the prospect of trying to capture well-trained military personnel; they would not give up without a fight, which was for sure. Don wondered if more help was required and perhaps he should contact Dr Ngama again.

To capture South African military poaching in Tanzania would create a serious diplomatic incident. He thought it through again, and came to the conclusion that the poachers had to be ex military, and therefore, classed as ordinary poachers. He could not imagine the South African government sanctioning such activities, especially in the new South Africa.

"These are pro's Jonathan; do we have the capability to capture these poachers?"

"We have twenty-two men at our disposal; there are only three of them. I see no reason why we should not be able to capture these men."

"We must immediately deploy our forces in two teams as a front along the river which Samuel is certain they will try to cross."

"I suggest that we send five scouts, and drop them off with Samuel, behind the poachers. Samuel can track them, and determine their course, and your radio operator can call back to base the anticipated cross over point. We can then concentrate our forces over a smaller area."

"If we cover a semi-circle of their probable cross over point, then we can trap them and close the net. We could cover an area of five kilometres in groups of five, at one and a half kilometre intervals. We should pick them up when they try to cross the river."

"I would prefer to place the men on a narrower front to say five hundred meters in groups of three. Should one group come under attack or detect the poachers, then the other group is in easy range. Samuel can track them and indicate their direction with fair accuracy."

"Let's discuss it with Toby," Don said and reached for the radio.

Captain Khumalo had heard the plane and recognised its search pattern. He hoped that they had not found the tracker. They had made excellent time and covered more ground that he had anticipated. Moses for once had worked well and not complained; he guessed he was thinking about a Tanzanian jail. They all knew what the conditions would be like, and he secretly trembled at the thought.

They had covered thirty-five kilometres the previous night and had not, as far as he could determine, been detected. He found their position on the map; they were now only sixty-five kilometres from the river crossing. The nearest town of any size was Mkowela, and they had taken a wide path around it. They would run for Chitowe and cross the river where the Lumesule River and the Ruvuma River converged.

The river was wider, but shallower; they would probably still need dug out canoes to cross the river, as it could be too deep to wade across. This would be the most dangerous time, as they would be exposed on the crossing. Once across the river they would be able to hire porters to carry the tusks, and they would not have a problem with any scouts. They would move quickly to the rendezvous point and transfer the tusks to the professional hunter waiting for them. It would then be a straightforward matter to get home, as they would be collected at Mueda and flown home.

He allowed himself the luxury of thinking of home and then quickly removed the thought from his mind. There was still a long way to go, and he needed to concentrate on the job at hand. The sun was setting and it was time to move out. He confirmed his compass bearing and led the group towards Chitowe.

He hoped that they would make the same distance as the previous night, as this would leave them in striking distance of the river. They did not attempt to cover their tracks, as he knew that if they had found the tracker, this would be a futile exercise. All he could do was rely upon speed and believe that he had at least a day's head start.

They marched through the night and passed Chitowe just before dawn. They had done better than he had anticipated. Again, there had been no contact and no need to slow down the march. They found a thicket and decided to rest up until sundown. Their luck was holding out.

Chapter 8

Angela Murchin sat at her desk, reading the list of names of the terrorists. She knew that she was onto a compelling story, and would not let it go. Thomas had been away from the office all day yesterday and was still not back at his desk this morning. He obviously was working hard on the information required, and knew he had a far better chance than she would ever have, at finding the truth. The terrorist's relations would never talk to her, a privileged white of the old era.

Thomas was back in the office by two in the afternoon but brought disappointing news; he had not gleaned any information other than the names of the next of kin. He would follow his investigations also via contacts in the army and the police.

She covered her disappointment and thanked him for his efforts.

"Miss Murchin, did you really expect me to find out something so quickly?" He asked.

"I suppose not, it was just that I was hoping to have something to work on that was all."

"Please call me Angela; we do not need formalities here."

"OK Angela, but think about it; if this was a straight forward faction killing, why should it be so difficult to find out information?"

"The police and relatives of the murdered and the murderers are never so secretive. Information is normally so easy to come by. I mean it is going on all the time."

"Why do you think they are being so secretive?" She asked.

"I do not know, but my contacts will find out for me."

"Do you have any spare cash?" he asked.

"How much do you need?" she asked, understanding immediately why he asked.

"I need about five thousand Rand,"

"Are you serious?"

"Yes, it will cost at least that. I can arrange to have cash for you by tomorrow morning; will that be OK?"

"Fine," he responded.

"What are you two discussing," demanded the assistant editor.

"The proposed plant in Durban; you know, that Korean crowd," she responded quickly and gave him an innocent smile.

"What has Thomas to do with it; I gave that assignment to you."

"He has contacts in the local government office and can assist me with the information we need."

The assistant editor looked at Thomas, and then Angela and did not believe a word of it.

"Employees in this office are not at your disposal," he retorted.

"In future, if you wish to use someone in this office, discuss it with me first."

"Sorry," she said. "Next time I will do that,' she gave him her best smile."

"How far have you got then," he demanded.

"Well, we only discussed it yesterday, and he has not had a chance to consult his sources yet. He will also need money for bribes," she added quickly.

"How much do you need?"

"Say five thousand Rand."

"Piss off. He can have one thousand, and I will expect results."

The assistant editor stormed off to his office.

Thomas smiled at Angela, and said, "Nice try."

"Nothing ventured, nothing gained," she said laughingly.

"You can get cash from accounts now that dickhead has approved it; at least it's a start."

"I would advise that you also come back with some information on the proposed plant, just to cover our tracks so to speak."

"I will," he assured her.

Angela discarded the list of names and looked over the notes for the proposed car factory in Durban. Soong Industries owned by a Chen Yoo Soong. He was the sole owner of this gigantic corporation that employed twenty five thousand people in Korea alone. Turnover was estimated to be fifty billion dollars per annum, with a growth rate of seven point two percent per annum. It was a remarkable success story.

The Company's central business was steel and steel products. They had branched out into chemicals and pharmaceutical. Their latest ventures included a shipping line acquired in Hong Kong, a household appliance manufacturer in Germany, and they had installed a fully computerised car plant in Korea. Their markets were based in the Far East and Europe. Chen Yoo Soong had no holdings or any sales in the USA. It was inferred that he detested Americans, yet no reason was given.

Under personal notes, Angela found that Chen Yoo Soong was sixty-three years old, and had one son, Yamamata, who was twenty-four. He must have married late she mused. He was virtually unknown in Korea until after the Korean War.

It was rumoured that he had sold weaponry to both sides and made a small killing in the process. She smiled grimly at the pun. He acquired his first steel plant in nineteen fifty-five and had never looked back. He was a ruthless man, expecting and receiving full loyalty from his top managers. They never left his Company, and the occasional manager had even died under mysterious circumstances. He was renowned for his business acumen, and the ability to be in the right place at the right time.

He ran his Company with an iron rod, and was indefatigable. He had a private jet, helicopter, and houses in Switzerland, Rome, London and Brussels. He commuted regularly between his houses, and spent less than four months a year in his native Korea. His only indulgence was his son; he had tried to buy his way into Eton, and was unsuccessful. He settled for Brooklands in Dorset.

His son had been educated along the lines of the British aristocracy and spoke perfect cultured English. His son, Yamamata, had been an excellent student, and had been sent to Oxford and majored in economics.

His son was an outstanding athlete, but had been crazy about motor racing. Chen Yoo Sung had bought him a red Ferrari for his eighteenth birthday, which Yamamata had driven with gusto, and was often on the verge of being banned from driving, due to his high-speed exploits along the motorways.

He had formed a formula one racing team, ostensibly to promote the new car in Europe, but also to indulge in Yamamata's dream of becoming a racing driver. The team had been met with derision initially, but later with respect when the team had secured podium places.

They had bought the best team manager available, and their number one driver, Adrian Smythe, was considered to be the up and coming driver in Europe. The success of their second season of racing was unprecedented. They had been pursued by Bridgestone, to use their tyres, whilst Goodyear had made a dismal offer to the team.

Chen Yoo Soong had made a mental note of Goodyear's apparent lack of enthusiasm towards the team. As they became more successful, the

Goodyear management, tried in vain, to convert the team to Goodyear tyres.

There were few photographs of Chen Yoo Soong, and none of these, were clear pictures. He avoided publicity. Yamamata was the opposite; there were many photographs of the smiling handsome young man. The photographs showed the vibrancy and enthusiasm of Yamamata.

Angela was coming to the end of the summary and was at the heading 'General Information'. There was little about Chen Yoo Soong. On Yamamata, there were volumes; speeding fines, women he had dated, racing successes.

A final comment stated that a Korean prostitute had been beaten to death, and Chen Yoo Sung was implicated. Nothing ever came of the investigation, but there were strong rumours that Chen Yoo Soong had done the beating.

Angela closed the dossier, which had said everything and nothing. Chen Yoo Soong was a successful industrialist, and was not without faults. He sounded typical of most successful men, as she believed that you could not be that successful without breaking laws somewhere.

The footnote intrigued her, and she pondered whether to investigate the matter further. She doodled on her note pad, successful, ruthless, indulgent, murderous and influential. It was obvious that power was the key, and not the money involved in the ventures. He, like many billionaires, lived an austere life; his only indulgence being his son, an Achilles heel perhaps.

He was building a substantial corporation, and one could see how his various businesses had synergy. What would he buy next she thought, and why build a car manufacturing plant in South Africa? She could imagine the immense incentives being offered by the South African government. He would certainly know about the high violence levels in South Africa, and the often intransigence, of the black workforce. They would be in for a culture shock.

She stood up and stretched, which thrust her breasts forward provocatively; all the men stopped and stared. She suddenly realised what she was doing, and straightened up, collected the notes and dossier, and walked towards the exit. She had an athletic gait that enthralled the men, and made the women jealous. She passed them all, neither caring nor trying to play down her sexuality. She had decided to go and see the police officer in charge of the case of the terrorist attack, and then on to the municipal council buildings for information on the new car plant.

Chapter 9

Don Scales, after his discussion with Toby, suggested a council of war in the base camp. He did not anticipate that the poachers would be anywhere near the river crossing for at least another two days. He landed, and collected Toby, then returned to base.

"Toby, Jonathan and I have discussed our options on the way back, and would like your input."

"What have you discussed already?" Toby asked.

Don outlined the discussions already held, and sought Toby's advice on the options proposed, or any viable alternative.

"The problem, as I see it, is not whether we make contact, but how do we successfully apprehend the poachers."

"They will be armed, most probably with AK47's, and we have the old bolt action Lee Enfield .303 with a three bullet magazine. If they are military, as you seem to suggest, they will be well trained, and probably have night sights. Our scouts are not badly trained, but they are not military, and they do not have night sights."

"They are used to poorly armed, and untrained poachers; they do not have the skills to fight a military unit, even if there are only three of them."

"Have you thought of the possibility of them having reinforcements at the river crossing? If the South Africans dare come this far, then it is possible that a back up unit could be waiting for them," Toby concluded.

Don listened to Toby intently, and had to admit he had not considered firepower or the possibility of a back up unit. The position did not look promising.

"It is not as if they are not expecting us," said Toby.

"Look how easily they caught our best tracker. Remember I lived in South Africa for four years whilst I was at varsity. These guys patrolled an area from the coast in Namibia to the east coast at Cosy Bay. They bordered Angola, Botswana, Zimbabwe and Mozambique."

"You can count the number of successful attacks from across their borders on one hand. They are past masters at setting up an ambush, or taking out terrorist infiltrators. If the poachers are from a recognised anti-terrorist unit, then we have big trouble."

"You must also remember that if they are Zulu's, then they probably worked in these units, as they were as eager to prevent the ANC coming to power, as the whites."

"We have twenty two scouts, and the three of us," Jonathan said. "These are blacks, and you always insist that the blacks can do nothing without white support."

Toby gave Jonathan a withering look but declined to comment.

"Let's look at what we know, and try and find a solution," Don said.

They both nodded assent.

"OK, we assume they are South African, they are armed with AK47's, they could be military, and they are extremely fit," Don said.

"There is also one amongst them that can face two charging elephants without panic, and coolly shoot them both. He is also an excellent shot to place that bullet, under immense pressure, in the brain box of the elephant," Jonathan said.

"For once I agree with you Jonathan," Toby said. "These are not the normal poachers that we have come up against. They will not throw their weapons away, and run for it."

"So, do we just let them cross over the boarder," Don asked testily. "You cannot be surely suggesting that."

They both responded together, that they did not believe that letting them cross the border with impunity was the answer.

"All I am saying Don, be sure you know what you are up against, and plan accordingly. It is too late to bring in the military, in any event. I would doubt that Dr Gama would even consider such a proposal."

"I agree with that," Don said. "I do appreciate what you are saying, but how do we capture these men without loss of life on either side?"

"I can tell you now that the possibility of no loss of life is impossible. They know exactly what will happen to them in a Tanzanian jail, and they will not surrender without heavy resistance. Is the elephant worth it? Now that they know we are on to them, will they ever come back again?" Toby asked.

"If we do nothing and just let them escape, they most certainly will return; we cannot allow that," Jonathan said.

"How many lives are you prepared to lose for the sake of two elephants, which are already dead," Toby asked. "And while you are thinking about it, ask yourself another question; last year twenty two elephants and ten rhino were poached. As part of our culling operation, to control the population we have shot nearly as many ourselves."

"I understand that," Jonathan said, "I understand the need to cull, but you cannot allow it to go on anywhere, are you suggesting that we allow the poachers to do our culling for us'?"

"Stop it now," Don said with authority, "What we privately believe in is of no concern. At this moment in time, our problem is how to capture the poachers with minimal losses. I do not wish to suggest a number." He looked directly at Toby.

Don brought out the map and laid it on the table, and plotted the course the poachers had taken. He estimated that they could travel a maximum of twenty kilometres per day, with the heavy burden of the tusks, slowing them down. This would indicate that they could not be in a position to reach the crossing before Thursday, two days hence.

Toby disagreed, and suggested that in a forced march, they could easily cover thirty maybe forty kilometres a night. They could be lying up within striking distance now.

"Jonathan, do you know Samuel's current position?" Don asked.

"I will call up the radio op with his unit and find out where they are and the direction of the poachers."

Jonathan left the room to call the operator. Toby studied the map, and searched for the most likely crossing point.

"If I were they," he said, "I would take the shortest route, and cross where the rivers Lumesule and the Ruvuma meet."

"We picked them up near Makungivro, and we know they were headed for Mkowela, that's about a hundred kilometres, they have covered that ground in only three days."

"That makes them some sixty to seventy kilometres away from the crossing point you suggested."

"Correct," Toby said.

"We have to assume that they will not cross at, Gomba, Masuguru or Negomane as they would be at risk of detection. My guess is they will cross where I said, or at a direct line from Chitowe."

At this point, Jonathan returned and made his report. The poachers had made a straight line for Mkowela, and had not bothered to cover their tracks. Which meant that they did not know we had recovered Samuel?

"Or they thought pace was better than covering tracks."

"We need to know what direction they took from Mkowela," Don said.

"How far does he think he is behind them?" Toby asked.

"Samuel believes he will catch up with them before nightfall, they have left a trail a blind man could follow."

"He must not overrun them Jonathan. That could be fatal."

"I will get him to hold back until dawn, they cannot reach the river tonight regardless of which point they choose. He can give us their direction tomorrow," said Jonathan.

Don felt uneasy about the whole thing, and realised the tremendous responsibility on his shoulders. He had never fully considered the risks to his scouts before, and he now realised how little he knew about what went on. What could he do? A germ of an idea started, and slowly grew into what could be the answer.

Chapter 10

Captain Khumalo knew that by now they were being followed by the anti-poaching units, and pondered his position. He came to the same conclusion as Toby that, in all probability, the scouts would be ill equipped, and poorly trained. He thought how easy it had been to catch their best tracker. What concerned him was that he did not know the number of scouts pitted against him.

He estimated that they were fifty to sixty kilometres from their designated crossing spot. They would force-march to within twenty kilometres. They would leave just before dark tonight.

He called sergeant Khubeki to him, "Sergeant, we are going to march for at least forty kilometres tonight."

"I am not sure that we can, we have been pushing hard now for five days. Moses looks stuffed," he said.

"We have to do it, tomorrow night I will go forward, and reconnoitre the river, and you must circle back, and determine who and what is following us."

"That will mean leaving Moses alone, is that wise?"

"What else can we do? He would be in the way if either of us took him with us."

"Then we must tie him up," said sergeant Khubeki.

"No need for that. Where would he go, he cannot give himself up as he would go to jail regardless of what deal he tried, we just have to risk leaving him."

They called Moses over, and explained the plan to him, and told him that they would have to march forty kilometres that night. He looked at them incredulously but said nothing; he was learning that his point of view held no sway in their plans.

They left half an hour before nightfall but, this time they carried the tusks turned down over the backs of both men. They had to walk a meter apart, and keep in step to prevent tripping each other up. The sergeant was behind Moses, and carried more of the weight of the two tusks, and also set the pace.

Captain Khumalo led the way taking compass bearings at regular intervals. They moved at a brisk walk that the sergeant could keep up all night. The ground was flatter now as they moved closer to the river making the task a little easier.

They covered the forty kilometres one hour before dawn, and decided to walk until daybreak. They skirted Chitowe, and hid in an acacia thicket six kilometres from Chitowe, and only twenty kilometres from the river crossing. Again they had done better than anticipated, but they were all weary, and could have gone no further.

The forced marches were taking their toll, and Moses had developed a cough from heavy sweating and rapid cooling from the cold dawn. Moses water bottle had run out two days earlier, and he was surviving on the water given to him by Captain Khumalo. He was dehydrated, and close to collapse.

"You have done well Moses," said Captain Khumalo. "We will make a man out of you yet."

Moses scowled but said nothing, as he was too tired to argue. He fell into a deep sleep.

"Sergeant we cannot rely on Moses for sentry duty, so we must share it between us. I will take the first watch."

The sergeant nodded and understood. He also was exhausted, and was soon fast asleep.

Samuel and his five scouts were tracking at dawn, and they reached the outskirts of Mkowela at midday. They followed the clear spoor past Mkowela, and on towards Chitowe. The radioman called Jonathan, and advised him of their direction. Jonathan reported this to Don, and they studied the map again

"They are going to cross the river somewhere between Negomane and the Mbangala River," said Jonathan.

They all agreed that was most likely, they had an area to cover of forty kilometres of riverbank, and they had seventeen scouts, and themselves.

"I have to make a phone call," said Don.

He had tried to make the call the night before, but the person he called would not be back until the early afternoon.

"Who are you calling?" Toby asked.

"I have an old friend that can advise me."

They both looked at him, but no further explanation was offered.

Don had remembered his old friend Allen Beatty; they had been at school together in Dundee, and had met up year's later and swapped stories. Alan had been evasive about his work in the army, and had been posted to Ireland several times.

Allen had worked under cover, and was a member of the S.A.S. anti-terrorist force that dealt with the release of hostages. He had done duty in Zimbabwe when a small group of British tourists had gone missing. They had been killed, but the S.A.S caught the killers, and exacted revenge. There had been no survivors.

Allen had not volunteered this information. Don put it together over a period of four years. Allen had not told him out of bravado, but more the need to talk to someone he could trust. Don had never mentioned his activities.

They had kept in touch over the years by occasional letter and phone calls, but their friendship was intact. It was a strange bond unique to few men, as they knew that they had complete faith in each other.

There had been many times after a mission that Allen had stayed with him. Don could tell by the eyes how terrible it had been, as they were often wild looking for days. Then Allen would relax, and the tension would go out of his body, and the wildness would leave his eyes. He would sometimes talk about it, but not always.

Don dialled the number, and heard the familiar voice on the other end of the line giving his number only.

"Hi Allen, its Don."

"Hi Don, how the hell are you," came the reply.

Don went through the usual pleasantries, and then moved onto the reason for the call.

"Allen, I have a problem, and I wondered if you could advise me."

Allen heard the anxiety in the voice, and said. "Fire away."

Don explained his situation with the poachers, and the problem of the firepower stacked against him. Allen's response was quick and decisive.

"Forget it Don, you have neither the training nor the ability to carry out such a mission. They will eat you for breakfast. I know about the South African Special Forces. They are nearly as good as the S.A.S. and do not be fooled by the skin colour, they were all superbly trained, and are very fit. Ask yourself could you carry tusks of that weight plus your food, water and rifle at that pace over the distance you have told me."

"I know that, but I have to do something."

"All you will do is get yourself, and a good number of your scouts killed. These guys are pro's, and it would take pro's to handle them. Sorry kid, but you are not in their league."

"To co-ordinate a capture of this nature, you require skilled anti-terrorist squads that understand the others actions generated from years of training. They may be burdened with the tusks, but they will probably slip through your net without you even knowing."

"Tell your tracker to back off, he, and the scouts with him, will be taken out, if they get too close again. Your tracker was lucky the first time, and this tells me whoever is leading them had complete discipline from his squad. The tracker will not get a second chance."

"Don, promise me that you won't take them on, please."

"Allen, what can I do? I cannot stand by, and let them slaughter the game at will. I have to do something, or they will keep coming back again."

"Don you can do nothing! Do you expect them to come back again after being chased halfway across the country?"

"Yes I do," he said.

"How will you know if they are back?" Allen asked.

"We will only know when the dead game is found."

There was silence over the phone for ten seconds or so, and Don thought he had lost the connection.

"Are you still there?" he asked.

"Yes, I am thinking."

"Allen I need your advice, please help me."

Allen heard the cry for help, and his heart went out to his friend. He was concerned that if he did nothing Don would get himself killed, and he could never live with that.

"Don, I suggest you concentrate your forces in two groups of eleven, and have your two assistants in charge of them. You stake out the river at two points only, and let them make a lot of noise. That way you will alert the poachers and survive, and you will have done your level best."

"You are asking me to give up without a fight, and I am not sure I can do that," Don replied.

"Don if you are lucky, maybe you will either capture, or kill, one or two of the poachers. They will certainly kill or wound twelve to fifteen of your scouts, and if that should happen, the normal poachers will have a field day as you will have no staff to control your area. Do you want that?"

"Of course not!"

"Killing people is not easy Don, or being shot at. You are not mentally or physically equipped to handle this situation. You are outgunned and will be outmanoeuvred. I implore you please do not try."

"Allen what else can I do?"

"You can wait for me."

"I beg your pardon?"

"Don, I cannot help you this time, but definitely the next time they strike. You will have to be patient. I know a couple of buddies that would help, we would need no more than three of us, and we will take them alive."

"You could be on another mission."

"If they come back within six months I will not be on another mission. My buddies and I cannot go on another mission for six months."

"Where have you been to get that kind of time off?" Don asked.

"Not on the phone," was Allen's reaction.

"'Do you think they will be back within six months?"

"I am certain that they will," Don replied.

"Then do as I suggest, and wait until they come back, and call me immediately."

"O.K. Allen, I see the logic in what you say, I will follow your suggestion."

"Thanks buddy, and please do not try to be a hero."

"I won't," Said Don "Thanks for your advice."

"Cheers," Allen said.

"Cheers," Don said, and replaced the receiver.

He looked out of the window but saw nothing. The phone call had left him drained, and feeling guilty. He knew that Allen was correct in his assessment and recommendations, but was not sure that he could follow the advice given. He thought of Jonathan who would be expecting some action to prevent the escape of the poachers. He knew that Jonathan respected him, and he did not want to lose that respect. Toby, on the other hand, had already suggested the same course of action as Allen.

He stood there full of doubt, and felt the burden of responsibility on his shoulders. He would not let his scouts be killed, as Allen suggested, they certainly would be. He wondered if the uncertainty was created due to his ego, or the actual fear of a disaster. He did not like being told that he was incapable of handling this situation. He rationalised the situation the same as Toby, the elephant were already dead, and it was not worth risking his team's lives over it. He concluded that he felt better now that he had made his decision.

He went back into the ops room where Toby and Jonathan were waiting. They both looked up at him as he went into the room, and they both saw the anguish in his face.

"What is the problem," Jonathan asked.

"I have just called a friend of mine that has experience in these matters. He suggests that we split the scouts into two groups and cover two areas only."

"But that will leave a huge gap in our line," said Jonathan.

"I know, but I need to concentrate my forces in the event of a contact," Don said.

Toby gave him a wry look, and then it dawned on him what Don was proposing. He was going to let them get away. He said nothing.

"Don if we do as you say the poachers will almost definitely get away. We have worked damned hard to keep in touch with them, and box them in," Jonathan said.

"I know, but that is the way I see it, and that is what you will do," ordered Don brusquely.

"Now let's look at the map, and no more arguments."

Jonathan was about to open his mouth and protest, but Don gave him a warning look that said to be silent.

They studied the map, and selected the most likely points for crossing the river. The teams would be located five kilometres apart having chosen a point equidistant between Negomane, and the convergence of the two rivers, Lumesule and the Ruvuma.

They called off the trackers, and arranged for them to be picked up. The scouts would be redeployed as planned. Jonathan did as ordered, but without enthusiasm, as he felt he had been let down by Don. He would confront him later about it. They got up to leave, and Don asked Jonathon to stay behind.

"Jonathan, I know that you are disappointed with my decision, but you must understand that I cannot risk lives unnecessarily. These are not ordinary poachers; they are a highly trained military unit. We must regroup and retrain our scouts such that they can handle a similar event in the future."

"But Don," Jonathan started to say.

"There are no buts," Don said, "I understand your need to protect the wildlife, understand my need to protect the lives of my scouts and you."

"Don, when we take on this job, we know the risks."

"That's correct, I know you know the risks, but I am not about to see my scouts slaughtered. If you lose a large portion of your scouts, then who will keep control of the game parks? Moosa will have a field day."

"But what is to stop them coming back."

"We want them to come back, but next time we will be equipped to deal with them."

"Why is that?" Jonathon asked.

"Trust me you will see."

Jonathan appeared to be ready to ask another question, but Don held up his hand to stop him. "You will see," is all he said. Jonathan looked at Don, and then resigned himself to following the plan as given. He would never dream of disobeying Don. He walked stiffly from the room, and called in the scouts.

The scouts were in their designated positions just before sunset. They were puzzled why they had taken up a defensive position rather than an ambush position. They did not question the judgment of their superiors, as a life of following orders was second nature to them. They posted sentries and lookouts, and waited for events to unfold.

Captain Khumalo was shaken awake by sergeant Khubeki. He sat up, and looked around him, to see Moses still fast asleep.

"Wake him up," said Captain Khumalo.

Sergeant Khubeki gave Moses a kick up the backside, and he woke up aggressively.

"Can it," said Khumalo.

Moses looked at the sergeant and thought that one day, on his own terms; he would make this man suffer. The sergeant read his thoughts and smiled.

"Moses you stay here and watch the camp, if you move off on your own we will find you and kill you. Do you understand?"

"I understand, where the fuck would I go to, I cannot get home without you two, so I will stay here, don't worry."

"Sergeant, you back track and find the tracker, if they are still following us, dissuade them."

Sergeant Khubeki grinned from ear to ear and asked. "How many should I take out?"

"None at all if possible, just disarm them and give one or two of them a good beating. Then return here. I would like you back here for two am, O.K."

The sergeant nodded.

"I will reconnoitre the river and find out where the patrols are. We can then move out to the crossing."

The sergeant set off at a steady jog that would eat up five kilometres an hour, it was five pm, and he had nine hours to get there and back. He would run for three hours and then start scouting an additional five kilometres. If he could not find them in that range, then they were too late to catch up with, at least on foot. If they travelled by vehicle, they would hear them from miles away and have a nice surprise for them.

Sergeant Khubeki found no traces of the trackers during the night. They were either too far back to matter or they had given up. He turned and jogged back.

Captain Khumalo jogged at the same rate as the sergeant and was within ten kilometres of the river by seven in the evening. He slowed down, took his bearings, and ran on at a slow jog with his rifle at the ready across his chest He ran to within a kilometre of the river and stalked forward. He reached the river without seeing or hearing the scouts. He was puzzled as he thought they would be well spaced out to detect his presence.

He decided to scout back up the river to ascertain the exact positions of the scouts. He moved with the utmost caution. He had travelled for an hour when be heard a cough. He froze instantly and then bellied towards the sound. He moved silently, careful not to disturb the branches of neither the acacia's nor the reed patches that he had to move through. He caught sight of the man who coughed, and another, some ten meters to his right.

He withdrew and then circled around them. He found the main group sat around a camp making no attempt to hide their positions. He counted nine in all and a white man who sat away from the scouts on his own. He was smoking a cigarette. It was with some relief that he realised that these scouts were amateurs, and though he must not discount them, they were actually no threat to him or his team. He withdrew undetected and headed back to their camp. He ran smoothly and efficiently and was not even breathing deeply when he reached the camp.

He decided to have some sport on his way back to the camp. He stopped a kilometre short of the camp, and stalked Moses he knew that the sergeant would not be back, as it was only just after midnight. Moses was watching the track, which the sergeant had taken and was oblivious to the captain's approach. Captain Khumalo tapped Moses on the shoulder. Moses jumped out of his skin and spun round to see his attacker.

Captain Khumalo realised he had made a grave error as Moses was so uptight whilst waiting on his own that he went to pull the trigger on his AK47. Khumalo knocked the gun to one side, but a burst of fire went into the night. After the silence, the noise was deafening.

He quickly disarmed Moses and put the AK back on safety, and single shot, not automatic.

"You stupid bastard" roared Moses, "I could have killed you"

"You never could or will be able to," Khumalo said.

"Now get ready to move out."

"What about Khubeki?" Moses asked.

"He knows where we are going, he will find us. Now get moving."

They loaded the tusks as the night before, but this time Captain Khumalo was leading. They moved off at a fast march. Sergeant Khubeki was five kilometres from the camp when he heard the shooting. He immediately increased his speed and was at the camp in thirty minutes. He circled the camp slowly and warily but could not detect either Moses or the Captain. He stole into the camp without making a sound and found it deserted. He saw a spent cartridge on the ground and picked it up. He searched for more and found another five casings. One tap on the auto he thought; six rounds. He searched for tracks and found the direction they had headed and set off after them at a steady lope.

Chapter 11

Angela Murchin arrived at the police headquarters, flashed her press card and asked the duty sergeant for the officer in charge of the terrorist attack.

The sergeant gave her a look of appraisal and asked," What terrorist attack, I am not aware of any terrorist attack."

"Last Tuesday in Alex, there was an attack, and one of the local ANC bigwigs was murdered."

"Oh, that one" why did you call it a terrorist attack, it was just another faction killing. Warrant Officer de Bruyn is the officer in charge, I will see if he is in."

He picked up the phone, and dialled a three-digit number, it rang for a couple of seconds, and he asked for Warrant Officer de Bruyn. He was in, but he was busy, he said. The desk sergeant turned away from Angela and said, "You will want to see this one believe me."

"Why?" asked de Bruyn sounding puzzled.

"She's got legs a mile long, and tit's you would die for," he said.

De Bruyn laughed and said, "Send her in. I could do with a little light relief'," then as an afterthought, "Who is she, and what does she want?"

"Press and murder in Alex last Tuesday," he replied.

"Ah no," he groaned, "Send her in any way."

He sat at his desk chewing over what the sergeant had said, "Legs a mile long and tit's to dream about."

He had better be right or he would crap all over him later.

Angela smiled and walked down the series of offices following the sergeant's directions. She guessed what he had said when he turned away and once again thought how foolish men are. They are so easily manipulated with a little flash of leg, and a bit of pouting.

She knocked on the door, and a gruff voice said, "Come In."

She opened the door and stepped inside.

Warrant Officer de Bruyn was sat at his desk. He was middle to late thirties and was studying her intently. She gave him her best smile.

Warrant Officer de Bruyn said, "How can I help you?"

"My name is Angela Murchin, and I am with the Metropolitan. I am investigating the murders in Alex last Tuesday; I was surprised to hear how the attackers were caught and gunned down so quickly."

"Isn't that just typical, we have been badgered by the press on the level of crime and in particular unsolved murders. You people are never satisfied," he said angrily.

"They were unlucky, or we were lucky we had a patrol passing in the area, and they heard the gunfire, and went to investigate. The attackers opened fire on the police, and the police returned their fire, and killed them all."

Violence in Johannesburg had reached unprecedented levels and car hijacking, rape, robbery and murder were commonplace. High levels of violence had always been confined to the black townships during the Apartheid regime. With the new South Africa came a crime wave that sent fear, and trepidation, throughout the white suburbs.

This was due to the removal of the repressive pass system and the release of thousands of political prisoners and the revoking of the death penalty. Exiles returned in droves from various European countries and the rest of Africa.

The exiles expected to live as the white population had previously; with big houses, fancy cars, and swimming pools. They were returning to a promised land bolstered by the promises of the ANC. They returned in reality to a South Africa virtually unchanged. They did not have the means to purchase their dream houses, and rapidly became disillusioned. Their only hope of survival was to turn to crime. With ensuing corruption, the most experienced and capable police officers left the force to create a plethora of security companies, and left the police forces across the city seriously depleted. Affirmative action promoted unqualified black police officers to levels, which were beyond their training and experience.

The killing of police officers reached levels that drove fear into the heart of the most dedicated officer, and they sought other employment in private industry. The morale in all the forces was at its lowest. This was further exacerbated by the Truth and Reconciliation Commission, which hounded the police for crimes against humanity. There were few officers in the special branch that did not have some blood on his hands. The Apartheid regime had been cruel and efficient, and had held a minority population in power through fear. These barriers were removed overnight, and a more deadly, and ferocious system took its place. The gangs!

Even the special investigative branch of the past had masters, and laws to contain it. The gangs knew no laws. They slaughtered black and white with apparent impunity. Taxi wars broke out driven by gang leaders controlling the taxis in Johannesburg.

The only effective system of transport in South Africa was the taxi from the townships into the industrial areas and offices. This was a large business, and the gangs, through fear and mayhem, were taking control. Rival gangs fought for this business and killed indiscriminately. Pick up points, loaded with passengers, were mowed down by automatic fire. The centre of Johannesburg was under siege with daily murders, robberies and hijacking. Businesses created a building boom in the suburbs, building new offices for their staff, as they would not venture into the "no go areas," created in central Johannesburg.

The world famous Carlton hotel saw its occupancy rate drop from an average seventy percent to less than twenty percent. Other hotels in the area declined so rapidly that bankruptcies were commonplace. The CBD changed in six months, from white dominated businesses, to black dominated crime.

The government withheld this information, as with the advent of the new South Africa, tourism was booming. Yet tourists were mugged on an almost daily basis, and quickly embassies from virtually all the European countries, advised their tourists to stay out of Johannesburg. This only added to the decline of the area, which even the police would not dare to patrol except in armoured cars, and in force.

The police had been slated for their inability to control the CBD, and were criticised daily in the local press. Any success in apprehending or wiping out a gang or part of a gang was music to the ears of the whites, and a good deal of the black populace.

There was open hostility against the police, who had an impossible duty to perform, and attacked by the press which sensationalized every aspect of crime. The Metropolitan was one of the most vitriolic of the local press.

It was against this background that Angela was attempting to obtain cooperation from Warrant Officer de Bruyn.

"It is a bit unusual not to get at least one back alive, isn't it?" She asked.

"That depends upon the willingness of the attackers to give up, In this case they made no attempt to surrender, and we had to protect ourselves. You have no idea what it is like to face a group of thugs armed with AK47s," he concluded.

"That's my point," Angela said, "We are not convinced that they are thugs, but actually a trained and experienced military unit."

Warrant Officer de Bruyn groaned, and said, "Please do not start assuming that these men are the so called Third Force."

There was a theory expounded by the ANC that a Third Force existed which was attempting to destabilise the country making it impossible to govern. This Third Force was supposedly made up of disenchanted military personnel who still dreamed of white supremacy.

The Third Force was allegedly connected to the old National Party, and included the military personnel, at the highest level, military intelligence, and the old disbanded ISS, which was the secret service. In the old Afrikaner society, the Broederbond was also implicated.

The Truth and Reconciliation Committee had found numerous instances of hit squads that took out prominent leaders opposed to Apartheid prior to the election of the Government of National Unity. The TRC, as it was known, heard heart-rending stories of brutality and murder. The purging went on for eighteen months and was given full coverage at the now ANC controlled South African Broadcasting Company. The National party, to ensure that the policies of Apartheid were broadcast, had used the SABC unmercifully. The sycophantic directors of the SABC only held the government appointed positions for as long as they supported the government, and extolled the virtues of separate development.

In this respect, nothing had changed, only the allegiance and the colour of the directors. Apartheid was a class structure based on colour first, then home language, Afrikaans, and then position in society. Each individual was classified and recorded in that order. The blacks were slaves in their own country.

Education was for whites only. This was clearly evidenced by the low levels of literacy amongst the black population. This was done by decree; they did not want any clever Kaffir rocking the boat.

The English-speaking sector was no more than tolerated, and they had never come close to holding power. Most had gone along with the system, deriving all the benefits, without getting their hands dirty.

Even those that opposed Apartheid made little effort to make changes. It was a system so loathsome and degenerate that it had no hope of survival.

It always amazed the outside world that the black population tolerated Apartheid for so long. There was no choice, townships were created to enclose the black population, prevent adequate communication, and deter uprising. It was only possible to live adjacent to, never in, the cities of South Africa, if you had a job there, and a pass. The rural blacks were not allowed to move to the centres and were tied to farms. They were paid a pittance, but knew no other life. The control was total.

The floodgates of anger and hate were opened when the ANC came to power. Even they had not anticipated such a release of hatred and mayhem. They had neither the desire nor the resources to control the backlash of this bloody coup.

The pendulum hand swung one hundred and eighty degrees to the left. It would take little to bring this situation to flash point, and this would probably lead to civil war with the armed forces, still controlled, by white generals.

Nelson Mandela had recognised this possibility and had tried to pull the teeth of the armed forces. He had stopped conscription, reduced the personnel, put out to grass many prominent generals and placed his own key men in power. He knew that this was superficial. The MK (armed wing of the ANC) he had drafted into the armed forces were no match for the well-trained professionals already entrenched. The armed forces had spent their lives fighting the blacks across an impossible border with a success only matched by Israel.

The Zulu nation, renowned world wide for its fighting spirit, was purposely infiltrated to create disorder.

An alliance of the armed forces and the Zulu nation would to most, be unthinkable, and yet if this happened, they would probably be unstoppable. The ANC had applied the same tactics as Apartheid to ensure that the two sides never met successfully. They did this in many ways, but the most damning was the use of the MK, to kill and maim in Natal.

Prior to the election, atrocities in Johannesburg townships were reported worldwide. Atrocities of whole villages wiped out in Natal were not even given coverage, and information was not released. More people died in Natal under the banner of faction fighting than in any other province. Yet little was known about it. It was alleged that thousands had died at the hands of the ANC who astutely turned the situation round in their favour.

A Third Force feeding on such hate and suspicion could be the catalyst required for civil war. The only solution for the white supremacists, and a disaffected Zulu nation, that was losing power.

"You do not believe there is a Third Force?" Angela asked.

"Absolute rubbish," was his response, "We have released too many so called political prisoners, and when we catch them again, they are released after spending only months in jail."

"What about the TRC revelations then?" She countered.

"More bullshit from a government that has lost control, and needs to find something else for the population to feed on," he said with feeling, "Just ask yourself who would gain from a third force action."

"Whites! And the Zulu's of course."

"The ANC are out of control, and knew it, they have to have a scapegoat as it is unthinkable to the rest of the world that they are incapable of governing this country."

"South Africa is yesterday's news," Angela said, "How many foreign correspondents do you see nowadays."

"Domestic issues do not sell papers overseas."

"What do you know about Samuel Dlamini," she asked, Angela noticed a slight flinch at the name, but de Bruyn was soon under control.

"Nothing, why do you ask?"

"We have information that he was with the anti-terrorist squads based in Natal."

"Then your information is better than ours, where did you obtain this information?" he asked.

"We never reveal our sources, as you well know."

De Bruyn became officious, leaned forward towards her and said, "If you have any information on this matter you will tell me now, or I will arrest you for withholding evidence, and obstructing justice. I can hold you for forty eight very unpleasant hours," he warned.

Angela felt a twinge of fear, "My information is common knowledge, and I am surprised that you do not know of it. A colleague at the office knew a Samuel Dlamini, and said the one he knew was in the antiterrorist squads in Natal."

De Bruyn noted with satisfaction the fear that she could not hide from her eyes. He also knew that she was unsure of the source or the validity as she parted with the information too easily.

"What is your colleague's name?"

Angela now realised that she had said too much and felt uneasy. "I can't remember," she said weakly.

"Listen lady, do not talk shit to me, and now give me the name."

"Why are you so interested in my colleagues name when you believe that the case is closed?"

"The case is still under investigation, and any information that you have you must disclose. We may wish to interview your colleague, so he can help us further with our enquiries. There is nothing sinister in this, we would also like to get to the truth," he said persuasively.

He appeared genuinely concerned and had dropped the aggressive attitude of earlier. Angela was not sure she could trust him, and studied his face intently for anything untoward. He remained impassive and almost genial. Angela felt her resolve diminishing.

"His name is Thomas Msibi. He has been with the Metropolitan for six months now."

"Thanks. Now, can I help you with anything else?" he asked.

"I do not think so," she said, and stood up to leave.

"Can I give you a word of advice?" he asked.

"On what?"

"On your investigation," he said.

"If you must."

"You have been lucky today, do not trust all the police officers you meet and never disclose a name again, these are difficult times that we live in. If you are remotely close with your theory, and what you publish, you could be in grave danger."

He gave her his card, which had his office and home number.

"If you need help, please call me," was all he said.

"Thanks I will," her opinion of him was improving; Angela turned to leave then said, "What will you do with that name?"

"It will not leave this office," he said.

"Thanks again, and Tot Siens," she said.

He smiled, "Mooi bly, go well," he replied.

She walked out of his office and down the corridor past the front desk where the desk sergeant looked at her curiously. He would call the commandant tonight and advise him of the papers interest and who was involved.

He picked up the phone and dialled de Bruyn's number.

"De Bruyn"

"Were you disappointed?" he asked lewdly, "a real cracker hey."

"A corker," he agreed.

"Did she know anything of interest," he asked casually.

"Nah, nothing. She was just fishing. I told her that, for once, it was an open, and shut case," he said.

"Well I hope she comes back, I need distractions like that."

They chatted about nothing for a couple of minutes, and then put their telephones down. The sergeant was not convinced, and thought that de Bruyn was being evasive. Similarly, de Bruyn noticed a professional interest by the sergeant in Angela Murchin. Not merely a passing sexual discussion. He did not mention her legs or tit's again, curious he thought. He would keep an eye on the sergeant.

He looked at the name on his pad, and decided to remove the page and throw it away. He ripped it into small pieces and threw into his wastepaper basket. He would know how to find him if necessary. He felt a shiver of pleasure at the prospect of seeing Angela again.

That night the sergeant rang his commandant, said the code word Phoenix, and replaced the receiver. He walked three blocks from his house, and waited for the call at a public telephone. The phone rang, and the sergeant gave his call sign, and received the correct response. A familiar voice on the end said, "Give me your report."

In a distant office in central Johannesburg, a tape clicked on, and recorded the discussion. The tape had seventy-three other calls made from the same public phone. In the same room were twenty recorders covering a further twenty public phones. They were all turning slowly, listening to conversations across the city.

The selected public phones were, in reality, known call points for the operatives of the Third Force. The phones locations and numbers were changed at monthly intervals, as designated by the Third Force command. Yet, the ANC had penetrated the security of the Third Force and had long been recording their clandestine operations.

The same network existed in Pretoria, Cape Town, Durban, Bloemfontein and Pietersburg, and the ANC had access to many of these calls.

The ANC knew or suspected, most of the Third Force hierarchy, but not yet the supreme leaders. They could not move until they had that information. Electronic and manual surveillance had been placed on the four key suspects. A politician, an army general, a commandant in the police force, and a leading member of the Broederbond. The Third force was still elusive due to their codes and passes which had, in large part, proved indecipherable to the ANC.

The mole could still not find out the names of the supreme leaders, but knew they were positioned in the upper echelons of government and industry. The President, and his two vice presidents, was the sole recipients of his reports, to ensure that there would be no leaks, and the Third Force would not realise how far the ANC had penetrated their ranks.

The Third Force network stretched the length and the breadth of the country covering all levels of society both black and white. It was developing into a considerable force, and was a significant threat to government.

They had ruthlessly dealt with the informers they had found, and had sent out hit teams across the country causing destruction wherever they went. It was not a random effort. It was coordinated to generate maximum impact as the violence spread from one main city to another. And all the time the membership of the Third Force grew.

The disillusioned white population became particularly susceptible to the wooing of the Third Force. There was no application form, just a friend of a friend who knew the feelings of the applicants, and recruited them into the organisation. It was expanding exponentially, at a terrifying rate. They were often recruited as vigilantes, or as special police; they were watched closely for months before induction into the Third Force.

As membership grew secrecy became more difficult, and information inevitably leaked. The perpetrators of indiscretions were dealt with severely, and seldom acted with indiscretion again. Those that did, disappeared, and were never seen again. Training camps for special operatives were organised on the vast game farms of the Northern Province.

They were never held twice at the same venue. The combined knowledge of the special services, and the ex ISS members, created a formidable operative trained in disinformation, assassination, explosives and surveillance.

They operated in individual cells and were never linked. The maximum number to a cell was six, but some operatives acted independently. They covered all the occupations from process operator to factory managers; they were in the armed forces, police force and the civil service. They were coded by number and never by name.

The ANC had realised that it had to be purged at all costs. Before it was too late!

Chapter 12

His name was Nathaniel Molefe. He had been tried for three cases of rape, including torturing his victims, as well as strangulation. He had been acquitted on all three charges, due to lack of evidence. There was no clear evidence of guilt, and though all the court knew he was responsible, there was nothing they could do.

The parents of the girls, who had been murdered, were sat at the back of the court, and all cried in despair at the verdict. The mothers sobbed and the fathers consoled their wives, looking angrily at Molefe.

The public prosecutor turned to face the parents, who were sitting behind him. He saw their anguish and anger, followed by outrage, and knew that he could not provide any comments. He knew he had failed them. He had tried, but due to incorrect procedure in gathering evidence, the major part of his case against Molefe had been inadmissible. He had the feeling that this was done deliberately, but could not prove his theory.

Molefe was well known to the police, and the Department of Justice, and was one of the most wanted men in South Africa. He headed up the equivalent of the local mafia and was virtually untouchable. His contacts and pay offs ran deep in the judiciary, and the police. He had been connected with a number of rapes and murders throughout Natal, but no concrete evidence could be found.

Molefe's followers cheered at the verdict, and the Magistrate called for silence, and repeatedly banged his gavel. His followers would not be subdued. He ordered the court to be cleared, and the security guards and police moved in to clear the court.

Molefe was unmoved, and shook hands with his attorney. His attorney, Neil Marriot, of the local firm Marriot and Venter, regarded him coolly.

"You were lucky this time," he said.

"I only employ the best," Molefe said.

"You will not use our firm again," Marriot responded.

"We will see," Molefe said.

Marriot felt dirty and disgusted, he knew his client was guilty as hell. He honestly believed that all people deserved the best defence, but in this case, he had serious doubts. He would not ever take another case for Molefe, regardless of how lucrative it would be. He also knew that there would be plenty of other attorneys who would. He should have been a farmer like his father, he thought to himself. He glanced across to one of the mothers, whose daughter had been brutally raped, tortured, and then strangled. She caught his glance and gave him a look of pure hatred.

Molefe was jubilant and walked out of the court believing he was untouchable. His followers chanted his name. He swaggered out of the court into bright sunshine, which temporarily blinded him. His eyes adjusted and he saw the press waiting for him. Cameras were flashing, and the SABC reporter was moving towards him for comment. He was revelling in his notoriety.

"I am pleased to have been acquitted on all the charges laid against me," he said in a voice deep and resonant. He looked like a priest addressing his followers.

Two of his lieutenants moved forward to clear a path for him, and he strode forward with his arms raised in salute. He stopped in front of his followers; they had now left the court and were spread out in front of him. He stood to address them.

A mother of one of the victims moved forward screaming, "You fucking animal."

The lieutenants quickly moved forward to cut her off, and the police moved in to prevent any further violence occurring.

Molefe smiled wickedly, "Which was your daughter?" he asked.

The mother couldn't answer. She broke down and cried. Her husband moved in aggressively and a constable cut him off and advised him that it would serve no purpose. The man collected his wife and started to move away.

Molefe stood there admiring his followers. They parted as if he were the messiah. His lieutenants moved alongside him, as if to protect him; he merely brushed them aside. "Give me space," he said.

One of his lieutenants then noticed a small red spot appear on his chest. He pointed to it, not understanding what it could be, and the spot moved up towards Molefe's head. Molefe now noticed the spot but mistook it for a fly, as he went to brush it away. This was the last move he would ever make.

A neat round hole appeared in his forehead. Molefe looked surprised, and then his knees gave way. He fell flat on his face, kicked spasmodically for three or four seconds, then lay still. The bullet had smashed into his skull and then disintegrated into his brain. The tissue was minced, and there would be precious little of the bullet left to identify the assassin.

The crowd was stunned as recognition dawned slowly upon them, and then panic ensued. The lieutenants dropped to Molefe's side, and could immediately see there was nothing that they could do. One of the lieutenants looked around the crowd in an attempt to identify the assassin. He fixed his eyes on the parents, who were stood on the edge of the crowd. He stood up and moved towards them. A neat hole appeared in his forehead, and he stumbled forward. The crowd then dived for cover.

The police on duty had drawn their firearms, and were searching the crowd for a target. They were trying to fix the direction of the shots, and could only assume that they had come from an office block on the edge of the court square. The sergeant quickly took control.

"Call the Captain," he said to a constable next to him.

"You two come with me; I think the shots came from the office block across the square." He turned to the court security guards.

"You keep this crowd under control, and make sure that the parents of those kids are not attacked." The guards stood there stunned by what had happened. "Do it," yelled the sergeant, "and keep those people away from the bodies."

The press moved forward, taking photographs continually, and the television crews were filming the events as they unfolded. There was panic and fear written in the faces of the observers. People were running away from the square, whilst others were running into the square to see what had happened.

The calmest person was the assassin. She felt no remorse for her actions; sincerely believing that this was the only way justice would be served to the likes of Molefe. She also knew that the second shot was not authorised, and would cause her problems later. She shrugged and said to herself, 'One less animal on the streets.' Of more concern was the delay the second shot had made for her. She should have been out of the building already, and she had wasted precious seconds watching the events unfold, and then taking out the second man. In her business, she had to flee whilst confusion reigned; she could not allow the shock to subside and the direction of the shots to be located. She calmly took the scope off the rifle, broke the rifle down and packed it in her briefcase. She removed the plastic overall and gloves and packed these in a plastic shopping bag, and left the office, she had rented some two weeks earlier. She was dressed in a business suit that revealed her athletic shape, but was so well cut that it added an air or respectability. She was obviously a lawyer amongst the many that were now circulating outside, asking what had happened. She shrugged and looked equally mystified. She passed a rubbish bin and dropped the plastic bag inside. There would be no evidence on the bag as she had worn gloves, and any fibres would be untraceable to her. She joined the rush down the stairs that led outside, just as the sergeant entered the building.

"Nobody leaves this building," Shouted the sergeant.

He could not stop the first half dozen, and she was amongst them. A Mercedes pulled up outside the building, and she got into the car. She knew that the sergeant would not suspect a businesswoman as an assassin, and she was correct. The sergeant was searching for a man, and did not even consider the attractive businesswoman as she glided past him. He quickly sealed the entrance and stopped any other people leaving the building.

"Constable, find the back door and seal it off," he shouted to the constable next to him.

The constable ran through the lobby and shouted, "Where is the door to the parking area?"

A man pointed to a corridor that led to a fire door. As he went through the door, a car raced away into Smith Street. He noted the make noted the license plate numbers, as the car sped away at high speed. A man, an obvious suspect, was driving the car. He radioed his sergeant and gave him the make colour and number of the car being driven by a white male. The sergeant contacted his captain, and relayed the details. The police cars were now converging from all directions, with sirens wailing; ambulance services were hot on their heels.

The Mercedes cruised down West Street, and picked up the freeway to Pietermaritzburg. The driver stuck to the speed limits, and watched with amusement as the police cars with sirens wailing, were flat out on the other side of the freeway, headed into the city. He looked in the rear-view mirror at his passenger. She sat there calm as you like, reading magazines, as if nothing had happened. He knew better than to talk to the lady, he was just the driver. He had never seen her before, but would never forget the woman in the back of the car. She was incredibly beautiful. He shuddered when he remembered what she was capable of. He drove towards Pietermaritzburg, taking the turn off to Pinetown, to avoid the toll road. He rejoined the freeway at Inchanga, and drove on towards Cato Ridge. He maintained a steady speed of one hundred and twenty kilometres per hour, and only used the outside lane to overtake slow traffic. The vehicle was just one of many cruising down the freeway. He saw the police roadblock and slowed down; he cruised between the cones, used to divert the traffic into a single lane. Armed police guarded the lane, and they were checking the cars as they went past. He looked in the rear-view mirror, and the lady was still reading her magazine.

"Could be trouble ahead," he said.

"Just stop as required, and tell them you are my chauffer, you are taking me to a meeting in Pietermaritzburg. If they ask any questions, I will take over."

They approached the stop sign, moving to a crawl. A police sergeant was looking into the car ahead, and then waved it on. They came to a stop, and the sergeant took one look, and then waved them on. He was looking for a blue Volkswagen Jetta driven by a single male. These two didn't fit the description in the slightest. She gave the sergeant a beaming smile as they went past. She could see that he would never suspect her as an assassin.

As they sped away, she saw him watching the car in the rear-view mirror. The driver saw the turn off to the farm, and took the dirt road to the farmhouse. He parked the car at the back of the farmhouse, and got into his Nissan bakkie (pick up truck), and roared away.

The assassin watched him leave, and then opened the door, and walked to the back of the farmhouse. A helicopter was waiting, and fired up the moment she appeared. She sat beside the pilot, who gave her a cursory nod, and then lifted off, heading towards the Northern Transvaal. The flight took two hours, and they landed at a game farm in Ellis Rus. The journey was completed in silence. She alighted from the helicopter and went into the hunting lodge.

General Kobus Lauberschagne was there to meet her.

"What the hell do you think you were doing?" he exclaimed. "You were only authorised to take out Molefe."

She saluted and said, "Good afternoon sir."

"Answer my question."

"The man was about to attack one of the parents, what should I have done?"

"You were damn well nearly caught, you stupid woman."

"I was never in any danger, as the police would never suspect a mere woman as being capable of murder in such a manner."

"It was unprofessional, and you know it. We cannot jeopardise this operation because you wish to be the protector of all people. We have a far bigger agenda, and you cannot allow yourself to be sidetracked by events that you cannot control."

"I am here, and the job was done; added to that there is one less animal to concern ourselves with," she responded angrily.

He realised the futility of further discussion on the matter and started the debriefing.

"How did you dispose of your coverall and gloves?"

"I dumped them in a waste bin on the second floor."

He looked exasperated. "They will have found them by now and have them over to forensics. You would be amazed at what they can find nowadays. They will almost certainly determine that you are a woman by traces of perfume, hair and God knows what else you left on the gloves."

"I had no option; I had to get out of there quickly."

"Precisely my point earlier; you cannot afford to deviate from the plan."

"I am sorry."

"Not good enough. You will now lay low, and will be suspended for six months, and during this period of suspension, you will have no further involvement in this operation."

"What" she exclaimed.

"You clearly understand, and you will obey my orders Major."

"Yes sir," she replied.

"In all other aspects, you did well, and your shooting was excellent. They will not be able to get much from the bullets, except calibre. Is the rifle in the briefcase?" he asked.

"Yes sir."

"Then give it to me. It will be destroyed as well as the briefcase. The rifle used will be a dead end for the police."

"Yes sir," she said as she passed him the rifle.

"You will go to detox now, where you will shower and leave your clothes, which will also be destroyed. We will test for any traces of gunpowder when you have finished. The helicopter is refuelling and will return you to the farm, where you will be driven to your office in Durban. Do not do anything out of the ordinary, and this time, stick to the plan. If you are in any doubt about your security, you will call your operative and give the code Venus. He will have you moved out to a safe house if this is required. I sincerely hope that it is not."

"Can I go now sir," she asked laconically.

"You can major."

She got up, left the room, and walked towards the detox room. As she left a man entered from a cubicle built adjacent to the room. He was thirty-eight years old and the youngest ever General in the history of the South African Defence Force. "That young girl has guts, sir."

Although they were the same rank, the young General had respect for the man sat in front of him.

"Sit down Allen."

"Yes Sir."

"Allen, you do not have to call me sir. I would prefer you to call me Kobus or General."

The young man smiled, exuding confidence and power. He was charismatic and knew it. He liked this old man and could see similar qualities in him; he was an old warrior with strict discipline for himself, and his subordinates.

"Kobus, that girl is one hell of a lady, and has just pulled off two very difficult hits. I agree with you about sticking to the plan, but you have to admit she did not wilt under pressure."

"I agree Allen, but at best our present position is precarious. We cannot afford any loose cannons bringing attention to our operation."

"I agree with her on one aspect though."

"What's that?"

"I do not believe anybody would ever suspect her of assassination; a beauty queen, model or even a high class hooker, but never an assassin!"

"You have a point I must admit she is far too feminine and could talk her way out of most predicaments. But, she must always obey instructions; you of all people know that."

Allen sat back and reflected upon the narrow escape he had experienced, due to a rookie getting over enthusiastic. It had happened in Angola when he was a captain, and a squadie had been sent forward to provide covering fire if needed. He had been given clear instructions not to get involved in any action.

They had parachuted in at night and were a squad of ten. The operation was to sabotage a fuel store, and get out quick. The squadie was over enthusiastic, and had taken a shot at a sentry as they were leaving, and had brought the house down on them. They had been chased for two hundred kilometres, fighting a rearguard action all the way. He had lost four men, the squadie who had fired the shot being one of them. The only satisfaction out of the raid was the fact that the enemy did not find all the explosives in time, and the fuel dump had been destroyed. It had been a blot on his otherwise exemplary career in the armed forces.

"I take your point."

"Discipline is everything in the armed forces. Just remember the Boer War; what a difference it could have made if the armed forces had the discipline of today."

"Kobus, you know as well as I do that that war could never have been won by the Boers, you also know why."

"Ach man, you are right, but I can always dream."

"I still say the girl is one of the best operatives we have, and to leave her tied up for a few months may not be in our best interest."

"What do you suggest Allen."

"I would suggest that we set up a court of enquiry, have her disciplined, and then get her back into active service."

"Why are you so interested in her?" he asked with a smile on his face.

"I would say that we are not using all her skills to our best advantage. She is articulate, a lawyer, bi-lingual, extremely attractive, and very cool headed under pressure."

"Have you read her file?" Kobus asked.

"Not yet."

"She was raped when she was fourteen and, as far as we can ascertain, never had a relationship with any man since."

"Now I understand her fanaticism against women beaters and rapists. Hell of a waste though."

"How is Maria?" he asked sardonically.

Allen laughed and said, "Are you reading my mind?"

"To business, Allen. The new Internal Security Department is recording the networks phone calls from pay phones in Johannesburg, Pretoria, Cape Town and Port Elizabeth. There is a leak in the network that we have created. They know our codes and the telephone numbers."

"Any idea who could be leaking this information?"

"We suspect a warrant officer in the Booysens Special Branch. We have not yet set a trap, but are almost certain it is Warrant Officer Johannes Kobus Kriel."

"I know him; why do you suspect him?" Allen asked.

"As you well know, our people are positioned throughout the whole business sector, as well as the armed forces and police. We have searched

Kriel's bank account, and there have been some strange deposits. We have put Kriel under surveillance, and he has three other bank accounts with substantial sums deposited, way beyond his earnings."

"This does not necessarily determine whether he is a bent copper or a spy, does it?" enquired Allen.

"Kriel has a major problem in that he has a proclivity for Asian and black prostitutes. We suspect that he has been set up, photographed and turned, he is on a roller coaster that he cannot get off."

"If he has been turned, then we can use this to our advantage. We can feed him false information, and have the ISD running round chasing their tail," responded Allen.

"The danger is that he still has a broad outline of our plans; I am not sure we can risk this."

"What do you suggest?" Allen asked.

"Our first problem is that we do not know how much ISD know about the plan. We have a guy inside, but he needs time to establish himself before we can really use him to gather intelligence. We cannot risk him too early."

"I understand, and then what do we do about Kriel?"

"We were considering setting up a similar trap, and trapping him between ISD and ourselves. This would mean that he would then be at risk from both sides, and most likely would return to the fold. We would also search for and destroy any similar evidence held by the ISD."

"There is one downside to your plan; the prostitute used could well be a danger to us afterwards."

"Yes, we considered this and thought the best solution was to take her out afterwards."

"I am not keen on that idea, as then we become as bad as the people we are fighting," Allen said.

"Allen, this is a silent war, and there will be casualties. It cannot be helped."

"Spare me the detail then please."

"You agree in principle then?"

"Yes," Allen replied despondently.

"Moving on, we are talking to General Mkondo in Natal. He has set up a strange operation to raise funds for their armed forces. As you know the ANC has made sure that they cannot afford a sizeable force, and have thus been incapable of any serious military action. They are now actively poaching in Tanzania, and selling rhino horn and elephant tusks." General Kobus said.

"You must be joking, that wouldn't fund any kind of army, and it is ridiculous."

"I agree, but they have just raised two point five million Rand on their first operation, and they are scheduling more."

"Two point five million Rand is peanuts, it's a hopeless case."

"Not so, remember that they pay next to nothing to their regulars, as they have no other opportunities. This two point five million Rand would feed, and pay for nearly one thousand troops for two months. They have bought many AK's for peanuts from the Mozambique rebels, now that they are at peace."

"The numbers do not stack up; this would mean it would only cost forty five Rand a day per squadie. It is not possible, ammunition and weapons would cost more than that."

"The weapons they have, I know this to be a fact. It is manpower that they are short of. If you work as a casual worker in Durban or Pietermaritzburg, you will only earn sixty Rand per day; there is no difference for the average guy in Natal."

"Incredible," was all Allen could say.

"You must also remember the Zulu's come from a tradition of warriors and have always been well disciplined."

"I know their anti terrorist squads were well trained, and excellent soldiers, but the rank and file have long since lost the discipline you refer to."

"General Mkondo is absolutely ruthless, and he would not tolerate indiscipline. Do you remember that incident where the ANC representative, and his family were murdered in Alex?"

"Is that where they were all shot down leaving the scene?" Allen asked.

"Yes that was Similane's doing. He is working for Mkondo, and used the Swazi Dlamini to his own ends, and then he organised for them to be taken out to ensure no loose ends."

"A charming man," Allen said in distaste.

"He saw it as necessary, and another act of the silent war that we are fighting."

"Could you possibly trust such a man?" Allan asked.

"No more than we have to. You must remember they are all the same. Mandela and Mbeki both sacrificed their supporters for the greater cause, and the new leaders, are no better."

"Politics are a dirty business," Allen remarked.

"I agree. In politics, there is no coming second, winning is all that counts," Kobus said.

"Kobus, if we look at the General plan, where would these people fit in? They have proven that they are not the least trustworthy. How do you maintain control?"

"That is the dilemma, we cannot do it without them, and we cannot do it with them. In the rest of Africa, in fact, the world, the only way to maintain peace and stability is to make any action against you so devastating, that it would ruin the entire country in taking that action. Clinton and Thatcher understood this, and they ensured that any attack from the then Soviet Union, would result in such heavy retaliation that the Soviets could not contemplate such a scenario. The west spends billions of dollars on defence even now, why?"

"I see your point. You are suggesting that we would be so powerful a nation that to attack us would be suicidal. What of the scenario of peace keeping forces in South Africa, sent by the UN?"

"We have run that scenario. They know that we have the potential to manufacture tactical nuclear warheads, and this would be deterrent enough. In any event, who cares about Africa anymore, the moralists has achieved their objectives, and we are no longer worthy of attention."

"I think that would change with what we are planning."

"It is a question of priorities. We would be headline news again, but not for long."

"I believe fully in the plan, and support it one hundred percent. I also know that many of the other senior Generals and commanders also support the plan. For it to be completely successful, we will need the support of the police."

"We already have a network of officers in all positions currently supporting the plan, and they will come to the party when asked. We also have support from the NFP that is currently being developed."

"I am not sure that the Zulu's are totally reliable. I know that they are disappointed by the level of support for the ANC within their nation, and they are currently acting independently to secure their future. For it to be successful we need to have all the people in place, and the co-ordination must be incredibly accurate."

"I agree," said Kobus. "We will have more diversionary tactics over the next six months leading up to the summer recess of parliament. Most of the senior politicians will be overseas or on holiday abroad. So when we strike at the government buildings, this will make it doubly difficult for them to organise any meaningful resistance. This will give us three days to a week to tie up loose ends."

"How do we keep a lid on this when we are involving all the senior military personnel? I am concerned that there will be some loose talk, and the further we push out the action, and then almost certainly someone will do or say something which points towards us."

"The government suspects something already, which has already been confirmed by the recruitment of Kriel. What they do not know is when and how deep the conspiracy is. They have responded by retiring generals and admirals, and replacing them with their own people. They have kept their troops out of the trouble spots, as they do believe that there is a Third Force currently active in South Africa."

"We can step up the campaign if necessary; we have all the people in place. We are daily planting rumours of fraud and corruption, from our sources within government. We are actively creating strike action in three major companies in Johannesburg, and organising faction fights in Natal, and on the Cape flats. As fast as they get one area under control, we are creating problems in another. Even they can see that this is not a coincidence."

"What of the business front?" Kobus enquired.

"The banking sector, where possible, is making loans to black entrepreneurs, and then calling in the loans before they are able to make payment. We have senior finance guys lobbying to maintain the high interest rates, and stop the flow of capital out of the country. The Rand is slipping, but not at the rate we would like. The business community is helping at every opportunity, claiming that lack of investment is driven by the violence in the country. We have organised complete disruption in most CBD's, but most of the muggings and hijacks have not been our responsibility," he concluded. "We have to get the public really pissed off with this government, and I would say that we are nearly there. We still need a major incident to spark the intended action. Something so disgusting that all mouths will say 'get rid of these people'. Have you any ideas Allen?"

"We have run a number of scenarios, and looked at what would dramatically affect public opinion, not only here, but overseas, as well. We looked at leaking a false document that suggested nationalising the gold mines and diamond operations. We would couple this with indisputable evidence that virtually all the cabinet have considerable offshore funds in Swiss banks, which more than contravene the current exchange control laws. This is easy to fabricate, although, in some instances, it may well be true. We have our own civil servants wading through the myriad transactions to find some dirt. Another option would be to link these actions together with a hidden land reform bill, which clearly indicates that the maximum holding of any one family would be one thousand hectares of land. Businesses would have to prove that they needed more than this figure."

"A useful set of scenarios. Have you have worked on any others recently?"

"We have run the likely responses both locally and overseas, to our intended coup. Our major trading partners would immediately place an embargo on trade with South Africa. We believe China, and to some extent, the rest of Asia, would still do business with the new government, but under stricter, and more difficult terms. The African countries would suspend any kind of contact, and obviously call for an immediate return of government to the ANC. There would be discussions within the UN to have a directive against South Africa, the Rand would plummet, and imports would be dramatically reduced. To counter these measures, we would decrease the production of gold and diamonds, and all exports of coal and iron ore would be stopped. We have a number of financial analysts that suggest the first six months would be critical to our successful reintegration of government. They say the economy is like the Queen Mary, once rolling it takes a long time to turn it around."

"What of overseas assets of South African companies?"

"They would be frozen by the governments concerned."

"But surely this would cripple most international companies in South Africa?"

"Our analysts think not. Most of the big multinationals have moved offshore in any event. As you know, I am no expert on financial matters, but we have some of the countries top people researching the possibilities."

"When will they report?" Kobus enquired.

"I have arranged a presentation by van der Linde from the Reserve Bank."

"Excellent."

The Generals sat quietly, each having their own thoughts about the risks and possibilities. They sat and thought for some minutes.

"This is a high risk scenario for you Allen," Kobus said.

"And what of you then?" Allen responded.

"Ach man, I am an old warhorse, past my prime, I have little to lose. Whereas you, my friend, are young and in your prime. You have much to lose."

"I don't think so Kobus, I only see a short horizon for me before they replace me with one of their own."

"I am not so sure Allen. You have the ear of the president and he certainly respects your view."

"It is too late to go back Kobus, even if I wanted to, which, by the way, I do not."

"I agree, but why do you need to take the risks that we are taking. You are not an Afrikaner, you are from English stock."

"I am a third generation South African, from English stock, and I consider myself as South African as much as anyone else."

"Enough talk, let's have a drink,' General Kobus Lauberschagne rang the bell for the orderly."

The female assassin meanwhile took her shower, and was tested thoroughly for any traces of gunpowder residue, and was passed clean. She could return to Durban and pick up her life as if nothing had happened. Her name was Annette Venter, and she was the daughter of the senior partner in Venter and Marriot, in Durban.

She had been raped when she was fourteen years of age, by a black burglar that wanted more than the TV and video. Her parents were at a function, and she was left on her own with the maid in the large house, in Durban North. The black man had never been caught, and she had been in trauma for close on three years. Even now she had nightmares. She had matriculated late due to the trauma, and had then gone to Wits to study law. She was first in her class and shunned all male contact, having become a virtual recluse.

She was accosted one night by one of her fellow students, who had a drink too many, and she had screamed and yelled until he ran away. After that night, none of the other male students bothered her. She had made a friend with one of her fellow students; he was no threat to her, as he was homosexual. He was a keen follower of karate, and encouraged her to join his class. She attended the first lesson, and enjoyed the discipline, and the release that it gave her. She quickly became proficient. She had always been athletic, and was soon testing for her black belt, which she achieved easily.

They had asked her many times to compete locally, but she had always refused, not wishing to attract attention. With her looks and figure, this was a near impossibility. She was spotted by a member of the Special Forces, and approached to use her skills for the cause. She thought the man was ridiculous, and told him so. The man persisted and eventually she attended a training session held secretly on a farm in the Northern Transvaal. At this time she had qualified top of her class, and had taken a position as an articled clerk in her father's company.

The commandant watched her carefully, and was impressed by her composure, and obvious ability in self-defence. He introduced her to the rifle range, and both he and she, were amazed, at her ability with a rifle. She was a natural. Slowly, but surely, she was inculcated into the local commando.

She was twenty-eight, and worked for women's rights in Durban. Her office was the meeting place for women who had been beaten or raped. She gave legal advice and opinion for next to nothing, unless the client could afford the costs. She was becoming well known for her appearances in court, seeking injunctions and restraint orders for battered wives, and raped women. She could not tolerate the indifference given to battered wives, and the general lack of interest when rape was mentioned.

She had made her first hit some two years earlier, and had nearly passed out afterwards. Molefe and his lieutenant had been her fifth and sixth. She was now poised and calm following the hits. She wondered if she was getting blasé, and that she no longer had any feelings. She reconciled this with the fact that each hit she made was against an animal with a known criminal record, and had continually committed robberies, rape and murder. Each case was thoroughly researched prior to her acceptance of the hit. She would not take on any contract unless she was convinced that there was no other route.

She had many arguments with her father over the representation of obvious rapists and murderers. He had countered that it was not for him to judge, and that, however, heinous the crime, there had to be a legal defence. His partner Neil Marriott also chipped in with the same defence. What about the victims Annette would counter; there was no money in the victims and the practice was operated like a business, was their reply. Her father was mercenary about the practice, but Neil showed more concern for the reputation that they were gaining.

That Neil was attracted to Annette was not difficult to see. He had tried to get close to her, but with little success. He was not married, and, at thirty-two, this was a little strange, as he was considerably wealthy and extremely handsome. Annette felt that she was not capable of a relationship, and although she enjoyed Neil's company that was all it would ever be. Neil, on the other hand, never gave up trying to get her to go to dinner with him.

"Your helicopter is ready, Major," an aide called, this broke her reverie, and she sighed and moved towards the door.

The aide was outside the door and said, "The General wishes to see you before you go ma'am. Please follow me."

She followed the aide into the drawing room and saw the General sitting on an armchair. Opposite him, she could see another person, but only the back of his head.

"Come and sit down Major, I wish you to meet someone."

The man with his back to her stood up and turned to face her.

The man smiled, and she felt her stomach go liquid. He was six feet plus, incredibly handsome and had a smile that would melt butter.

"I have been looking forward to meeting you Major," he said in English that was obviously his home language.

"Let me introduce you, this is General Allen Doyle."

She stood to attention and saluted the General.

"At ease, Major Venter. Come and sit down."

She sat on a sofa opposite the Generals. She had never heard of General Allen Doyle, and was amazed a man so young could become a General.

"I have discussed your actions today with General Doyle, and he agreed that you were very foolhardy. He is more forgiving than I, and suggests that you are severely reprimanded, but kept on active duty. You will attend a disciplinary hearing held at the farm in Cato Ridge. General Doyle will be the commanding officer present. This hearing will take place on the 8th of October. This will be placed on your record."

She looked at General Lauberschagne with anxiety; "What is the probable outcome?" She asked.

"That is up to General Doyle."

General Doyle smiled. She felt an overwhelming attraction for Doyle that she had never felt before.

"At the hearing we will discuss your actions, reasons for those actions, and your state of mind. I wish to know whether you are safe to be used again, or if we have a better use for your talents."

She was about to ask another question, but the General stopped her; "You are late and must leave now."

She came to attention, saluted, and then left the room. She was feeling giddy from the experience.

The man Doyle had penetrated a barrier that she thought was impregnable. In a curious way, she was looking forward to her disciplinary hearing with General Doyle.

Chapter 13

Sergeant Khubeki caught up with Captain. Khumalo, but gave a low whistle to warn him that he was approaching.

"What was all the shooting about?" He asked.

Captain Khumalo explained what had happened, and they both looked at Moses with disdain.

"What of the scouts, tracking us?" Captain Khumalo asked.

"They are well behind us, and appear to be falling back, I cannot understand why, they have been close to, us but now seem to have given up," he reported.

"They must know where we are heading, and must be concentrating their forces at the river crossing," he concluded.

"I am not so sure," said Khumalo. "They are at the river crossing but in two groups with huge gaps between them. They appear to be very amateurish in their approach."

"That's good for us surely?" said Khubeki.

"This is too easy, and I do not like it," said Khumalo.

"What could they be up to then?"

"That's the problem, I do not know."

"We are less than ten K's from the crossing, and the scouts are making so much noise that it is almost as if they want to be detected, so that we can easily bypass them. I cannot imagine why they would chase us for so long, and then make it easy for us to escape."

"Do you think they know who we are?" Khubeki asked.

"I have thought about that, we know the scouts are poorly armed and not well trained. They are used to undisciplined poachers, and if they suspect that we are a military unit, and even more disciplined than the normal poachers, perhaps they want no part of a fight with us. Let's hope we are right, but we must move forward with the utmost caution."

"Could they be funnelling us into a channel where an ambush could take place?" Khubeki asked.

"I do not think so. I doubt that they are that well organised, you go forward now and scout the river and come back with your report."

Sergeant Khubeki slipped away from Moses and the Captain and moved quickly across the ground towards the river.

"What's going on?" demanded Moses.

"Nothing to concern you," retorted Captain Khumalo.

"My skin is on the line as well, so tell me what is going on."

Captain Khumalo explained to Moses the current position and why he distrusted such an easy escape.

"Sounds good to me," said Moses.

"It sounds too good, and we must make sure that this is not a trap which we blunder into."

Sergeant Khubeki closed rapidly on the river. He was helped by a perfect night, which was as black as coal with low cloud, which blanked out even the stars, visibility was down to thirty meters; it would conceal him from the scouts unless he blundered directly into them.

He knew he was close to the river as he could smell the water and the temperature was dropping. He dropped to his stomach and crawled forward, listening at one-minute intervals for any sound of the scouts. He reached the river without detecting any of the scouts and started to move up the bank heading east. He heard the scouts after some ten minutes had passed. The scouts were surprisingly noisy and easy to detect. He moved in close to them and saw that there were ten scouts and a white man. They were all sitting around a fire with the white man sitting well away from his scouts. He knew that he could have taken them all out with little effort.

He slipped away back along the track. He had come about and headed west up the river. It took him a further forty-five minutes to detect the second group. They appeared more attentive and had posted lookouts at two hundred meters from their camp. The sergeant detected the lookouts without being seen himself, and easily bypassed them. At the camp, the scouts were quiet but also highly visible as the campfire could be detected from a kilometre away. There were also ten scouts in this camp but no white man.

The scouts had left a gap of seven kilometres between them, more than enough for the unit to slip through without being detected. He searched the riverbank for a likely crossing and found a section of the river, which opened out to eighty meters. He entered the water and started to move across to the other bank. He carried with him a stick to test the depths, and found that by moving diagonally across the river the level never came above his waist. The current was not strong and would not present a problem even when carrying the tusks. He headed back to Captain Khumalo.

Captain Khumalo and Moses had continued towards the river carrying the tusks between them. They had moved slowly and cautiously but when sergeant Khubeki found them they were a little over four kilometres from the river.

"I have found an ideal crossing point," reported Khubeki.

"What about the scouts?" Khumalo asked.

"It is just as you said. They appear to want us to find them, the group to the east is so noisy you could not help but locate them. The group to the west is a little more attentive but again they are easily detected. I do not understand it."

"What is the distance between the two groups?" asked Khumalo.

"At least seven K's, it would take a minimum of thirty five minutes for the two forces to regroup. It will take us no more than five to ten minutes to cross the river."

"Why do you think that the scouts have made their positions so obvious?" asked Khumalo.

"They do not wish to have contact is the only possible answer."

"Then the next question is why not?"

"What do they know that would deter them from their obvious goal from the beginning?" Khumalo said out loud, more for himself than Khubeki.

"What knowledge could they possibly have which would make them behave the way they are doing?"

"Perhaps they have a reception party on the Mozambique side and are just funnelling us into them," Khubeki said.

"I do not think so as we have clearance at the highest level to pass through Mozambique. I do not expect any trouble once we are in Mozambique as there will be some porters waiting for us at Nazombe which is fifty K's from the river crossing. We are about four K's from the river and can be across to the other side in thirty minutes. We must play it by ear and approach both sides of the river with caution. Let's move out."

Sergeant Khubeki moved ahead and continually monitored the ground in front of them.

They reached the river without encountering the scouts and were at the crossing well ahead of schedule. They regrouped at the river and remained concealed for thirty minutes, expecting at any time to encounter the scouts. This was the most dangerous time for them, as they would have to move out into the open to cross the river.

"Check the river bank to the east sergeant and I will check to the west," said the Captain. "Moses you stay put; do not move from this position."

Moses just nodded. He wanted out of this situation. Being shot at as they crossed the river was the last thing he wanted.

Captain Khumalo and sergeant Khubeki moved out and checked the riverbank both east and west. They found nothing had changed since their earlier survey. The scouts were still in their original positions and were making no attempt to detect the poachers. It was most puzzling to captain Khumalo.

Both Khubeki and Khumalo returned to their rendezvous simultaneously.

"Can you see anything?" Captain Khumalo asked.

"No change and you?"

"Nothing different," said captain Khumalo.

The tensions were building, as they would now have to commit themselves to the crossing and were exposed and vulnerable.

"Sergeant, cross the river and check the bank on both sides for at least a kilometre," ordered the captain.

"Can't we get on with it," said Moses impatiently.

"Be quiet, you know nothing of these situations, most missions fail due to impatience, there are no second chances, if we get it wrong," Captain Khumalo said.

The sergeant moved down the bank and slipped into the water. Moses and the captain watched him go and could clearly see him for the full width of the river. It merely highlighted how exposed they would be as they crossed the river.

Sergeant Khubeki made the crossing without incident and reconnoitred the bank in both directions. He found nothing.

Moses and the Captain clearly saw him return from the bank across the river towards them.

"There is nothing on the other side," reported the sergeant.

"Then let's go," said the captain. "I will cross the river first and give covering fire if required. Once I have crossed the river you must follow quickly."

Moses and the sergeant nodded.

Khumalo entered the river, and was initially shocked by the cold water. He moved slowly, continually checking the depth with his stick, keeping his eyes on the bank ahead of him. He reached the opposite bank without incident.

Sergeant Khubeki, and Moses entered the water, and Moses heart was racing. He did not enjoy being out in the open, even in the darkness. The sergeant was leading, and Moses was bringing up the rear.

Some fifty meters away a pair of eyes lifted out of the water without making a ripple. The crocodile had been hunting well downstream, but had been attracted by the vibrations through the water of the crossings made by captain Khumalo. It had moved down the river to investigate. It had seen the first man cross the river but was too far away to take advantage of the opportunity.

It had clearly seen the two men enter the river burdened with the tusks. It moved slowly and imperceptibly below the surface of the water.

Moses and Khubeki were making excellent time across the river, urged on by their precarious position and the need to get to the safety of the far bank. They were ten meters from the far bank when the crocodile struck.

The crocodile had glided under the water following the vibrations of the men. It had closed to within ten meters of the pair when it had gathered itself for the final charge. The crocodile was thirty years old and had grown to a length of eight meters and weighed just less than one ton. It was a formidable killing machine and held no fear of man. It had accounted for many of the villagers on both sides of the bank.

Captain Khumalo was watching the opposite bank for any movement or sign of attack. He was keyed up, and his senses were heightened. Out of the corner of his eye he noticed a ripple in the water behind his two men who were now ten meters from the bank. He looked intently at the water, perplexed, and not yet fully encompassing the danger.

The crocodile lifted its head slowly out of the water to guide the attack. It then lunged forward at an incredible rate and caught Moses around the waist.

Moses knew nothing about the attack until he was knocked off his feet and felt a vice like hold around his waist His back was broken instantly and he screamed in terror and pain. He was dragged under the water, and he died without knowing what had killed him.

Sergeant Khubeki felt an enormous pull on the tusks and instinctively grasped them tightly. He heard the scream from Moses, and only then heard the shooting from the captain from the bank in front. His first thoughts were that they were under attack, and he dropped the tusks and went under water. He came up to see Moses floating away on the current and captain Khumalo calling him to grab the tusks. He wrestled with the first one and got it to the captain who was, by now, in the water with him. They got the tusk to the bank, and looked for the second one. They were lucky in that the second tusk was stuck in the mud close to the bank. They pulled it out, and they laid on the bank gasping for breath. Sergeant Khubeki was first to see the movement on the opposite bank.

Jonathan had sat by the campfire with little enthusiasm for the proceedings. He felt let down and could not forgive Don for not attempting to capture the poachers. To sit in camp and allow them to escape was not acceptable to Jonathan. He had been brooding for hours and felt he had to do something.

It was three in the morning when he called three of his scouts to follow him on patrol. He intended to walk down towards Toby's camp and at least try and do something. For all, he knew the poachers had already crossed the river either above or below his position.

They had walked for fifteen minutes when they heard the shooting almost directly ahead of them. Jonathan froze at the sound of the shots and then instinctively worked the bolt on his rifle to put a round in the breach. He heard his men do the same. They heard the agonised scream of Moses and assumed that Toby's scouts had been attacked.

They ran forward with rifles at the ready to where the terrified scream had come from.

"Terr's on the opposite bank," whispered sergeant Khubeki using the signal acquired in past missions.

Captain Khumalo took in their position at a glance. They were still partly exposed on the bank and would be seen at any moment by the forces across the river. The tusks were exposed and would be clearly seen by the men on the other side of the river. They were still some distance away but were searching the opposite bank for sign of the poachers.

"Move slowly up the bank," Captain Khumalo said, "I will cover you, take a tusk with you."

Sergeant Khubeki caught hold of the hollow end of the tusk, and moved crabwise up the bank into cover. He made the top of the bank and moved into cover without being seen. He slid down the bank slowly, and retrieved the second tusk, and again started crabwise back up the bank.

Captain Khumalo judged the range of the scouts to be one hundred and fifty meters and they were still out of sight. The scouts were slowly moving to a position opposite to where he lay. He saw that there were only four of them He knew be could deal with this situation if the shooting started.

Jonathan searched the bank for any sign of the poachers. He moved forward cautiously, expecting contact at any moment. He was fearful that the poachers would cut them down if they remained exposed on the bank.

He signalled for his team to stop. He listened intently for any noise that may give away the position of the poachers. There was nothing, just a deathly silence.

The usual cacophony of insect noise had stopped, and the air was filled with tension. Nothing moved or stirred; he could clearly hear the breathing of his men but nothing else.

He moved forward again, alert for any approach or sound of danger. Something stirred on the opposite bank and he clearly heard a sliding noise. He indicated to his men the direction of the noise and they all stared intently at the opposite bank. There was something incongruous about the opposite bank, but he could not see clearly what was out of place. There were no further sounds and the tension increased.

Sergeant Khubeki had seen the men stop and knew they were obviously listening for movement. He was two meters from the cover at the top of the bank, and he froze immediately. The scouts opposite him started forward again, and he moved closer to the protection of the cover that the ridge provided.

Captain Khumalo had taken up a defensive position behind an exposed root and was covering the approach of the men opposite. He clearly heard the scrape of the tusk as the sergeant moved forward. He saw the men opposite freeze and stare intently in their direction. He slowly turned and looked back at the sergeant. He was now meters from cover and would need a couple of seconds to reach the safety of the bush. He watched as the sergeant set off again and then returned his attention to the men opposite.

Jonathan heard the scrape again, and moved forward towards the place were the poachers had crossed the river. He clearly saw the footprints of where the poachers had entered the water and scanned the opposite bank for any sign of them.

Captain Khumalo watched the men opposite lie down, and they stared directly at him. He knew that they could not clearly see him but also realised that the other scouts would have heard the shooting and would be upon them shortly. He had to do something.

He turned to look at the sergeant who was now partially in the bush with half of the tusk sticking out. The sergeant looked at him and to his disbelief smiled and nodded.

He knew that the sergeant would be ready to cover him should he make a dash for the bank. He first had to buy time for the sergeant to get under cover.

Help came from a strange quarter.

The body of Moses was tangled between some roots and the blood from the body had attracted a whole load of crocodiles. They had glided down the river unseen and unheard by the poachers or the scouts. They attacked the body of Moses with primeval ferocity and smacked their tails on the water. The noise in the silence was deafening as they twisted in the water with flesh being torn from the body of Moses.

Sergeant Khubeki heard the slap on the water and started. He quickly realised what had happened and pulled the tusk into cover and made ready to cover the captain.

Captain Khumalo spun round at the sound of the slap on the water and then glanced quickly back at the scouts.

All the scouts were up on there feet racing down the bank towards the noise.

He took advantage of the confusion and quickly joined the sergeant in the cover of the bank.

Jonathan had started at the sound and had immediately headed down river. His men had followed him. He stopped when he realised what had caused the sound and cast a glance back in the direction of where the poachers had crossed. He was just in time to see the captain disappear into the bush. He swore in frustration. It was one thing to shoot the poachers on the opposite bank, but entirely unacceptable to follow them over the river. They could have recovered or captured the poachers from the bank edge, but to follow them into Mozambique would create an international incident. He would not be able to follow the poachers any further now.

He turned away in frustration and called his men over. They would return to base.

"Call base and tell them the poachers have escaped across the river," he said to the radio operator.

Captain Khumalo watched the scouts leave and indicated to the sergeant they could move out. They balanced the tusks on their shoulders and walked out towards their rendezvous. Captain Khumalo thought as he was walking, that in his last two missions, he had lost two men. He had been through hundreds of missions against terrorists without losing a man. It was strange that the enemy had not killed the men he had lost, but rather the animals they had been sent to hunt.

Chapter 14

Angela Murchin was sitting at her desk when Thomas walked by and said,

"See you later in the Keg, OK."

"Have you got something?" She enquired feeling the excitement building up.

Thomas just touched his lips and said, "Later"

There was two hours to work through till lunch, and she found she could not concentrate on the assignment she had been given. The car factory held little excitement for her when there were far more interesting projects at hand. She looked again at the dossier of Chen Yoo Soong and again read the piece about the prostitute. She would call the local paper that published the story and get more information. The file indicated that the Korean paper was based in Seoul and was called the "Korean Daily News". The journalist was called Lee Chen. She obtained the number from records.

Angela placed the call, and heard the phone ringing on the other end, and a voice answered in Korean. "Can you speak English please?" She asked.

"This is the Daily News, how can I help you?" Was the accented response.

"I would like to speak to Lee Chen," she responded.

"Hold please," the voice responded.

Angela waited, and a couple of seconds later she got through.

"Chen."

"Mr. Chen my name is Angela Murchin from the Metropolitan paper in South Africa."

"Yes, how can I help you?"

"I am sure you know that Soong is proposing to build a car factory in South Africa. I have a dossier on the chairman of the company, Chen

Yoo Soong, and this includes an article written by you about a murdered prostitute. Can you give me further information on this murder please?"

"What is your interest in this case?" he asked.

"I would like to know more detail about the murdered prostitute and why you believe that Chen Yoo Soong was involved or linked to the murder."

"Could you give me a number to call later?" He asked. "I will also check your credentials; you did say the Metropolitan in South Africa, what is your press card number?"

"I did say the Metropolitan, and my number is W2396195. You can call me back: on 011 872 3218 after six our time."

"Thank you, I will call you then."

Angela replaced the receiver and thought about the conversation she had just had. Why he was so evasive or at best guarded? Why call back later? She found his response particularly puzzling.

Angela worked on the dossier until twelve thirty and then went to lunch at the Keg. She saw Thomas sitting in the corner of the restaurant. She moved across and sat opposite him.

"So Thomas," she said." What news do you have for me?"

Thomas looked around the room as if to check that there were no eaves droppers and then said, "Angela I hope you know what you are getting into. Once you start on this road, there will be no turning back. And it will be dangerous."

"What am I getting into Thomas?" she asked.

"Samuel Dlamini was a member of the Natal anti-terrorist squad, he had accounted for many terrorists crossing the Swaziland border either directly or indirectly. He was based in Swaziland and fed information to the anti-terrorist squads. When the ANC came to power the records of these squads, were destroyed for the safety of the people involved. I have talked to the relatives of Samuel, and they believe he, and his squad, were eliminated. They believe that he was set up by an informant inside the NFP who appear to be running an operation of disruption prior to the elections. There are a number of units operating in Gauteng and Natal."

"Are you saying that the leaders of the NFP know and approve of these actions?"

"That is not clear, but there are indications of elements within the NFP that want destabilisation, and to undermine the ANC. The word is that there is a Third Force acting within the country and that a coup of some sort is being planned."

"You can't be serious." Angela responded.

"I am deadly serious, and if you persist with your enquiries you will be in grave danger. They have people in all positions of society and they are intent on taking over the country."

"How did you find out so much so easily if the operation is so clandestine that the newspapers, police and the intelligence service do not know about it?"

"The rumours have been around for years about a third force, and apparently a unit were sent into Tanzania, and one member of the unit was killed. The family did not receive any compensation and they had been complaining bitterly to the Natal police. They have kept this under wraps, but it took very little persuasion for the relatives to talk to me."

"Why Tanzania, what could be there for them?"

"That I do not know, but I am still trying to find out."

"Are you safe to carry on? I mean if the people concerned are so ruthless you could end up being there next target."

"I agree it is risky, but how can we stop now?"

"Don't you think that we should alert the authorities?"

"What would we tell them? We would also be showing our hand to this Third Force, and they have apparently people placed everywhere. We need much more information before the authorities would take us seriously."

"Could they know about our inquiries already?" She asked feeling a ripple of fear in her gut.

"I cannot say, but if I found the information so easily, then you can bet your bottom dollar that the authorities already know more than we do. It could be beneficial to both the ANC and the NFP to keep this information out of the media."

"Shit, we are caught between a rock and a hard place; whatever we do we are in danger from both sides."

"That is correct."

"What I do not understand is why the ANC would react adversely to this knowledge?"

"It is simple," he said, "The ANC is terrified of a threat of a military coup, particularly if the coup is inspired by the Zulu nation linking with the white dominated military. This could be an unstoppable force."

If the information came to light that these elements existed, and could be confirmed, it could expedite tensions, and possibly even result in a civil war. There are many people out there that would like to see a return to the old days. If they could be united as a single force, who knows what could happen. The ANC is employing the same tactics as the old Apartheid regime of dictatorial control. They have no alternative. The current levels of violence and corruption in the country could be used by the third force to call to arms all the old commando forces."

"The rest of the world would never accept such a regime."

"Why not? It happens all the time in Africa."

"Business would collapse in South Africa, there would be no overseas investment, and we would just go backwards."

"The forces concerned would not worry about such issues. In any event, businessmen are pragmatists and they would still deal with South Africa. They always have, even through the sanctions," he said.

"It's a frightening scenario."

"Where do we go from here?" Thomas asked.

"I do not know to be honest. We have stumbled onto something too big for us."

"Well I cannot give up now; I will carry on regardless of your decision."

"Let me think about it for a while, and Thomas, please be careful."

Angela and Thomas then headed back to their respective desks for the rest of the afternoon. Angela was just clearing her desk and preparing to leave when her phone rang loudly, startling her for a moment. Angela reached for the phone and said.

"Angela Murchin speaking."

"Good evening, this is Lee Cheng speaking, returning your call, as agreed."

"Oh, hi, why couldn't you speak to me earlier?" Angela enquired.

"The phone lines are not necessarily secure. Is there any chance of your phone being tapped?"

"I don't think so," Angela said.

"It is important that you are sure that your phone is not tapped, if you have any doubts then I will give you a number to call me back."

"I am sure," Angela said, "There is no reason for anybody to tap my phone."

"O.K., what specifically do you want to know about Chen Yoo Soong and the murdered prostitute?"

"I would like to know why you think Chen Yoo Sing is involved with the murder."

"The girl was a high class prostitute, and she only worked for the upper echelons of business and government people. It was known that on the night in question she had been hired by Chen Yoo Soong, and taken to his private apartment in Seoul. She was never seen alive again. A friend of hers, who had previously also been hired by Chen Yoo Soong, had been badly beaten up, but was supposedly paid a fortune to keep quiet about it. She did not dare inform the police of the incident, but she spoke to me off the record."

"What did she tell you?"

"Chen Yoo Soong likes flagellation. He does not get beaten, the girls do. For the sum involved she, thought she could take a minor beating. She agreed, and he stripped her and chained her to the bed face down. He brought a strap and began to lightly beat her across her back and buttocks. He increased the intensity of the beating and after half an hour she blacked out from the pain. She believes that this saved her life. When she had recovered from the beating, he was standing there, smiling, and admiring his handiwork."

"He was obviously aroused by her fear, and got really excited when the girl told him she could take no more. He smiled at her and told her he had hired her for the night, and had just begun to have fun. She survived the night by being totally acquiescent, and he finally let her go in the early hours of the morning. She honestly believed she was going to die that night."

"My God," was Angela's response, "I don't believe it."

"It was common knowledge with the local prostitutes that he was getting worse with each girl. None of the locals would go with him after the girl I am talking about went with him. The prostitute that was murdered was from out of town, and did not know his reputation."

"But surely the police would know?"

"They would never arrest him despite what they did or did not know. He was the Korean businessman of the year, and the saviour of Korea. They would not have him arrested or allow him to be maligned by a common prostitute's death."

"You printed the story and implied that he was involved, so your editor must have agreed?" Angela said.

"The story lasted one edition and then was canned from high. That was the end of it. I was quietly advised to forget about any further investigations."

"Even so, I still pursued the case until one night two goons jumped me, broke a few ribs and threatened to cut off my fingers if I persisted with the story. I did not."

"Now I understand the need to ensure my phone is not tapped. Sorry if I seemed a bit thick at the beginning, but I did not anticipate such a story," Angela said.

"What are you planning to do with this information?"

"I do not know yet," Angela said.

"Be very careful, and please use what I have told you judiciously."

"I will I promise, I will never use your name or contact you again. And, thank you for you input."

"You are welcome, but again, please be very careful."

"I will be and thanks again, Bye," Angela put down the receiver.

Angela sat silent for a minute and sifted through what she had found out over the last two weeks. It had all started with the murders in Alex and then the quick annihilation of the hit squad. Then there was Thomas' information about exploits into Tanzania and the existence of a third force planning a military coup. It was all so confusing and where in all this, if at all, sat Chen Yoo Soong. Her gut told her there was some connection but she had no idea how or why. She needed to talk to someone but whom could she trust with this type of information.

She wrote out the names of her associates and slowly ticked them off, without finding a person that she had total faith in. She would have to talk to Thomas tomorrow.

Chapter 15

Captain Khumalo was busy giving a detailed report to General Mkondo. The General sat quietly through the report and for a moment after while he digested the information.

"They know who you are in Tanzania?" he asked.

"I do not think so but they know we are not an ordinary poaching force. Why else would they back off and let us through with no attempt at capture."

"Do you think that they know you are South African?"

"I cannot see how they would come to that conclusion. I do know they will be better equipped if we were to return to Tanzania," Captain Khumalo said.

"It would appear that the wildlife is more dangerous to you than the locals," he said laconically.

"It was unfortunate in both cases."

"So it would appear," responded the General, "We cannot afford to lose any more people and your reputation of always bringing your people out is somewhat tarnished wouldn't you say?"

Captain Khumalo stared angrily at the General, but said nothing.

"Do you think you can go back again?" the General enquired.

"Not for a couple of months."

"Surely they wouldn't expect you to return immediately."

"It would be very dangerous to go straight back."

"Unfortunately, we do not have time to worry about the increased dangers of such a mission. Anyway, your missions have always been dangerous. That is why you are so well recompensed"

"We have always balanced the need versus danger in the past. It would be high risk to go back immediately."

"That is understood. But we have an enquiry from Korea for high-grade Rhino horn. The deal is that it must go through in three weeks and the horn must be fresh. The customer concerned is of great importance to our cause and will pay way over the market price for the horn. We have no alternative but to send you back again. This time you will be travelling light, as the horn cannot weigh more than twenty kilo's. You can be in and out in less than three weeks."

Captain Khumalo sighed and realised the futility of further discussion. He would have to go back regardless of the danger to himself or the sergeant. This time there would only be two of them. "When do we leave," he asked.

"Tomorrow at 0 Three Hundred, you will be dropped ten K's short of Nazombe by helicopter, you will be collected eighteen days later at the same spot. Is this enough time for you to get in and out?"

"Yes it will, but this time I require an inflatable dinghy to cross the river as I cannot cross close to the same location, and the currents will be too dangerous."

"O.K. it will be provided. You will also have a new Rigby 450, please try and bring it back with you this time."

Captain Khumalo stood up, saluted, and left the room.

General Mkondo watched him go, sat pensively for a moment, and then picked up the phone. The number he dialled was in Johannesburg. The phone rang for five rings and a voice said, "Yes."

"Phoenix 321."

"O.K." was the response. The general put down the receiver.

He left his office and drove out of Babanango towards Eshowe. At exactly six thirty he was standing outside the Eshowe post office waiting for the return call. The phone rang; the general picked up the phone and waited for the correct response.

"Bullwhip."

"Phoenix, still rising," he responded.

"Make your report," the voice said in heavily accented English.

"We have made delivery; we are already on the way for our next collection."

"What have we earned from this delivery?"

"Two million Rand."

"The next delivery will gross how much?"

"Three million Rand."

"Excellent, report again when you have further information."

The call had taken less than fifteen seconds and was untraceable.

Chapter 16

Don Scales sat in his office reviewing Jonathan's report. He was angry that Jonathan had disobeyed him and even angrier that Toby, on hearing the shooting, had not left his position to help Jonathan. It could have been a disaster. Jonathan was waiting outside his office and Don was thinking how he would handle the interview. Don stood up and walked to the door; he opened the door and beckoned Jonathan to come in.

"I will see you later," he said to Toby who was sitting next to Jonathan.

"O.K. Boss," Toby said with a wry smile.

Don was further angered by Toby's insubordination, which was reflected in his tone and demeanour. He returned to his desk chair, and looked sternly at Jonathan, who still stood up in front of his desk. Jonathan looked defiant, but also sheepish in the same moment.

"Sit down," Don said.

Jonathan sat down.

"Now can you please explain to me what the hell you thought you were doing?"

"We had sat by the river until 0 Three Hundred when I assumed that the poachers would already have crossed the river. I decided to lead a patrol down the river to ascertain where they had crossed for future reference. I heard the shooting and went to investigate. We very nearly caught them."

"You very nearly got yourself and three of your scouts killed. You left your position in direct contravention to my instructions. I cannot believe that you would be so irresponsible to do such a thing," Don said angrily.

"I assumed that they had already crossed the river and that there would be no danger to myself or my scouts."

"Then why did you follow up on the shooting?" Don asked.

"I thought that Toby had come under attack and went to help him. What should I have done?"

Don saw the futility of reprimanding him further. He could not discipline Jonathan for going to the assistance of his colleague. He was more disappointed with Toby that he made no move to help Jonathan. "If you wish to remain my deputy you will do as I ask. We had plenty of time to discuss the action taken and agreement was reached. I need to be able to trust you at all times."

"You can, and it will not happen again," Jonathan said.

"Call in Toby, please," Don said to Jonathan.

Toby entered the room with a smile and swagger knowing that Jonathan had just been given a grilling.

Don knew he could not berate Toby for following his orders implicitly but also realised that he needed a team that had faith in each other. He could not see how he could bring the two men together. There was a huge gulf between them.

"Toby you followed my instructions to the letter, the other night, and for that I am grateful. I am also concerned that a colleague could have been in trouble and no assistance was offered. Why would you not wish to help a colleague," he asked.

"I cannot win," whined Toby, "If I go to help him and lose my scouts you would be jumping all over me, I wish you would make up your mind."

"I understand what you are saying but you are reliant upon each other to be successful, you must have total trust in each other otherwise you will never make a team."

"I can look after myself'," Toby said.

Don looked at Toby with disdain and said, "In this business, if you only look after yourself, you will be looking after no one pretty damn soon!"

Toby said nothing.

"I believe the poachers will return again and soon," Don said. "What can we do to have the earliest warning that they are back?"

"I would suggest that we stake out the river at the point where they crossed into Mozambique," Jonathan said.

"That would tie down our resources and leave the reserve open to Moosa's poachers," Don said.

"Why not use Samuel to patrol the river?" Toby asked.

"I need him myself," Jonathan said.

"Hang on Jonathan that is not a bad idea, Samuel could cover a range of fifty kilometres per day, and Toby's Jeremiah could cover a further fifty kilometres per day. We could cover a hundred K stretch of the river with two men."

Jeremiah was the tracker assigned to Toby's scouts.

"It could work," Jonathan agreed.

"This way we should never be more than a day behind the poachers said Don. And the rest of the reserve can still be patrolled."

"What do you think Toby," Jonathan asked.

"I agree it could work," Toby said.

"When can they be in position," Don asked. "Tomorrow morning?"

They both nodded assent.

It was pitch black, and the army base was deserted as Captain Khumalo, and Sergeant Khubeki boarded the helicopter to take them into Mozambique. The helicopter took off exactly at 0 three hundred and beat its way north across Natal towards the Border. The range of the helicopter was fifteen hundred miles and would need to be refuelled before crossing the border. It touched down at Cosy Bay and refuelling took forty-five minutes.

"What are we going after this time?" Sergeant Khubeki asked.

"Rhino."

"Same place?"

"Yes."

"Jeez isn't that a bit risky. I mean we were lucky last time."

"I doubt they will expect us again so quickly, and, in any event, they are not equipped to deal with us."

"I hope you are right."

They carried on in silence and made their rendezvous by o-five-thirty. The sun was rising and cast a red glow on the surrounding bush. They alighted, collected their gear, and were gone into the bush in five minutes. The pilot watched them leave, and wondered what these people are actually up to. He knew he would not be the one to collect them, and knew he would never know the purpose or results of their mission. He did not want to know in truth, as in this case information was dangerous.

Captain Khumalo and sergeant Khubeki moved silently through the bush. After a couple of hours they stopped and made an interim camp. They were now some three kilometres from the river. Approximately 100 kilometres from their previous exit point. They would cross the river at dusk.

"It should be easier this time," Captain Khumalo said, "We are here for one Rhino and we saw plenty in the crater. The horn will weigh about twenty kilo's and we can cover the ground quickly with only that weight."

We have light packs, and we can cover sixty K's a night on forced marches. We should be in and out in twelve, maybe eleven days.

"How far is it to the crater?" Sergeant Khubeki asked.

"From the river I would say five hundred and twenty K's."

"If we push hard, we could be there in seven days. Maybe six and a half", said the sergeant.

"We must rest now as we have a long night ahead of us." Captain Khumalo said.

As the sun dipped low in the sky, they carefully made their way down to the river. They arrived just as the sun was setting and inflated the dinghy. They carried a spare gas cylinder, and they would be able to let the air out of the dinghy, and bury it with the cylinder on the opposite bank.

They entered the water and paddled upstream for two hours to make certain they were far from their previous route, which they were certain, would be closely watched by the scouts. At last the captain called a halt and they dragged themselves and the dinghy up the riverbank and back into Tanzania.

Captain Khumalo deflated the dinghy whilst sergeant Khubeki covered their tracks as best he could. They had chosen a place to leave the river where there was a shale bank. This made the covering of their tracks a little easier. They buried the dinghy and the air cylinder beneath a bush near the river. They set a small barrier of branches that would look like flotsam from the river, but if anyone came close enough to discover their dinghy, the branches would be disturbed. And then the poachers would know that the heat was on them.

Captain Khumalo took a compass bearing, and they immediately headed off at a fast trot towards the crater.

They ran throughout the night with no attempt to cover their tracks, but they did avoid the villages that dotted the landscape. This time, speed would have to be their ally. Occasionally dogs barked at their passing but they were convinced that the villagers had not seen them.

They found a hiding place just before dawn and fell down exhausted. They had done far better than they had anticipated, and captain Khumalo estimated that they were only thirty K's from Mbarangandu. If they were correct, they had covered eighty-five kilometres in the first night. He knew that the terrain would change very soon, and their speed would decrease markedly as they started to run uphill to the crater.

Captain Khumalo took first watch and sergeant Khubeki slept soundly for four hours. In turn, Captain Khumalo slept. They were both ready to move on dusk having eaten their meal from their backpacks. They drank water lightly so as not to induce thirst later.

They ran through the night again and passed Mbarangandu around midnight. They kept up this rate for the next two days, then the terrain changed, and the uphill slog began. They were only one hundred and seventy five Ks from the crater when they finally called a halt at dawn. Again they were both exhausted, and they knew that they were pushing themselves to the limit. They were fortified by the fact that they would reach the crater ahead of schedule by at least half a day. It was an incredible feat.

They lay up for the day, and as anticipated, they made the tip of the crater four hours before dawn of the fifth day. They would have one day to reconnoitre, one day to shoot the rhino and then they must dash for the border again. It was a formidable task, but they were confident that they would achieve their mission.

Chapter 17

Samuel had discovered the tracks of the poachers one day after they had crossed the border. He had found scrape marks in the shale and then come upon the spoor of the two men. The information was with Don Scales by midday of the poachers second day in Tanzania. He immediately called his friend Allen.

"Hi Allen, how's it going?"

"Hi Don. I assume your poachers are back, correct."

"Correct," Don said.

"How many?"

"Two."

"Is that all? What can two men carry with comfort? It cannot possibly be Tusks."

"It must be Rhino horn or a trophy buck," Don said.

"O.K. my buddies are on standby, and we can be out there in twenty four hours. We obviously cannot travel with all our gear, as they would not even let us into the country. You will have to get some supplies for us."

"This is what we will need." Allen reeled off a whole host of things and asked Don to read them back to him.

"That's fine. You have gotten everything on my list. Now the question is, can you get all that is required?"

"I don't think so; this is not like the UK. There are a few items on your list that will be impossible."

"Such as?" Allen asked.

"The Uzi's, the infrared sights, the stun grenades and night sights, the rest is O.K."

"That leaves a big gap," Allen said, "These items are issued to your armed forces."

"How do you know that?" Don asked.

"It's my job to know Don. Try your military people, explain your situation, but under no circumstances inform them of our involvement."

"I will try, but I am not sure that they will comply with my request."

"We will worry about that when we arrive. See you tomorrow, and, by the way, we will be travelling on a package holiday, organised ten weeks ago, to your Selous Game Reserve. We will be travelling as Bill Simms, John Preston and David Wesley. Please take note of the names, and we will contact you once we are through customs and immigration. And don't worry; we will catch your poachers. What number can I contact you on, and where can you collect us?"

Don gave a number and location some eighty K's from the airport. Allen did not wish to be picked up at the airport for obvious reasons.

Don braced himself for the required call to Dr. Gama and went over the reasons for the required weaponry. He lifted the receiver and made the call.

"Good afternoon Dr Gama, this is Don Scales."

"Good afternoon Don, how is it going down there," he asked pleasantly.

"You will recall I talked to you about some professional poachers, well, unfortunately, they slipped through our net. They came back into the country yesterday."

"How many?" Dr. Gama asked.

"Two," Don replied.

He could sense Dr. Gama's irritation, and pre-empted his response.

"Dr. Gama, these are not ordinary poachers. They are a disciplined military unit from South Africa."

"How on earth did you come to that conclusion, and why didn't you tell me before?" he demanded.

"We were not sure, but now we are convinced because of weapons and tactics used, and reliable information provided by one of our trackers."

"Are you suggesting that a white military unit from South Africa is actively poaching in Tanzania," he scoffed.

"They are not white. They are black, and they are extremely resourceful."

"How do you know they are military?" He asked.

"They referred to their leader as captain and the second in command as sergeant."

"It could be a renegade outfit not attached to the military at all."

"Even if that is the case these men are highly trained, and capable of killing a lot of my scouts."

"There are two of them, and you have twenty four trained scouts, and you know I do not wish to involve the armed forces."

Don knew exactly what he was talking about. There was no love lost between the Minister of Defence and the Minister of the Environment. The rivalry had started when the Minister of Defence had questioned the President on the need for low-level ministers (aimed at Dr Ngama) to attend meetings of national security. The rift between them had never healed.

"We can handle the job if we have the tools," Don said.

Dr. Gama thought of the points he could score at the next meeting when he advised the President that his men had captured a South African military unit in the heart of Tanzania. This would totally undermine the Minister of Defence. The possibility made his head spin. If Scales failed, then it was just another group of poachers that he had let escape. He could not lose. He could not pass up this opportunity to settle an old score.

"What tools do you need?" he asked, with undue emphasis on tools.

Don read from his list.

"Impossible, we could never supply such equipment to your scouts."

"If we are to catch these men we have no choice," Don said.

Dr. Gama felt the opportunity slipping away from him and was quiet while he considered who owed him favours.

"Are you still there?" Don asked.

"Yes, I am thinking," he said testily.

"How long do you need the tools for," he asked.

"Seven days," Don said.

"Wait by the phone; I will call you back in ten minutes."

Don waited by the phone for three trying hours when, at last, it rang.

"Don Scales," he answered.

"Your tools will be delivered to you personally at o-five-hundred tomorrow. You can have them for seven days, and they must be returned personally to me. Do you understand?" Dr. Gama said.

"Clearly," Don said.

"And Scales, do not fail."

Dr. Gama put down the phone before Don could respond. He did not mind, as he was elated. He thought of ringing Allen with the news but realised he would be on his way already. He must obtain as much information as possible about the whereabouts of the poachers. They must also do this quietly so as not to alert the poachers. He was saddened that he must let another of the animals in his charge die such that he could catch the poachers. But it would be worth the sacrifice.

He went across to the ops room where Jonathan and Toby sat looking over a map.

"Where do you think they are headed this time?" Don asked.

"Back to the crater," Toby said.

"Why do you think there again?" Don asked, "Surely if they are chasing a buck or a Rhino they could obtain that in the Selous Reserve."

"They know the ground, they know the whereabouts of the game, they know that Rhino are abundant within two kilometres of the crater rim, and they know the way back," said Toby.

"I agree," Jonathan said, "It makes sense."

"Where is Samuel now Jonathan?" Don asked.

"He is tracking them, and he believes he is some thirty to forty K's behind them. They will not catch him a second time," Jonathan said.

"Show me on the map where Samuel is right now."

Jonathan pointed to Luguruka, "Right there," he said.

"Samuel must not get too close, as we cannot risk him being caught again."

"What have you been up to?" Toby interjected. "You have been chatting away on the phone for some time now. Are you going to let us in on the secret?"

"Not yet," Don said, "I am sorry to be so secretive but all will be revealed in due course."

"Can't you trust us then?" Toby asked.

"It is not a matter of trust as you will be needed later, now please bear with me."

"Jonathan, advise Samuel to stay well back from the poachers but keep in touch with them. He must not be seen or detected. We want complete surprise when we take them."

"We are going to capture them this time?" Jonathan asked, excitedly.

"We are going to try our utmost to do so."

"Why now, and not before?"

"Just trust me Jonathan. This time we will be ready and will be able to take them alive."

Toby looked at Don, quizzically, but said nothing. Perhaps here was an opportunity to drop Don in it, and get him replaced by himself. Don felt the intensity of the stare that Toby gave him. I had better watch him closely thought Don.

"No one will leave the ops station until the capture is in progress, and I mean not even you two, Toby and Jonathan."

They both started to protest, but Don held up his hand to stop them.

"I have made my decision; you will be cut off completely from the outside word until we are finished."

"Could you say why?" Toby asked angrily.

"No loose tongue will jeopardise this operation. It could easily be done by accident, and I will not take that risk."

"Do you think we are children that you can order about at will," Toby asked.

"I have made my decision. You can make the necessary grievances after the operation is concluded. Until then, you will do as I ask."

Don could see the hurt in Jonathan's eyes and anger in Toby.

"The meeting is closed," Don said firmly, "There will be no contact with anyone outside of this building, and do you both understand this?"

They both nodded but looked uncomfortable for totally different reasons, Jonathan thought Don did not trust him anymore and Toby saw his chance slipping away.

Don went back to his office and on the way collected all the phones in the building and the radio's. He would not be undermined by Toby and Jonathan would just have to suffer, he would explain it all later.

Chapter 18

Captain Khumalo and Sergeant Khubeki reached their old base camp under the fig tree, silhouetted on the craters edge. They rested until fifteen hundred hours and then set off in pursuit of their Rhino. The Rhino population in the crater was high due to the lack of poaching in the area. Captain Khumalo was confident that, at the latest, he would have his Rhino horn before the end of the next day. They had already been in Tanzania for nearly six days. They must shoot the Rhino and get back to the rendezvous in a maximum of nine days or the helicopter would leave without them. He felt sure that they could do it.

Within an hour, they picked up the spoor of a large Rhino and Captain Khumalo checked his rifle. He also carried a spare round between the fingers of his left hand. The spoor was fresh, and thirty minutes later they could make out the grey hulk resting below a shady thorn tree. Captain Khumalo checked the wind and moved to a position where the wind was blowing from the Rhino towards them. They moved slowly through the bush, making no sound at all.

The Rhino was oblivious to their approach and was enjoying an afternoon siesta.

The Rhino's slumber abruptly ended at the sound of the Grey Lourie (the Go- Away bird, as the locals called it). The cry is the warning given to all animals in Africa and hunters were often thwarted by the bird's warnings. Every animal instinctively responds to that call. The Rhino was up and away in a flash racing through the bush. As with all animals unused to being hunted, the initial action is to race away, and then stop to detect the exact danger from a distance. The Rhino stood amongst the bush one hundred meters away from the poachers. His ears were pointed forward, and he was trying to detect the danger that the Lourie had clearly seen. The Rhino's eyes are poor, but he has the most acute hearing of any animal, and his sense of smell is also unsurpassed. His size and strength mean he has no natural enemies in the wild.

Captain Khumalo cursed in frustration, the Go-Away bird was still in the tree ahead, and any further movement might precipitate another call, and the rhino could well charge them, or worse, run away. The Rhino was only partially visible through the thick bushes.

Khumalo raised the rifle slowly to his shoulder and set the cross hairs of his telescopic sights on to the area directly behind the ears. He pulled the trigger, and the recoil knocked him backwards, and for a second, he did not see if the bullet had found its mark.

The Rhino collapsed on its front legs. The bullet had entered the fleshy area behind the ear, but had just missed the brain. The impact of a 450 bullet equates to four tons of stopping power, and it will even knock down an Elephant in full charge.

Captain Khumalo ran forward with his rifle ready to where the rhino lay. The Rhino was trying to stand, and it was lashing out with its horn in pain. Captain Khumalo shot the Rhino again behind the ear, and this time found the brain. He reloaded his rifle and shot the Rhino for a third time. There would be no surprises and no mistakes this time. There was no reaction from the Rhino as the second bullet had killed it outright.

"Cut off the horn sergeant," Khumalo said, impassively.

The sergeant set to work immediately whilst the captain scanned the adjacent veldt. There was nothing moving. Sergeant Khubeki removed the horn without even the slightest remorse. It was just another job to him.

The horn, though not overly large, had a beautiful shape and was perfectly formed. It was twenty-two centimetres long, seventeen centimetres at the base and curved back at sixty degrees. He estimated that it would weigh a little over twenty kilograms whilst wet but that this would dry down to seven kilograms when dry. As a poachers reward, it would be worth a maximum of a thousand U.S. Dollars for the locals, yet he knew that his superiors would be able to fetch at least a thousand times that price, if not more. And when converted into a sexual potency powder, it could fetch up to one hundred U.S. Dollars a gram. It is a massive business that to all, but the native poacher was, extremely lucrative. A native poacher with a thousand U.S. Dollars in his local currency was a rich man indeed; He could never comprehend the value of the horn once it left his hands.

To Captain Khumalo he was doing his duty and fighting for his country. He did not understand the politics behind the killing of the Rhino. He accepted it was necessary. To explain to him that this was an endangered species, he would simply have responded that so is the Zulu nation. He would kill whatever, and whenever he was ordered. There was no thrill of the hunt. It was just a job done on foreign soil, and the need to get the hell out of there before being detected.

They returned to their base camp routinely checking that they were not being followed. They waited the customary hour in the bush before entering their base camp. Sergeant Khubeki was posted as look out whilst captain Khumalo rested. At nightfall, Captain Khumalo and sergeant Khubeki started off on the long journey back to the river. There was no need for compass bearings, as they both knew the way from the landmarks they had noted on their previous trips. They were ahead of schedule and would be out of the country well before their nine-day deadline.

At almost exactly the same time of the shooting of the rhino, a Boeing 747 landed at Dar es Salaam with three gaudy English tourists. They wore colourful and patterned shirts, baseball caps, sunglasses and shorts. In short, they stood out from the crowd, but also were part of the tourist scene, and therefore, anonymous. Their passage through customs and immigration was uneventful but lengthy. They did not try the usual trick of U.S. Dollars in their passports to ensure that their passage through customs was hastened. This invariably put them to the back of the queue.

Outside the airport, Allen used a public phone to call Don.

"Don Scales," Don said.

"We are down," was Allen's response.

"I will collect you, as arranged, it will take about two hours," Don said.

"That's O.K. We will need a couple of hours to hire a car and meet you at the rendezvous."

"See you later Allen."

"Cheers," Allen said.

Don Scales left the base camp and flew north towards Morogoro and then due east to a private airstrip at Ngerengere. He landed without incident and waited for Allen and his colleagues to arrive. He did not have to wait long when he saw an old Volkswagen mini-bus heading towards the airstrip. He raised himself from his chair and followed the mini-bus path to the office at the airstrip. It was Allen. The mini-bus parked in front of Don, and Allen got out of the passenger seat to meet him.

"Good to see you again," Allen said. He shook Don's hand firmly and with obvious friendship.

"And you; how was your trip?"

"No problems and quite a good flight, we managed to sleep most of the way. Let me introduce you to my buddies," Allen said.

The two men strolled over, and Don studied them intently. To him they looked like a couple of athletes as he could sense the confidence in their walk and they exuded fitness. He was conscious of his own lack of athleticism and envious of their more than apparent trim waist and broad shoulders. They were not tall or huge men; they were no more than medium height and build. Yet, they exuded a quiet confidence and an understated strength.

"Don, this is Mike and Ralph."

Don shook hands with both of them and felt the silent strength behind the gaudy outfits. They looked him straight in the eye and went through the normal pleasantries. Mike was sun tanned and blonde with deep blue eyes, whereas Ralph was only lightly tanned with deep brown eyes and brown hair.

"Very good of you to come," Don said.

"Anything to help a buddy of Allen's," Mike said, with a slight Scottish brogue.

"Likewise," Ralph said, with the obvious London accent.

"I don't know how to thank you enough. I know you are always busy men and to give up part of your holidays to help me with my problems is more than I could expect," Don said, feeling rather foolish and inadequate.

Allen noticed the inflection in Don's voice and said, "Don, it is a pleasure to help if we can. I still remember you helping me with my officer's exams when I couldn't make head or tail of the English, let alone the true meaning. I do not know what I would have done without you," he said kindly.

"Yeah. We have heard a lot about you," said Mike, "This guy is always going on about you."

They all laughed, and it broke the ice, and made Don feel a lot better.

"Let's get back to base then."

He helped them load their luggage, three suitcases, and a grip, a cine camera in its own case and three other assorted cameras and tripods.

Don went through his routine ground checks and thanked the traffic controller for coming out at such short notice. He filed his flight plan before setting off and taxied down the slip road to the dirt runway. He turned into what little wind there was, brought the revs up to the maximum on both engines, and held the aircraft steady with the brakes. The aircraft shuddered with restrained power, and then he released the brakes and roared off down the runway. They were airborne in seconds and climbed to two thousand feet and headed west to Dodoma.

While they flew, Don was able to talk to Allen, who was sat next to him. Ralph and Mike were lazing in the cabin aft.

"Did you get the tools we requested?" Allen asked.

"Yes I did, all of the tools that you requested, much to my surprise."

"Allen. I do feel a little foolish calling you in for two poachers," he said.

"Don't," Allen said.

"Let me tell you a story just to let you know what you are dealing with."

"In 1982, a platoon of the Reccies, the South African equivalent of the S.A.S., was parachuted into Zambia, to take out an ANC base. Somehow the ANC heard of the raid and set up an ambush at the DZ, sorry "drop zone". There were fifteen men, and two Reccie officers in the middle of nowhere, and they parachuted right on top of the ambush. The ANC had over one hundred men on the ground, and they shot three of the guys as they dropped. The other twelve regrouped and were completely surrounded and caught in the crossfire. Yet somehow they fought there way out and in the process lost two more men, but they took out more than half of the attacking force. It seemed that they had no means of escape as their pick up had been shot down. So these guys ran across Zambia with virtually all the Zambian army chasing them until Victoria Falls, where they eventually slipped back into South Africa through Zimbabwe. They did not lose another man, and they caused numerous casualties on the Zambian forces as they raced for the border. This is the type of people you are facing now".

"Well", Don said, "I knew we were out of our league, but I think that is an understatement!"

Allen smiled and then said, "Don, can we take a detour and fly over the area concerned, particularly the river section where you believe they will try to cross the border."

"Of course," Don said.

They flew on with Allen and his friends watching the ground below and admiring the scenery. As they approached the river Allen turned and said, "Mike, Ralph. Have a good look below you. This is the terrain that we will need to cover."

Mike and Ralph got up and moved to the windows. "Can you take her down a bit?" Mike asked.

Don put the aircraft into a shallow dive and levelled out a hundred feet above the river and held the plane just above stalling speed. The dense bush clearly indicated the path of the river, and it was possible at this height to get a good idea of the depth, and breadth of the river.

"Looks interesting ground," Ralph said.

They flew for fifty kilometres west down the river, turned, and then flew back another seventy, the vegetation changed little along the river except where there was a village, and the timber alongside the river had been cleared.

"We can go to your base now," Allen said, "I think we have seen enough for now."

Don turned the aircraft and headed north, back to base. They landed as the sun was low in the sky. The new arrivals quickly settled into the base, stowed their gear, and went to meet Jonathan and Toby.

Don introduced the team starting with Allen, then Mike and Ralph. Jonathan and Toby were perplexed as to whom these people where. They could tell that they were not tourists, and they could also sense the inner strength of these men, which was unsettling.

"We have come to help you catch the poachers," Allen said.

Toby stared at Allen, and knew instantly that these guys were military regardless of their relaxed demeanour. He could smell Special Forces, and they looked very, very capable. The eyes always gave it away, there was no softness. These guys could be Reccies, he thought. Jonathan was also going through the same thought processes and had come to a similar conclusion. He did not know how to feel about it. It made him feel rather inadequate.

"This is Ralph and Mike," Allen said, introducing his two colleagues.

"Nice to meet you," Jonathan said, feeling uneasy, though he did not quite know why.

"Hi," Toby said, and weighed them up mentally. Hard, unforgiving and bloody fit were his thoughts.

"Don, could you take us through the events so far, beginning with the first time you became aware of them, and the timing of the subsequent visit. Please give as much detail as possible, and ask Jonathan or Toby to fill in any of the gaps."

Don started from the beginning and discussed the tracker finding the Elephant, and the subsequent events. "Jonathan, could you tell them what happened at the river, please?"

Jonathan went through his story in great detail.

"Toby, have you anything to add?" Allen enquired.

"Nothing more than has been already stated," Toby said.

"Toby, did you hear the shooting as the poachers crossed the river? I need to know to determine how far the sound travels through the bush at river level?"

"Yes I did," Toby said.

Allen looked hard at Toby and asked, "how far away from the shooting were you?"

"I was, say, seven kilometres away."

"How long did it take you to get there?" Ralph enquired.

Toby squirmed in his seat and was about to say something when Don chipped in, "I told him to stay where he was."

"Then you heard the shooting as well?" Mike asked.

"Actually no," Don said.

"Then how could you have advised Toby to stay put when you didn't hear the shooting," Mike asked.

"Toby was following my original instructions."

"I am confused," Mike said, "Toby you heard the shooting. Don, you did not, correct?"

"Yes." Don said.

"I assume then that Toby thought nothing of the shooting or decided not to help," Mike said bluntly. He looked straight at Toby.

"Leave it," Allen said.

"I was following instructions," Toby whined, "I do not have to listen to your accusations." He got up as if to leave.

"Sit down," Allen commanded.

His voice left no room for disobeying. It was a threatening command, which shocked both Don and Jonathan. Don was about to try to reassert his authority when a look from Allen stopped him in his tracks. The man had changed from the amiable Allen, into a commanding officer that would not accept any further discussion.

The mood had changed completely. These men were now in control, and the rest were purely advisory. Allen indicated to Don that he would like to speak to him privately. Jonathan and Toby left the room.

"Don I am sorry about that incident, but we need to know who we can trust, and who are not suitable for this type of operation. We were hard on Toby, but our lives could depend upon him. I would not trust him as far as I can spit. What are your thoughts?" he asked.

"He is a competent game ranger but is somewhat bitter that he did not get my job."

"I cannot believe that he did not go to the aid of Jonathan. What kind of man is he?"

"He lost his family to the blacks in Kenya; he has never forgiven them."

"Christ, that is hellish dangerous for you and Jonathan. Now Jonathan looks a good type, how far would you trust him?"

"Totally," Don said.

"Mike, Ralph, any comments?"

"Yeah," Mike said, "I don't trust the guy called Toby either."

"I think it is worse than that, I feel he is actively trying to undermine you. His whole attitude is one of conflict. He does not like you and obviously despises Jonathon. Who looks a good guy, by the way," Ralph said.

"Don, we cannot have him in the team. He would be too dangerous," Allen said.

"How the hell do I remove him from the team and prevent him from jeopardizing the operation, which he could so easily do."

"Leave that to me," Allen said, with hardness in his voice.

"Allen. I still have to work with Toby when you leave."

"Don, we can leave him in the team, but we will talk to him privately. We will not hurt him, but we will threaten him with bodily injury if he so much as steps out of line, now, or, after the operation," Allen said.

"That is Mike's department he is very persuasive when he wants to be."

Don was suddenly reminded of the time he ran the management meeting with total authority until the managing director arrived.

The MD would say to Don, "Don't mind me. I am only sitting in."

He would then promptly take control of the meeting, questioning all Don's departmental heads monthly reports. This situation felt much the same, except, possibly more humiliating.

"Allen, I realise that I am expecting you to risk everything to capture these poachers, and I know that you will. For that, I cannot thank you enough. I still do not know what to do about Toby. You have only seen his bad side, and he does have some redeeming qualities," he concluded.

"Don, we have been friends for ten years or so, and we have always trusted one another, haven't we?"

"Yes."

"Then trust me now, please, we will do what is best for you and us, I promise that we will not harm him or cause him unnecessary grief, O.K."

"OK."

"Now let's get down to the serious business of eating! We are all starved."

"We are having a braai, the African equivalent of a barbeque," Don said.

They all left the room; Jonathan and Toby were waiting patiently for them to come out.

"Have the guys got the Braai going?" Don asked.

"Yes," Toby said, with enthusiasm, "The fires are ready and the beers are cold."

"Excellent," Allen said, "Let's get on with it then."

They moved outside and there were the two braai's already with glowing coals. The scouts who were not on duty had also been invited. The cook came out staggering under the weight of the meat and sausages, and all the SAS men laughed.

"Good God," exclaimed Ralph, "Who will eat that bloody lot, there is enough meat there for a battalion."

Allen took in the appearance of the scouts at a glance. They were smartly dressed with not an ounce of fat on any of them.

"They look a good bunch of men," Allen said to Don.

Don felt a flush of pride, "They are. All they need is some training from you guys, and they will be a very effective force against these poachers."

"I can see that," said Allen, "Do you think we could make anything out of these guys?" he asked Mike.

"Don't see why not," he said.

The men could not understand a word of English, but stood there beaming. Their gleaming white teeth were practically glowing in the dark. They snapped to attention and saluted the three men as they approached them. That the three strangers were impressed was obvious, this only made them more rigid in their stance.

"Tell them to stand at ease please Jonathan," Don said.

Jonathan gave the command, and they stood there expectantly.

"What are they waiting for?" Don asked.

Jonathan smiled and said, "This is a special occasion and they are waiting for you to address them."

Don felt embarrassed, then said, "Will you translate for me please Jonathan."

"Of course I will."

Don made a short speech feeling quite embarrassed in front of the SAS men. He welcomed Allen, Mike and Ralph and explained that they had come to help them catch the poachers. They brought expert knowledge from overseas and would make their task easier. The scouts stared at the three SAS men with awe; they could see that these men were not tourists with the plump bellies and lazy eyes. They had learned to determine the response of wild game from the way they behaved, and the look in their eyes. They could see the same subtle power in these men. There was a surge of anticipation.

The sound of the meat spitting and sizzling on the braai broke the trance. An occasional flame would shoot up from the fire where the fat from the meat and sausages had ignited, lighting up the place.

"Tell them the talking is over, and it is time to eat," Don said.

Jonathan translated, and there was a tremendous whoop of joy as the men dashed to the braai. They all laughed at the antics and the debate around the fires. Some wanted their meat barely cooked, and others wanted it almost burnt. Most of all they wanted to enjoy themselves.

"How many beers should I allow them?" Jonathan asked.

"Four each,"

At the mention of beers, the noise stopped at the braai. They did not understand English, but they clearly understood the word beer. They did not understand the word four, and they waited in anticipation.

Jonathan held up four fingers, and they whooped for joy again.

"These guys know how to enjoy themselves," Mike said.

"They certainly do," Don said, "They would drink most Europeans under the table and still carry on. They have a prodigious capacity for liquor. I can tell you now that before the meat is finished; the ration of four beers will be long gone. They will ask for more," he said laughingly.

"How will they be in the morning?" Allen asked.

"If they drink four beers, it has no impact. With eight beers, they will be slightly under the weather. Anything above that and they will be useless."

They sat down at a wire table and watched the scouts enjoy themselves. They laughed and talked amongst themselves and even Toby joined in telling tales of his childhood in Kenya. He was most enthusiastic about the early days, describing a farming paradise where crops would grow in profusion. They had to fight the bush to keep the fields clear and the occasional Elephant. It sounded idyllic and showed a side to Don he had not seen before. He became bitter when he talked of the death of his family and then became quiet again.

"I think we had better cook some meat before it all disappears," Allen said.

"No need," Don said," They will deliver our meat just now."

"Like the bloody Ritz," Mike said.

They all laughed.

The food, when it came, was an incredible sight for the SAS men. They laughed, and said they could never eat all that. There was sausage, chops, steaks, sweet potato, potato salad, a spicy bean salad and lettuce and chopped onion salad. The cook watched them eat like a school matron, and was delighted when they, much to their disbelief, consumed everything. They washed the meal down with a lovely South African red wine. The SAS men ate their part but drank remarkably little. They praised the cook a thousand times as they tested his delights. Jonathan interpreted, and the cook, a small fat man, beamed and smiled so wide with pride that his face must crack. They all laughed loudly again and applauded the cook.

"Don you are a lucky bastard to land a position like this," Allen said.

"I know," Don said, "This could really be a paradise if they ever sort out the politics."

"I thought Tanzania was stable nowadays," Ralph said.

"The bloody kaffirs are power mad and never stop trying to top each other," Toby said, "as long as the strongest man is in power then there is a kind of peace. But they never stop plotting against each other."

"Mike, it could be a good time for you discussion with Toby now," Allen said.

"Yes, I agree, Toby, could I have a word with you please. I want to run over some details for tomorrow."

"O.K.," Toby said, completely unaware of the mood.

Mike and Toby left, and Jonathan looked on curiously.

"Jonathan," Allen said, "you are obviously the most relevant person to explain the politics in your country, and I would like to hear what you think."

"It is always difficult for the European to understand the African, but you should look at your own history. Europeans have slaughtered more people this century than Africa ever will. How many people were killed in two world wars in the so-called educated and sophisticated West? Africa has been a tribal society, and the boundaries of every tribe were clear in the past. The Europeans discover Africa and come to colonise. They have no understanding of the tribal chiefs or their domains; they literally split up the continent in nice little pieces, and in the process, split the tribal lands. They then have had enough of Africa, and they leave."

"These tribes can be traced back as far as your Monarchy. They do not sit well together and conflict starts. Their first targets where the whites, who stayed behind, as these colonialists were seen as the oppressors. They drove them south. Having their country back, the tribes that had been split wished to be reunited. The new regime did not want to part with their lands and wars broke out everywhere. Only this time it was a tribe against tribe."

"Europeans could never understand this behaviour, but the new regimes were ruthless men who saw a powerful opposing tribe as a major threat. As one tribe reaches ascendancy over another, it attempts to wipe out the opposition. It has to maintain power, and as you know in the west, power is everything.

"How do you see it being resolved," Allen asked.

"Through time and education," Jonathan said, "Just look at South Africa, most of the black people are illiterate and that has been the policy of the apartheid regime. They were cannon fodder for the armed forces or for industry. It will take years to heal."

The only country in Africa, which appears to be stable without ethnic conflict, is Botswana. The reason being, that blacks are well educated, and always have been.

There was a bloody civil war, which went on for ten years. There was much posturing at the end of the war, but the blacks in Botswana have put that behind them. There are more whites returning to Botswana than any other African country. This gives the rest of Africa hope," he concluded.

"What of Tanzania," Don asked?

"There are more than 120 tribes in Tanzania, of various ideologies. It will take time for all the tribes to forget their roots and live like Great Britain. Even in Britain the old tribes are still resisting. That is why there is still conflict in Ireland."

Allen was going to interject, but Jonathan held up his hand and said, "Please let me finish as I will forget the point I am trying to make."

Allen agreed by holding up his hands and saying, "Continue please."

"In Ireland your army subdued a country by force. They were not your tribe yet you tried to become part of that nation, and they could never accept you as such. They are a proud people with strong ties to their history. The island was split and a compromise sought. The people on the wrong side of the division could never accept that they were not part of the free island so what did they do? They revolted. They fought the might of the British Empire, and your army could not subdue them. They are still fighting your army now. What happens when the island is returned back to the Irish, which you most certainly will have to do? You will have a disenfranchised Anglo-Irish, which will not be able to accept the change. They will become the new IRA, what will your army do then? They are like the Afrikaner in South Africa; they have nowhere else to go. Will the mainland welcome them back into the UK, will they want to go when they have a history in Ireland stretching back four hundred years, I doubt it. Gentlemen, you have your own Africa on your own doorstep. Then you have the arrogance to advise Africa how it should resolve its problems."

"Phew," Don said, "I am impressed with your level of understanding, and I do not mean that condescendingly," he added quickly. "Where did you learn all that stuff?"

"Don, with the best will in the world, and I mean no harm from this statement, all Europeans believe that Africans are thick and cannot work out the problems for themselves. I was educated in Dar es Salaam and most Europeans would conclude that there is no political or modern history taught. Most Africans believe that the Europeans cannot learn from their history, you are a first world country we are third world."

"Would somebody explain to me what third world means? You assume that we are incapable because we do not have the infrastructure to educate our people. Why didn't the Europeans install the infrastructure to educate the masses? "

"You raise many pertinent issues," Allen said, "Most of what you say I believe to be correct, I cannot argue on the politics of Africa, I take your point on Ireland, I have never ever heard it explained that way before."

"I do not mean to offend," said Jonathan, "but please judge each African as you meet him. We are as different as any European country."

They debated without rancour the difference in culture and beliefs. Jonathan was pressed on many points, and he responded with honesty.

The SAS men were extremely impressed with his understanding of Europe and realised they knew nothing of Africa except that depicted by the media. They never noticed Mike return for some time.

Allen noticed Mike had returned, and asked, "How did it go with Toby?"

"Quite well actually, he will be joining us again shortly."

Don looked at Mike quizzically but could glean no information from his impassive face. He held Don's stare until Don turned away.

"Mike, Jonathan has been educating us on the African mind and politics. It was most interesting, a pity that you missed it," Allen said.

"I caught some of the end of it; it sounded very plausible, especially that bit about Ireland."

"Don. It is now twenty one hundred, and I would like to go over the actions for tomorrow with you, Toby and Jonathan. We will then put together an action plan and present to you and your staff at o-five hundred tomorrow. Is that O.K. with you?"

"That's fine," Don said, "Let's go back inside and look over the maps."

All the men filed inside and found Toby waiting for them.

"Everything O.K.?" Don asked.

"Fine," was his only response.

Jonathan took centre stage again and indicated on the large-scale map where Samuel had found the river crossing, the route the poachers had taken and their probable route back. Allen, Mike and Ralph asked questions about terrain, weight of a Rhino horn, speed that his scouts would cover the terrain. Jonathan answered succinctly and clearly. Toby was asked his point of view and gave a similar view to Jonathan. Don was asked for the final say and what resources he could utilise. Don outlined the scouts available and the fact that they would have the use of the Cessna.

"O.K., have you got enough Mike?" he asked, Mike nodded, "and you Ralph?" Ralph also nodded.

"Then Don would you mind bringing in the tools and then you and your staff can leave us. We will meet you all in the morning."

Toby, Jonathan, and Don filed out.

"What are these tools?" Toby asked.

"Just a bit of equipment they asked me to get them," Don said evasively, "I think we should all get to bed now. There will be a long day tomorrow."

Goodnight, they both said. "Goodnight," Don said.

Don went to his private locker and took out the tools. He was back in five minutes, and the three SAS men were in deep consultation.

"I have your tools," Don said.

"Put them on the table please," Allen said, "You can stay if you like."

"I would be in the way, but I would like you to check the tools first please."

The three SAS men went to the bag and took out the tools, the Uzi's' were stripped down in the blink of an eye and all the parts laid out separately. The three spare magazines per Uzi were emptied, and the ammunition checked. Don looked on in awe as these professionals checked their equipment.

"These look fine," Allen said, "just need a bit of cleaning, that's all."

"Right I will leave you to it then, goodnight."

Goodnight the three SAS men said simultaneously. Don left the room.

The three S.A.S. men studied the map of the region and in particular the riverside section where the dinghy had been hidden. They had seen the density of the bush adjacent to the river and knew it worked both for and against them. They had the latest in detection technology, which determine movement up to a range of three kilometres. The infrared cameras would beam up to a satellite and back to a visor receiver worn like a night sight. The person wearing the visor would only see the picture. No light would or could be detected externally.

They studied the map and determined where they would place the cameras and movement sensors; there was no point in moving more than three kilometres from the section where the dinghy was buried. The area to be covered was too large and needed to be placed in a grid that would cover the maximum area adjacent to the dinghy. Allen indicated on the map the position of the sensors he thought would most likely cover the area to give maximum surveillance.

"Are you in agreement?" Allen asked.

Ralph and Mike indicated that they were in agreement.

"The dodgy bit is we do not know exactly where the poachers are now. How much ground they have covered and when can we anticipate them arriving in the area. We know that they are exceptionally fit, well trained and presumably well armed. There are too many unknowns for my liking," Ralph said.

"I am always concerned when the full intelligence is not available," Mike said.

They both looked at Allen.

"Then let's look at the facts," Allen said.

"They killed the Rhino here," Allen pointed to the marked section of the map.

"They killed the Rhino yesterday, and presumably set off back to their point of crossing which is here," Allen pointed to the site of the buried dinghy.

"We assume that is where they are heading," Mike said.

"Why bury a dinghy if you are not planning to use it again?" Allen asked.

"There could be the fact that they intend to cross at another point and suspect that the dinghy may be found," Ralph suggested.

"I would not agree with that," said Allen. "They have easily eluded Don's regular scouts, and that was with a couple of very heavy tusks to weigh them down, I doubt that they will be concerned again."

"If they are professional soldiers then they are trained to assume that they have been detected, and they will approach the dinghy with extreme caution," Ralph said.

"I agree," Mike said.

"If we were to use the same method of escape, we would have at least three options already planned, and we would have the flexibility in the use of these options," Mike said.

"Agreed?" Allen asked.

"The problem is that we can only cover one site, I dare not use the scouts to capture these poachers. We have worked with the South African Reccies, and we know their capabilities. We have to settle for the most likely area of retreat and plan accordingly."

Mike and Ralph nodded in agreement. They talked through their layout of sensors and how they would hopefully capture the poachers without having to fire a shot. It was vital to capture them alive.

The sensors, twelve in total, would be placed in a grid reference that would cover an area of thirty-six square kilometres. Any movement through the area covered could not go undetected. At a range of five kilometres, their point of crossing would be pinpointed down to a matter of meters, and the thick riverside bush would shepherd the poachers towards the awaiting SAS. The SAS men would have time, and flexibility, to be in a position to capture the poachers long before their arrival.

They discussed the method of capture and agreed that stun grenades were preferable to the darts that they also carried. The darts were coated with a fast acting anaesthetic that would put a supremely fit man down in three seconds. The problem is that a well-trained soldier, who is extremely fit and mobile, can do a terrific amount of damage in three seconds.

The method of capture was agreed, and the decision on who would be point, and back up was formulated. Each man knew exactly what he would be doing and there would be no changes to their plan unless circumstances dictated a change. They discussed all the probabilities and formulated three back up alternatives to their main plan.

"I think we have just about covered everything and might as well call it a day." Allen said.

"One last point Allen, how reliable is their tracker Samuel?" Mike asked.

"He has been in the business a long time, and Don believes that he is reliable. In any event, we will be using our own detection systems which are far more reliable than any tracker," Allen said.

"I know and understand that, but the question refers to their current whereabouts, and how far they are away from the crossing site. If we are to be successful, then we need at least a day to prepare and double check equipment. If Samuel is not accurate we could be detected whilst placing the sensors and the whole plan would be blown."

"Don indicated that the poachers were at least three days away from the crossing site. That was at seventeen hundred hours today. They estimate that they will attempt the crossing in four days time sometime between twenty two hundred and o-one hundred. The moon is new, the area will be very dark indeed, and they will have maximum cover."

"Then we have at least three days to set up."

"Correct," said Allen.

"Are we all agreed then?" Allen asked.

Both Mike and Ralph nodded agreement.

Chapter 19

Captain Khumalo and sergeant Khubeki cleared their base camp of all evidence of their presence and set out for the river. They had discussed where they should cross and concluded that they would push hard for the river, and then lay up for a day to reconnoitre the area. They had to be able to detect and avoid any of the scouts that could be positioned adjacent to the river crossing. If need be, they would abandon their dinghy, and cross further downstream.

"If we push hard we can make the river in four days, we can move by day, for the first day, as the area is practically uninhabited," Captain Khumalo said.

Sergeant Khubeki looked at his captain and said nothing. He merely nodded his head. The rhino horn was wrapped and placed in a backpack; the design of the backpack distributed the weight evenly across the shoulders and back. The weight of the pack was lighter than their normal backpacks and would not hinder their progress. They moved out with captain Khumalo leading and sergeant Khubeki following, carrying the horn.

They travelled at a steady jog that would eat up the ground but not tire them. They could jog for eight hours without a break and in that time easily cover 50 kilometres. They felt that they had no need for caution, as they were certainly undetected so far. And even if the rhino were discovered they would be long gone. They had seen no evidence of scouts or anti-poaching units in the area.

They rested after ten hours of jogging and ate a meagre meal of bananas and cold, precooked mealie meal. They rested till dusk and then set off again.

They were still a great distance from the river, and running through savannah, patched with Mopani and Acacia trees, growing in clusters randomly across the plain. The game path that they were following meandered across the plain and although longer in kilometres, was preferable to running through the grass, which at times was chest high. They made no effort to cover their tracks, as it was impractical to do so.

Captain Khumalo led the way, and they changed backpacks every two hours. When they stopped to change it would take less than a minute.

They did not speak at all, when changing or during their spells of running. There was no need to do so, both understood what was required, and talk was superfluous.

The first day and night passed without incident and as they came closer to their crossing a sense of urgency was ever present. On the fourth night, they were forty kilometres from the crossing, and as they got closer to the river, more and more villages were present. They had abandoned their daytime running to avoid detection, and so far they had covered the terrain without, they believed, having been detected.

They had now been in the country for over nine days. There had been no evidence of a search for them. The fifth day they hid in a Mopani thicket and slept till late afternoon. On the evening of the fifth night, they ran up to a small Kopje, which they knew was twenty kilometres from their crossing point. Captain Khumalo gave the signal to stop.

"I will go forward and reconnoitre the river crossing. If it is all clear, then we can cross tonight. If we have to detour then, we will cross tomorrow night."

"We have seen no evidence of being detected or followed," Sergeant Khubeki said.

"That does not mean that our trail has not been found. Let's hide the horn in the bush, and you can backtrack ten K's, and see if we are being followed. It is now nineteen hundred hours. We will rendezvous back here at twenty two hundred."

The men separated without further discussion.

Captain Khumalo set off for the river crossing at a steady jog. The nature of the terrain was changing, and he was moving through denser bush, the closer he got to the river. He moved with caution, but did not see any of the scout patrols on the river until he was seven kilometres from the crossing. He had chosen to take a game trail through the thickest bush to avoid any possibility of detection. He heard the scouts long before he saw them.

He crawled close to their camp and watched them for thirty minutes. If he needed evidence that they were not detected, then what he saw confirmed this. It was obviously a routine patrol with no effort of maintaining silence or posting guards. The camp was noisy and relaxed. None of the men were carrying firearms and all appeared to be ready to sleep. It was a normal bush camp and not a search party.

He withdrew cautiously and proceeded to the crossing area and found the area intact. The branches that he had set to notify him if they had been discovered were still in the same place, and he could see that there had been no movement in the area. He began to relax and withdrew quietly. He made his way back to the rendezvous, and found sergeant Khubeki waiting for him. He had arrived minutes earlier.

"Anything to report?" Captain Khumalo asked.

"I went back down the trail for about fifteen kilometres, and the only tracks I found were ours. There is nobody following us."

"I found a river patrol some seven kilometres or so from the crossing point. They were not on the alert and were not expecting company. I do not believe that they know we are here," Captain Khumalo said.

"I worry when it is too easy," Sergeant Khubeki said.

"I know what you mean, but these scouts are not army and their ground intelligence is not good. They always chase and apprehend after the event, and seldom catch poachers prior to them poaching. Still we must always assume that they know we are here and act accordingly."

"Should we split up and meet on the other side?" Sergeant Khubeki asked.

Captain Khumalo thought about this option.

"If we split and we do run into any kind of resistance, then we run the risk of being taken due to the inability of protecting ourselves. It is wiser to stay together and cover each other at the most dangerous section of the river crossing. We will be most exposed at this point."

Sergeant Khubeki looked at his captain and nodded agreement.

"We must leave now," Captain Khumalo said.

The time was precisely twenty-two thirty three hours, and it would take no more than an hour to reach the crossing at the pace that they would take. They would exercise the utmost caution in approaching the crossing. Captain Khumalo led the way through the dense riverside bush. They could hear the river long before they could see it, and a recent spate of rain had turned the river into a torrent. They circumvented the scout's camp, and again they saw that there was only one guard, and the rest of the camp was evidently asleep.

They only had seven kilometres to go before they would be at their crossing point. They were both aware that this would be their most dangerous seven kilometres, as if they had been discovered the most probable place for ambush would be here. They both automatically checked their AK47's, captain Khumalo adjusted the sling on the Rigby 450 to ensure it was tight to his body, and would not impede his ability to move freely. They moved off cautiously through the bush.

The three S.A.S. men were ready at dawn and were pleased to see that the scouts and Don were waiting for them.

"Good morning Don," Allen said.

"Can we discuss today's events with you please?"

"Good morning, sure, let's go to my office, do you need Toby and Jonathon," he asked.

"Not just yet."

Ralph and Mike greeted Don, and they all moved to Don's office.

"Don, we want you to place two sets of scouts in these locations," he pointed to crosses indicated on the map. "They are to stay there until you receive our call that the poachers have been arrested. You are to advise them not to place sentries other than normal and behave as if they were on an ordinary patrol. The poachers must be able to find them and bypass them easily."

"You are using them to guide the poachers to the crossing site?"

"Correct," Allen said.

"The poachers must not suspect or see anything out of the ordinary," Mike said.

"I see, and then they will have no involvement in the capture of the poachers?" Don asked.

"No they will not. We cannot afford any mistakes and the fewer people involved the better," Allen said.

"Can you tell me what you are planning?" Don asked.

"Yes, the plan is a simple one. You will place one group of scouts seven kilometres to the East of the crossing and the second group seven kilometres to the west of the crossing. We will have detection sensors fixed at two kilometre intervals set up in a grid," Allen indicated on the map the positions of the sensors.

"Each sensor has a range of three kilometres and transmits infra red pictures to these head sets," Allen indicated the headsets they had carried in their kit bags.

"The sensors will pick up movement, and automatically lock on until instructed otherwise by the control button on the sides of our visors. If animals create the movement, they can be reset at an instant. Once we detect the poachers all the sensors will automatically focus on the poachers, and we can track them right into our collection point."

"The bush is pretty thick out there. How will you be able to determine which movement is an animal and which is human?" Don asked.

"There are two aspects to this little baby," Allen said. "Once movement is detected an image intensifier takes over. The outline of the image is plotted and intensified to give a graphic representation of the object moving. This is based on the heat given off from the body and a clear shape can be determined. The other sensors then lock on to the shape and give a three D picture of the object. This is then translated into a clear picture and even the armaments can be seen clearly. We can plot their movement down to a centimetre, and we can be in position accordingly. We then have visuals on them from our normal night sights and image intensifiers. It's quite simple really."

"It sounds far from simple to me," Don said.

The three SAS men smiled and said nothing.

"Where do we get involved?" Don asked.

"When we have the poachers in custody your men must take over. We will collect our gear and be gone the next morning. It cannot be known that we were involved, or there will be hell to pay."

"What about Toby, Jonathon and your men. Can they be trusted to keep quiet about this?" Ralph asked.

"I think so, you put the frighteners on Toby, and he would have been the risky one," Don replied.

"Do we need to talk to him again?" Mike asked.

"I do not think so, but maybe a reminder before you leave might help."

"We will need transport to the areas marked on the map, and we would appreciate it if only you took us."

"The equipment that we are using is classified and not for general observation. I do not need to tell you that what you see can never be discussed with anyone, do I?" Allen asked.

"Of course not, I can only thank you for coming to help me; I would never ever discuss this with a soul."

"Then let's get on with it, shall we? It will be a busy day."

The men left the room and collected their gear. Don explained to both Toby and Jonathon that he and he alone, would accompany the SAS men to the ambush site. They objected, but they quickly realised that objection was futile. They accepted with some resentment being left out of the picture.

It took the SAS men all of the day to set up their sensors in the positions that they were happy with and to ensure that they could not be seen. The testing was relatively quick, and the only final testing would be later in the evening, to ensure that there were no faults with the equipment after dusk. They returned to the river in the late afternoon. Nothing could now move through the bush without being detected for thirty-six square kilometres.

The outer sensors were placed seven kilometres from the river on both the east and west side of the river crossing site. The grid was marked out similar to a naught and crosses game, with nine squares. Each square had a sensor, but on the outer squares, the sensors were placed at the edge of the square, and on the inner sections in the middle of the square. The three squares adjacent to the river had two sensors to reduce the area covered and intensify the image proportionately. It would also be possible to see the exact location of the three SAS men, so each man knew where the other was at all times, and more importantly, where they were in reference to the poachers.

"Don, can we have a meeting with you and your two lieutenants now please," Allen asked.

"Sure," Don said, and called Toby and Jonathon to his office.

"We wish to discuss with you tomorrows events, I will hand over to Allen now," Don said.

"Thank you Don," Allen said.

"We have devised a plan to capture your poachers unharmed. This plan requires your total co-operation, and cannot be deviated from for any reason whatsoever. Jonathon, you will take your scouts to a position east, seven kilometres from the crossing point as indicated on the map. Toby, you will take your scouts seven kilometres west of the crossing point."

"You will behave as if you are on a normal patrol and you will not post more that the usual amount of guards. We would prefer you to make plenty of noise such that the poachers can hear you and easily avoid you. Do you understand these instructions?" Allen asked.

Toby and Jonathon nodded their heads; Jonathon started to ask a question but was prevented from doing so by Allen raising his hand to quieten him.

"I know what you are going to ask and yes, we will handle this situation alone. This is no reflection on you or your scouts. It is just that we have our methods and prefer to work with people who have been trained the same way. We cannot afford any mistakes, and we do not wish to see anyone of you harmed."

"We have been in many tight situations before with armed poachers, and we have handled ourselves very well. What is the problem now?" Jonathon asked, insisting to be heard.

"The difference this time is that these men are highly trained army personnel. They are capable of things you would not even believe possible. On their last foray, they eluded all your scouts and were carrying tusks that must have weighed two hundred pounds each. They forced marched four hundred and seventy five kilometres with three men carrying the tusks between them. They captured with ease your most capable tracker, and they could have killed any number of your scouts, and still escaped. Need I say more?"

"You make them sound superhuman," Jonathon said.

"In a lot of ways they are. They are incredibly fit. Each man has an individual skill that complements the unit, and they are trained to the highest level. That alone is enough, but if they have been in any action, they know how to use their skills because they survived. The Reccies in South Africa where always pitched against superior numbers, sometimes considerably superior numbers. You cannot come through these experiences without carrying that experience forward."

"Toby, you must have seen or heard about the Reccies, surely," Don asked.

"Everyone's heard about them, but nobody knows who they are. They were considered the most efficient fighting unit in South Africa; the SADF was no mean fighting force itself, so they must have been good."

"You are quite right," Allen said, "The SADF was respected around the world for its fighting prowess even if the objectives were unreasonable, and the Reccies were the elite of the SADF."

"I get the picture," Jonathon said.

Allen explained the rest of the plan to them and asked for further questions, none were forthcoming.

"Jonathon, any report from Samuel your tracker," Ralph asked.

"The scout with him calls in every four hours, I have instructed them to leave a distance of at least four hours walk between them, so far they have not been detected. The poachers are moving very quickly, and are estimated to be two days from the river, and they should arrive tomorrow night, and we estimate that they will attempt to cross the river between midnight and 0 two hundred hours."

"Don, I would suggest that you call off the tracker when they are within one day of the river crossing. If I were they, I would double back, and ensure that I was not being followed. I can only assume that they will do the same. We cannot afford to warn them" Allen said.

"We will confirm their direction tonight and then call in Samuel and the scout," Jonathon said.

"So far they appear to be heading for the river crossing where they hid the dinghy," Don said.

"We will have a fourteen kilometre section of the river covered. If they choose another crossing, then there is nothing that we can do about it. We take our chance based on probability, but there is always a possibility of an alternative route."

"Allen, if they take an alternative route, then are you saying that they will escape?" Don asked.

"I am afraid so. It is not possible or practical to extend the area we are covering. We would not be able to react quickly or selectively. We must be in the strongest position, not the poachers."

"I understand, but it would be very disappointing to lose them now after all this effort," Don said.

"Sometimes it can't be helped, that's life as, they say. I would like your men in position tonight please Don."

"We will leave immediately."

"You will not see us tomorrow until we have either captured the poachers or they have crossed elsewhere. We have your radio frequency, and we will call you once they are in the bag," Allen said.

"Good luck and good hunting," Don said.

"Thanks," said the three SAS men simultaneously.

Don and his lieutenants left the room, and soon the SAS men could hear the scout's vehicles moving out. They were on their way to the selected place and would be in position before sunset. They checked their equipment and prepared to leave. It would be a long wait, but rather too early than too late.

The SAS men were in position just after sunset and were spaced twenty meters apart. The contact between each man was by a prearranged signal via a vibrator on the chest of each man. Allen represented one tremor, Mike was two and Ralph three. There was no other discussion required, as they had prearranged their movements. If, for any reason, they had to relocate, then Allen would determine this. He would indicate the required movements to ensure that the poachers were covered in a "v" formation.

The sensors supplied all three SAS men with the same 3D picture of their environs. The movement of the SAS men would be determined by arrows on the frame of the picture, moved by Allen on his console. He also knew that Mike and Ralph would predict these moves and would be following up automatically.

The sensors were tested in the darkness of night, and the pictures they received where crystal clear. The area could be scanned at will, not by rotating the sensor, as this could create noise and detection. But by raising and lowering shutters on the nine lenses that made up the sensor. They had three sixty degree capability but normally only one eighty degrees were required. This could be programmed to change at regular intervals but was seldom done. The motion sensors determined when and which lenses would be opened or closed.

The three men had been in many similar situations before, but this did not stop them from feeling tense. Even with the best planning in the world something can go wrong. You could only minimize the risk; you could not take the risk away altogether.

They had done all they could and left nothing to chance. They were accomplished in camouflage and even at five meters in daylight; they would not have been detected. In the darkness of the night, they were entirely invisible. They lay in wait.

The poachers did not come on the first night, and as this was anticipated, there was no rancour. The day was spent in complete silence with each man busy with his own thoughts. At no time did they move from their hiding place. They knew that they could not be detected unless infra red detectors were used, and they were reasonably confident that the poachers did not have this equipment. They rested during the day in shifts of four hours, with two of the men always vigilant.

Slowly the day passed, and darkness enveloped them again. They knew that tonight was the most likely night, and the tension came back into their bodies and minds. Vigilance was everything and these men understood that there was no time to rest. Their weapons were checked carefully and were made ready for action.

The plan was straightforward enough. The poachers would be tracked into their path. The game trail was some twenty meters from where the dinghy was buried.

There was no other alternative route unless they forced their way through thick bush. If that should happen then the SAS men would retreat with them as agreed and take them as they emerged from the bush.

Allen would control the movements and would indicate when they were to throw their stun grenades by a vibration of five beats. The moment the stun grenades were thrown Mike, who was in the rear, would disarm and subdue the last man to enter the V. Ralph would do the same to the man leading. Allen would be on hand to cover both Mike and Ralph should the stun grenades not work perfectly, and, if one, or both, of the poachers managed to raise their weapons. Allen carried a nine-millimetre Beretta for this close up work and was deadly with this handgun. They all hoped he would not have to use it as he would have to shoot to kill. They had every confidence that he could shoot both men before they could raise their weapons if required; they had seen him in action before.

They waited patiently, and as the hours passed, the tension and worry increased. Doubts began to appear. When four hours after dusk arrived with no sign of the poachers, they began to fear that they had moved to another crossing.

Suddenly, a sensor opened, and an image was starting to form. It was the image of a man moving slowly through the bush. Allen felt a sudden rush of adrenaline and the excitement began to build. He knew that the others were receiving the same pictures.

All the sensors automatically opened the shutters in line with the movement observed. The image improved, and it was seen to be a man carrying an automatic rifle, with another rifle strapped to his back alongside a rucksack. He tested the communication with Mike and Ralph and immediately received a response. They had all seen the man coming through the bush.

The man approached with extreme caution and stopped frequently to check the area around him. The sensors tracked the man with precision. As he moved towards the river he came crouched, and slowly down the game trail, but he came alone. Allen was concerned, as by now, the other poacher should have appeared. He began to worry if they had split up, he would prefer to catch them both.

He put himself into the shoes of the man approaching and wondered why he would come alone. And then suddenly he realised why. The man was reconnoitring the ground prior to crossing the river. He was being ultra cautious as you would expect from a professional. This more than convinced him that they were dealing with soldiers who had seen a lot of action. Taking them would not be easy.

He signalled both Ralph and Mike not to take any action. The man must be allowed to reconnoitre without obstruction. They signalled that they understood, and they settled down to wait.

The man moved at a snails pace through the bush, and stopped frequently to check his surroundings. It took an hour for him to reach their positions and he passed within a meter of one of the SAS men without detecting their presence. He appeared on the bank and checked in both directions. He moved across to some branches and studied them carefully. He nodded his satisfaction and passed the SAS men the way he had come. He moved quicker now and was out of sensor range in thirty minutes.

Allen hoped that he had not made a mistake. He realised that they had been lucky not to disturb the branches he had arranged.

He pondered for a moment, had they been disturbed? He knew with certainty that the poachers would be back within two hours. The wait began again.

It was three thirty five in the morning when a man reappeared on the extreme sensor. Immediately all the shutters opened again to focus on the object moving. The man moved cautiously down the game trail towards the river. He had travelled no more than thirty meters when a second man appeared. This was obviously the second poacher, and he was carrying an automatic rifle.

They moved down the trail, always keeping the space between them to thirty meters. The leader frequently stopped to look and listen and always used hand signals to stop his accomplice. Allen was impressed by their professionalism. They had covered over five hundred kilometres but still assumed that there was danger ahead. They would not rush the last hurdle.

He signalled both Mike and Ralph who responded immediately. They would have to move slightly to accommodate the distance between the poachers, as they had anticipated no more than ten meters between the two men. It was imperative that both men were taken out simultaneously to prevent a shoot out.

The image of the two men were locked into the sensors and they were followed all the way down the game trail to where the SAS men where hiding. They were one hundred meters from the SAS men when the leader stopped, and organised for him to be covered whilst he crawled the last hundred yards to the river. Again Allen gave the signal to leave him.

The man crawled past their hideout and down to the rivers edge; he checked both ways and then returned to his comrade again passing within meters of the SAS men. The two men now appeared to relax and came down the game trail with confidence.

The leader passed Mike and came opposite Ralph. Allen gave the five-vibration signal and Mike and Ralph hurled their stun grenades at the two targets. Their visors automatically came down as the brilliant light dazzled all around and lit up the sky.

Allen watched Mike bring down the rear man and Ralph bring down the lead man. He rose from his hiding place with the Beretta in his hand.

It was not necessary as both men had been disarmed and were now handcuffed. It had been over in less than five seconds. He called Don and advised him of their success.

The two men sat there in shock, and their eyes were recovering from the blinding light. Their ears were still ringing from the blast. They were sat in a manner emitting as much defiance as possible.

The SAS men did not speak at all, as they did not wish to be recognised as British, and they sat and watched the captured men through their visors. Their faces were hidden and would not be recognised.

The leader had only been carrying the Rigby 450 and an AK47; the second man had been armed to the teeth. He had an AK47, a thirty-eight special, a hunting knife at his waist and a small knife attached to his ankle. They had been professionally searched and then their ankles were strapped together. It was impossible for them to move.

They heard the convoy of trucks crashing through the bush long before they arrived. The trucks could not penetrate the last hundred meters and the scouts had to stop and complete the journey on foot.

They burst into the clearing where the poachers were held, and rushed to see the poachers up close. They pointed and jabbed fingers at them and cursed them in their own language. The fact that it did not induce any response from the poachers did not in the least diminish their passion for verbal abuse.

Don arrived on the scene, and the scouts went quiet, and they parted allowing Don to see the poachers. He studied them carefully. They were dishevelled, to say the least, they had not washed or shaved for days, and they did not look at all like members of a crack military unit.

He looked across to the three SAS men, and they could have come from out of space. They were dressed in black from head to foot, and the helmet and visor were similar to those used by pilots. He walked across and was about to talk to them when they all held up their hands to stop him. Don immediately understood and turned back to the poachers.

Toby and Jonathon were going through the rucksacks, and they had found the rhino horn. Jonathon looked at the poachers with contempt but said nothing.

"Get them back to the vehicles and back to base," he instructed.

The poachers were dragged to their feet, and half dragged, and half carried to the waiting vehicles.

"No harm must come to them," he warned Toby and Jonathon.

They both nodded and followed their men back to the vehicles. When the clearing was clear of all his employees he turned to the SAS men.

"All I can say is, thank you, but it does not seem half enough," he said.

Allen unplugged his console and removed his visor, "It was a pleasure to help."

Mike and Ralph removed their visors and grinned at Don. It had gone far better than expected, and they knew that they had been fortunate to only receive minor abrasions from the scuffle.

"We need to clean up the area, and be gone by the morning; we are going to look around a game reserve, and behave like tourists for a week, to ensure our cover is maintained. We will return your tools tonight, after we have removed the sensors. We will meet you back at your base at around five in the evening," Allen said.

The three SAS men moved off into the bush and had disappeared in seconds. Don felt the anticlimax following such an action and walked back to his vehicle. The driver was waiting for him and, as soon as he appeared, he started the engine. Don, now feeling extremely tired, gave the instruction to get him back to the camp. He felt that at last it was all over and that the authorities would take over. He would no longer be required. He could not have been further from the truth.

Chapter 20

Reuters reported the arrest of two poachers caught in possession of rhino horn. They report stated:

SOUTH AFRICAN POACHERS CAUGHT IN TANZANIA
On Monday, two South African citizens were caught red handed in possession of rhino horns. They were apprehended attempting to cross the river Ruvuma into Mozambique. The two South Africans were named as Petrus Khumalo and Samuel Khubeki.

The Head Warden, Mr. Don Scales, who was not available for comment, masterminded the exercise. Dr. Julius Ngama, Minister of the Environment, released a brief statement congratulating Scales on the apprehension of the poachers. He also issued a warning to other poaching gangs that wished to cross the border into Tanzania.

"We have proven our ability to apprehend this highly organised gang of poachers that attempted to take game in our country." he said.

"Mr. Scales, a recent appointment to the position of Head Warden, has proven that the rhino and elephant can be protected using modern methods of detection and capture. I must congratulate Mr. Scales and his staff on the excellent work that they are doing to protect our most valuable natural resource".

It is rumoured that the two poachers are ex-military personnel-----

The two South African citizens were caught red handed in possession of rhino horns. Angela Murchin read the article and then read it again. This was it! This could be the connection she had been looking for they were apprehended attempting to cross the river Ruvuma into Mozambique.

The two South Africans were named as Petrus Khumalo, and Samuel Khubeki.

"A penny for your thoughts?"

She looked up and saw Tim Wells. "Sorry, I was miles away, can I help you?" She enquired.

"How are you getting on with research into the Korean car manufacturer," he asked? "I want to prepare my article for next week."

"I have all the background data of the company, and I will have it on your desk tomorrow." Angela said.

"Have you found anything of interest, or out of the ordinary?" He asked.

"Well. The chairman of the company has a bit of a reputation with the girls; there is also a question mark as to how he raised the capital to form such a major company? He seems to have appeared from nowhere and built up a huge conglomerate in just over a decade. His rise has been meteoric, to say the least."

"How sure are you of the facts?" he asked.

"The information is very sketchy indeed; I would not suggest you use any of the juicy bits until we have confirmation."

"How will you confirm your juicy bits?" he asked

"I have made contact with a journalist in Korea. He partially confirmed the stories about Chen Yoo Soong but was not prepared to go further. I think he was afraid of the consequences. Yoo Soong is very influential in Korea. There was a story about a girl brutally murdered, and Yoo Soong was implicated but nothing was proven."

"Wow, this could be dynamite. Please follow up and keep me informed."

"Will do," she said

Tim Wells winked at her, and as he left he said, "Keep this between you and I, O.K."

"Sure."

Angela sat and thought of the Korean industrialist and how she could explore the company and him further. She would call Lee Chen again. She checked her watch and realised it would be the middle of the night in Korea. She made a note to call at four thirty in the afternoon.

The capture of these poachers in Tanzania kept returning to her thoughts. She knew that there was a link somewhere. She read the Reuters report again. She would ask Thomas when she later saw him. He would perhaps shed some light on the matter.

She looked around the newsroom and spotted Thomas delivering mail to the assistant editor.

"Thomas, have you got a minute please."

Thomas waved and said, "Be with you in a minute."

Angela went back to her notes on Yoo Song; she felt that there was a story to be told about this man. He emerged only after the Korean War, and was suspected of dealing in arms on both sides. He developed a substantial business in ten years and for the last thirty years has created an enormous multinational company. This in itself was not unusual. There were many instances of Asian companies going global. Even in South Africa.

Anglo American and Rembrandt have also developed into substantial global players. Yet there was something about Yoo Soong that was not quite right.

"You are looking for me?" Thomas asked.

"Yes, what are you doing for lunch," she asked.

"Nothing planned, why?"

"I want to talk to you about something related to the information we have found."

"Is there something new?" he asked

"That's it, I just don't know. We have just received a news brief from Reuters, and it mentions South Africans being caught in Tanzania poaching, here read it yourself."

She passed him the brief.

Thomas read the brief and looked quizzically at her, "I don't understand the link," he said

"Neither do I, but I know that there is a link somehow. It must have been something someone said, or I have read a reference somewhere. You have no idea then?" She asked.

"Why would I?" he responded.

"I don't know why, but I know it is something that we have uncovered that makes reference to this Khumalo. That is why I thought you would know."

"I see," said Thomas.

"Do you have any leave due to you Thomas?" she asked.

"Yes, they owe me a couple of weeks. Why do you ask?"

"I think we could be onto the biggest story of our lives here, and we need to do the proper research, and we cannot do it safely from the office. I can link into the newspapers data banks from home using my access code. We need some time to put it all together."

Thomas saw the assistant editor coming out of his office, and heading towards them, "Can we discuss this over lunch Angela." He asked.

"That's what I was about to suggest," Angela said.

"What the bloody hell are you two gassing about? Don't you know there is work to be done?" demanded the assistant editor. "If you have nothing to do I can soon find you something. Now get on with your work."

"See you at lunch when this moron is not around," Angela said to the rapidly departing Thomas.

"What did you call me?" he said threateningly.

"A moron I think."

"Are you trying to get yourself fired?"

"No, but if you insist on behaving like a moron, it is inevitable that someone will call you one," she said smiling beautifully, and showing a bit of her thigh to him.

He took a long look at her thigh, and it was obvious his mind was working overtime, "Just you be very careful," he said.

"I will," she said.

The assistant editor scowled at her, then turned and walked away. Whilst his back was turned all the journalists and copy boys gave her the thumbs up. They would not have dared speak to the man that way.

Angela went back to Yoo Soong. Was there a bigger story here? She wrote down in random order what she knew about Soong:

(1) Wealthy
(2) Powerful
(3) Very low profile
(4) Appeared after the Korean War
(5) Murder suspect
(6) Dotes on his son
(7) Developed Multi-national Corporation
(8) Has a strange sexual proclivity
(9) Proposing to invest in South Africa?

She knew that she could flesh out all the above topics, but it would all be unsubstantiated. She needed to glean more information on the company and its associates. She would try the Internet.

She logged on the company provider and entered the search mode:
She typed
"Soong International Corporation"

The screen flickered and then came up with two million five hundred and twenty five sites. Do you wish to refine your search?

She typed
Soong\ownership\annual report
the screen flickered again and found twenty matches. Angela scrolled down the list
Soong Corporation
Soong Corporation latest annual report
Website and information
Soong International
Globalisation of the corporation
Soong Steel and Ferrous Products
A division of Soong Corporation
Soong Motor Corporation
The manufacturing divisions Asia, Europe
The Soong Corporation Racing Team
Objectives, current position, drivers, team manager
Soong Banking Corporation
Corporate banking and risk assessment
Soong Shipping Ltd.
Details of the fleet and ports
Soong Asia
Corporate structure
Soong Europe
Corporate structure
Soong China
Corporate structure
Soong Computer Division
Manufacturing bases in Asia and Europe

The rest on the list were similar names to Soong, but not related to the company Angela wanted to investigate. Angela opened each web site and copied the information on to her hard drive. She had downloaded seven hundred megabytes before she was finished. Angela then copied the files to a flash stick and put the disc in her handbag. She deleted all the files from her computer. She would read through them later at home. Angela doubted that she would get much information from the websites, as it would be highly unlikely to find anything incriminating. Yet it would be perfect background information, as she would be able to plot the time and dates of Soong Industries global expansion. There must have been acquisitions along the way, and this might lead to other areas of interest. If there had been hostile bids, then there could be some dirt hidden amongst the companies that were taken over. It was patently obvious that whatever business Yoo Soong bought or developed, they always outstripped their opposition. The achievements in such a short time were incredible.

"Are you ready," Thomas asked, who had suddenly reappeared.

"Oh, sorry, I didn't realise that it was one o clock," she said.

"You were so engrossed, what were you doing?" Thomas asked.

"Just some research for Tim, I will meet you downstairs."

Thomas left, and Angela shut down her computer, and followed him out to the street door. Thomas was waiting for her and asked. "Are we going to the Keg again?"

"I think so don't you, its close, and the food is very good."

They set off for the Keg that was only two blocks away. It was a hot summer day, and Angela was wearing an ordinary blouse, and a pleated skirt. It showed off her figure and many of the passers by ogled her, and then looked in amazement that she was walking through Jo'burg with a black guy. Thomas noticed the stares and the condemnation in the eyes of the white passers by, and wondered if the countries attitude would ever change.

"You realise we are causing quite a scene here," he said.

"Why?"

"It is still not acceptable for a beautiful white girl to be seen walking and talking to a black man."

Angela looked around and noticed people staring at them; she gave a couple of guys a hard look and decided to ignore them. "Take no notice of them Thomas. Tell you what, let's link arms whilst we are walking, and really give them something to talk about!"

"You are incorrigible," said Thomas.

"My, my, now that's a big word for a black man in Africa," she said mockingly.

"It must be the company I keep," he said.

They laughed, linked arms, and walked to the Keg.

They picked a table which was out of the way, and ordered a light bar meal.

"Have you thought any more about that Khumalo guy?" Angela asked.

"I have, and I must admit that I am no further forward. Why do you think there is a link?"

"I don't know yet, but I am sure it has something to do with that guy Dlamini. You remember the raid in Alex, where the ANC guy was killed."

"I remember the incident vividly, but I do not recall any mention of Khumalo."

"I know that there is a link, it may have been just something I have seen, but I am positive that the link exists."

"Is it women's intuition?" Thomas asked.

"I don't think so."

Their conversation was interrupted when the waitress brought them their meal. They ate silently, and when finished, Thomas asked.

"I am trying desperately to try and recall any link between Dlamini and Khumalo. I have to admit that I really see no link."

"Okay, let's look at the facts. Dlamini was a member of the Special Forces that were responsible for preventing terrorism."

"They were very successful, and there was tremendous resentment of these forces when the ANC took power. I am sure that Khumalo was also a member of these Special Forces, and they both operated on the Swazi border. Don't ask me where I have seen this but I know it to be true. I will find this information on file somewhere."

"Then let us assume that there is a link. Why would the capture of poachers be linked with a gang raid in Alex?"

"It is too much of a coincidence that these defunct units are popping up in different places performing strange tasks, but for whom?" she asked herself.

"Thomas, the other guy Mnini. Do you think he could be part of the same Special Forces?"

"If your theory is right he would have to be."

"How can we find out?"

"What you mean is how I can find out."

"Well, I suppose I do," she said laughing.

"I am sure I can, but where would I look for the evidence to link Khumalo and Dlamini?"

"I will try and find out where he lives, and you can visit his village."

"What makes you think that I would have more success than you?"

Angela lifted his arm and lay it alongside her own, "That," she said.

Thomas smiled and said, "You are impossible!"

Angela laughed and said, "Time to get back to the office, are we agreed then?"

"Yes," Thomas said smiling.

Chapter 21

Don Scales was doing his utmost to avoid the press and television, which wanted to know the full story about the poachers. Jonathon and Toby did not speak to the journalists for decidedly different reasons. Jonathon supported Don a hundred percent and would not talk because he was asked not to do so. Toby would not talk because he had seen the capabilities of the men who advised him for his own good, not to talk about the operation.

Don had managed to have a brief chat with Allen and his team before they left; they had spent a week touring the Serengeti, and behaved like the tourists they were supposed to be. Don had met them in a quiet camp at Mogana, and he had thanked them all profusely.

They were extremely modest and said it was nothing, just glad to help really. Allen had asked him about the poachers and what would happen to them now. He had responded that the courts would try them, and they would probably be jailed in Tanzania for a couple of years.

Allen asked to be kept in touch with events, and they parted after warmly shaking hands. Allen knew his friend well enough, and the moment Don sat and thought about it, he would start to explore the differences between the poachers of the past and the poachers captured by his team. Allen knew with near certainty that this would not be the end of the matter, and at some stage, he would likely be back in his official capacity.

Captain Khumalo and Sergeant Khubeki had been jailed in separate cells. They had not been allowed to see or speak to one another. They were a prize that Dr Ngama wanted to exploit to the full. His adversaries in the cabinet were embarrassed by the capture of armed forces on their own soil, and he was only the Minister of the Environment. This would not harm his career at all.

Dr Ngama was puzzled by the efficiency of the capture. Needless to say, there had been many poaching episodes in Scales' time, but he had not been involved in apprehending them. Why now? Why did he ask for all that equipment, and how did he know that these poachers were different to the ordinary everyday poacher? Curious indeed! He would have to talk to Mr Scales.

The interrogation of the poachers was to commence at 10 am. Don Scales was early, it was only 9.30 am. He had compiled a list of questions that he would ask and placed a tape recorder, pad and pencil, on his desk. He told the guard to bring in the first prisoner, the one called Khumalo. The prisoner was brought in shackled at the ankles and handcuffed. Don looked at the man and felt a twinge of pity. He was in a terrible state, filthy and obviously had not been allowed to wash or shave. Khumalo's clothes were covered in dirt, and there were bruises on his cheekbone, and around the eyes.

"Has someone beaten you?" Don asked.

The prisoner smiled and said "No more than I had expected."

He spoke with a deep resonant voice that showed neither fear nor sorrow. The man looked dishevelled, but his bearing was quite different; he was not as black as the Tanzanians, and had a bearing that was defiant. Don struggled for the correct word, it was not arrogance, it was confidence.

"If this man is beaten or maltreated in any way again, you will all be dismissed," he said to the guards. "I can only apologise for their behaviour." Khumalo looked at him as if he was weighing him up to find a weakness. He stared at Don for a considerable time and Don felt uneasy under the stare.

"I have suffered worse indignities in the past," Khumalo said.

"Guards, take this man away and allow him to shower and give him a change of clothes, something that is clean. If the other prisoner looks the same, then get him cleaned up as well."

He turned to Khumalo. "Do not try to escape or see this as an act of kindness. If you try to escape or create any disturbance, the guards will shoot you. Do you understand?"

Khumalo smiled. This man had surprised him once already. He still could not believe an amateur force had captured him.

"I will not try to escape on this occasion, you have my word." Khumalo was taken out and allowed to shower and change. He came back in fifteen minutes looking and smelling much better.

"Sit down Khumalo. My name is Don Scales, and I am the Head Warden of the Tanzanian Game Department. I will be conducting the initial interviews and dependent upon your co-operation, the only interviews prior to you being formally charged by the Tanzanian police," Scales said. "I must advise you that I will be taping this conversation."

"You have been charged with poaching and in this country that carries a minimum penalty of two years. You are suspected of poaching an elephant in June of this year; can you confirm this?" Scales asked.

"If I had, why should I confirm such an act when it would only lead to more trouble and a longer sentence," Khumalo said. "There is no logic in your question."

"If you co-operate now, then the sentence may well be reduced. We need to know the details of your previous visits. We have forensic evidence that the man found at the site of the dead elephant, was South African. We know that you are South African as well as your accomplice; we merely ask for confirmation of what we already know."

"If you know already, then why do you need confirmation?" Khumalo asked.

"It is always necessary, as you well know, to have first hand evidence to back up the forensic evidence."

"Then I can only assume that the forensic evidence is not conclusive, and why should I admit to a crime that would only injure me?" Khumalo asked.

"When the elephant killed one of your team, you attempted to burn the evidence; this was not successful, and the buttons on the tunic of your comrade clearly indicated that he was South African, and was, or had been, a member of the armed forces. We have contacted the South African authorities, and they have advised us that the buttons are from an army tunic."

"The army tunics can be bought in a number of army surplus stores in South Africa, or they could have been stolen. In any event, how can you link the dead man to my comrade or me?" Khumalo said.

"Khumalo, I can only help you if you co-operate fully."

Khumalo raised his hands to stop Scales, and asked, "Why would you want to help me?"

"Tanzanian jails are not the most pleasant of places. You will be locked away with other criminals who will not take kindly to South Africans invading their patch."

"I can assure you Mr Scales that I am quite capable of looking after myself."

"Do you deny that you slaughtered two elephants in the crater earlier this year?"

"I do."

Don Scales looked at the man with obvious anger, but he knew that anger would not get him anywhere. He had to recover his composure and start again.

"Khumalo, are you a member of the South African armed forces?"

"No," Khumalo said.

"Have you ever been a member of the armed forces?"

"That is no concern of yours."

"I am afraid it is. You may have created a diplomatic incident by entering Tanzania armed to the teeth and wearing South African army uniforms."

"When was this?" asked Khumalo.

Don turned away exasperated and said, "You still deny that the dead man was a member of your gang from South Africa."

Khumalo said nothing.

"Could you answer for the tape please; was the man found dead at the site of the bull elephant, one of your gang of poachers?"

"No," Khumalo said.

"Do you not think it coincidental that you are both from South Africa? Do you really expect us to believe that you are not part of the same gang? Have you forgotten already that you can both be identified by the tracker you captured?"

"There you have a point," Khumalo conceded.

"Can we now establish that you were the slayers of two elephants in June of this year?"

"You have the evidence."

"Then say it for the tape," demanded Scales

"We were responsible for the killing of the two elephants that you refer to."

"The dead man was part of your gang?" Scales asked.

"Yes."

"How many times have you entered Tanzania to poach game?"

"Three times. Twice to hunt and once to recover the tusks"

"Then you have crossed the border three times since June this year, is this correct?"

"That is correct."

"Where did you sell the tusks?"

"No comment."

"You realise that we will need to know all the details before we can help you. We know that you are the small guys in the chain. If you help us catch the big fish, then we will consider you turning states evidence, and will allow you to leave Tanzania as a free man."

"No comment."

"That is a pity Khumalo; we would like to help you, but cannot unless you give the names of the recipient."

Khumalo looked away and offered no further comment.

"Are you afraid of the consequences of telling me the names of the recipients?"

"I have answered all the questions that I am going to answer; there is no more to tell."

"We haven't even started yet. The police will use much harsher measures to extract the truth from you."

Khumalo smiled, "When all else fails, try brutality, is that it?"

"Those are not my methods, but you were born in Africa. I am only an immigrant. If my methods do not get the required results, the African way may succeed where we Europeans fail."

"I am an educated man; I understand perfectly what you are saying. I was born in Africa and know the ways of the African; I also have the stoicism of the African. You will never frighten me into saying more than I wish, assuming, that I had something to tell."

"If you have nothing further to offer; then perhaps your colleague will."

Khumalo laughed, "That is even less likely than me."

"We will see. Guards, take him back to the cells, and bring me the other poacher."

Khumalo was unceremoniously bundled out of the room.

Don watched him leave, and knew with absolute certainty, that he had received all the information that it was possible to extract from Khumalo. He wondered how he could break through the veneer of Khumalo. He seemed to have the same military bearing as his friend Allen. In many ways, they were similar. He, in spite of himself, felt a tinge of sorrow, of having to put this man away. There was no doubt in his mind that Khumalo was part of a bigger plan, and was following orders. He believed that Khumalo and Khubeki were still members of the SADF. The South African authorities would never admit their existence, let alone that they were members of Special Forces.

What puzzled Don was why a rich country like South Africa would have any kind of involvement in poaching, in Tanzania. It was not credible.

If the authorities were unaware, and one had to believe that they were, then for whom where these poachers working? They had crossed Mozambique without being detected, and it was implausible to think that they could have carried the tusks all the way to South Africa.

They must have had vehicles or have been flown in. If they were in vehicles, how did they cross the border between Mozambique and South Africa without being detected? There had to be complicity at the highest level for this to happen. If there was complicity, then Khumalo would never tell.

He would be expendable in any event. Khumalo knew who was involved, that was for sure, but he also knew the consequences of talking. He would have family back in South Africa, and they would be under threat. Khumalo or Khubeki would never talk willingly.

He pondered the question and wondered how Allen would deal with this type of situation. The guards bringing in Khubeki broke his thoughts. Don was despondent, as he knew he was wasting his time. Nevertheless, he would go through the motions.

He questioned Khubeki in the same manner as Khumalo and elicited the same result. He spent an hour trying to persuade Khubeki to give him more information than he already had. It was a waste of time and effort. Khubeki was less cooperative than Khumalo, and certainly was not as intelligent.

Don returned him back to the cells, cleared the desk, pulled the tape from the recorder and stood up to leave. He heard a commotion outside and thought that Khubeki was trying to escape. He ran to the door, and before he could open it, it burst open, and an army Colonel stood in front of him.

"What the hell do you think you are doing interrogating these terrorists?" The Colonel demanded.

"What the devil are you talking about? They are poachers, and as such fall under my jurisdiction," Don said, forcefully.

"As from now they are classed as terrorists, and will be taken into custody by the army."

"Under whose authority and what proof of this decision do you have, can you show me any written authority?"

"I need no proof or paperwork, if I say that they are terrorists, then that is good enough for you."

"I am afraid not, and you will not take my prisoners into your custody unless authorised by the President himself."

"Do not mess with me Scales. My men are here to take them into custody, and we will do so!"

"You will do no such thing, and we will defend the prisoners until such time that you come back with the correct paperwork. Until then, you can leave the prisoners where they are or face the consequences."

"Are you threatening me?"

"You may take it any way you like, but you are not taking my prisoners."

"You have not heard the last of this."

"I am sure I have not."

The Colonel turned around and stormed out of the room. His men followed behind him, and they left the compound in a cloud of dust.

What the hell was all that about, wondered Don? Why was it so crucial that the military took hold of the prisoners? He would talk to Dr Ngama later.

Chapter 22

The girl was pretty and of African origin. Kriel was immediately taken with her. He had called his usual agency, or at least he had dialled the exact numbers, but his call was intercepted, and transferred. He knew that there were lots of different receptionists and was not troubled when he did not recognise the voice.

"Sugar Plum Escort Agency," she had said.

"I need an escort for tonight," Kriel said.

"Yes sir, what is your preference?"

"I would like a young black girl."

"Yes sir, we have many. There is Angelique who is twenty and has a large bust, we have Blossom who is twenty two and has a trim figure, we have Annabelle who is twenty five and is well built, and Rose who is eighteen and well built; which one would you like sir."

"Is Angel there tonight?" he enquired.

"I am afraid she had to go home to see her sick mother, she will not be back for a week."

"Okay, send me Rose."

"Certainly sir, and where should we send her to."

"Send her to room 216, Crest Hotel, Sandton."

"She will be with you in half an hour, is that all right; her rate is two hundred Rand an hour, and the agency fee is also two hundred Rand. How long do you think you will you need her for?"

"At least three hours," Kriel said.

"That will be fine sir; can we have your credit card number please?"

"I will pay cash directly to her."

"Then whom should she ask for?"

"My name is Johan."

"Thank you sir, she is on her way."

The operator turned to general Lauberschagne, "we have contact sir and the girl he called is on her way."

Lauberschagne frowned and said. "Was he suspicious?"

"I do not think so, but then I have never done this before, sir."

"You did well sergeant Ames, and thank you. You may leave now."

It had taken three weeks to set up the room and the girl. It was well known that Kriel used the Crest Hotel in Sandton, and the owner was easily persuaded to make the room available to them. When Kriel booked the room, it was the only room available to him. It was all too easy and this worried Lauberschagne. It should not be this easy.

The video camera operator was sat in the room above Kriel's hotel suite, where holes had been drilled in four places; optic fibres had been inserted and then connected to a video and recorder. There was not any part of the room that could not be filmed. It was impossible to detect the fibre optics or the microphones that had been installed. The equipment was state of the art and could pick up a fart at a hundred meters, according to the technician. So why was he so worried? He did not like the idea of being a voyeur; he would have to watch events, and determine when sufficient material was secured, such that they could move in on Kriel.

They had to complete their mission, get him on track and back to work for his next shift in two days. It was all a bit too much for the elderly general.

Kriel showered and prepared himself for the girl, who was on her way to him. He felt a thrill of excitement, and this caused an immediate erection. He felt the bulge in his trousers with satisfaction. He was going to have an extremely enjoyable night tonight. He sat and thought about his previous episodes with the girls that had been sent to him. He had screwed so many that he could not remember them all, but there was that black bitch last year, which had nearly blown his mind, she had been the best.

He was suddenly aware of a knock on the door and his anticipation heightened. He had no idea what she would look like, but if he were not happy he would just send her back. He got up from the bed and moved towards the door. The timid knock came again. He opened the door, and saw the girl and he was more than pleased with what he saw.

"Johan?" she enquired.

"Yes, come in," he said as he opened the door for her to enter. "Would you like a drink?"

"Please, whisky, with ice and lemonade."

Kriel poured the drinks.

The cameraman ensconced on the floor above had been recording from the moment the girl knocked on the door; there was no sound other than the beating of his heart as he watched the scene unfold before him.

"Shall we get the business out of the way first?" The girl said. This was obviously not a request, and Kriel finally appraised the girl.

She was dressed in a red dress which had a slit up the side to her thighs, there was lacing up the sides, which showed her chocolate skin off against the red of the dress. It also showed that she was not wearing any underwear. His erection was now blatantly obvious, and she smiled at him and pointed to his erection.

"You obviously approve of me," she said tartly.

Kriel went for his wallet and said, "Okay, its six hundred for you and two hundred for the agency correct?"

"That's right," she said.

"What do I get for my money," he asked.

"You get three hours of my undivided attention," she said.

"Can you be more specific," he asked.

"Okay, you get a massage, a blow job and a fuck; if you can keep it up after that you can stick it anywhere that takes your fancy. I do not do whippings or anything like that."

Kriel was just about bursting out of his trousers and knew he would get round to sticking it anywhere. "Sounds good to me," he said and handed over the eight hundred Rand.

Kriel lay on the bed and said, "I want you to undress in front of me first and then undress me."

The girl slipped out of her dress and showed at first her pubic hair and then her breasts.

"Great tits," said Kriel.

"Thank you," she said.

She joined him on the bed and undid the buttons on his shirt one by one and stroked his chest as she did so. He was moaning softly as she removed his shirt, then shoes, socks and trousers. His erection was protruding through the slit in his underpants, and she stroked it gently. He gave an involuntary movement and groaned. She removed his underpants and then turned him onto his stomach. She took some massage cream from her handbag and started to massage his back.

The general watched with fascination. He had never seen anything this erotic before and felt his own erection starting. He tore his eyes from the screen and started to admonish himself.

What a disgusting old pervert he thought, how can a man performing with a prostitute excite you? He wanted to leave, but he knew that there had to be sufficient evidence to ensure their operations success. He decided to look at ten-minute intervals and determine when enough was enough. His arousal disappeared when he thought of the consequences for the young girl.

He looked back and Kriel was now on his back, and the girl was massaging his chest. She worked her way down to his erection and massaged his penis with the oil; he exploded immediately and came all over her breasts. She got up from the bed and went for a shower. Kriel lay there and waited.

The general looked away and waited his prescribed ten minutes. The girl was just leaving the shower, and Kriel was about to join her in the bathroom. Kriel was already erect again, and the general admired his stamina.

The girl propelled Kriel to the shower and said "Get clean first." Kriel stepped into the shower.

The girl moved back into the room and searched for Kriel's wallet. She knew that this was a one off and would not meet the guy again; if she could rip him off and get out of there, then she would have earned well for the night. Unfortunately for her Kriel was too quick in the shower and she heard him turn off the shower. He walked through wearing the hotels bathrobe, with his erection protruding out from the robe. He advanced towards her, and she kneeled in front of him and took his penis in her mouth.

The general looked away and thought, how much more do we need. He knew that he would have to get Kriel having sex with the girl as well as any other disgusting act that he wanted to perform. He decided that he could not watch the couple's copulating, and that he would only take infrequent cursory glances. He felt embarrassed by what was taking place, and the fact that his subordinate knew he was watching.

The young prostitute quickly worked through her repertoire and satisfied even Kriel. They had been having sex in every different way imaginable for two hours; she was preparing to leave.

"Hey, where are you going?" Kriel shouted.

"You have had enough surely?" She asked.

"I paid you for three hours," was his response.

"You wish to have more?" She enquired incredulously.

"I don't know yet, maybe."

She sat opposite him and said, "OK, when you are ready."

He tried desperately to seek further arousal, but realised that it would not be possible. 'Okay, you can go,' he said.

The young prostitute left the room. The general gave a nod to his aides, and they left the room. The young prostitute was picked up outside, supposedly by a taxi. She thought it strange that a white man drove it. He turned the corner, and slowed down, and another man entered the cab.

"Hey, what's going on?" she shouted at the new man and the driver. A feeling of dread possessed her.

She tried to open the passenger door and was not surprised that it would not open. There had been something suspicious from the beginning, and her fears were being realised.

"What the fuck do you want," she asked aggressively.

The new man looked at her and said, "nothing girl, so just be quiet and we will see."

"We will see what?" she asked in real fear, feeling the cold prickle of sweat running under her armpits. She looked around her for help, but there was none available. She felt panic overtake her.

They drove on for nearly an hour, and she sat silently; she did not want to precipitate any action against her. They turned onto a dark gravel road, and she felt her bowels loosen; she desperately held on to control. She started to cry and shook uncontrollably. She looked desperately around the cab for a weapon to defend herself, but there was nothing she could use. She sobbed quietly now, almost reconciled to her fate.

The driver turned into an old farmhouse and pulled up outside the back door.

The man sitting opposite her moved quickly, and before she could even struggle, he had placed handcuffs on her wrists; she started to struggle and scream. He struck a blow to the base of her neck, and she went limp. They carried her to the house and into one of the bedrooms, where a doctor was waiting.

He quickly took vaginal swabs for DNA testing later. Kriel had not used a condom. The girl was then shackled to the bed post by both hands, and feet, and she would not be able to move.

Kriel was enjoying a scotch and soda in his room, when he heard a knock on the door. He had recovered from his sexual exploits and thought maybe the girl had come back again. He got out of his chair, and looked through the peephole, but saw nothing. Curious, he took the chain off the door and started to open it, when it crashed into him, knocking him off his feet.

"Hey, what are you doing?" he shouted.

Two men forced their way into the room and quickly subdued Kriel. Another man moved and plunged a syringe into his shoulder. He passed out almost immediately, but not before he voided his bowels.

The men quickly moved Kriel out of the room and into the service elevator. They went down to the basement and were out of the building in minutes. They had not been seen.

They travelled the same road as the cabbie and arrived at the same farmhouse. Kriel was unceremoniously dumped in another bedroom, adjacent to the prostitute. He was shackled and left to wake up.

Close circuit cameras were monitoring both bedrooms, and the rooms were bugged, such that any conversation or noise could be heard in the control room above; a room built into the attic of the old farmhouse.

The operators waited patiently for the general to arrive.

The General came into the control room, and the two operators stood to attention. He looked around the room and saw the large number of monitors.

"At ease man, where there any problems?" he asked.

"No sir, it all went according to plan. We have monitored the police frequencies and heard nothing. The room has been cleaned, and there is no evidence of a forced entry. The management of the hotel will believe that he left early. He did pay his bill in advance."

"I doubt that we will have a problem. His wife is not expecting him back until tomorrow midday," he concluded.

"Then we only have ten hours to complete our interrogation and show him the evidence. How long will he be out for," he enquired.

"We can administer the antidote, and he will be awake in ten minutes, sir."

"Then do it straight away," The General ordered.

The operative left. He saw the man enter the room and inject the serum into Kriel.

"What of the girl?" he asked.

The second operator pointed to another screen and said, "She is also sleeping sir."

"We do not need her for the moment; do not give her the antidote."

"We didn't administer drugs sir; Captain Venter slugged her as we were about to leave the car. She will come round shortly."

The general gave him a quick look, and the operative saw the disapproval in his stare.

The operative looked away. He thought what the hell, it doesn't matter anyway; they were going to kill her later. He said nothing but returned to monitoring the screens in front of him.

Kriel lay still for a further ten minutes, and the general was getting impatient.

"Are you sure that the antidote works?" he demanded.

In response to his question, Kriel groaned and tried to move. He must have realised that he was shackled as he then panicked and struggled against his shackles.

"Stay still," commanded the General, as he spoke into the microphone in front of him.

The microphone was a state of the art system, controlled by the computer. The voice pattern was changed, and it would be impossible to identify the user from voice analysis. To ensure total security, the distortion frequency was changed every fifteen seconds randomly by the computer. It would appear to Kriel that he was being interrogated by a whole host of different people. The only inflection that he would be able to determine was that the voice was supposedly male.

"You are Warrant Officer Johan Kriel of the special branch, based at Booysens, Johannesburg?" The General asked.

There was no response from Kriel.

"Shall I repeat the question for you Kriel?"

Kriel searched the room for the camera, and the microphone, but it appeared that the voice was coming from everywhere in the room, and he could not detect the camera. He started to think. He was trapped with no obvious means of escape, and he had been taken professionally. The equipment in the room was top class, so he was in deep trouble. He needed time to think. He felt the dried excreta in his pants, and now noticed the smell.

"I need to clean up," he said.

"Answer my question," the General demanded.

"Yes I am Warrant Officer Kriel. Now, can I clean up?"

"You will answer some more questions first."

Kriel groaned and tried to move, but his shackles held him firmly.

"What do you want with me?"

"You will find out in due course, now, do you know a man called Petrus Msini of the Internal Security Department?"

Kriel froze at the name; Msini had been his contact and all payments came from him. He went cold and then started to sweat. Keep calm, he said to himself.

"I know of a Petrus Msini."

"When did he make contact with you?"

"I don't know what you mean?"

"To be more specific, Kriel, when did you start working for the ISD?"

Kriel controlled his panic. "I do not understand what you mean."

"Oh, I think you do," said the voice.

Kriel never moved or said a word.

"Are you still with us Mr Kriel?" asked the voice.

Kriel's mind was racing. He knew now with whom he was dealing. He tried to think of a reasonable explanation. He had known this day would come, and he had planned a response. What seemed plausible then did not seem to hold water now.

"I have been making some money on the side with some of the gangs in Jo'burg; they paid that money into those accounts for me to look the other way."

He waited for the response with trepidation.

"A very interesting response, Mr Kriel, you have probably guessed by now that we are taping this conversation, and you realise who your captors are. We need to know how much information and detail you have passed on to Msini and we have many ways of extracting that information. We can make it easy for you or very hard, but be assured Mr Kriel; we will have extracted all information from you before, or if, you leave here."

"'What is it you think I have done?"

"We do not think Mr Kriel; we know what you have done, just not how much. We will find out Mr Kriel, I assure you."

"How can I co-operate?" asked Kriel.

"That is better Mr Kriel. You can co-operate by detailing your contacts, drops, codes and safe houses being used."

"And if I do, what is in it for me?"

"You may get to live," said the voice.

"I will co-operate fully."

"Good idea, Mr Kriel. We will send in a man now, who will release you from your shackles; he will allow you to shower and we have a change of clothes ready for you. I must advise you that if you try to attack this man or attempt to escape, he will kill you. I can assure you Mr Kriel that he is very accomplished at what he does, and you would not be much of a challenge for him."

"I will co-operate; I will not try to escape. I think that you know you have me whichever way I move."

"We appreciate your co-operation Mr Kriel and look forward to debriefing you; please do not try to renege on the deal and not reveal all, as we will dispose of you without compunction."

Kriel heard the key turn in the door and a man walked in; he was medium height but well built and Kriel knew that he was no match for the man in a straight fight. But then, Kriel had never been in a straight fight. He had to determine how many guards were out there and where he was located. He would need to keep his wits about him if he were to survive. He had already decided to give them only half of what he knew and drag that out as long as possible. He was due to start work at three tomorrow afternoon, and if he did not turn up they would immediately contact his wife. If they did that, then the ISD would know, as they had tapped his phone.

That would then be relayed to Msini, who would then start investigating his disappearance. Not because he would be concerned for Kriel, but because he would possibly be losing a valuable asset. Kriel had to stretch it out as long as possible because he knew his captors would have come to the same conclusion.

Kriel showered slowly in an effort to gather his wits, such that he would be able to respond to their inevitable questions. He cleared his mind and worked through what he knew. That the ISD knew that there was an internal insurgent force plotting against the new government was fact; what they did not know with any certainty, was who was involved. They also knew it had to be members of the old defence force that was inevitable. They even knew that the generals were involved at some level, but did not know how deeply involved they were, and which generals were plotting and what they were plotting. Kriel had vital information about the Third Force that he had gathered over the last two months, as he now knew the identity of at least two of the generals and their aides. This would be enough to start the operation against the generals and give the ANC the opportunity to squash the rebellion.

Kriel knew that his options were limited, and he could offer to work for the generals by acting as a double agent. The problem with this offer is that he would never be trusted by either side and would be eliminated the moment he became of no further use to either side. He was in a catch twenty-two without an apparent means of escape, or at least, no immediately obvious means of escape.

He knew he was not strong mentally or physically; and wondered if it would it be better to come clean immediately? He also knew that modern drugs would have him telling them his innermost thoughts in no time at all. What hope did he have of holding back any information, or of even misleading them? He would need all his cunning to get out of this mess. His warder broke his thoughts.

"Okay Kriel, time up, you are as clean as you need to be."

Kriel felt a shiver of fear. He stepped out of the shower and dried himself off with the towel provided by his captor, who watched every move that he made. He was given a white coverall and nothing else.

"Where are my shoes?" he whined.

His warder merely grabbed him by the arm and frog marched him out of the shower room and down a corridor, past a number of doors to a white door. His captor opened the door and took him into the room. It was not the cell that he had been in, and this room terrified him. The room was some six meters by six meters. In the middle, of the room was a chair that looked just like the electric chairs that he had seen in the movies. He gasped in horror. There was no other furniture in the room, no window; the walls were painted a cream colour. The electric chair held his attention. He froze.

His warder felt him resist and immediately pushed him towards the chair. Kriel started to fight back and pushed hard against the man. It was no contest.

The man merely pinned his arms and forced him into the chair. Kriel could not fight back as the man was far too powerful.

"What the fuck are you going to do?" he shouted.

"You will find out shortly," said his warder and clamped his arms and legs to the chair.

His head was held firm by a metal cap that fitted over his skull and electrodes and wires were attached to his wrist, chest, legs and head. He struggled against his restraints but was unable to move. He felt his bowels trying to give way, and he forced himself not to give them the satisfaction of shitting himself again.

His warder left and closed the door behind him. Kriel could not see the door and tried to turn in the chair to see where the man had gone.

"Sit still," a voice commanded.

Kriel responded, "What are you going to do?"

"If you answer our questions truthfully you will see the sun rise tomorrow," said the voice.

"I do not know what you want, I know nothing that would be of interest to anybody other than the police force, you know I am a policeman, you saw my uniform, this could get you into serious trouble," he tried to bluff.

"We know exactly who you are Warrant Officer Kriel. We know your station, your address, your wife's name, your date of birth, your ID number, your history from birth, schools you attended etc etc. Do you need me to carry on and give you more detail Kriel?"

Kriel remained silent.

"'In front of you Kriel is a screen that is part of the wall. Just watch what we know and then we will ask you some questions later."

The whole wall in front of Kriel became a screen that lit up but displayed nothing other than a slight snow affect. Suddenly it burst into life and displayed a photograph of Kriel as a baby, being held by his mother. It rapidly moved on to various stages of his life, through school, the army and his police graduation day. All were still photographs. Suddenly the screen showed Kriel walking down the street where he lived. The camera followed him and picked up the noise of the traffic going past and followed him for three blocks, then stopped.

Kriel sat there mystified by what he had seen and could not understand the relevance of the sequence.

Another sequence came up showing Kriel parked inside the multi-storey car park at Johannesburg International Airport. Another car arrived and parked alongside him, it was driven by Msini, an operative of the ISD. Kriel got out of his car and crossed over to the other car and sat beside Msini. It showed both men in conversation, and then Msini passed a package to Kriel. Kriel nodded and then went back to his own car.

"We believe that this was one of your earlier meetings with Msini, and, unfortunately, on this occasion we could not get audio," said the voice.

Kriel said nothing.

The screen changed again, and showed Kriel sat in Msini's car, and suddenly he could hear Msini talking to him.

Msini, "Well Mr Kriel, we have your recent information that clearly shows that your station commander is part of this conspiracy to overthrow the government.

This in itself is useful, as we have tapped his telephones both at home and his office and this has given us further leads. As you well know, this is only the tip of the iceberg; we need further intelligence on the following people."

Msini gave Kriel a sheet of paper that presumable had a list of names that the camera could not detect.

Kriel studied the list.

Kriel, "Some of these names you have given me are not even police related, how do you expect me to gather intelligence on people that I have no direct contact with?"

Msini, "You are the detective, you tell me?"

Kriel, "I suppose that I can access their files, assuming that we have any, and take it from there; but surely you can do the same and your information must be better than mine?"

Msini, "That may well be true, but you can get closer to these people, easier than we can. What we propose to do is organise burglaries at these homes, such that you have a legitimate reason to search their houses and place a watch on them."

Kriel, "I would have thought that you guys were far more capable of turning over a house than I would be, given your resources."

Msini, "This will happen, but we are looking at the bigger picture and even we, with all our resources could not gather the intelligence that a police officer could when held in trust by the people concerned."

Kriel, "There are some high-profile people here; it will not be easy to get close to them."

Msini, "We have considered this and the burglaries will be followed up by threats on their lives. This will mean police protection to some degree and we will ensure that you are responsible for that protection. We will sacrifice a couple of people that work for us, by tipping you off when they are about to strike and then you can play the big hero."

Kriel, "That does not mean that they will reveal any information to me."

Msini, "You have to convince them that you are against this government and over time they will bring you into their circle. To advance this the officers you must use for surveillance will be those that we know are part of the conspiracy, these are the officers that we know about at your station."

Msini gave Kriel a similar piece of paper to the first one.

Kriel read the list and said, "Shit, I had no idea that these officers were involved."

Msini, "Because of the complexity of this operation, you will only give information to me; this will be done via our normal drop, which you will mark when the information is gathered. Do not wait until you have gathered what you believe to be the full story, but send information as soon as possible. We will raise your fee to ten thousand rand per drop, so it is in your interest to give as much information as you can."

Kriel, "That is very generous of you."

Msini, "Mr Kriel, do not think that we are stupid. If you give false information or withhold information, we will deal with you accordingly. Do you understand Mr Kriel?"

Kriel, "I fully understand Mr Msini; I will not try to cheat you."

Msini, "For your good health, I hope not."

Kriel smiled at Msini and got out of the car.

The sequence stopped and then immediately moved on to Kriel walking down a street in Edenvale, Mooi Street. He stopped at house number 322, lifted the post box and deposited an envelope. He raised the flag on the post box to indicate his drop.

The time on the recording said 14.55.23. At 15.30.35, Msini arrived, and emptied the post box, lowering the flag to indicate that the drop had been received. Three times they followed this sequence, each time showing the drop by Kriel and the collection by Msini. Kriel sat silently through it all.

"Kriel, perhaps you now know the extent of our knowledge," said the voice.

Kriel remained silent.

"We have intercepted all your drops at this location. What we do not know, and you are about to tell us, is what drops have we missed."

Kriel still remained silent.

"Kriel, we can do this the easy way or the hard way; it is entirely up to you. Be assured of one thing, we will get the information that we require. You are strapped to a rather unique chair Kriel, all your senses are being monitored, and we can detect when you are not telling the truth."

Kriel still remained silent.

"Kriel, we are going to ask you some simple questions, and we will monitor your responses. If you lie, we will know immediately and will take the appropriate action to ensure that you tell the truth."

Kriel said nothing.

"Is your name Jacobus Kriel?" asked the voice.

"Yes," Kriel said.

At the back of the room where Kriel was being monitored, was an operator with a series of screens in front of him. There was a screen that looked directly at Kriel, another indicated his heartbeat, and another screen showed the moisture on the skin, a screen was measuring brain activity and another measuring voice modulation. Each screen had a standard measure as a control point whilst interviewing Kriel; even the eye movement was monitored. Sat next to the console were a psychiatrist, a doctor and an experienced interrogator. The general turned to the interrogator.

"Are we getting the base data required?"

The only answer was a nod of the head.

"Kriel, are you a warrant officer in the South African police?"

"Yes," said Kriel.

The general looked across to the interrogator, and he again nodded his head.

"Are you married to Maritke Bezeidenhout?"

"Yes,"

"How long have you been married Kriel?"

"Twelve years."

The general looked across at the interrogator; the interrogator nodded.

All the functions on the screen were displaying stress, but it was evident that he was not lying. Heart levels were constant, sweating showed a constant. The general asked a further five questions on Kriel's life and family, each elicited a true response as shown on the screens and the intelligence gathered on Kriel.

"Kriel, how long have you known Msini?"

Kriel's heartbeat shot up to one hundred and twenty but settled at ninety-eight. His sweating increased, and his brain activity suddenly soared.

"One year."

The monitors, without exception, showed massive reaction, and it was evident that the response was a lie.

"Kriel, that is not true, and we will give you one more chance to answer the question correctly, or we will take corrective action?"

Kriel was determined, to know the extent of the accuracy of their equipment.

"Eighteen months," he said.

Again the monitors showed that he was lying.

The screen in front of him came on; it showed a Catherine wheel effect that started moving slowly, then spinning faster and faster still. Kriel found that he could not look away. He tried closing his eyes, but the wheel seemed to penetrate into his brain. As the wheel intensity increased, a sound that seemed to blow out his ear drums suddenly came on. The wheel revolutions where increasing rapidly and with each revolution the ear-splitting screech intensified. Then suddenly it stopped. There was total silence for thirty seconds. The image and the sound still penetrated Kriel's brain, and he could not shake it off.

The monitors again showed a massive reaction to both the sight and sound. The general waited until Kriel's vitals had settled down. He looked across to the interrogator, who merely nodded. Kriel was holding up better than expected, as all his vitals returned quickly to their previous levels.

"Kriel, how long have you known Msini?"

Kriel did not respond immediately. He was disorientated by the wheel and the screen and was trying to gather his thoughts. He realised that they had some specialised equipment and that they would eventually obtain the information that they wanted. How much they knew, he was not sure about, and he would try to be as cooperative as possible until he felt that they had obtained enough. It would be a game of cat and mouse.

"Kriel, how long have you known Msini?"

"Just over three years," said Kriel.

The general looked towards the interrogator who nodded. Kriel had told the truth.

"Thank you Kriel that was the correct response. How long have you worked for Msini?"

"I have worked for Msini for over two years."

The monitors remained unchanged.

"We are making progress Kriel. Tell me, how did you meet Msini?"

"We met at a function given by the station commander at a Christmas party."

"How did he recruit you?"

The questions and answers went on for two hours, establishing the background of both Msini and Kriel. Kriel did not try to deceive, as the questions asked were obviously known to the interrogator. It was pointless to lie.

"Kriel, the list that Msini gave you with the names of your colleagues, what did you do with it?"

Kriel's heartbeat and brain activity went through the roof.

Kriel remained silent.

"Kriel, I will not ask the question a second time!"

"I threw it away."

Kriel's vitals went through the roof again.

The room suddenly changed colour, and the colours were at different levels, it was like a rainbow, but the colours moved from one segment to another, creating a kaleidoscope of alternating colours, and direction. It at first appeared to settle Kriel, then the colours started to rotate in difference directions and it appeared to be at the same pace as his heartbeat. He started to breath heavily, and his pulse rate increased. The colours increased with the increase in a heartbeat and then suddenly started to take over; he found that as the colours changed and rotated, his heartbeat started to follow suite. His heartbeat was now up to one hundred and eighty and still the colours rotated and increased in intensity; he was losing control of his bodily functions and then suddenly it stopped. There was total silence; he could feel his heart pounding in his chest.

Kriel shouted, "Stop, I have had enough, I will tell you what you want to know."

Chapter 23

Captain Andries Els and Sergeant Jay Ramasey were assigned to the murder of Molefe. They were called to a meeting at City Hall to meet the Commissioner of Police and the Mayor of Durban. Els knew that the meeting would be a tense affair and was not looking forward to it at all.

"We can't win on this one," Els said to Ramasey as they sat outside the Mayor's office.

"I know Molefe was well connected and hated at the same time. He paid off half the police force. Why did they pick us for the investigating officers?" he asked.

Andries Els had not had a brilliant career in the police force. He was slow but disciplined and without much initiative. Jay Ramasey was just beyond a rookie, having been in the police force only three years. He had performed well and shown promise but did not have a lot of experience in murder investigations. They were an unlikely couple.

"For my brain and your good looks," Els said, jokingly.

"They obviously do not want the murderer caught quickly."

"Thanks," Jay said.

"I was only joking."

The door opened, and the Commissioner, Pieter Verkramp, beckoned them to come in. The Mayor was sat behind his desk and did not stand up to greet them.

"Sit down officers," he said.

The Mayor had an unpronounceable first name, so he was referred to only as Mayor Singh.

"You all know why we are here. The assassination of Molefe, though probably well deserved, has a major impact on this city. We are almost totally reliant upon tourism to ensure the city's survival. People being shot in broad daylight; outside our court is just not acceptable! Commissioner, can you tell me what are you doing about it, are these your best men to solve this case?"

"We have every confidence in these officers to solve this case," the commissioner responded.

"Then what do you have so far Captain Els?"

"We were assigned to the case this morning your honour, and have only had time to read the report from the Sergeant on duty, before coming to this meeting," Els said.

"Then what will be your approach," The Mayor asked.

"The facts are that Molefe and Mangope were shot from an office block across the square from the courts. All the offices have been checked, but no evidence was found of any discharge of firearms. The tenants of the office block are all attorneys, or companies associated with the attorneys. We cannot determine the exact office from which the shots were fired, but on searching the building, we did find a coverall and a pair of gloves in a waste bin on the second floor. These are currently with forensics and to date we have not received their report. The autopsy report is still outstanding, and when we ascertain the angle of entry, we can then narrow down the number of offices it was possible to shoot from."

"In other words, you have no idea," replied the Mayor.'

"That is unfair and uncalled for Mr Mayor," The commissioner said. "It is still early days, and the hit was done by a professional. This wasn't an act of vengeance; it was a planned take out of Molefe. The suspects or possibilities are endless. There are many people who would like to see the back of Molefe."

"Does that include the police?" Mayor Singh asked.

"Sir, with the greatest of respect, that was uncalled for. Sure, we would have liked to have nailed Molefe in court, and we were not his friends, but we do not organise and commit hits on the general public or known felons."

"Yes, I am sorry. We need to get to the bottom of these murders quickly, to ensure that the tourists can see that we are capable of finding and prosecuting acts of murder in this city. What resources have you applied to this case Commissioner?"

"We have appointed Els and Ramasey to head up the investigation, and they will be assisted by ten officers, to do their legwork. If we find that we require more, then they will advise me. It is still early days."

"Captain Els and Sergeant Ramasey, you must put your best efforts into the resolution of this case. The Commissioner will supply whatever you need. If you need anything further then contact me directly. I want a written report weekly, of your progress."

The mayor stood up, and it was the signal for all to leave, "Good day gentlemen."

"Good day," they all said together as they left.

"Els, Ramasey, come with me to my office," instructed the Commissioner.

They followed him through City Hall to his office on the fourth floor. He sat down but did not invite the officers to sit down.

"Now, if you find out anything at all, I want to be the first to know; do you understand that?" demanded the Commissioner.

"You wish us to bypass normal channels sir?" Els asked.

"You just report it to me as instructed."

"Is this before we report to our Station Commander or do we do it simultaneously?" Els asked.

"You will report directly to me and only to me. Is that clear enough for you?"

"Yes sir," Els said. "Could we have that in writing please sir?"

"No, I will talk to your Station Commander and make arrangements. I have allocated an office in my department in City Hall; this will be your incident room. It will accommodate you and the officers helping you."

Els and Ramasey looked at each other uneasily, "When will this take place sir?" Els enquired.

"With immediate effect, and you can move your current files and information into room 316 A/B as from tomorrow. These rooms are more than adequate and computer terminals, phones and all the surveillance equipment you need has already been installed. You heard the Mayor; we need a fast solution to these murders. I will be on hand to ensure that there is no slacking and that you have all the support that you require. Do you have any further questions?"

"No sir,"

"Then you may leave."

The officers stood up, and walked towards the door. Before they got there, the Commissioner said, "I see there are no black officers assigned to the case."

"That is correct sir," Els said.

"Tell me why not?"

Els wanted to say, because they are as thick as shit, as old prejudices die hard. But he said, "I do not know why, you should ask the Commandant, sir."

The Commissioner just waved them away and went back to reading his report from the Commandant.

Once out of the door, Els said, "That prick thinks he is going to be running this investigation from his office. Well, he has another thing coming to him."

"Be careful Andries. You know what he is like, and he wants to fire a Captain, in order to achieve his quota of black officers. Tread carefully, my friend."

Ramasey knew his own rapid promotion to Sergeant was part of an affirmative action programme. They were actually, an odd couple. Andries, the Afrikaner with all the inbuilt prejudices and Ramasey the typical Indian, and managed to be all things to all men. That Ramasey was the brighter of the two was patently obvious. Els had been promoted at the time when only whites achieved officer status, regardless of ability. In some respects, Els was a dinosaur within the South African Police Force. But, Els was a survivor and had been a policeman for twenty years. He knew how to get by.

They found rooms 316 A/B and found them to be more than spacious. There were two computers already in place with laser jet printers connected. There was an incident board, a pin board and roster board, for controlling the investigation personnel. They looked at the set up and admitted it was much better than they would have given back at the station.

Ramasey switched on the computers and saw that it booted up on the latest Microsoft Windows. On the screen were all the usual icons and one that gave them direct access into police files countrywide. There was even an Internet programme.

"Captain, they have given us all the bells and whistles here," Ramasey said.

"No expense spared," Els said sarcastically.

"There is your office over there," Ramasey said, pointing to a glass cubicle office across the room. Else walked over to the office, opened the door and walked in. There was a fair sized desk with four draws and a comfortable office chair behind it.

A notepad sat in the middle of the desk, surrounded by a pen and pencil rack, ruler, stapler and a series of felt tipped pens. The telephone was to the right of the desk, adjacent to another computer terminal, for his private use. There was a bookshelf, a small conference table and a coffee maker with bags of ground coffee beans.

"Wow, so this is how the other half live," Ramasey said. This was a far cry from the shared desks and computers back at the station.

'I ask myself why?" Els said. "This is too good to be true. The Commandants office is not equipped as well as this."

"Molefe must have been more than high profile," Ramasey said.

"He was low life that deserved to die," Els said with feeling. "As far as I am concerned, the end was too quick for him, he was a real kaffir."

"Captain, be careful what you say, for all we know this room is bugged."

"I don't give a shit. I won't get any further promotion, that will go to the under privileged amongst us."

"Are you referring to me Captain?"

"Hell, no Jay. In my opinion, you deserve more than Sergeant, and if we crack this case quickly, which I doubt, you will surely be up for Warrant Officer."

"You do not see me as the under privileged then?"

"You must be joking, yours is the only nation to be able to play in both teams and ensure that you win. You okes are past masters of not rocking the boat and coming out on top."

"I am not sure that you are paying my people or me a compliment. We have learned how to survive in the most difficult of regimes."

Els gave him a quizzical look and headed out of the office towards the door, "Enough of this crap, we have a job to do, so let's collect the files and photos and set up shop."

They left the building and drove round to the station, to collect their files. It was already four thirty, and the traffic was heavy as they moved up West Street.

The Commissioner replayed the tape of their conversation. So Els was a typical racist, and that would be easy to deal with. Ramasey was a different kettle of fish; He showed intelligence and may become difficult. He would have to watch him carefully. If they dug too deep, they might find out that there was a connection between the hit and the armed forces. This could not be allowed.

He did not particularly want the crime solved, and they could possibly stumble across the connection. It was remote, but still a possibility. He had the room bugged and the phones tapped. Even the computers were linked so that he could follow any line of investigation. No point in leaving anything to chance.

Chapter 24

Angela Murchin sat in her office and mulled over the facts that she had written down:

1. South African poachers caught in Tanzania, possibly military.
2. Soong Corporation looking to invest in South Africa.
3. Ex Special Forces personnel used as insurgents in Gauteng linked with the NFP.
4. Possible force in South Africa, white dominated, looking to plan WHAT?
5. Many assassinations of known criminals, done professionally, WHY?'

She felt that the above were all linked but could not see a common thread. If they were linked, then what would be the objective? Who would benefit? She could not just go out and interview people, as they would not readily disclose this information. Could she go to print without better and more complete information? Her boss would never print a story without further verification.

If she went on the Internet, could they trace her? To whom could she send her information and why should she believe that they did not already know. She could be exposing herself and Thomas to unnecessary danger. To what end?

Her doubts and fears stayed with her for some time, and she knew that she was about to capitulate, when her cellular phone rang.

"Angela, I have found more information. We must meet.' Thomas said excitedly."

"Tell me where you would like to meet?"

"At the Keg for lunch," Thomas suggested.

"'I will be there at one o'clock, is that okay?" she asked.

"That's fine by me, see you later. Bye," he said.

The phone went dead, and she sat there wondering what could have materialised to get Thomas so excited. She would have to wait and see. She checked the time; it was eleven thirty, not too long to go.

She went back to her list of unanswered questions and tried to get a feel for the basic story and then as if out of the blue, a possibility struck her.

"My God," she exclaimed.

"And now what is bothering you?" asked the assistant editor, Byrand Meyer.

"Nothing in particular," she responded.

"Are you still messing about with that faction fighting," he asked aggressively.

"Not at all, I am researching the Korean industrialist for Tim Wells, if you must know," she said.

"Bullshit, let me see your notes," he demanded.

"Piss off, they are mine and I am not about to give you four hours of work so that you can use it and claim it as yours," she answered.

Meyer leant forward and tried to pick up her notes, but she was too quick for him, and placed them in her drawer.

"Do not make a total arsehole of your self, as people are watching," she said.

Meyer looked around the room and saw that the other journalists present had noticed the little skirmish. They had all stopped working and were watching the events unfold.

Meyer glared at her and said, "Be careful. Be very, very, careful, that you do not upset the wrong people."

"Get back to work," he shouted to all in the room, and then strode off to his office.

That was more than professional interest she thought. Wonder why he is so uptight? Could he be involved? There were more questions than answers today! She removed the list of events from her drawer and looked again. She believed that she could now see the connection between all of the events, which at first glance seemed unrelated. The common theme was the Special Forces, an offshoot of the old military. But why the poaching, that did not fit into any likely scenario. There was only one way to find out, she must go to Tanzania.

She doodled again, writing.

Poaching

Power

Armed forces

overseas investor
Government
Third force
Finance
Insurgents
Assassinations

They all fitted together, other than the poaching, and this thought niggled her as she went to meet Thomas at the Keg. Thomas was already there and had reserved a table in the corner of the room, where they could talk privately, and observe who came into the restaurant.

"Come sit down," he said urgently, "I have some incredible information."

"Okay, okay, calm down. People will notice."

He smiled and led her to the table. He could not wait to tell her what he had found out and was obviously extremely excited.

"I have got the final piece of the jigsaw," he said, "I know now why the poaching is part of the conspiracy."

This was his moment of glory, and he wanted to drag it out as long as he could.

"You know that I went to Natal last week and managed to talk to some people that knew the captured poachers. There were three of them."

"But there were only two reported as captured, did one escape?"

He smiled at her.

"Go on, go on," she encouraged.

"One was killed," he replied.

"Killed by whom?"

"He was killed by an elephant, by all accounts."

"How do you know this?" she asked.

"Because I tracked down the relatives, and they are pretty pissed off with the army. They have not received any compensation or outstanding salaries from the Natal government, who they say these men were working for."

"But why would the Natal government want their army personnel poaching in Tanzania?" she asked, "It does not make sense at all!"

"Oh, but it does when you know why," he said smiling.

"Are you going to tell me or not," she asked testily.

"Of course," he said.

Thomas started to tell his story and was interrupted by the waiter. They ordered coffee, and sandwiches, and Thomas continued his story. He had driven to Natal, and had used their sister paper, the Natal Metropolitan, to look up recent events of the insurgency in Natal, but in particular around Port Shepstone. She made a move to interrupt him, but he held up his hand, and said, "Let me finish, and you can ask questions later."

Thomas had found a number of references to acts of violence and the repeated request for more staff from the police force. This had not happened, but military personnel were drafted into the areas to help keep the peace. The inference was that the ANC were stirring up trouble in a number of areas and were taking out the political leaders at the lower levels. This intimidation was such that the locals, who knew where the violence emanated, were too frightened to vote for any party other than the ANC.

As the military and police quelled problems in one area, they would flare up in another. The Richmond area and Pietermaritzburg were the main areas of violence. Little violence was taking place near the stronghold of the NFP in Babanango. The net effect of all this violence was that the police and military were stretched to the limit, and close to breaking point. If this happened, then the violence would escalate further, and the local government would not be able to cope. This would mean that the ANC led government would have to step in, declare a 'State of emergency,' and essentially take control of the province."

"As you know, the province is in the control of the NFP alliance, and they have a slim majority of 53%. The balance of power would shift, and the Zulu nation would be forever under the control of the ANC." explained Thomas.

"Yes, I understand all this, but what has that to do with the poaching," she demanded.

"Be patient, you have to know the background before you fully understand."

"The violence was escalating out of control, when suddenly more than five hundred armed forces personnel appeared. This impacted immediately upon the situation, and at the same time, the violence flared up in Gauteng. These occurrences are inseparable. It shows that the NFP was going on to the offensive against the ANC. I believe these additional troops were financed by the proceeds of the poaching."

"Don't be ridiculous, how could poaching finance five hundred new army personnel and all the necessary equipment?" She said.

"It is simple really. Have you any idea what would be paid for trophies out of Africa. I have done some research, and the yanks will pay up to two hundred and fifty thousand dollars for an exceptional set of tusks, and the Far East will pay much the same for rhino horn. What would it cost to finance five hundred men in Natal, when the unemployment rate is around forty five per cent?"

"That is too incredible for words," she responded.

"Incredible yes, but it is actually happening. I have irrefutable proof. I talked to the widow of corporal Msini and to the wife of captain Khumalo. Although she was not that helpful, it transpires that the three men operated as a unit in the old defence force and were Reccies. They accounted for a lot of terrorists back in those days. There is also one other remarkable fact, and that is that captain Khumalo was a marksman, and believe me, that is rare in the armed forces for a black man."

"Isn't this evidence a little flimsy," she asked.

"Not at all, it puts the final piece together, and now we can see the full picture," Thomas said.

"I still think it is a bit weak, though, how can you be so sure?"

"It is easy, really. I interviewed Mrs Mnini, and she told me the full story, as she knew it. Her husband had been a little loose with his tongue, and he told her he was going on a special mission into Tanzania. In any event, how else would they get transport up to the border of Tanzania and back again, if the army did not support them. They could not have walked across Mozambique, and be back again in the time frame that she gave me. It would be impossible, even for the Reccies."

"How long were they away for?" she asked.

"On one of their trips they were away for twenty days, they travelled a distance of three thousand kilometres there and back; it would not be possible on foot!" he said.

"I take your point. So they must have had assistance. If a man is willing to pay two hundred and fifty thousand dollars for a trophy, why couldn't he have financed the trip?" She asked.

"That's a good point; I had not thought of that possibility. In that case, why use army personnel for the job? The person paying such large amounts could well afford a professional hunter, and many would do it for such a fee."

"I agree, why use army personnel. There can be only one reason, and that is that the Natal government is the beneficiary of the sale. It would also be easier to ship the trophies out of Durban when the government is involved," she said.

"Quite," he agreed.

"Where is the tape of the interview?" She asked.

"I put it into a safe deposit box with the First National Bank in Braamfontein, I believe it will be safer there than my home. I have a spare key for you, should something happen to me," he said.

"That's a bit melodramatic isn't it," she said.

"Not at all, between the ANC and the NFP, hundreds are being killed every week, due to faction fighting. What would one more murder mean? We are talking about people with real power, and they have proven that they are not afraid to use it."

"So if we put all this together, we have insurgents in Natal, trying to undermine the NFP. We have the NFP reciprocating in Gauteng. We have the NFP organising poaching in Tanzania for a third force, considered to be plotting against the government. This sounds like a recipe for civil war, and we thought how well we had done with the transition to democracy. Politicians are the same the world over, it always boils down to power and greed!" she said.

"Let's just work through what you have just said. Supposing there are two active groups in opposition to the ANC, what would be their objectives?" asked Thomas.

"I would have thought that would be obvious, they both want power or control of the country, surely," she said.

"Yes, but what happens if one or the other overthrows the government. Surely they would then face the same possibility from the opposition, whether it is black or white inspired. In fact, if it was white inspired, all the blacks would unite to overthrow the new government again. Nothing would have changed," he said.

The penny dropped for both of them at the same time, and they both said together, "What if the Zulu's and the white generals are in alliance, what would happen then?"

"Oh my God, what a scenario! It could mean the partition of South Africa into splinter states or countries, with their own government and controls. What could the ANC do about it?" she asked.

"They could go to war, but they would not be equipped to win. They would rather sue for peace and accept some power in another transitional government. It's too fantastic for words. It would never happen; the rest of the world would not allow it. The new government would be castigated, and sanctions would be imposed immediately," Thomas said.

"Would they? The new government would not consist of whites only; there would be the blacks from Natal too. And the two combined would be an irrepressible force, especially if properly equipped and trained. Just think of all the commando forces that were disbanded. If they could be reactivated, there would be thousands of trained men armed to the teeth, spread strategically throughout the country. It's a frightening thought," she said.

"I agree, it would set South Africa back a number of years!"

"We need more evidence to support this conclusion before we blow the whistle on this conspiracy. I intend to go to Tanzania to try to interview the people that apprehended the poachers." She said.

"Is that wise?"

"Thomas, this could be the story of our lives, almost as big as Watergate. If we can prove our theory about this conspiracy; surely the risk is worth it?" she asked.

"Is it worth our lives?" he asked.

"Then what do you propose?" she asked.

"I don't know," he said uncertainly.

Angela was caught up in the enormity of the story and was not thinking of the consequences. She knew that this was significant news, and you could not just walk away.

"I will go to Tanzania, and you put your research together on the widow and Khumalo's wife. We will meet when I get back and discuss where to go from there," she said.

"How will you explain your time away to Meyer?" Thomas asked.

"Simple, I am due some leave and will just take it. They cannot complain as personnel have been complaining about the amount of accrued leave that I have. I have no major deadlines at the moment either," she said.

"What about the Korean Industrialist that you are supposed to be researching for Tim Wells?" he asked.

"I have just about completed my research on Chen Yoo Soong, Tim can fill in the gaps," she said.

"Good luck then. How long do you think you will need to be away for?" he asked.

Angela thought for a second or two, and said, "About two weeks should do it."

Thomas looked at his watch and said, "Hey, we're late, we best get going."

"You go first, and I will follow later; this will help keep the nosy editor off our backs," she said.

Thomas stood up and said, "Shall I get the bill?"

Angela smiled and said, "My treat, see you later."

Thomas left the restaurant and waved goodbye at the door.

Chapter 25

The disciplinary hearing was conducted at the farm just outside Pietermaritzburg. There were only five people present. General Alan Doyle was presiding, and there were two people prosecuting, with Annette Venter defending herself, and a female typist recording the hearing.

The prosecutor Captain Gerry Le Grange read out the charge, 'failing to comply with orders, and thus, endangering the lives of other army personnel, sir.'

"How do you plead Major Venter?"

"Not guilty sir," said Annette.

"Who is defending you?" General Allan Doyle asked.

"I will defend myself, sir," she said.

"Are you sure about that?"

"Yes sir," she replied stiffly.

"Very well, carry on Captain Le Grange, please present your case."

The captain went through the events of the assassination of Molefe and his Lieutenant Mangopi. He related the orders given and also the risk of making the unauthorised hit on Mangopi. The premise was that the delay taken by Major Venter made her capture more likely, and the resultant interrogation would have endangered the lives of those in the Third Force. He concluded that it was an unnecessary risk that served no purpose other than to gratify Major Venter.

Annette sat through the whole evidence with a stoic expression. Neither acknowledging what was being said, nor even looking as if she agreed with what was being said.

"Major Venter, will you please respond to the charges against you," General Doyle said.

Annette began by giving the court the background to the sanctioned hit and how she planned the timing and the escape. She admitted that she had taken a chance by making the second hit without direct orders.

In mitigation, she asked that the court realise that her decision to take the second hit was based on her assessment at the time. She felt that the parents were in real danger from Mangopi, and acted accordingly. She knew that this would delay her escape but had calculated, correctly, that the disruption caused by the second hit would help her escape. She pointed out that had been the outcome. She finished her defence by saying.

"When operating alone in the field, one has to make decisions that cannot be calculated at the inception of the operation, I could not walk away from the danger as I saw it. Thank you sir, that is all."

General Allan Doyle looked long and hard at Major Venter; she had tried desperately to play down her sexuality, by not applying make-up and wearing her army uniform. Yet she had failed miserably. He could not help but admire her coolness and restrained beauty.

"Captain Le Grange, do you have anything further to add," he asked.

"No sir," was his response.

"I will then retire to my chambers to deliberate," he said.

He stood up to leave, and the whole court rose with him. He went back to his chambers smiling to himself. "What a woman," he thought. To look that beautiful, and be able to hit two men through the forehead at two hundred meters was incredible shooting.

He could not afford to lose such an asset, but he had to make certain that, in the future, she would obey their orders implicitly. "What", he thought "was the best punishment"? This was not like the regular army where the laws were strictly adhered. No, he had to be much more thoughtful on this issue. Old man Kobus would not want too light a sentence, whereas he could not afford to lose such an asset.

What was making his dilemma worse, was the fact that he would have done the same; if only he could shoot that well, he mused. Bust her to Captain, give a rollicking, and that should be sufficient. That would probably satisfy all parties. He decided that it would be best to put her on probation for nine months, and if any further discipline issues arose, then he would take a decidedly different attitude. He stood and smiled. Kobus would not be happy, but he had been left to make the decision. He set off back to the court.

The court rose as he entered via the side door, which led to his bench. He sat and shuffled his papers, ensuring that the Major felt uncomfortable, and he wished to prolong her discomfort. He set a stern face, and said, "Major Venter, the charges against you are of a serious nature and show lack of discipline on your part."

He continued from the notes that he had made about the incident, outlining where the breach of discipline had taken place, and in particular the risk that she had taken, that could have jeopardised the organisation. Annette stood and appeared unmoved by what he was saying. This annoyed General Doyle, as he wanted her to show some response.

"You appear unconcerned by the charges Major Venter," he said icily.

"I am sorry sir, I was merely trying to listen to what you have to say and was not, I hope, showing a lack of concern. If that is how you read my behaviour, then I apologise most sincerely to the court, sir."

"Major Venter, are you indeed concerned about the fact that you disobeyed orders and jeopardised the safety of this organisation, because if you are, then you do not display any concern," he said.

Annette looked at the General and was not sure how she should respond.

"I am familiar with courtroom conditions sir, and this may give the impression that I am not concerned. Whereas, in fact, I am petrified that the decision you make, would seriously diminish my usefulness to the organisation. I believe strongly in what we are doing."

The General looked at her but did not respond. He felt that he had made his point, and there would be no further benefit in labouring the point any further.

"Major Venter, you have been found guilty of misconduct and failing to follow orders implicitly. You behaved rashly and put the whole organisation at risk. I have decided that you will serve a nine month probationary period, and if, in that time, any further misconduct should occur, then the minimum that will happen is that your rank will be reduced to Captain, and you will be removed from operational duties in the field. Is that fully understood Major Venter?"

Annette could not believe her luck and was smiling inside, "Yes sir," she responded.

"That is the decision of the court, and you will start your probation from today. Clerk, draw up the papers for my signature, then attach them to Major Venter's file."

Allan Doyle stood up to leave. The assembled court rose, and watched the General leave by the side door.

Captain Le Grange looked across to Annette and smiled, she responded in kind. "You were lucky today Major," he said, "He must have been in a good mood."

Annette looked at Le Grange but said nothing. She gathered her papers and left the courtroom. As she was leaving, the clerk came to her and said, "General Doyle would like to see you."

"What, now?" she questioned.

"Yes, Ma'am, right now, please follow me."

Annette followed the clerk to an annexe at the back of the house. The clerk knocked on the door. "Come in," said General Doyle.

The clerk entered the room with Annette, and they both saluted the General.

"Thank you Corporal," he said and then, "Sit down Major Venter."

Annette sat down.

"Major Venter, I wished to talk to you about your actions and conduct in private. We are not at all pleased with the way you behaved, but you are considered a necessary element of our campaign."

Annette made a move to talk but was immediately stopped by the General. He held up his hand and said, "For once major, just shut up and listen!"

"You may think that you have all the answers, but patently you do not. Did you ever consider that the man that you shot could have been working for us; no of course you did not," he said angrily. "There are many people out there that are as equally unhappy with the current state of affairs, and they are not all white. You assumed that the second man that you shot was also part of Molefe's gang. How do you know that he was not working for us? Did you ever consider this possibility?"

"No sir, I did not!"

"This is why your targets are very specific and you could have taken out a valuable asset to this organisation."

Annette again tried to speak but was immediately told to sit and listen.

General Doyle went on to explain how the organisation had many assets in the most unlikely places that gave invaluable information on what is happening, both in government and throughout the country. These assets had to behave like the other members of their respective groups, or it would be obvious that they were operatives. Her actions had not been fully thought through, as she could have been caught and she also put the driver at risk.

"There are many people that help this organisation, similar to you, that accept the risk as part of what they believe is necessary for this country and its future. They do not expect maverick actions from a senior member of staff. In the future, you will only take out the targets that we give you, and nothing else, regardless of what you feel is necessary. Only when your own life is threatened, and you believe that it is the only way to escape personal injury, will you be allowed to use your weapons on anything other than the target specified. Is that understood Major Venter?"

"Yes sir," she said.

"You may leave; we will be in touch with you shortly."

Annette stood up and looked at the General, but he had already returned to his papers, and did not even respond to her salute. She found that she was perspiring profusely and could not be sure if it was because of the man or the berating that she had just had. She concluded it was both.

Chapter 26

Don Scales was sat in his office thinking about recent events with Khumalo, when his phone rang. 'Don Scales,' he said.

A female voice on the other end of the line said, "Mr Scales, my name is Angela Murchin and I work for the Metropolitan in Johannesburg. Do you have time to talk to me please?"

Don was curious and said, "What is this about Mrs Murchin?"

"It's Miss actually" she said. "I am investigating a series of events that appear to lead to Tanzania and some poaching that is taking place."

"Whoa there, we cannot discuss this case, as the case has not gone to trial yet," Don said.

"What would you say if I told you that it never will go to trial," she said.

"Bullshit, would be what I would say, Miss Murchin."

"Then you will be making a grave mistake, and I would really like to discuss this with you."

"I bet you would. You reporters are always looking for sensationalism, and I do not suppose that you are any different. If you wish to discuss this case, then I suggest that you talk to Dr Ngama, who is the head of tourism in Dar es Salaam."

"I desperately need to talk to you, as I believe that you, perhaps unwittingly, hold the key to a conspiracy taking place in South Africa," she said.

"My God, you really are trying it on; do you really expect me to believe you?"

"I can understand why you would not, but I would ask you one question and then if you are sure that I am mistaken, I will not bother you again."

"What is your question?"

"Has any person or government body tried to take your suspects away?" She asked.

This was just a shot in the dark, but worth a try, and she could tell by his intake of breath, that she had hit pay dirt.

"I do not understand the relevance of your question," he said, having regained his composure.

"I am sure that you do, otherwise why the pause between answering?" she asked.

"I was just surprised by the question," he said.

"Now I can say bullshit. Somebody tried, and I bet it was military." She said.

"How could you possibly know that," he stopped abruptly, realising that he had inadvertently confirmed her suspicion.

"We need to talk," she said.

"I do not see why, as the matter was just a case of jurisdiction," Don said.

"My question was not a wild guess, as you probably realise by now, the two poachers that you caught were almost definitely military or ex military personnel."

Don was intrigued by what she had said, and also the knowledge that she had of the poachers. She was no longer fishing, but telling him what he already knew. He knew himself that the poachers were not the run of the mill poachers that they had had to deal with in the past. There was undeniably something strange happening, and he would like to know what it was.

"Do you propose to come to Tanzania?" he asked.

"Will you see me if I do?"

"You have stirred up my interest, and yes, I will see you."

"I will take the next flight to Dar es Salaam, could you meet me there?"

"How will I recognise you? I assume that you do not wish me to hold up a card with your name on it?"

"Do you have cell phone reception where you are?" She asked.

"Yes, why do you ask?"

"I will send you a recent photo," she said.

"That should work," he said.

"See you tomorrow then, Bye."

Don put the phone down and called Jonathon to his office.

"Jonathon, tomorrow I am going to Dar es Salaam. Can you arrange the flight for me, and ensure that the prisoners are well looked after."

"Will do, may I ask why you are going to Dar es Salaam?"

"Let's keep it between you and me for the moment, but I am meeting a reporter from Jo'burg."

At that precise moment, his phone bleeped to inform him that he had received a message. He picked up his cell phone and opened the message. It was a photograph of Angela Murchin. He whistled and showed the photograph to Jonathon saying.

"Quite a looker, don't you think?"

Jonathon looked at the photograph and smiled.

"Not my type, far too thin!" He said laughingly.

"It appears that you like her though."

"This is all business Jonathon as I will explain later."

"I am intrigued, why not tell me now?"

"I need to think first and sort out a few ideas in my head. I will need your help. In the meantime do not discuss this with anyone, OK."

"No problem boss, you can trust me."

"I know, but I think that you are the only one that I can trust, so please do not let anything slip. As far as you are concerned this is an old girlfriend that is coming to see me."

"You wish," said Jonathon.

Then Don said, "Bugger off and do some work."

Jonathon laughed and left the room.

Chapter 27

The Lear jet landed at Durban Airport and taxied to the apron. The passengers looked tired after the long flight with the exception being Chen Yoo Soong, who appeared well rested. The stewardess advised them that they had arrived at Durban Airport and opened the door and lowered the steps to the apron.

There were four passengers on board, and they moved towards the door to disembark. Chen Yoo Soong was first, followed by his director of development, then the chief accountant and finally the production director.

They were dressed in business suits and ties that were obviously too warm for the Durban climate, and the heat and the humidity hit them immediately. Again, it appeared that Chen Yoo Soong was not perturbed by the change in climate as he alighted to the apron. His directors looked very uncomfortable and were pleased to see the large black Mercedes waiting for them.

The driver of the Mercedes had the doors open and waited until they had got into the car before closing the doors, turning the air conditioner on full, and then driving towards the VIP lounge. Not a word was spoken on the short journey to the lounge.

They were met by the Natal Interior Minister - Justice Nkabo, the Minister of Land Affairs - Petrus Nkumu, the minister of Development - Johannes Mchunu, and the Minister of the Environment Precious Cele.

Justice Nkabo stepped forward as soon as they entered the VIP lounge and said "Welcome to Natal Mr. Soong. My name is Justice Nkabo, and I am the Interior Minister for Natal. Can I also introduce you to the Minister of land Affairs - Petrus Nkumu, the Minister of Development - Johannes Mchunu and finally the Minister of the Environment - Precious Cele?"

As he introduced the ministers the visitors bowed and acknowledged the ministers, but not a word was spoken.

"I trust that you had a good flight gentleman?"

The minister was acknowledged by the director of finance Soo Yen Ling who said, "Thank you, it was long and tiring but as you see we have arrived safely. Unfortunately, Mr. Soong does not speak English, and I will be translating for you".

His accent was clipped British upper class, and it was more than obvious that he had been educated in England, and probably Oxford or Cambridge.

"May I have your passports please," asked the minister, "Just a formality you understand, you have to have the stamp of arrival," he said apologetically.

"In the meantime can we offer you some refreshments? We have a long drive to Babanango, what would you prefer?"

Soo Yen Ling translated to his colleagues and said, "Do you have any iced tea?"

"Of course, we will organize it immediately, please take a seat whilst you are waiting."

He summoned the waiter and asked the other ministers what they would like. They all settled for ice tea.

The group sat down and made light conversation that was somewhat stiff due to the constant need for every statement to be interpreted. It was clear from the beginning this was to be all business without the usual pleasantries when hosting diplomats.

The iced tea arrived, and they slowly sipped their drinks. The Interior minister said. "When you are ready we can go to the cars that will transport us to Babanango. I am sure that you will enjoy the scenery on the way."

"If you do not mind we will split into two groups with Mr. Soong and Mr. Ling travelling in my car with the others following with our ministers. We will have an escort all the way, so we will have no delays." He was about to say no hold ups but thought better of it.

"I will take you through our itinerary for the next four days whilst we are driving to Babanango"

The party looked at Mr. Soong who in turn looked at Mr. Ling. He said something rapidly in Korean and waited for Mr. Ling to interpret.

"That will be fine," said Mr. Ling following the response from Mr. Soong.

They finished their tea and walked to the cars parked outside. There were two Mercedes and 4 police cars and 4 motorcycle outriders. The cavalcade left the airport with a cacophony of sirens that would clear the road in front for them. It was 2 pm in the afternoon, and the traffic was light. They made good headway to Pietermaritzburg, and on down the freeway to Melmoth

"Mr. Ling, could you please interpret for me as I wish to discuss the itinerary with Mr. Soong," Justice Nkabo said.

Mr. Ling nodded assent and quickly explained to Mr. Soong.

"We propose to spend today talking to Mr. Mabuto - the Chief Minister of Natal." He waited for Mr. Ling to translate.

Mr. Ling nodded and said, "Proceed"

"We will follow initial discussions with a banquet at 19.00hr, with traditional dancing afterwards."

Mr. Ling again interpreted with a conference taking place, in Korean, between the members of the party. They appeared unhappy with something and Justice Nkabo waited patiently. Eventually, after much discussion, Mr. Ling said.

"We appreciate your invitation to your banquet, but we are very, how should I put it, particular about what we eat. We are all vegetarians and do not eat any meat. Will this be a problem?"

Justice Nkabo did not even flinch although his mind was racing; he had seen the preparations and knew that a bull had been slaughtered specifically for this occasion. He had three hours to put something else together.

He brought out his mobile phone and spoke in Zulu. He suspected that Mr. Soong understood perfect English, and he thought, "Well, two can play at that game".

He rang his office in Babanango and spoke to his PA, "We have a problem", he said in Zulu, "These guys are all vegetarians and we need to cook up something good, without meat, Get hold of Rashid. He will know what to do, oriental vegetarian. You had better advise the chief and get moving quickly as you only have three hours. And please, keep me informed and when speaking to me only speak in Zulu."

"That will not be a problem, as we cater for all needs and diets at our headquarters," he said.

"Tomorrow we will travel to the proposed site for the factory and allow you to see the access and the infrastructure available," Justice Nkabo said.

Mr. Ling translated and replied, "At what time will we be leaving tomorrow?"

"We are to have a light breakfast and leave at 09.00; we will arrive on site at approximately 11.00."

Again there was a delay whilst the translation took place and further discussion. Mr. Ling said.

"Would it be possible to leave a little earlier, as we feel we must spend a good deal of time surveying the site, and ensuring that it meets our requirements? This may entail a number of visits to the site."

"What time would suit you as we are in your hands?"

Mr. Ling turned to his colleagues, and they discussed the issue for a while then Mr. Ling said.

"We would like to be on site by 09.00 this would mean us leaving at 07.00 and having breakfast at 06.30, would this be acceptable?"

"That will be fine as we are all early risers in South Africa."

Mr. Ling interpreted and got a nod of approval from Mr. Soong.

"We assumed that you would want all day at the site and we have, therefore, booked the group into the Royal Hotel in Durban for the evening."

Mr. Ling interpreted and again Mr. Soong, nodded agreement.

"On Wednesday, we will meet at headquarters to discuss the project and timing," Justice Nkabo said.

Again Mr. Ling interpreted and said, "We would like to see the site first and then reserve our decision to meet in Babanango as we may need more than one day, would this create a problem?"

"Unfortunately, it would, as the Chief Minister is only available on that particular day."

Mr. Ling interpreted at length and much discussion took place in Korean with the whole group talking and clearly unhappy.

"Mr. Soong asks how often is it that you have a project worth US$ 2 billion with other benefits to be discussed."

"As you well know the Chief Minister's time is of the essence and his diary is set for at least three months. It would not be easy to rearrange his appointments."

Mr. Ling looked at Justice Nkabo and said, "It is quite straightforward, if we need more time, we take it. If your Chief Minister is not available, then we will leave and maybe come back another day. We have several projects, and we always research them carefully and only deal with the decision makers. Please pass this on to your Chief Minister."

"I understand the importance of your visit and the need to meet with the Chief Minister, but I cannot say that he will agree to what you ask. I realise that we need the investment and the difference it would make to our party. Nevertheless, I would have to consult with the Chief Minister and then give you his answer."

"Then please advise our party as soon as possible, as we have to be able to make a decision as soon as possible," Mr. Ling said.

They drove in virtual silence for the rest of the journey with only occasional talk about the weather and the scenery. The Koreans showed little interest in either social chat or the scenery. They would occasionally discuss a topic in Korean but were generally very quiet and preoccupied with their own thoughts and discussions.

Justice Nkabo was pleased when he spotted the sign to Babanango and said. "Nearly there now, and you will be honoured by a kilometre of our Impi's in traditional dress."

As they approached their headquarters, the Zulu warriors were lining the road, and as soon as the first warriors saw the cavalcade approaching, they began to beat their assegais against their shields. This was then picked up along the line to the Babanango base. The lead police car turned off the siren, and all the other cars followed suit. They could now clearly hear the rhythmic beat of the assegai on the shields. The warriors looked impressive as they all wore the Zulu regalia with the ostrich feathers and hides of the impala cloaked with the skin of leopards. They were lean and obviously extremely fit and athletic.

As the cavalcade went past they raised their assegai and shouted, "Bayette Nkosi" (welcome my chief.) The Koreans only tacitly acknowledged the Zulu impi.

The cavalcade drove into the Babanango camp and drew up outside the main building where a guard of honour was waiting. Chief Minister was waiting with his aides to receive the Koreans. He was the consummate politician with an immense smile even though he was annoyed by the antagonistic approach of the Koreans. Chen Yoo Soong disembarked with his aides directly following. He was immediately greeted and welcomed to Babanango by the Chief Minister, who indicated to them to follow him through the line of soldiers in full military dress.

They made their way through the parade and turned at the end of the rank to inspect the next rank. There were three ranks in all, and Soong showed little if any interest in the soldiers standing for inspection. The

Chief Minister quickly moved them inside the air-conditioned building and up to the first floor to the boardroom.

The Koreans sat on one side, and the ministers flanking the Chief Minister, on the opposite side of the table. They went directly through the pleasantries and then on to business with the Chief Minister opening the discussions by saying."

Mr. Soong, we have set aside what we believe to be the perfect site for your proposed car factory. This has excellent access to the port of Durban such that imported parts can be readily delivered, and any exports can be easily transported to the docks. The site consists of 10 hectares of land for development solely for the purpose of Soong Industries. The infrastructure is in place with power and water requirements allocated according to the needs that you indicated to my department last year. However, there is more than adequate power and water should your needs have changed."

"Excuse me Chief Minister Mabuto, but I will need to interpret for Mr Soong as his English is not adequate for this type of meeting," said Mr. Ling.

"By all means Mr. Ling, please go ahead."

Mr. Ling interpreted, and the Koreans held a conference for a further five minutes.

"Chief Minister we appreciate what you have said, but we have a number of questions, if you do not mind?"

"Please go ahead."

"If we planned to expand further would there be more land available?"

"The developed area is 30hactares, and expansion would be possible."

"Is there labour readily available?"

"Yes, there is a township not more than 5 kilometres from the site."

"Is there skilled labour in the area?"

"Yes. In Durban, which is only 15 kilometres from the site, there are plenty of artisans and operators from major industries."

The group talked between themselves in Korean, and Mr. Ling said.

"If there is skilled labour and the accessibility is to our liking, then we think that we can do a deal. What incentives would be given to our company for such a major investment?"

"There would be a tax break for ten years, and low rentals for the ground itself. But there could not be any financial assistance from the province, but perhaps some help from the central government."

"Our primary market would be Southern Africa; would the local governments of the SADC offer any assistance?"

"To obtain the best advantage it would be preferable to our province to not involve other countries, until all aspects of the deal are concluded. It would be premature to involve the SADC, or at this stage even the South African government."

The group discussed the comments and Mr. Soong dominated the discussion. Then Mr. Ling said.

"We assume that when you talk of all aspects of the deal, you are talking of the assistance that you require from our arms section?"

"That is partially correct, but other aspects, such as the time frame, your power requirements, labour levels, raw material requirements, still need to be discussed."

After discussion, Mr. Ling said.

"We would install a plant that would produce one hundred cars per day, and this would require a staff of eight hundred people. The power requirements would be ten megawatts; we have prepared a document for you that explain our needs." He reached into his briefcase and took out a file and passed this to the Prime Minister.

"Thank you, Mr. Ling. We will pass this document over to our projects department. As for the power, we have set aside a reticulation of twenty megawatts for your use. On the more sensitive matter, perhaps we could discuss our military needs?"

"Chief Minister, perhaps we could discuss your requirements when the site has been seen and approved. At this time, it may be premature to discuss such a sensitive subject."

"That is quite so, Mr. Ling. We will discuss the whole project, and it's implications on Thursday after you have visited the site. I have left my diary open for you until Friday at mid-day. Now I suggest that we retire to our rooms such that we can prepare for the banquet tonight."

Chapter 28

Don went through to the holding cells to talk to Captain Khumalo. The guard on duty stood to attention and saluted.

"I want to see the prisoner Khumalo in the interview room. I wish to see him alone, but you can post two guards outside the door." Don turned around, and went to the interview room, and waited for the Captain.

There was a knock on the door, "Bring him in."

The door swung open, and captain Khumalo was brought in. He was handcuffed and had chains around his ankles. Don wondered if this was necessary, but realised he was dealing with a man as capable as Allen in the SAS. It would be wise not to give him any opportunity to escape. The guards brought the captain to the chair, and made him sit down.

The captain looked at Don with a smile on his face and said, "You wish to see me sir?"

"You can go now," he said to the guards, "I will look after Khumalo now."

The guards left the room and Don turned to the captain and said, "Believe it or not I need your help."

Captain Khumalo said nothing.

"I need your help in unravelling what is going on here as it is obvious that you are not the normal run of the mill poachers. So what is driving you, or more to the point, who is driving you?"

"Mr. Scales, we have been through this already. We may not be the run of the mill poachers as you put it, but we are still poaching to make some money."

"I do not believe you, and quite frankly, you are not very convincing."

"I can't help that, but the reality is that we are poaching to make money, why do you want to make it any more? You caught us in the act, you have evidence, case closed."

"You do not want to help me understand then?"

"There is nothing to understand."

"Tomorrow I will return with more information, and we will repeat this discussion."

"And you will receive the same answer."

Don smiled and said, "We will see."

"Guards, you can take him back now."

Don watched Khumalo being escorted out of the room and realised that he was a true professional and was unlikely to give away information under any circumstances. He found that he was almost beginning to like the man, and admired his will power. He must know that he would be sentenced to at least two years in prison, yet his determination to not cooperate did not waiver. He did not seem to be interested at all in his fate and had total allegiance to his commanding officer, or whatever unit he was operating for. Don would have to seek information from the reporter and try to put things together that way. 'What would I do with the information anyway', he asked himself? Who would believe me? Perhaps he should just hand his prisoners over to the military and forget all about it. Then he realised that this was not an option, as he would be abdicating his responsibility. The problem was, there wasn't anybody that he could discuss what was happening with, as he could not trust him or her to keep quiet. He would call Allen after discussions with the reporter. He was quite looking forward to meeting her.

The flight to Dar es Salaam was uneventful, and he arrived well before the flight from Johannesburg. He checked the arrivals board and saw that the plane was due to land on time at 10.45am. He went to the coffee shop, purchased a cappuccino and a newspaper, took a seat, and waited for the journalist. He thought about how he would approach the discussions. How much could he tell her and what would she tell him? She had more knowledge than he had on the situation in hand, but she needed his help to put it all together.

He started to read his newspaper and saw that the poaching incident was still being reported, with Dr. Gama taking all the credit for apprehending the poachers. His photograph was right above the article, and he beamed towards the camera. Don smiled and started to read the article in more depth, when he heard the flight SA188 from Johannesburg had landed.

They had agreed to meet in the arrivals hall. He did not notice that he was being followed and was blissfully unaware of the surveillance. Don saw her coming through the automatic gates, she was carrying nothing more than a holdall, not much larger than her handbag.

She was dressed in jeans and a loose fitting top that did little to hide her figure. Her hair was pulled back tightly and was tied in a ponytail at the back. She had obviously made an effort to dress down, but it only made her seem more attractive. Don moved towards her and said, "Angela Murchin I assume?"

Angela quickly assessed Don and saw a classic game ranger in the standard issue of neutral colours and well-worn shirt and trousers. He was tall, slim and appeared extremely fit. She liked what she saw and gave him her best smile. "You must be Mr. Scales," she said.

"Please call me Don, and I trust that you had a good flight."

"Yes thank you Don, where have you parked your car?"

"We will be flying back to my base in Dodoma and my plane is parked through those doors at the side."

"Do you fly the plane?"

"Yes, does that bother you?"

"Not really, provided that you are a good pilot. I hate flying at the best of times, even with the big airlines. You hear of so many accidents nowadays, particularly with small planes, that it makes you wary of flying, and I have never seen you fly."

"I have over three thousand hours of flying time, and have made this flight many times, and I am still here. Trust me you will be OK."

"I suppose we could not hold our discussions here by any chance?" She enquired.

"Afraid not, we need to be somewhere where we cannot be overheard, nothing better than the remote bush for that, the only bugs are wild ones."

Angela laughed at his joke and said, "OK, what must be must be, I notice an accent there, and it sounds that you are from northern England, is that correct?"

"It bloody well isn't. I am not a Sassenach. I am a Scotsman and proud of it." He said.

Angela laughed again and said, "You and the English seem to be old enemies and yet you still call it the United Kingdom, makes you laugh hey."

Don smiled. He was enjoying Angela's company and was attracted to her despite his reservations on reporters. Watch yourself old son, he said to himself, don't get involved now. You just want information, and then she goes home.

"When is your return flight?" Don asked.

"I have booked a holiday for one week, and I return next Monday at three in the afternoon. I have arranged accommodation in Dar es Salaam for tonight and will decide where to go tomorrow."

"Well, I can advise you where to go if you want to see the big five or, perhaps, sunbathing on the beach, it depends on what you are looking for?"

"No, definitely not sunbathing, I would love to see the game parks and wildlife. I am not too concerned with seeing the big five. I just enjoy the bush veldt."

"Well there is bush veldt aplenty in Tanzania of that I can assure you. There we are that's the plane to take us to my base," he said, pointing to the twin engine Cessna standing in the shade of an acacia bush.

"Not very big is it!" said Angela, "Are you sure that it is safe?"

"Perfectly," said Don, "Safe as houses, relax my girl, you are in safe hands."

"I have heard that before." She said. "Many guys tell me that at least you dare not run out of petrol," she said laughing.

She knew that she was flirting a bit, but could not resist teasing this very interesting man. I had better be careful here, best not get involved, all I want is the info for my story she thought. Mind you, it could be fun winding him up, and, who knows she might just enjoy a holiday romance. He is quite handsome in a rugged way, she thought.

"How long is the flight?" she asked.

"About forty five minutes," he said.

"Thank God, I abhor long flights!"

"There will be plenty to see along the way and we can always drop down to look closer if we see anything interesting."

"You're OK," she said, "The sooner we get down to terra firma then there will be less terror."

"My goodness you're a cry baby aren't you, where is your spirit of adventure?"

"It comes back after I have landed," she quipped.

He opened the door to the passenger side of the aircraft and helped her into the plane. He could not help noticing her figure and the athletic way she climbed over the wing.

Don went through his checks around the aircraft and climbed into the cockpit. He contacted the traffic controller and got permission to take off. The flight to Dodoma was uneventful, and Don pointed out the game below as they saw them. He explained the symbiotic nature of the animals, and why they grazed at different levels. This helped to calm her nerves during the flight and it seemed to reduce the time taken to arrive at Dodoma.

Don spotted the landing strip and said, "Nearly there now, I will just take a pass over the runway and make sure that there isn't any game in the way."

Angela said nothing and Don could see the tension in her eyes.

He roared over the runway and banked over the trees to commence his run in to land. The g forces pinned Angela to the window and she looked even more uncomfortable.

Don turned the plane into the wind and brought it down gently leaving it till the last second before flaring. The plane gently touched the gravel strip and then bumped to the end of the runway. As the reverse thrust was applied the whole plane vibrated and shook.

"There we are safely down," he said, and he gently steered the plane towards the hanger. He could see Jonathon waiting with the Landrover and he gave a wave through the cockpit window.

Angela looked at Don and said, "Thank God for that, that was an awful landing!"

Don laughed and said, "That my girl was a very good landing, and I would not normally come in so gently."

"Then thank God I am not going to experience one of your normal landings," she said, emphasising normal by using her fingers to depict inverted comma's.

"You really are a spoilt little bugger aren't you," he said laughing, he was really enjoying teasing her and she knew it.

They alighted from the plane and Jonathon was waiting for them and appeared agitated

"Is there something wrong Jonathon?" asked Don.

"Yes, I have just been informed that the army are coming to collect the poachers for further interrogation at the barracks in Manyoni."

Don looked at Angela and said, "Looks like we are too late Angela."

"Shit, are you happy with them taking them away?" she asked.

"Of course not, but what can we do?"

"Who was it that told you Jonathon?"

"Dr. Gama, and he was none too happy about you not being here, he also knew that you had flown to Dar es Salem, and picked up Miss Murchin."

"How the hell did he know that?" asked Don.

"Apparently they have been expecting Miss Murchin and were going to keep her under close surveillance whilst she was here."

"It would appear that the ANC or NFP have good contacts with their counterparts in Tanzania. How else could they have known of my flight?" she asked.

"When are they coming to collect the poachers?" asked Don.

"They said either later today or first light tomorrow."

"Let's get back to base and discuss the situation there." Don said.

Jonathon opened the door of the Landrover for Angela and she slipped into the back seat. They place her luggage on the back seat with her.

Don drove the Landrover to the base and pulled into the main yard with a cloud of dust and parked outside the main entrance to the offices. They alighted from the Landrover and hurried in to Don's office without a word.

Don went behind his desk and motioned Angela to sit down opposite him and said, "Angela, we must think of the alternatives that we have as we cannot just allow this to happen. I know what their barracks are like and I doubt that either of the poachers will emerge alive."

"I suggest that we swap information on the poachers and their activities and I will give you the background to what we believe is happening."

"OK, I will go first and then you add your half-penneth and see what we have."

"Jonathon, can you ask Constance to organise some tea for us. And then you must join us for this discussion as you will be able to add what you believe."

"What about Toby" asked Jonathon?

"I don't think so, he knows very little and he cannot keep his mouth shut."

"Who is Toby" asked Angela?

"Toby is the other senior ranger but he has a bit of a chip on his shoulder about me getting this job as he thought he should get it. Do not worry yourself about Toby. We need to crack on as if they come this afternoon then we must have a plan of action"

"Let's first determine what we know as fact and then move on from there," suggested Angela.

Jonathon returned to the room and sat next to Angela.

"Let's use the white board to write down the sequence of events as we know them," said Don.

Don moved to the white board and picked up the black pen that was lying in the tray below the board. He started to write.

(1) Poachers ex South African army

"Actually they were reccies," Angela said.

"What is the significance of that," Jonathon said.

"Well, they are from Natal, and they accounted for quite a lot of ANC insurgents at the border of Swaziland, where they used to cross into South Africa. This would suggest that they are not working for the ANC, but more likely the NFP," she said.

"That would suggest that the NFP would want to keep them quiet and not the ANC," Don said.

"Exactly," Angela said, "And the significance of that I will explain later."

Don went back to his board and altered the first line.

(1) Poachers ex South African Defence Force pre elections in 1994, probably/possibly working for the NFP in Natal

(2) Transport to Tanzania had to be provided impossible to cover the ground on foot in the time frame, who assisted? Private or a political group?

(3) Why does the Tanzanian army want these poachers?

"That's easy," Angela said, "There must be a link with the army here and the NFP, though I do not understand why as Tanzania assisted the ANC with camps in Tanzania?"

"Do we have any evidence of that?" Don asked.

"It stands to reason, there has to be a link at the highest level otherwise why take the poachers as the ANC would definitely want them returned to South Africa for interrogation."

"Then how do we know it isn't ANC inspired and the Tanzanian government aren't working with the ANC."

"Good point that, we do not know," Angela said.

Don turned to look at Jonathon and asked, "What do you know of the camps in Tanzania that the government provided for the ANC?"

"Not a lot, as I was too busy studying to take any notice of what was happening with the ANC in Tanzania. I do know that at that time we had our own problems and it was rumoured that ex- reccies did some work for the government in the 90's. This was never admitted, but the locals knew as it put a stop to a lot of the poaching gangs at the time."

"That would suggest that there is a link between the reccies and the government here," Don said.

"That's a little tenuous isn't it? Angela said, "How could we determine such a link?"

"At this late a stage it would be impossible," Jonathon said.

"I agree, in any event we do not have the time to discover such a link, we have to assume that it is there or we will be going round in circles all day, and we do not have all day!" Don said emphatically.

"We know these guys were reccies and I am curious that you captured them so easily, Angela said.

"It was not that easy at all; in fact we missed them at the first attempt," Don said.

Don turned to the board and wrote.

(4)

"Angela, it is your turn now what do you know?" Don said.

Angela went through her investigations that she instigated when the poaching was first reported and the events that followed. Her assumption that there was a Third Force operating in South Africa to destabilise the government and that there could be links between the NFP and the Third Force. This could well lead to a military coup in South Africa supported by the Zulu nation.

"Wow!" Don exclaimed!

"What a scenario?"

"What would be the outcome?"

"It could lead to the partitioning of South Africa into splinter states based upon tribal lines." She said.

"Impossible, the rest of the world would not allow it."

"Wouldn't they?"

"They have seen it happen across Africa, just another event that nobody would particularly care about. You have to remember it would be mainly black on black, very similar to India and Pakistan."

"Angela may well be right,' Jonathon said.

"Would these poachers know any of this, I would have thought they are too junior to be privy to such information?" Don said.

"They would not know the detail, but captain Khumalo may know enough to help the ANC put the plot together."

"Angela. That is too fantastic for words," Don said.

"I know, but all the evidence is pointing that way and there are rumours of an assassination squad in Natal that are taking out the heavyweight criminals that the police and the ANC are using to destabilise Natal."

"Why should we intervene?" Jonathon asked.

"If these people are planning a military coup then surely we must report this to our superiors as this is outside of any remit that we may have," Jonathon said.

"This is the biggest story of my life and probably I will never get a chance to ever record such events again. I know this is a bit mercenary, but the fact still remains that an attempt to overthrow a government will be made. Would it not be better to report the whole story as handing over these poachers will not resolve the problem, only push it further underground," Angela said.

"Angela, do you have a leaning towards these right wing elements?" Jonathon asked.

"I do not agree with everything that the ANC are doing, but corruption is rampant the violence in South Africa grows worse every day, and the infrastructure is failing at unimaginable rate."

"Does that justify a military coup in a country that has been repressed for over fifty years?" Don asked.

"No, it does not! The problem is that unless this plot is uncovered totally then it will only delay the coup not stop it in its tracks."

"And of course, you will get your story of a lifetime," Jonathon retorted.

"Yes, that is the motivation for me," she replied.

"Not very noble," Don said.

"But honest," she replied.

"Regardless of the motivation we have to try and prevent the coup. Would we be doing this by handing over the poachers to the army?" Don asked.

"You and Jonathon both know that they will not survive, they will be shot trying to escape or something similar, and then where are we?" Angela asked.

"What are the alternatives?" Don asked.

"We have to get them back to South Africa to a safe house, and then we can expose the whole plot," Angela said.

"And how do you propose to do that?" Jonathon asked.

"What is the range of your plane," Angela asked.

"That is unthinkable," Don said. "I would be accused, and rightly so, of stealing the plane and helping criminals to escape justice."

"For the greater good," Angela said.

"Don, I cannot get involved in this as my career would be ruined, and as you know, I support my whole family," Jonathon said.

"It is a difficult situation for all of us I realise that," Don said.

"The difference for me is that I would still have to live here, and you could always go back to Scotland. Angela would be the conquering hero, and I would be a pariah in Tanzania. I would never get another job assuming I survived the interrogation that I would be subjected to."

"I agree with you Jonathon, and I think the solution for you is to leave these discussions, and go on a patrol of the northern district. That would take you well away from here, and you would not be involved in whatever we decide to do."

"I agree," Angela said.

"I see no alternative for me, but the ramifications of you doing what you propose is that you would never be coming back to Tanzania. That would mean that Toby would probably get your job, and my position would then become untenable in the game department. All the last few years of work would be undone in months."

"As I see it we have only two alternatives, these are to either give up the poachers to the army, and life goes on the same for us, or to help them get back to South Africa and hand them over to the authorities there."

"Don, you are overlooking one very important point. They will know your intentions and will almost certainly be capable, at some point, to either escape or, worse still, kill you. How do you propose to keep them under control?"

"Angela, is your mobile working in Tanzania?" Don asked.

"Yes but it won't in the remote areas as you do not have full cover in Tanzania."

"Is it working now," Don asked.

Angela looked at her phone and could see that she had two bars on her phone and said.

"I have two bars and that should be enough to make a call. What are you thinking," she asked.

"I cannot use my phone to make an international call as the military may well be listening. Is there a possibility that your phone is not clean?" he asked.

"I don't think so, as I have just taken out a new contract. What are you thinking Don?"

"I want to make a call to a friend overseas and ask him his advice. We don't have much time left, and we need to make a decision now on what to do."

Angela opened her purse and passed the phone over to Don.

As Don took the phone, there was a knock on the door. Don quickly erased the writing on the whiteboard and said, "Come in."

It was Constance bringing in the tea.

Don saw his opportunity and said to Jonathon.

"Jonathon, I am concerned that there is increased poaching activity in the northern district, and I would like you to assemble your team to leave in one hour. Please do a thorough investigation, and this should take you about a week. Is that OK?" he enquired.

"Certainly boss, I will get on to it straight away."

"Have your tea first," Don said.

Constance placed the tea on the desk and left the room.

"Quick thinking there," Angela said.

"What do you propose to do?" Jonathon asked.

"I would rather not say, and then you can honestly say that you had no idea," Don replied.

They drank their tea in silence.

"Don, I am leaving now and whatever course you take I wish you luck. You have been an inspiration to me, and I sense that I will not see you again. Please be careful."

The room was now charged with emotion. Don secretly knew what he was going to do, and also realised that he would never be allowed back to Tanzania. He looked at Jonathon, and could see that he was close to tears and said.

"Don't worry about me laddie. I will be OK, and we will meet up again. I think that I have a solution that will solve all our problems."

Don and Jonathon shook hands, and Angela stood up and said.

"Jonathon. I have not known you long, but I am sure that we will meet again, and I will look forward to that day."

She went to him, gave him a kiss on each cheek, and gently hugged him.

"Until we meet again," she said.

Jonathon took a long, last, look at Don. Then turned and left the room.

Don was despondent and took his seat behind the desk. He had said he knew exactly what to do, but the truth was he had no idea. The easy solution was to allow the military to take the poachers and carry on with his life. It would not harm his reputation, only his sense of responsibility.

Angela, aware of Don's dilemma, said nothing and waited for Don to speak. They sat in silence for a while and finally Don said.

"I cannot hand them over to be slaughtered. We have to get them to South Africa and to a safe house. Do you know where we could hide them safely?" He enquired.

"Yes, I know of a place, but what is your plan?"

"I don't have one," he said.

"But you just told Jonathon that you had a solution."

"I was trying to make him feel better."

"Well you convinced me. Who is this friend of yours that you want to call?"

"He is in the SAS, but I do not even know if he is at home."

"The SAS, how would that help?" she enquired.

"I don't know! All I know is that I need some advice."

Don opened the phone and dialled the international code for the United Kingdom and followed this with Allen's phone number. The phone seemed to take an age to get a ringing tone.

"Hello."

"Hi Allen, its Don."

"Hi Don, is everything ok?"

"Sorry to bother you again but we have a situation here that I need some advice on."

"If I can help, then you know I will. Please explain."

Don outlined the situation to Allen and the predicament he was in.

"Shit, it is never boring in Africa is it?" Allen said.

"'Fraid not, my mate, have you any ideas for me?"

"Yeah, get the hell out of there and get back home where you belong, how certain are you that this conspiracy is not just a figment of someone's imagination?"

"We have sufficient evidence to convince the most ardent disbeliever."

"This is way beyond your capabilities, and is just not a risk, but makes you a certain target. You are not trained to handle such a situation, who else knows that you have uncovered this conspiracy?"

"I have a reporter from Johannesburg with me that put the whole story together."

"Don, are you mad? If you have a reporter there now, get rid of him immediately!"

"It is a she, actually, and I cannot get rid of her without endangering her life."

"Shit! You certainly don't make things easy for yourself, do you?"

"Such is life in Africa, Allen."

"Look, I know that you are not foolhardy, but before I take this upstairs, I have to have some information that at least indicates that such a conspiracy is being contemplated. Can you send an email from that phone?"

"Angela, can I email from your phone?" Don asked.

"Yes you can." Angela responded, "Shall I show you how?"

"You can show me later, when we have finished our call."

"What is the address?" Angela asked.

"What is your email address?" Don asked.

Allen gave his address and Angela wrote it down in her writing pad.

"What details do you need?" asked Don.

"I need names, positions, places and when and how you believe this will happen. I will also give you a secure number that you can contact me on. I will talk to the boss now and transfer your message. I am not sure what his reaction will be though. I will get back to you shortly. In the meantime, do not do anything that would get you involved. Do you understand?"

"Allen, I am not sure that I cannot get involved as the army is on their way to collect the poachers. I cannot allow them to take them away."

"And how do you intend to stop them from taking them from you?"

"I don't know and hence my call."

"Well. You could get them into your plane and head for the capital. The Tanzanian police should help you."

"Allen, this is Africa, they would arrest us and then hand us over to the army. In any event, it is too late to go back now. I will head for the border in my plane and hide in Mozambique until you get back to me."

"It will take me a couple of hours to get back to you, but send the email now."

"Will do."

"Don, I want you to switch off your cell phone to save the battery and so they cannot trace you. In fact, can you charge it up now?" Allen asked.

Don turned to Angela, "Did you bring your charger for the cell phone?"

Angela nodded.

"Then put it on charge as soon as you can." Don said.

"We will charge the batteries as soon as we have finished our discussion." Don said to Allen.

"Good, once it is charged, turn it off. Then once you are down in Mozambique find somewhere to hide. That guy Khumalo can show you how. Then on every stroke of the hour switch your phone on for twenty seconds, that way we will be able to locate you."

"Are you coming out to help us?" Don asked.

"If I can, but this time I will need permission, and that will not be easy."

"I would feel so much better if you were coming out to help us."

"We will see, but in any event, we will contact you. Look after your bloody self and hang on as long as you can before you run for it, how will you keep control of your two prisoners?"

"I will get them to agree to cooperate, as they have no other alternative."

"Don, be careful. Can't you use some of your scouts as guards?"

"Not if we are going for the border I can't."

"OK. I will be back to you as soon as I can."

Don turned to Angela and said, "He needs names, details, places and anticipated timing of the conspiracy. Do you have this?"

"We," She emphasised the "we". "Have enough to convince your friend but whom will he tell?"

"He will consult his commanding officer who then presumably will take it to the British government."

"I am not sure that we have enough evidence to convince the Brits. It's more of a set of coincidences that are obviously related. The names that we have are not the top guys but would eventually lead to the top guys."

"We must send through what we have and then wait for his response."

Don and Angela sat together and composed the email giving all the information that they had. It did not seem so convincing, once they had written it out.

"We need to do something in the next two hours or it will not matter as the army will make a decision for us."

"We are about to make a decision that will affect us both for the rest of our lives and could even get us both killed. We must be certain that we are taking the correct action and have at least a semblance of a plan put together."

"You are right of course, but, unfortunately, we do not have the time to put together a detailed plan, so we will have to, "Suck it and see". There is no other way."

"Angela, I have now spent a few years in the bush and know how dangerous it is. You, on the other hand, have been brought up in a city with little, if any, experience of roughing it in the bush. Can you handle it?"

"My family have always owned land and in particular game farms. I have spent many days in the bush, and I have always kept myself fit. Yes, I can handle it."

"Let's get the prisoners in and explain the situation to them."

Captain Khumalo sat and listened to Don as he explained the position that they were in. He then asked for his comments.

Captain Khumalo looked at sergeant Khubeki and said in Zulu, "What do you think sergeant?"

"I think we are in the shit, whichever way we go. If we go back to South Africa, then we will receive the same treatment from the ANC. If we go back to Natal, we will be a problem for the NFP."

"Yes, but if we stay here, we will be dead by the end of the week."

"We are dead whichever way we go," he replied.

"Please speak in English," Don said.

"It is simple, Mr. Scales. It does not matter which way we go, we are dead anyway. The ANC will treat us the same as the Tanzanian army, the NFP will not want any evidence of their plans to be leaked. So what does it matter to us?"

"There is the possibility the once the story breaks that they will leave you alone."

"Bullshit and you know it!" was his response. "Even if we escape they will threaten to kill our family in Natal to dissuade us from blowing their cover, and to make an example of us."

"My newspaper can transfer your family to a safe house, and then organise relocation under different names," she said.

"All our family, do you realise what that would entail? There are ten members of my family and around twelve of sergeant Khubeki's family. They would find us whatever you tried to do."

"The army will be here in two to three hours to take you away. This is your only chance to get out. We can think of the best solution for you whilst we are on the move, there are no easy answers."

"Why do you care Mr. Scales? You are not South African; this is of no interest to you."

"You are my prisoners, and I do not allow my prisoners to be killed by any government. Just call me bloody minded but I do not accept that you warrant being condemned to death for poaching."

"But your men do this every day when tackling poachers."

"That is only when fired upon. We do not shoot unless we have to."

"And you actually believe that?"

"Yes I do and until I hear otherwise; I will always believe that."

"Then Mr. Scales, you have not been in Africa long enough."

"You may be right, but that does not change your circumstances here and now."

"Then what is your plan Mr. Scales?"

"Well there lies the problem. To get you out of Tanzania I have to trust you, is that possible?"

"You want my word as an officer and a gentleman that we will not try to escape and in the process harm you. Is that correct?" he asked with a smile.

"Something like that," Don said.

"Mr. Scales. We are condemned to death whichever route we take. Why would you trust a condemned man?"

"Out of necessity we need each other. We do not have the experience to evade capture. You do."

"We were trained by the best in the world, and it took years to perfect our skills. You believe that we can teach you how to survive and evade capture in the time we have available to us. It is an impossible task. Another question, what firepower would we have?"

"We wish to evade capture not cause a minor war. We would take a rifle each with us for protection from the wildlife, not to kill our pursuers," Don responded.

"And the lady here, how would she cope in the bush? There are no toilets, we would not allow you to wash or even clean your teeth. We would be travelling light and would have to cover fifty K's per day. I don't think so."

"I am fitter than you think, and I have even trained for the Comrades road race, so do not underestimate me," Angela said.

"You will be virtually running a marathon every day through dense bush and hilly terrain. That is a bit different to the Comrade's marathon."

"I will survive," Angela said.

"The people chasing us will be hardened bush fighters with a stamina that you would not believe. You would be the prize that would drive them on. If you were caught, the whole army would enjoy their pleasure with you. Believe me, you would not survive that."

"Ok, Ok, I hear you," Don said. "What if we take the plane and get as far away as possible, we must surely have a chance then?"

"That is a far better option," Captain Khumalo said. "I know of a landing strip that we used when we went into Mozambique on our sorties. Do you have a map of Southern Africa Mr. Scales?"

"Yes I do."

Don went into his drawer and found the map that he was looking for. He placed it on the desk so that they all could see it.

"Where is your airstrip?" Don asked.

Captain Khumalo looked at the map and pointed to a place called Msebi in the southern part of Mozambique.

"There it is," he said.

Don measured out the distance and said, "That is one thousand six hundred K's. That is just within the range of the plane."

"Then there is you solution," Captain Khumalo said.

"What will we need to take with us?" Don asked.

"We will need plenty of water and three days of food. We will only have one hundred and twenty K's to get to the border and into South Africa.

"Then let's get organised," Don said.

"There is only one problem," Captain Khumalo said, and rattled his shackles and handcuffs.

"Can I trust you," Don asked.

"We have no choice and neither do you. At least we stand a chance with you. I will give you my word we will not try to escape until we reach South Africa."

"That is not good enough," Don said, "I need your assurance that even when you get to South Africa you will not try to escape."

"And you will protect us in South Africa?"

"I give you my word," Angela said.

Captain Khumalo turned to sergeant Khubeki and spoke in Zulu to him. After a lengthy discussion, sergeant Khubeki nodded.

"We agree," Captain Khumalo said.

"Then let's get on with it," Don said.

Captain Khumalo rattled his chains again.

Don smiled and said, "Once we are on the plane, we have to make it look like we are taking you to Dar es Salaam for further questioning. Anyway, that is what I will tell my staff."

Don called for the guards and told them to take the prisoners to his Landrover. He then informed them he was taking the poachers to Dar es Salaam for further questioning. He instructed the senior guard to refuel his plane.

They all moved out to the Landrover, and the poachers were unceremoniously dumped in to the back. Meanwhile, Don collected four of the five-litre bottles of water, tea and sugar, and twelve cans of bully beef. He placed these in a rucksack and threw it over his shoulder.

"What about my holdall," Angela asked.

"Take only what you need and leave the rest behind,' Don said.

They drove to the landing strip, and the senior guard started filling the aircraft with aviation fuel. They quickly loaded the rucksack of food, and put the poachers in the rear of the aircraft. Don went round the plane doing his usual checks and he noted with dismay an immense cloud of dust in the distance. I could only be the military coming to collect the poachers.

"Is the plane refuelled?" Don asked the senior guard.

"Not quite boss," he replied.

"Then hurry up will you," Don said.

He noticed that the cloud of dust was rapidly moving towards his headquarters and that he did not have much time.

He checked his fuel gauges and saw that they were more than three quarter full, probably enough, but he would give the man a further two minutes. It seemed an interminable two minutes, and he shouted to the guard to finish what he was doing. The guard withdrew the feed line and closed the tank cap.

Don shouted, "All Clear."

The guard moved away, and Don started engine one, then engine two, and revved them to half revs. He then throttled back and released the brakes the plane started forward.

He taxied to the edge of the strip, applied the brakes and went to full throttle. He held it for ten seconds, then released the brakes and started to speed down the landing strip.

He had travelled halfway when he saw a Landcruiser appear near the end of the strip and then the vehicle was racing towards them. He saw the machine gun on the back of the Landcruiser, and he desperately urged on his plane. He knew that it would be close as the Land cruiser was closing fast. His speed was just too low to take off, but he had to evade the Landcruiser, now only one hundred yards away.

He pulled back on the stick and the plane shuddered but slowly rose from the ground. It was very close to stall speed and the alarms were sounding in his cockpit. He soared over the Landcruiser with only metres to spare and was airborne.

"Shit, they are shooting at us," Exclaimed Angela.

Don could not see anything and he was concentrating on clearing the trees at the end of the runway. As he went over the trees, he felt the undercarriage catch the top of one tree, and then they were away.

"Check for damage at the back," Don shouted above the noise of the plane.

"A few holes, but nothing vital as far as I can see," Captain Khumalo said.

Don levelled the plane and steered a course for Dar es Salaam. He would travel on this course for ten minutes and allow time for the radar to pick him up and establish his course. He then planned to drop below the radar and head for Mozambique.

His radio burst into life, and a voice said, "This is General Mfundi, and I am instructing you to return to base immediately."

Don looked at Angela and saw that she was petrified. He smiled and said.

"Don't worry love, we will look after you. We are certainly not returning."

Angela smiled and said, "I think we may have upset someone back there, I have never been shot at before."

The radio exploded into life again, and this time the tone was far more belligerent.

"Mr. Scales you will return immediately or I will instruct the air force to shoot you down. We have already scrambled two Mig fighters to intercept you. If you do not respond then, they will shoot. Do you understand Mr. Scales, you cannot escape."

Don ignored the threat and still held his course for Dar es Salaam.

The radio burst into life again, "Mr. Scales you have made your choice, and the Migs will be with you soon."

"Will they shoot us down Don?" Angela asked.

"Yep, if they can find us," he responded.

"My God, why are you so cocky?"

"That is simple my girl, saying it and doing it are two different things. We will go to tree height shortly, and we will be a bugger to find. Their radar will not be able to locate us, and the onboard radar is old hat. These planes are the original Migs, and they can only stay up for one hour. They will take some time to try and locate us. Then all we have to do is dodge them for about twenty minutes, and they will not have enough fuel."

"Twenty minutes being chased by jets does not exactly appeal to me," Angela said.

Don did not answer, but he brought the plane around in a turn towards Mozambique, and dropped to two hundred feet.

He observed the terrain around him then took it down to one hundred feet and knew, at this height, he would not be detected by radar.

"Keep a good watch out for the Migs," he said to Angela.

"I most certainly will," she responded.

"How are you doing in the back?" he shouted.

"We're OK," responded Captain Khumalo.

"Well hang on guys; we should be safe in another forty minutes."

"I am not sure, but is that a plane on your right," Angela asked.

Don turned in his seat and saw the Mig high in the sky but not headed in their direction. He knew if he kept low then it would be difficult for the Migs to see him. He was curious how they got there so fast. He must concentrate hard and use Angela and captain Khumalo as the spotters.

Keep your eye on that plane and tell me if it gets any closer." Don said to Angela, "Khumalo you keep a watch on the left for the other Mig."

Angela nodded but said nothing. It was evident that she was petrified and would be watching the aircraft to their left closely. Nothing would distract her as her life depended on her being observant.

"I see nothing on my side," Captain Khumalo said.

"If you see either of the Migs change direction towards us, let me know at once," Don said.

They flew for five minutes when Khumalo shouted, "The plane on your left hand side is turning towards us. I think that they have spotted us."

"How far away is he?" Don shouted.

"He is closing fast, probably 5 K's."

"Hold on everybody," Don shouted.

He went into a tight turn and saw the Mig at three o clock diving towards them. He quickly turned right into the flight path of the Mig and moved to full power to accelerate towards the Mig. They were closing fast, and Don saw the first cannon burst from the Mig. The cannon shells flashed overhead and the Mig immediately banked, and turned for a second run. Don followed the turn and dropped to fifty feet just clearing the trees below him and then flew in a zigzag pattern.

"Watch that Mig," Don said.

"He is turning towards us again and closing fact," captain Khumalo shouted.

Don turned again towards the Mig, and saw the Mig straight ahead at no more than 500 feet. He knew it would be close. He was desperately trying to guess when the first pilot would shoot again and judged it to perfection. He made a tight right hand turn and the cannon shells flew harmlessly by on his left hand side.

"Where is the other Mig?" Don asked.

"I cannot see him," Angela reported.

"Keep you eyes peeled. I do not want any surprises," Don shouted.

Don saw the river ahead and turned towards the middle of the river, putting the plane so low that he was almost touching the water. The trees on both sides of the bank were so close that he had barely 50 feet of space at each wing. He slowed the plane down and followed the river as it twisted and turned ahead of him. The Migs did not have the manoeuvrability to follow him and would wait for a straight section of the river were they could attack again. The river twisted and turned and then suddenly straightened for over a kilometre ahead of him.

"Can anyone see the Migs?" Don asked.

"Not on my side," Angela replied.

"I cannot see them," Captain Khumalo said.

"Do not relax," Don ordered.

The Mig suddenly appeared ahead of them coming in a straight line down the river towards them. Don reacted immediately and banked to his left and applied full power. The Cessna screamed and pulled up slowly with vibration from the straining engines shaking the plane. They cleared the tree line at the edge of the river, but the Mig was already shooting his cannon, and Don felt the plane shudder as the shells smacked into the tail wing of the Cessna. He felt the controls stiffen and become less responsive. He knew that they would not survive another attack, as he was now limping at tree height with very little manoeuvrability

"We have been hit," Captain Khumalo shouted.

"Can you see the damage?" Don asked.

"It looks like the tail wing is shredded but hanging on," Captain Khumalo replied.

"We need to go back to the river. That is our only hope," Don said.

He turned the plane back towards the river, but the plane was labouring, and would barely turn. They took a wide circle just as the Mig flashed past them with their cannon roaring. Again the shells flew harmlessly past, but the Mig pilot would have surely seen the damage inflicted from his previous run, and would know that they could not escape.

Don turned to the centre of the river and was following the twist and turns again and knew that this would make them a difficult target. The Migs could only have enough fuel for a few minutes or they would not get back to their base.

Don was in luck as the river was turning every 200 meters, and he knew that provided this continued, they would probably make it. The river was the border between Mozambique, and Tanzania, but he could not rely on crossing the border, as the Migs may well follow.

"Can you see the Migs?" Don asked.

"Yes, they are on our left but very high. Oh shit, they are both turning towards us," screamed Angela.

"How far away are they?" Don asked.

"I don't know," she replied.

"Khumalo move over and give me a range," Don ordered.

Khumalo moved across and shouted, "I would say about 2 clicks but closing fast."

Don had to think quickly as the two Migs would almost certainly shoot him down. What had the guy at combat school told him about manoeuvrability versus speed? You had to get close to them or have a twisting route. Don saw the river ahead of him and turned the plane across the line of the Migs and headed for the river. It would be close as the Migs were now screaming towards him.

He pushed the plane as low as he dared and could hear the tops of the trees hitting the undercarriage. As the Migs got closer, he turned hard to his right, and down to the river. He was heading towards the Migs but was following the twists and turns of the river. The first Migs cannon fire erupted around the plane but did not hit, the second Mig was waiting for the first to clear and then he opened up on the plane.

Don could do no more, it was either his time or he would be lucky. He was lucky, again the river twisted and he could follow the contours but the Mig could not. Now what? He would not keep getting away with his evasive action; he had to think of something else. The river twisted, and turned in front of him, and the riverside bush was closing in on both sides.

"Can you see the Migs," he shouted.

"They are banking round and forming up for another attack at about three clicks," Khumalo said.

"I am going to try and get under the bush so that they cannot see me."

"Do you mean land?" Angela asked, incredulously.

"No, I will try and fly under the overhanging branches as they stretch across the river here."

Angela was about to say something when Khumalo said, "I would suggest that you stay quiet so that he can concentrate on what he is doing. It may be the only chance that we have."

Don could see that overhanging branches from the trees ahead covered the river. He would have to be skimming the water and hope that none of the branches would hit the plane.

He brought the plane to just above stall speed, and set her as close as he could to the water. The overhead cover would only last for a couple of seconds, but this may be enough for the Migs to overshoot. The engine was labouring, and the controls were sluggish. Fortunately the trees gave the aircraft a couple of meters head clearance, provided he concentrated hard, he could maintain control.

Up ahead he could see that the river opened up to one hundred meters wide and the overhead cover would disappear.

"Chaps, keep a close watch as we will be coming out of this cover in a couple of seconds. Angela you look to the right and Khumalo you look to the left." Don said.

They broke through the trees and Don immediately opened up the throttles and lifted above the trees. Don spotted the Migs at altitude in front of him and raced down the river using the twists and turns as best he could.

"The Migs are high and in front of us," Don said.

"I see them," said Khumalo, "You carry on flying and I will watch their progress."

Don followed the river as low as he dared, but noticed that the plane was sluggish in the turns, and would be an easy target in the open. He was thinking what next to do when Khumalo shouted.

"The Migs are turning, and heading our way, they are closing fast."
"What now?"

"We keep evading by following the river course. Keep me updated on their approach, as we have to get our timing just right."

Khumalo watched the Migs and then shouted.

"They are coming in very fast and are lining up on the rear of the plane. I think they intend to attack from behind."

"How close are they?"

"They are about 2 clicks out but closing fast."

Don counted to five, and then swung the plane to his left as hard as he could. He felt the plane shudder, as it was hit, and sergeant Khubeki, who had been silent all the time, suddenly screamed.

"He has been hit." Khumalo shouted.

Don ignored Khumalo and kept the plane in a tight turn until he was well over the Mozambique border. He levelled the plane out and felt it shudder and vibrate across its length. There was nothing else that he could do. They were now sitting ducks with no hope of escape.

"Where are those fucking Migs," Don shouted his voice heavy with apprehension.

"I can't see them," Angela shouted above the racket of the plane.

"Khumalo, where are they?" Don shouted.

"They are very high, and seem to be leaving. I think we have got away with it." Captain Khumalo said.

"Watch them carefully as we need to be sure." Don said.

"They have gone," Captain Khumalo said.

"Then we were incredibly lucky," Don said.

Angela looked across at Don and saw the sweat on his face and the strain that he had been under. She felt a surge of feeling for this man and started to slowly weep.

"I, I am sorry," Angela said.

She was overcome with emotion, and Don looked at her and said.

"Don't worry gal, just let it all out. How is Khubeki?" Don asked.

There was a silence in the back of the plane, and Don had to ask again.

"How is he?" Don felt he knew the answer already.

"Dead." Captain Khumalo said.

"I am so sorry Khumalo; I had hoped we could all have escaped in one piece." Don said.

"So am I." Captain Khumalo said. "We go back a long way."

"Khumalo, we have to check the damage, or we will all be dead. Can you tell me what you see?" Don asked.

Captain Khumalo looked around the plane and reported what he could see.

Don took the plane down as slowly as he could. He was just above stall speed. The ailerons were shot out and the tail plane holding together by pieces. He was searching desperately for a flat landing spot. He estimated he could keep the old Cessna going for a couple of hours, but the wing fuel tanks had been ruptured, and were bleeding fuel.

He looked at his fuel gauges, and both wing locker tanks were displaying nearly empty. If he let them drain out, he would be down to his main tanks, and they would only have ninety gallons left. His predicament was that he had to get as far as possible into Mozambique to ensure that they were as close as possible to the South African border.

They managed to fly for just over three hours, and he calculated that he had travelled well over nine hundred kilometres. This would leave them close to six hundred kilometres from the border. He had to try and get closer, but he had to balance this with the inherent problem of lack of fuel, and the need for a safe place to land. They had to fly low to avoid radar. They flew on with the plane becoming less responsive and maintaining control was very difficult.

Don spotted a relatively flat area and said,

"We will have to land as soon as possible. There is a flat spot ahead, and I will try to land. We will first have a look round and see if there are any hidden obstacles."

Don moved the plane in a flight path that would cover the area. He circled the area and felt the poor handling of the plane. It was difficult to turn and was almost stalling. He pushed the throttles forward and felt the plane pick up speed. It would be a close call.

"Look to your left," captain Khumalo shouted, "It looks like an old landing strip."

"My God, you are right," Don said. "We may get away with it yet."

"Hold on to your seats, we are going to land."

Angela cried, "Oh my God," and gripped Dons arm.

Don reached out and grasped her hand and said,

"Listen my girl, we will get this bloody plane down in one piece or my name is not Don Scales."

Angela looked at Don with admiration, and she felt an unjustifiable confidence in this man. She knew at that point that should they survive, she could want to spend the rest of her life, with this arrogant Scotsman. He appeared implacable in the direst of circumstances and totally in control. As she watched him fighting with the aircraft, she felt an overwhelming affection for this man that she had only known for less than a day.

Don brought the plane round and could see the dark area of the old runway.

"It must have been used in the war," Don said.

"I think I know where we are, I think this is Dindiza," Captain Khumalo said. "I remember using this strip when we attacked the ANC training camps. We are about two hundred kilometres from the border."

"Are there any other bases nearby?" Don asked.

"No, if I recall, the nearest base is about fifty kilometres from here. I know this because that was the distance we would cover in one days march."

"What part of the border is two hundred kilometres away?" Don asked.

"The Kruger National Park." Captain Khumalo answered.

"Shit," said Don "The fence is electrified isn't it?"
"No, when the ANC took power they switched off the fences."
"OK, brace yourselves, we are going in."

Don could clearly see the outline of the old runway. He decided to make a pass over the old runway to see if there were any obstacles and look at the best approach. He banked the plane round and lined up with the old runway.

"I am going to have a look first so don't worry when we overshoot."

He took the plane down so low that it seemed that he was skimming the grass. He looked down the runway looking for anthills or similar obstructions. There was the odd anthill, but nothing that he could not avoid. He decided to bring the plane in as slow possible before he touched down.

He banked and turned and immediately felt the imbalance in the Cessna. The starboard engine was slowing down and was coughing for lack of fuel.

"Hang on guys; this could be a bumpy landing as we have lost the starboard engine."

He wrestled with the plane, but got it back on an even keel, and slowly turned towards the airfield. He had little power to straighten the aircraft and this was exacerbated by not knowing what fuel he had left. He brought the plane round and set it straight for the runway. The Cessna responded and slowly came in line. The plane almost glided towards the airfield.

Don fought the plane but kept it steady. The wheels touched down and Don brought the nose up by pulling on the stick and the plane gently settled on the grass. They hurtled down the runway, and Don applied the breaks slowly but surely. They came to a stop only ten meters from the bush. They had landed safely.

Angela leaned across, and gave Don a kiss, and said.
"You were bloody marvellous."
"Hardly a good landing, but I would suggest that we get out of here as quick as possible."

They all clambered out of the aircraft and stood by the plane.
"Can we make it look like a crash?" Asked captain Khumalo.
"What do you mean?" asked Don.
"Well if they find a burnt out plane they may assume that we did not survive, and this could give us precious time."
"They would be expecting four bodies and would soon see that there is only one."

"Then we need three more," said captain Khumalo laconically.

"Where would we find three more bodies?" Don asked.

"I could always find them." He replied.

"How and where?" Don asked.

"Look over there," he said.

Don and Angela looked to where captain Khumalo was pointing. There was evidence of an old graveyard.

"I noticed the graveyard when you were checking out the runway. We could use the old corpses as the other occupants."

"There are a couple of problems with that idea, in that we do not have the tools to dig up the graves,' Don said.

"They are only shallow graves, and we could use some old branches to get to the bodies."

"That is sacrilege," said Angela.

"It would give us valuable time to evade capture. I would risk upsetting God for the time it would give." Captain Khumalo said.

"I agree," said Don. "Let's get on with it. Angela, keep watch please."

Angela gave Don a severe look and was about to say something when Don said.

"Angela, we are not in a normal situation, and circumstances dictate how we survive. I appreciate your concerns, but I wish to get back safely, not just for my sake, but I feel responsible for your safety too. Please, for once, forget your disgust and work with us."

Angela grimaced and said.

"One day my man, I will make you pay for this, big time."

"If we survive this day then you can do as you wish." Don said.

"I will remember that," Angela said.

They moved quickly to the grave site and captain Khumalo located branches needed to dig up the shallow graves. They chose three graves that were closest to the bush as these would be the easiest to disguise. They began their macabre work and finally exposed the remains of the three bodies chosen.

The bodies had no flesh and were merely skeletal. They did the best that they could and carried the skeletons into the plane.

"To make this look like a crash we need to upend the plane. I suggest that we make a pit and turn the plane into it. This would at least look a little authentic." Don said.

"I agree," Captain Khumalo said.

They set about with their tools to excavate a small hollow in which they could upend the plane. They stripped the plane of its contents and stacked them neatly to one side.

"We do not have a compass." Captain Khumalo said.

"We can navigate by the stars," responded Don. "How much food do we have?"

"We have the bully beef, water and biscuits. More than enough to get us home."

"Will they not be suspicious if all the food is gone," Angela asked.

"Bloody good point," Don said.

"Put some back," Captain Khumalo suggested.

They replaced half of the food that they had brought with them, back into the aircraft.

"We need to drain some aviation fuel from the tanks to cover the aircraft. Otherwise, it will not burn." Don said.

They drained a couple of litres from the tanks and poured it over the engine. They used the branches to pitch the aircraft into the rift they had widened. They poured the remaining aviation fuel over the plane and looked for matches to set it alight.

"There is one small problem," Captain Khumalo said. "If we burn the plane they will be able to pinpoint our location. Is there any way we can delay the ignition?"

"We do not have timers," Don said.

"Then, before we set light to the plane, we have to clean the whole area as they will soon see the smoke. I would suggest that you leave that to me. I will clean the area and join you on that Kopje over there."

He pointed to a hillock some two kilometres away.

"How do we know that you will come back?" Angela asked.

"You do not," said captain Khumalo. "All I can say is that I give you my word that I will join you. We need each other. You would not last a single day evading the troops of Mozambique; I would not survive a day in South Africa without you. Trust me, I will return."

"How will you find us?" Don asked.

"That will be easy; I will simply follow your tracks. I will then erase them as I follow your path."

"We have no better option," Don said.

"In that case move out, take the food and water with you and I will see you shortly."

Don and Angela moved off at a good speed. They carried the food and water that was necessary for their survival. Don carried a Rigby 454 and Angela was carrying the BRNO 375. They had ammunition that weighed heavily on their back.

They soon came to the kopje, and Don said.

"We need to get about half way up, are you OK?"

"I am fine. I will follow you."

Don climbed up the Kopje until he reached natural cover that allowed him to see in all directions.

"We will settle here," Don said.

Don and Angela sat behind the rocks.

"I will move over there, this will give us an advantage if one of us discovered."

"Please don't leave me," Angela said.

Don looked at her and realized this seasoned journalist was vulnerable. He knew at that moment that he was desperately in love with her. He looked at this beautiful girl, and all he could think about was protecting her. He would give his life to see her safe. This was a most extraordinary feeling for him, never in his life had he felt this way.

Don leaned forward and took Angela in his arms and said.

"Lassie, nothing on Gods earth would ever take you away from me."

He kissed her gently and felt her body mould into his. She responded without even thinking and kissed him back. They held each other, and both felt incredible comfort in their closeness.

Their lovemaking was both reckless and dangerous, becoming a frenzy of desire. But, it was perfect for both of them. Angela had never felt so much love for anyone before, and Don was totally captivated by Angela.

Chapter 29

The Minister of Safety and Security, Petrus Madula, assembled his team around his boardroom table. Those present were his chief of staff Jacobus Ndlovo, his operations director Joseph Moroku, and agents John Marais, Peter Josephs and Petrus Msini.

There was tension around the table, as they knew that they were about to pass on some seriously damaging information that could be disastrous for the ANC.

"Gentlemen, what have you got to report on the activities of the group of generals that are planning an insurrection of some sort?" Petrus Madula asked. "Mr. Moroku, you will go first."

"Minister, we have infiltrated the Afrikaner group and have information that is quite disturbing. They are training in military camps in the Northern Province, the exact location we have not discovered, for ex and present military personnel in guerrilla warfare. This we know as fact as one of our agents, a man called Johan Kriel who is a warrant officer in the SAPS, has been working on this group for the last two years. He reports that the generals concerned are senior players in the SADF and are capable of raising a small army across South Africa."

"What are there names?" The minister asked.

"Unfortunately, we do not know the leaders yet, as they are operating under deep cover and have excellent security systems that prevent them from being identified. We do, however, suspect two generals, and they are General Lauberschagne and General Naude. They have both been under surveillance, but this has proven not to be beneficial to date."

"This is impossible, how the hell these generals can put together an operation the size that you are suggesting without direct communication?" The minister asked, angrily.

"They are professional's minister, and also privy to a good deal of the information that we are gleaning from our own sources. The worst problem is that Kriel went missing for two days, and we do not know where he went, or whether, he was taken somewhere."

"What is your prognosis on this group?"

"They are capable, and appear determined to overthrow the ANC by military means, if necessary. Our concern is that they are not operating alone."

"What do you mean," the minister asked belligerently, "is there another group at play here?"

"We suspect the NFP could be involved, but this is mere speculation at the moment".

"Why do you suspect the NFP?"

"We have been informed of an ex military group being captured in Tanzania while poaching elephants. We believe that they are trying to fund their operation by illegal poaching, and then selling the ivory overseas."

"Impossible, there would never be enough funds generated by such an operation. It is a ridiculous theory."

"Unfortunately, not, the selling price of prime ivory would net them one hundred and fifty thousand dollars. This would only have to be achieved four or five times, and then this would equate to around two to three million Rand, at the current exchange rate. This would go a long way to funding a small army."

"Who would pay such ridiculous sums for the ivory?"

"There are many rich Americans that would consider this an acceptable price for such a trophy. They could also make similar amounts by trading rhino horn in the Far East. This would be further augmented by the lion and leopard skins."

"How certain are you that this is happening, and do we have any Intel on these operations?"

"I will refer you to one of our agents that have been investigating these rumours.

John Marais is based in Natal and has been following up on these rumours. John, can you update the minister please."

"Yes sir."

"I heard the rumour of these operations in February and tried to determine who was responsible. I needed to know if it is an organised crime syndicate or something far more sinister. I hit a brick wall and could not bribe or extract any information at all on this operation."

"As you know, our operations to destabilise Natal have been ongoing. In the regions where we believe the anti-government operations are being organised, there are staunch NFP supporters. Yet, they will not give any information, not even to the moles that we have planted there. We do know that two men were captured, and another killed by an elephant in Tanzania. We know their names, and they were Reccies in the old regime. They were a particularly successful group and accounted for many MK soldiers prior to 1994."

"What are there names?" The minister asked.

"They are Khumalo, who is the leader, and had a rank of captain, Khubeki who was a sergeant, and Mnini who was a corporal. They were the best group in counter terrorism in Natal, and I am surprised that they were even apprehended while poaching."

"What do you mean?" The minister asked.

"These guys trained with the SAS from Britain and were seen to be as good as they are. It is unthinkable that amateurs would catch them. It just would not happen. We tried for years with our best operatives to catch them out and never succeeded."

"What are you implying?"

"They could only be caught by a similar group as themselves."

"Are you suggesting that the SAS are involved?"

"No, but it could be some ex SAS acting as mercenaries. This goes on all the time across Africa."

"The more I listen to this supposed plot the less plausible it sounds. This sounds like some idiotic plan by madmen."

John Marais gave a questioning look across to the operations director.

"Minister, I think we should not take this too lightly as we have evidence that there is subversive activity taking place. We have managed to stop most of their operations to destabilise Gauteng, but, that does not stop them trying again and again. You know about the Director of Internal Affairs who was murdered recently. We could not prevent it, but we managed to clean up the insurgents. They were all from Natal. Unfortunately, none of them survived, and we could, therefore, not interrogate them," said the operations director.

"That was rather careless, director," The minister said.

"They were all armed with AK47's, and did not intend surrendering. There was nothing that we could do."

"Is there anything further to add?"

"Yes, from our sources throughout the country, we have a list of a number of people that could be involved and we are tapping their phones and maintaining surveillance twenty four hours a day. This is stretching our resources, and we need a bigger budget to continue."

"Tell me, how much more?"

The operations director went through the detail and concluded, "three million Rand would cover the next six months."

"It will be allocated tomorrow. Is there anything further to add?"

"One last point minister, we have learnt of a couple of journalists that are following up on the poaching story. They appear to be operating freelance as their deputy editor told them to drop the story. The deputy editor is one of the people on our list and is under surveillance. He appears to be concerned by the reporters and they had a bit of a row in the main office, overheard by one of our agents."

"Are we following these journalists, and can they be helpful to us?"

"Yes they can, and we are letting them gather their information as they are able to talk to informants that would not talk to us. When we believe they have all the information, we will bring them in for interrogation."

"Do I know these reporters?"

"Probably not, one is a junior reported named Thomas Msibi and the other, Angela Murchin. She has been around for a couple of years."

"No, I do not know them. I am concerned that we need investigative reporters to do our job for us especially when you consider their resources compared to ours."

"We will keep a close eye on them minister and keep you updated."

"Do that. I want to take this to cabinet, but I need much more detail than I have so far. Make this your top priority and move quickly, I will, however, advise the president of your investigation and the results so far. Work with my secretary and organise a weekly meeting to suit my diary."

"Gentlemen, if that is all, then the meeting is closed."

The party stood and waited till the minister left the room.

"Sit down all of you," The Director of Operations said.

"You have all the resources that you requested, and I expect some answers sooner than later. Can we bring in these generals Lauberschagne and Naude?" he asked.

"We could, but we do not have enough evidence to hold them," Msini said.

"Since when did that bother this department?" The Director asked.

"These are not ordinary people. We cannot detain them. There would be uproar across the country!"

"Then get me the evidence, by whatever means, and get it fast."

"I can lean on Kriel a bit and see where that leads us. I have recorded every payment to him and all his dealings with the gangs in Jo'burg."

"Do that and also follow up on these journalists, where are they now?"

"Thomas Msibi has just returned from Natal and Murchin flew out to Tanzania yesterday where she is meeting the game ranger that caught the poachers."

"Why haven't we done that?"

"That would make it an official request from the government and that would warn the NFP of our investigations."

"Is there anything else that I do not know?"

"Not really. There is clearly a lot of detail in the surveillance reports and from the phone tapping. This has to be worked through and sifted for factual information.

The generals involved do not use their own telephones lines to communicate but use public phones at all times. It is difficult to know which phone they would use, but we managed to tape a portion of one conversation when one of their groups used the same public phone on three occasions. This is how we obtained names of the generals, but it was all coded and nothing conclusive."

"Well, I suggest that you try harder as the stakes are high and we must find out who are involved and what they are planning!"

Chapter 30

It was a long and difficult shot, and they had been hunting this man for three months. She knew that even if it were not a killing shot, she would disable him so that she could then make sure he was finished.

It was three hundred meters, and there was a cross wind and she would need to compensate for any deflection. She placed the cross hairs on his head and slowly breathed out. The man in the cross hairs was in deep conversation with another across the table. He was in the perfect position for the shot.

She gently squeezed the trigger and the rifle spat its deadly load. There was no need for a second shot as the bullet entered the side of the forehead and did not exit. The man was thrown off his chair, and then all hell broke loose.

There was screaming, and pandemonium, as the occupants of the shebeen, tried to escape in any way that they could. The only person that the target had been talking to remained as he checked on the condition of his fallen colleague. He could give no help.

Major Venter quickly broke down the rifle and placed it in her brief case that had been designed with a concealed base to hide the rifle.

She moved quickly and quietly through the veldt to the waiting car by the road. The driver had not heard the shot and jumped when she opened the car door. Without a word, spoken he just started the engine and drove off, only putting the lights on when he had cleared the confines of the township.

Major Venter stripped off her coverall and gloves, and dressed in her office clothes of a trouser suit, and high heels. She hid the coverall gloves and rifle in the hidden compartment under the passenger seat and combed her hair using the driver's rear view mirror. She felt no remorse for killing the man.

The target had been one of the biggest drug dealers, human trafficker and racketeer in Natal. He had paid off the police to leave him to his crimes, and had never been arrested or convicted of any crimes. The syndicate that he controlled would fall apart as soon as they heard that the boss had been killed. They would fight each other for leadership, and many would die in the process.

In the New South Africa people should not get away with such crimes against humanity. This was her reason for taking his life. This was now her ninth hit and all had gone successfully. She had never left a trace, and she would never be suspected of any of the assassinations. She suddenly realised that she had not picked up the cartridge case and had left if at the scene. As the rifle would never be used again, this was of little consequence, except that they would see the brand of the cartridge. From that, they could check the suppliers, but it was a 30.06, and thousands of hunters used this calibre rifle, so little of importance would be gained. Nevertheless, she was disturbed by her unprofessional conduct and would ensure that it did not happen again.

The driver took her to her rendezvous and dropped her off at the restaurant and drove off. He would destroy the rifle and the evidence of the clothing. She walked into the restaurant and sat at the bar with a gin and tonic. She could hear the police sirens howling as they raced past the front of the restaurant.

She finished her drink and slowly left the restaurant, and saw the waiting car. She opened the back door and slipped into the car. The driver, as before, did not speak, but started the car and moved off to the next rendezvous.

She repeated this procedure three times before the last driver dropped her where her car was parked. The car was hidden in a lock up garage, and even the last driver could not give any details of the car if caught and questioned.

The drivers that operated never knew more than three others in their cell. They never ever saw the other cell operatives and did not ask or seek to identify them. They were allotted a time and place with a final location. They were instructed not to communicate with any of their passengers except in an emergency. This had made the cells almost impenetrable, and even if they cracked one cell, they could not expose any others. Police radio frequencies were monitored, and an emergency plan of action was in place should they be detected. Each car used was supercharged, and the drivers were highly trained on evasion techniques. At all costs, they must protect the passenger, with maximum force if required. It was a sound anti-capture technique, and provided that they stuck to the plan, they would be untraceable.

Major Venter went into her house and straight to the bathroom to shower. She had a long, hot soak and scrubbed herself almost raw to remove any trace of the powder from the shot. She then settled in her lounge with a gin and tonic and watched the news.

The report of the shooting was headline news with a photograph of the victim, Benjamin Mtwetwe. The police report stated that it was a gangland hit and police, at this point had no suspects. They were investigating the murder, and the Chief of Police was adamant that an arrest would be made soon.

In the ensuing days, four more murders were reported as gang warfare broke out. All the gangs' members were now trying to consolidate themselves as Mtwetwe's successor. Major Venter had accomplished the removal of five leading criminals with her one shot. This at least made it worthwhile for her.

Chapter 31

Chen Yoo Soong watched as the dancers stamped to the rhythm of the drums. He particularly watched the female dancers, as they were topless and had sublime breasts that were firm and shapely. He was almost mesmerised by the rhythm and the dancing.

They had had the banquet and many speeches had been made welcoming the Koreans to Natal. Ling had responded on behalf of the Koreans and said that they looked forward to manufacturing their cars in South Africa. He expanded on this to state that many jobs would be created, as the plant would need support from the local manufacturers, which would almost triple the eight hundred locals the plant would employ. If the plant were successful, then they would expand output from their nominal one hundred cars per day to two hundred cars per day. This was greeted with a round of applause and Ling bowed and thanked the audience for being so attentive.

Meanwhile, Chen Yoo Soong was getting aroused by the dancers and would have to control himself. He would wait until they were in their suite at the Royal Hotel in Durban. He watched attentively throughout the dances.

Justice Nkabo said to Precious Cele, "You had better watch out, see how intently he watches the female dancers."

Precious laughed and said, "He is either very attentive or he is getting it off watching these young girls. Fortunately I am safe as I am much older and less attractive than these girls."

"They are a strange bunch don't you think?" Justice asked. "I will put money on the fact that Mr. Soong can speak perfect English, and uses the interpreter to give him time to think before he answers."

"We need them Justice, and you must not say anything that might rock the boat on this deal. There is far too much at stake."

"I know, it's just that they come across all high and mighty, and we have to cow tow to them. It irritates me that is all. They will never know how I feel about them; it is just their superior attitude, dealing with the natives!"

"For a new and better South Africa, I will put up with being a native for a couple of days."

"Yeah, I know that you are right, but, they just irritate me," he said.

"You are supposed to be a diplomat and the leader of this group. Behave man!"

Justice laughed and said, "As always you are quite correct."

The grand finale of the evening was the final explosive dance of the charging impi. This involved over two hundred warriors that were dressed in their tribal regalia, and enacted the encirclement of the enemy. The warriors were strung out in a line three deep, and were beating their assegais against their shields, and slowly advancing. It was a thrilling sight.

They moved in perfect unison with the regular beat against their shields. Their teeth and eyes were flashing in the dark as the large bonfire semi lit the area. All other lights were extinguished to add to the drama.

They moved forward in a rush and halted after ten meters. They increased the pace of the beating of the assegai and the front row started stamping the ground in the traditional dance. They rushed forward again, and then a single voice rang out and gave the order to initiate the bull's horns (an attack formation). They moved quickly and started to chant their war song. The assegais were raised and lowered with the chant and the blades glistened in the light of the bonfire. They stood and chanted whilst beating their shields again. And the threat of the dance was obvious.

It was impossible to remain impassive against such a magnificent sight of the impi performing their war dance and slowly inching forward. The Koreans were mesmerised by the spectacle, and nobody moved. Almost as if to do so would provoke an attack from these warriors. The war dance lasted more than three minutes, but it seemed no more than a moment. Suddenly the spell was broken, and on the single command of the leader, the spears were raised, and the impi charged the final fifteen meters across the courtyard, and encircled the group in the traditional bull formation.

The Koreans gasped as the spears were no more than a meter from them and each warrior were chanting their war song. The Koreans remained seated and did not move. There was another command and all spears were lowered as one and the chanting stopped.

The warriors slowly turned and moved away. There was a silence for almost a minute until Chen Yoo Soong stood up and started clapping. This was the signal for all the party to start clapping and the whole group rose to salute the warriors.

The rest of the evening was an anticlimax and the Koreans wished to go to bed to be ready for an early start the next day.

"Minister, what time will we be leaving tomorrow?" He asked of Justice Nkabo.

"As early or as late as you wish, we are in your hands and will leave whenever you are ready."

Mr. Ling turned to his colleagues and had a brief discussion in Korean.

"Minister, we would like to leave by 07.00hr tomorrow morning, we would like a small breakfast at 06.15hr. Will that be possible?" he enquired.

"Of course, I will arrange it immediately, would you like an early morning call?"

"That will not be necessary as we are all early risers and will no doubt be up and about by 05.30hr."

"As you wish Mr. Ling, then perhaps we can show you to your rooms for the night?"

"Yes that would be acceptable. But we may wish to meet tonight to discuss our plans for tomorrow. Do you have a conference room that we could use?" He asked.

"I will organise it straight away, and we will have an orderly there in case you require any refreshments tonight."

"Thank you."

The Koreans left the room talking to themselves, without so much as acknowledging the Minister. They got to the door and finally realised that they had not thanked their host.

Mr. Ling turned and said. "Sorry Minister, we have been rather rude by not thanking you properly for a wonderful evening. Please accept our apologies and we all wish to thank you for the banquet and entertainment that followed. It was an unforgettable evening, and we hope that we can have many more."

"Thank you and we look forward to hosting you again soon," the Chief Minister said. "Have a good nights rest and we will meet again on Thursday once you have surveyed the site."

The Koreans left the room.

"Unusual people," said the Chief Minister, "Can we do business with them?" he asked.

"I think so, they are the best opportunity for the NFP and the future of Natal," replied Justice Nkabo.

"This business with the poachers, whose idea was that," he asked?

"That was a collective decision sir, we were all aware of the operation. We did not tell you so that if it was raised you could in all honesty deny any knowledge," replied Justice Nkabo.

"I see, didn't work out too well, did it? And these were your best men?"

"There is no excuses sir; they were the best at that time. They cannot implicate the NFP as they were working on their own."

"All well and good, but what if they talk and implicate any of you, which would be disastrous for the party, particularly with elections coming up."

"That was the reason for the operation, sir. We had hoped to raise funds to fight the ANC at the next election. The Koreans will be a better bet I think."

"I hope so. We must ensure that there are no hiccups and that we give them everything that they need."

"We most certainly will, I want to raise another point with you, in private, if I may."

The Chief Minister looked at Justice and said, "Why in private?"

"It is a sensitive issue that I wish to run past you before we make it open for discussion."

"Very well, we can talk in my office."

They both left the room and walked to the minister's office. They entered the Chief Ministers office, and he motioned for Justice to sit down. "OK. What is so delicate that you cannot discuss this matter with the other senior ministers?'

"We have been approached by an anti-government group run by the old generals. They are planning to overthrow the South African government and are seeking our assistance."

"Are they mad? We could not possibly be seen getting involved in such a matter. In fact, we should report this immediately."

"I understand your apprehension, yet we have nothing to lose by talking to their representative."

"You are talking about treason, for that you can lose your life in South Africa!"

"We are already embarking on a campaign that could hardly be called pro ANC. We have solid reasons to fight the ANC both in Natal and their own backyard in Gauteng."

"Our issue is restoring our position in Natal, not planning to take over South Africa."

"It is not the generals plan to take over South Africa. They only wish to remove this government that appears hell bent on ruining this country. Corruption is rampant, crime is the worst in the world and nepotism is rife. You cannot obtain any government contract without giving incentive payments to the board that approves such contracts. Black empowerment is for ANC cadre only, and all other groups are excluded. Is this why we struggled for liberation?"

The Chief Minister looked closely at Justice Nkabo and said, "You make your point well Justice, but that is emotion talking rather than logic."

"My logic suggests that we take the time to talk to these generals and see what they say. In the event of us not deciding to choose their side, we will at least be able to report who they are. For us, it is a win: win situation. How can we lose? On the one hand, we throw our lot in with this group and achieve supremacy, or, on the other hand, if we do not get what we want, we expose them, and win that way."

"You really are a cunning bastard Justice. But I agree with your reasoning as long as we can distance ourselves from any possible ill consequences."

Justice Nkabo smiled. The Chief Minister was actually giving the go ahead. "I will attend to the matter and keep you informed. You will at no time be associated with the generals and there will be no trace back to you. I will guarantee you that."

"Then so be it. I will leave it in your capable hands."

"Thank you Sir."

"Now it is time to retire as we have a long day tomorrow. Good night Justice."

The Chief Minister rose and walked off towards his office door ushering Justice Nkabo before him. He then said, "Justice, be careful, as you must not underestimate the capability of the ANC."

"I will try not to," he replied. "Goodnight."

The Chief Minister walked down the hallway to his chambers and Justice watched him until he was out of sight around the first corner. He felt a shiver of excitement, as the games were about to begin. This was politics at its best, and he would enjoy the negotiations, and the action that would most likely take place. I will send word to General Mkondo tomorrow, he thought.

The Chen Yoo Soong parties met Justice Nkabo, at the reception of the Royal Hotel, in Durban and were taken to the proposed site in Isidingo. They had police outriders on motor cycles, clearing there way. They had a police car in the front and at the rear of the two cars heading towards Isidingo with sirens blaring out.

The site was levelled, and had road access to the centre of the development site. The site extended to thirty hectares with plots of five hectares being marked for development with the Soong Corporation being allocated ten hectares. Each plot had its own transformer with the main pylons carrying the electrical supply running adjacent to the west side of the marked land.

The party walked around the site and inspected the transformers to ensure that there was adequate power. The development engineer took copious notes. They talked in Korean at all times and Justice Nkabo left them too it, and went and sat in his car. He had the car engine running and the air conditioning on, it was still early morning, but the temperature outside was still thirty two degrees. He looked at the Koreans they were unperturbed by the heat and were checking levels, infrastructure and access.

They were on the site for two hours and Justice Nkabo thought. "What the hell can you look at for two hours on a flat site?"

He watched Mr. Ling break away from the party and walk towards his car. Justice Nkabo opened the door of his car and stepped out into the oppressive heat.

"Is there anything else that we can show you?" He asked.

"That will not be necessary." Mr. Ling said. "We will take the site and we can start negotiations immediately."

"We have booked a conference room at the Royal Hotel for the next three days. We can return there now if you so wish?" Justice Nkabo said.

"Mr. Soong will be leaving immediately and we must drop him off at the airport. We would then like to travel around Durban to see the area and also the township where you believe that we can source our labour." Mr. Ling said.

"Very well, we can travel in my car and the chauffer can take Mr. Soong back to the airport." Justice Nkabo said.

"We would prefer to travel together to the airport and we will go on from there on our tour." Mr. Ling said.

"That is fine." Justice Nkabo said.

The entourage then left for the air port with the police clearing their way. They arrived at the air port and disembarked and moved into the VIP room. Justice Nkabo cleared the passport control for Mr. Soong. He returned with the passport and said.

"I trust you enjoyed your brief stay in South Africa Mr. Soong."

Mr. Ling was about to answer when Chen Yoo Soong held up his hand and said.

"It was what I expected South Africa to be like, Mr. Nkabo." He said in English.

Justice Nkabo smiled, and said.

"I hope that you will return soon, have a good flight."

The Korean party then had a five minute discussion in Korean with Chen Yoo Soong speaking to each man in turn. Then he bowed and left them to be transported to his aircraft.

"Gentlemen, can we now look at the township and then Durban?" Justice Nkabo asked.

"That will be fine. Please lead the way." Mr. Ling said.

Justice Nkabo led the men from the VIP room and took them to the waiting cars. The chauffeurs immediately jumped out of their cars and opened the doors for the party. The Koreans all sat in one car and Justice Nkabo entered the second car. The police escort moved off with sirens blaring.

They toured the township and Justice Nkabo called Petrus Nkumu, Johannes Mchunu and Precious Cele. He advised them that the Koreans wanted the site and would be coming back to the Royal Hotel in one hour. They would start the negotiations then.

They moved through the suburbs of Durban and then returned to the Royal Hotel.

The party disembarked and moved into the hotel following Justice Nkabo. He led them through to the conference room and said.

"Would you like some refreshments we have at least one hour before lunch?"

"We would like some iced tea." Mr. Ling said.

Justice Nkabo called the waiter and gave the order for iced tea for all the party.

"Can I take your order for lunch at the same time?" The waiter asked.

"No, we will look at the menu later." Justice Nkabo said.

They sat around the table, with the Koreans on one side and the NFP representatives on the other. They waited for their drinks before starting discussions.

"Mr. Ling, do I need to introduce to you again the members of our party?" Justice Nkabo asked.

"That will not be necessary, as we know all the people present and their positions. We would like to discuss what we have seen today prior to negotiating and contracts." Mr. Ling said.

"Please do." Justice Nkabo said.

"We have a number of concerns that we would like to table. These are."

He opened his notepad and consulted his notes.

"Firstly, the township that we saw was not of a very high quality with a good deal of shacks and poor houses. Does this reflect on the quality of the staff that we would be employing?" Mr. Ling asked.

"I do not think so." Justice Nkabo said. "The poor quality housing and the conditions in the township reflect the legacy of the apartheid years. They have not been upgraded as the level of investment is huge. We have electrified most homes and they do have running water and toilets. The demand is, at present, beyond our fiscal means. The people living there have no choice, and with investment from companies like yours, we will be able to uplift the area over time."

"Is the education standard of sufficient level to be able to operate complex equipment?" Mr. Ling asked.

"The general education level is lower than we would like, but is improving with each year. There are many other companies in the area that are manufacturing and they draw their staff from this township and others in the area." Precious Cele said.

Mr. Ling looked at precious Cele and said.

"Would it be possible to channel your answers through one person, this will help on speeding up the meeting; we have a lot to cover."

"Mr. Ling, we all have skills in different areas and will respond with the person that understands your requirements in each area. We are not perturbed by your questions being answered by the relevant person in the room as that is why they are here." Justice Nkabo said.

"As you wish, Mr. Nkabo. Do you have authority to sign any agreement that we conclude?" Mr. Ling asked.

"Yes we do." Justice Nkabo replied.

They discussed the other points that Mr. Ling had and that took them through to lunch. They ate there lunch and reconvened in the conference room. They started negotiations in earnest and they went on through till it was dark. They had been negotiating for six hours and still had not concluded a deal. There were problems associated with repatriation of profits that conflicted with the exchange rules of South Africa. They were not happy to have limitations on the repatriation of funds or dividends.

The tax burden they said was too high, and the cost of capital in South Africa was excessive, and they would prefer to finance the project from their own capital sources. The tax break that had been discussed earlier was not sufficient, and they said they needed at least a ten year tax break with depreciation over the same period. The Natal government would generate far more tax from VAT and employees tax than they would from corporation tax as the plant would not be profitable for a number of years. They would be generating over a thousand jobs at the plant and construction staff alone would be around five hundred people. The support industry required would create a similar amount of jobs and their total investment would be around two billion United States dollars. This would be the capital inflow for the natal government. This surely outweighed any short term gain in corporation tax.

They negotiated for the next day and finally reached agreement on the morning of the third day. Justice Nkabo had conceded many points but had also maintained the credibility of his government. The deal would bring a huge capital injection into Natal and the port of Durban would also see major benefits from the project. In all, he was happy with the agreement, and so where his colleagues.

"Mr. Ling, I think we have an agreement and we will get the contracts drawn up and they will ready for signature tomorrow. We have just one more point to cover and that is the supply of armaments to our party." Justice Nkabo said.

"Mr. Nkabo, on signing the contract we will ship ten thousand semi automatic rifles, they are similar to the AK47, and known for their durability. We will also supply one million rounds of ammunition. Included in the shipment are one hundred rocket launchers and one hundred hand-held anti tank guns. They are already crated and will be shipped immediately. They will be shipped as construction vehicles for the development of the site. I trust that you can manage them through customs?" Mr. Ling asked.

"That will not be a problem, please inform us on what ship they will be arriving, and we will ensure the rest." Justice Nkabo said.

Chapter 32

Commissioner of Police, Pieter Verkramp, called in his two key officers that were searching for the killer of Molefe. He had been following there progress and noticed, with some satisfaction, that they still did not have a clue about the assassin's identity. They had searched through all their data bases and found nothing. They had come to a dead end.

There was a knock on the door and he said, "Come in."

Captain Els and Sergeant Ramasey entered the office.

"How long have you two been on this case? The commissioner asked.

"It has been three months now," Captain Els said.

"And what do you have to show for the three months? He enquired.

"Well. We know that the rifle used was a 30.06 and that Molefe was shot from the offices of Bailey and Bailey Attorneys. We found the coverall and gloves, and forensics have identified them as a common brand that can be obtained locally in any number of stores. The size of the gloves and the coverall were small and that would indicate that the assassin was either very small or female."

"Which do you believe it is?" The commissioner asked.

"To be honest we are not sure, Jay believes it is a woman whereas I believe it is a small man."

"Why do you believe that it is a woman Jay? The commissioner asked.

"We found a long blonde hair on the outside of the coverall which forensics has suggested is a woman's hair. They are running DNA tests now but due to the backlog the results will not be available for another month."

"And why do you believe it is not a woman Captain Els?"

"The hair was found on the outside of the coverall and could have been picked up from the waste bin rather than left behind by the assassin. It is also difficult to imagine a woman being an assassin. In my entire working career I have never heard of a female assassin. She would require intensive physical and mental training to a level that would probably be too difficult for a woman."

"Is that just your prejudice against women or based on fact?"

"I was applying logic sir," Els replied.

"Jay, what convinces you that the assassin is female?"

"There are a number of factors, the assassin's height, the fact that the police would not be looking for a female. This would allow the assassin to escape, as the police officer searching the building would not necessarily take notice of a woman leaving the building. The mindset would be that they were searching for a man."

"And what of the arduous training that captain Els refers to, do you believe that a woman is capable of such training?"

"I have no doubt, the Israelis use woman very effectively in their armed forces."

"You make a good point," Els conceded.

"The rifle used is a 30.06 which has little recoil and is very accurate. The bullets used are soft nosed and they break up immediately on impact. The fragments found at the murder sites can give an indication of the rifle used but it appears that none of the rifle markings are repeated. This would indicate that the rifle is only used once," Jay said.

"And what of the latest killing?"

"We found a casing that clearly indicates that the rifle is a 30.06, yet so far we have discovered nothing else. We are still waiting for the crime scene report and when we get that we will investigate further," Els replied.

"Do you believe that it is the same assassin?"

"Without a doubt, the modus operandi is the same. The killing shot could only have been made by a trained sniper, so yes, I believe that the killing is the work of our assassin. There is also the possibility of it being a vigilante as all the people killed were well known gangsters." Els said.

"Jay, do you concur with captain Els?"

"I do sir." Jay responded.

"You both understand that the mayor is getting hot under the collar about your lack of progress. You have been given the resources to solve this case or at least make some headway. Captain Els, you need to get on top of this case and get me some results very quickly. Do you understand?"

"Yes sir, I do. We are working around the clock on this case and we are sure that we will get a break soon. Perhaps you could help sir by speeding up the forensics on the hair so that we can at least start a DNA search."

"I will look into this straight away. Now you may leave and make certain that by next week we have something concrete to go on."

Captain Els and sergeant Ramasey stood up and left the office.

The commissioner watched them leave and then also left his office. He left the building and walked two blocks to the public phones. He dialled a number and when answered, said, "Phoenix 224."

"Public phone number 45," was the response.

The commissioner checked his diary and saw that public phone number 45 was three streets away on West Street. He quickly walked the short distance and found the phone booth was already in use. He waited patiently until the caller was finished and then moved into the phone booth. He dialled the number and waited for the answer. He gave his code of 224 and waited for the response.

"It is a difficult day for the police."

"All days are difficult for the police lately." The commissioner replied.

It was a simple code that could be easily overheard but would not be suspicious. If the reply had been anything other than the exact words used, then they would know that the commissioner had been compromised.

"Make your report."

"They believe that they have evidence that the assassin is a female and they have a strand of hair that they can run DNA tests on. I cannot delay the investigation further as my position will become compromised."

"Agreed, we will handle it from our side. If you have any other information then call again using the call sign, Phoenix R22. If they find out the identity of the assassin then call immediately but use the code Phoenix X51."

"I understand."

The commissioner hung up and walked back to his office. He was trying to put a plan together that would slow down the investigation without arousing suspicion.

Chapter 33

The atmosphere was tense in the boardroom. There were five Generals and their adjutant sat on one side of the table, whilst four of the NFP representatives sat opposite them. There was no apparent chairman.

"Gentlemen, we are all here to discuss a very difficult topic. I understand the reluctance for any one party to begin proceedings, but unless we have an open and frank discussion, we will not achieve anything," General Lauberschagne said. "Perhaps it will be easier if we put forward our case and our plan of action, then General Mkondo, I would like you to respond."

General Mkondo merely nodded but said nothing.

The general looked around the table and decided to begin with the state of the country, the sectarian violence and the lack of control by the ANC. He also went on to explain how the whites had been marginalized and had little if any input on how the country was governed. He finished by saying. "It is time to do something about this situation and we know that the NFP feel the same way. You have taken serious losses in Natal and are currently seeking to rearm by utilising funds from poaching in Tanzania. There is also the rumour of a Korean industrialist investing in Natal that may be prepared to finance arms from one of his manufacturing plants in Korea. Is this correct?" General Mkondo looked at his colleagues and then said.

"That we are unhappy with the current situation is correct, we are looking to rearm to protect ourselves rather than looking at taking over the country. We have no desire to become the next government, but we will not be driven out by the ANC. What you are suggesting would be treason, and we are not prepared to take such a step."

General Lauberschagne smiled, and then said.

"Come now General Mkondo, we need to have an open and frank discussion. If your objective was merely to protect yourselves then why would you require heavy armaments to do so?"

"I do not know where you get your information from, but what heavy armaments are you referring to?"

"We have seen your shopping list, and field guns are not merely for protection."

General Mkondo smiled and said.

"I do not know what you are talking about, and your informant must be misinformed. We have no such shopping list, as you refer to it."

"General Mkondo, we have to be open with our discussion or what will we achieve? There is no point in trying to deceive when what we have said is obviously true. Nevertheless I will continue as if we do not come to some agreement today then both our positions is untenable. It would be obvious to any third party that you knew when you came to this meeting what the agenda would be and to try and deny it would only make matters worse."

"What is it that you wish me to say?" General Mkondo asked.

"That is simple general. Just state your position and we can then proceed."

"I thought I had," General Mkondo responded.

"In that case then there is no further need for discussion and we will proceed without you. We have the capability to raise the forces required to create a solution to our problem. We would have preferred to combine forces with the NFP, but it is not necessary to do so as we will still achieve our objective. If you had been prepared to work with us, much bloodshed would have been avoided. There would have been a greater acceptance of the new government across the world and recovery would have been much quicker. If you force our hand, then we will have to move quickly. We would have preferred to work with the Zulu nation to achieve a bloodless coup. This scenario would have been most preferable."

"What would you have proposed once we had achieved this so called bloodless coup?"

"Does your question mean that you are interested?"

"We came here to hear your proposals but not necessarily to agree with you."

"Come now, do you really expect us to believe that you would walk away and say nothing?"

"That is what we agreed to, and we would stick to that agreement. If your actions did not interfere in Natal, we would allow events to take their course."

"Oh, I See. You will be complicit, but you will not take part in any military action, is that it?"

"You are correct to a certain point, but we would want assurances that we would be left to rule Natal as the government."

"So you would win either way. If, for some reason, the coup were a failure, you would force a weakened ANC into concessions for Natal. If we were successful, then you would automatically take over Natal. Would this government then report to the military commanders or would it be autonomous?"

"We would see it as an autonomous government with all aspects of governance being controlled by the Zulu's."

"I understand what you want but there are not only Zulu's in Natal. According to our studies, Zulu's only represent 54% of Natals total population. You would be fighting not only the Zulu's that support the ANC, but all the other sections of the population that are not Zulu's. You would set family against family, and there would be insurrection daily. You would not have sufficient resources to put down any determined resistance. You would also not have the support of the Asians or the whites. It would be chaos."

"The same would apply to your forces if they tried to take over the country. The black population would never allow it to happen again."

"Do you not think that we have thought of all the possible scenarios? It would not be apartheid again nor would it be a white government, we all know that would never succeed."

"Then what do you propose as it seems that we may have misunderstood your motives."

"All I will say at present is that Natal would become a country within Africa and not a province. If you will sign a document clearly indicating that the NFP will become party to such a proposal, then we will reveal our plans. This document will be copied and stored in a number of different locations and will be released to the press if you default in any way, do you understand?"

"I am authorized to discuss with you your plans but not authorized to sign any agreement that would clearly indicate the NFP complicity in such a coup. I would need to talk to my superiors prior to signing such a document."

"How do you propose to get such authorisation?"

"I will need to call the ministers and get their approval, but I cannot call them without the detail, as this would be pointless."

"What was your brief before you came here?"

"To discover your plans and see if it would benefit Natal."

"It will most certainly benefit Natal, but before we release any further information I need to discuss your requirement with my colleagues."

"We now require you to leave all your cell phones with us and you will be placed in a room which will be guarded. Please understand that we cannot allow you to interrupt our plans, and we will prevent you from doing so."

"Are you arresting us?"

"Just call it taking precautions. You will not be in any danger at any time. We will merely prevent you from leaving until the coup is underway."

General Lauberschagne turned to one of his colleagues and said. "Captain will you please show these gentlemen to the room that we have put aside for them." The captain stood up and said.

"Gentlemen if you will follow me."

The captain led the NFP delegates away to an anteroom. He opened the door and said.

"Please place your cell phones in the tray."

The NFP delegates took out their phones and placed them in the tray.

"Please forgive me but I will need to check. Could you take off your jackets please?"

The NFP delegation took of their jackets and handed them to the captain. He quickly checked the pockets and then frisked each delegate. He found no phones.

"We just have one more test, and then we will bring you whatever refreshments that you require and leave you in peace."

He took out what appeared to be a metal detector and passed it over each delegate. On General Mkondo, it started buzzing.

"Can I have the bug that you have secreted away please general?"

The general smiled and said.

"One has to try."

He took hold of a small round pin from his shirt lapel and handed it to the captain. The captain looked at the bug and said.

"This would be useless in these offices as all signals are jammed and nothing would get through. I will just check again if you do not mind."

The captain checked the general again and found nothing.

"Now what can the orderly bring you?"

As soon as the NFP delegation had left the room General Lauberschagne asked.

"Any comments gentlemen?"

"Yes," said General Naude, "Do you honestly believe that we can trust these people, they strike me as being totally untrustworthy?"

There was mumbled consensus around the table.

"Do we have any alternative?" General Lauberschagne asked.

"When going into battle, the last thing that you want is an ally playing both sides to meet their objective."

General Naude said. "With the NFP in control of Natal, that would take away a great deal of opposition. We have, as you well know, various scenarios to cover all contingencies."

"I am concerned that they will at some point change sides to suit their own ends, do we have a scenario to cover such an eventuality?" General Beyer enquired.

"As you know it is difficult to cover all scenarios, but, in this instance, we have run what our best reaction would be, and we do have a plan of action. My adjutant captain Brooks will cover this when he returns. It is not an ideal situation but if we can get the Zulu's on our side, this would make life so much easier. The economists have run numerous scenarios on world reaction with and without Zulu support. They feel that our planned coup would be better received with a Zulu involvement rather than purely white versus black."

"I would suggest that we allow the general to talk to their ministers but monitor their conversation throughout. If there is any doubt about their sincerity, then we hold them on the premises until we have completed our missions." General Naude said.

"I agree," General Lauberschagne said, "Are there any dissenters?"

All the generals nodded their assent.

Captain Brooks re-entered the room and said.

"Could I speak to you Sir?" he looked at General Lauberschagne

"Yes captain, do we have a problem?"

"Possibly sir, I found a transmitter on General Mkondo and the technical guys say that it has a maximum range of 5 kilometres. This would mean there is a back up party somewhere out there that are on standby."

"I knew we could not trust these people!" General Naude said.

The other generals agreed by adding their comments.

"Can we locate the group by using the bug?" General Lauberschagne asked.

"They are in the process of doing that now sir."

"Ascertain their strength and then send out a group to capture them. Colonel Du Toit should be able to manage. Keep me informed of your progress."

He turned back to the generals and said, "Do not give any indication that we know that there is a back up group as we will use this against the ministers later once we have captured their team."

"Captain Brooks bring the delegates back to this room," he ordered.

The delegates filed into the room in silence and took up their positions opposite the generals. They waited for the generals to talk.

"Gentlemen, we have discussed your request and agree to allow you to council your ministers. I would also tell you that we will not leave these premises until we have an agreement. This may well be that we agree to differ, but it will not be left uncertain how we propose to move forward. I trust that you understand this."

"We understand perfectly, and we will do our utmost to settle with an agreement, that we can take forward." General Mkondo said.

"You may make a call, but I must tell you that the call will be monitored, and should there be any sign of treachery, the line will be cut. Do you understand General Mkondo?"

"Perfectly," General Mkondo said.

"Captain, take the delegates to the communication room and give them a secure phone to make their call."

"Yes sir. Gentlemen will you please follow me." The delegates stood up and followed the captain from the room. General Meyer, who had sat quietly during all the discussion, raised his hand to ask a question.

"Generals," he said, "I do not believe that we can totally trust these people and feel that we should have a plan to incriminate them by association should they try and walk away. If one studies the dynamics of this group, it is evident that, with the exception of general Mkondo, they are all expendable. We know from past experience that general Mkondo is totally and utterly ruthless. If events today were not to unfold to his liking, he would not think twice, about eliminating these delegates, such that he could cover his tracks completely. This is the kind of man that we are to form an alliance with?"

The other generals grumbled agreement and looked to general Lauberschagne for guidance.

"The problem as I see it," General Lauberschagne said, "is that we do not have a lot of other options in the matter. If we proceed without the NFP, we will be fighting across the whole country against every group.

With Natal secure, we can subdue the central and northern provinces. This I believe is why we should persevere with the current strategy and do our utmost to achieve this alliance."

"Our original plan did not include the NFP, and we felt then that we could achieve our objectives without them. I appreciate the advantages of having a secure flank but would it be secure with these people?"

"I believe so," General Lauberschagne said, "They would be supportive as they would benefit far more by working with us than with the ANC."

"For as long as it suits them," General Du Plessis said.

"Not if you work it through, they have to commit and involve their forces. They could not deny complicity after that," General Lauberschagne said.

"They would also have the benefit of our forces in Natal to support them. These, as you know, are highly trained commandos, that NFP does not have in any numbers. It would be madness not to optimise your forces to the best of your ability. They may be ruthless, but they are far from mad."

"Gentleman, we have chosen a course of action and decided to form this alliance as a group. We have come this far, and we should not be questioning that decision. Whether we like them, or their tactics, it is necessary to deal with them to achieve our objectives."

"You are correct, as usual." General Naude said. "We must establish a united front to achieve our goal.

"Thank you General Naude. Perhaps we can now move on to analysing the possible NFP responses to our proposal."

The generals discussed the possible scenarios and ultimately reduced them to three likely outcomes. They Zulu's would no doubt be difficult to negotiate with, as they knew that the third force troops would need assistance to achieve their goals. The Generals broke their responses down to three possibilities and these were:

(1) They would cooperate and become part of the plans to overthrow the ANC

(2) They would agree to have no involvement in the planned coup but would offer no resistance to the attempt, provided they would reach their goal of self governance

(3) They would decline all connection with the coup and would react totally against it

First prize to the generals was alternative (1), and they had already put in place the necessary plans in this eventuality. The second option they had discussed would not be perfect, but at least they would stop the ANC in Natal from participation. This would drastically reduce the forces against them, and they would control a large portion of South Africa. For this second option, the NFP would need time to rearm their forces and would be assisted by the generals. This would also show their collaboration, as the document trail would clearly indicate that they were involved.

They concluded that in reality options (1) and (2) were in essence the same with the probable same conclusion. Option (3) was their greatest concern. If they had to take control of the country, they would have to subjugate the whole of the country. They had their plans and strategies in place, but this would be a far more difficult campaign.

General Mkondo called Justice Nkabo.

"Nkabo."

"Minister, this is general Mkondo, and I need to talk to you, but I must warn you that this call is being monitored."

"Are you with the Generals?" Nkabo asked.

"I am sir, and they are proving to be very difficult. They wish for a document to be ratified that clearly implicates the NFP in the proposed coup. They feel that we are not committed and will sit on the fence until we can make our own moves. They will not give any information on their plans until they have a written document from us stating our involvement."

There was a long pause and General Mkondo asked.

"Are you still there?"

"I am thinking. Where are you?"

"I do not know exactly. They collected us at Lenasia airport and then took us in a totally closed van to this destination. We were driving for at least three hours, I cannot say exactly where we are, but I think it is in Limpopo or thereabouts."

"Do you know the Generals involved?"

Captain Brooks tapped general Mkondo on the shoulder and shook his head.

"We will disconnect you if you answer or try to answer that question." Captain Brooks said.

"As I said, this call is being monitored, and they will cut me off if I mention any names." General Mkondo said.

"I understand. We cannot be seen to be involved and hence we cannot sign any document. We can only give assurances that we will not interfere in their actions provided that they do not try to overthrow Natal."

"Unfortunately, that will not be acceptable to them. In my opinion, it would be in our best interest to work with them. They are very determined and also appear very capable. Can I suggest that you join us in these discussions?"

"I will call you back on your cell phone."

"That is not possible, as they have taken all our phones, and will block any attempt to trace them. They are very well equipped."

"In that case I will come immediately."

Captain Brooks tapped general Mkondo on the shoulder, and said.

"Sir, please advise the minister that he must not try and be followed. We have anti surveillance techniques that he will not be able to counteract. If there are any people following, or trying to follow him, they will be disposed of. Also, no bugs, as he will be checked."

"I am advised to warn you not to attempt to be followed or wear any transmitter or bug."

"You can tell the generals that I will come alone and without any monitoring equipment. I wish to conclude these discussions as soon as possible."

"When will you leave?"

"I will leave in thirty minutes and take the flight to Lenasia. I will be there at 15.30hr today. I will meet them there."

"Thank you sir we will see you later."

Justice Nkabo hung up. He pondered whether he should discuss this latest development with the Chief Minister. He decided not to.

Chapter 34

Allen received Don's email and read through it carefully. He read it again and could see that it was going to be a difficult problem. There was circumstantial evidence of a coup, but not conclusive evidence, and it would be difficult to take this to his colonel. He needed to think about the email and discuss this with Ralph and Mike.

He called Ralph and said.

"Hi Ralph, I need to discuss a problem with you and Mike. It is very urgent; can we meet in the Crown and discuss this?" Allen asked.

"Sure Allen, when do you want to meet?"

"Ten minutes OK with you? I'll call Mike to join us."

"Yeah, see you soon."

Allen went out to his car and drove the short distance to the pub. He went inside and chose a table in the corner opposite the windows. He would be able to see anyone passing or entering the bar long before they saw him. The need for constant attention was deeply ingrained. Mike and Ralph came in through the back door and appeared in front of Allen as if from nowhere.

They greeted each other, and Ralph said.

"OK Allen. What is the problem that is so urgent that you had to drag me away from my girlfriend?"

"You remember our little sortie in Tanzania with my mate Don?"

They both nodded their heads.

"Well it has developed into something far more serious, and Don is in grave danger. It appears that the poachers that we caught were part of a much bigger operation and that there is actually a plot for a military coup in South Africa."

"Wow!" exclaimed Ralph, "How did they get this information?"

"I have an email from Don, look at it and tell me what you think."

They both read the email through and then passed it back to Allen.

"Not really conclusive," Mike said.

"I agree," Ralph said.

"Yet I know Don" Allen said. He would not send me an email like this if he were not convinced it was so. You have met him, what was your opinion on the man?"

"A solid guy but obviously not trained in covert operations. Could he be misreading the signs and coming to the wrong conclusion?" Ralph asked.

"He is so convinced that he is prepared to risk his life saving these poachers, and he has a female journalist with him. She has been the one to uncover the whole story." Allen said.

"He has a journalist with him? He must be mad, how the hell did that happen?" Ralph asked.

"She came to see him, and the whole thing blew up when the army were coming to collect the poachers. He had no choice." Allen said defensively.

"What is he doing now?" Mike asked.

"He is waiting for advice from me on what to do. I advised him to take the poachers to the police in Dar es Salaam, but he said that they would just be handed over to the army. He believes that they would likely be shot to cover up the coup plans."

"That would suggest that the Tanzanian army or government support the coup in South Africa, which hardly seems plausible," Ralph said.

"But why would the Tanzanian army be so interested in these poachers?" Mike asked.

"We know that there is a history between some of the Reccies from South Africa and the Tanzanian army. They could be working together." Ralph responded.

"That's stretching it a bit, isn't it?" Mike asked.

"We never did understand the politics of Africa, they have always been confusing. With old allegiances and inner circles, you could never know for sure." Mike said.

"I agree," Allen said. "The fact is that Don is already running away with the poachers with a female journalist in tow. We know that these poachers are more than capable of taking out Don and the journalist if they so wish. There has to be some motivation for them to run with Don."

"Yeah, they just want to escape." Mike said.

"I think it is deeper than that. If they escape, and return to South Africa, they may well be picked up by the ANC, and made to talk. The whole NFP plot would then be revealed. What would happen then?"

"They could not allow the journalist to talk or print her story and Don would be right in the middle." Allen said.

"I suppose they would all have convenient accidents or they would be eliminated by the forces planning the coup, or even the ANC if they wanted to cover up such an attempt." Ralph said.

"Why would the ANC wish to cover up an attempted coup, surely it would help their cause to have the detail released?" Mike asked.

"Possibly, but that would upset a very fine balance in the country. They would have to be seen to react, and it would have to be punitive action. This may well precipitate the very scenario that they wish to avoid as the action taken would be against the whites." Allen said.

"Yeah, I understand your point.

"OK, lets assume that Don is correct in his analysis, how can we help when we are 5000 miles away and help is needed right now?" Mike asked.

"That my man, is the difficult question, and that is why I asked you to join me." Allen said.

"OK, let's look at the facts,"

"One: the Reccies that have been poaching to raise cash to rearm the forces controlled by the NFP in Natal."

"Two, we know that the Tanzanian army wishes to dispose of the poachers."

"That is an assumption." Mike said.

"I know but bear with me" Allen said.

"Three, we have the names of a general in Natal and a general in the SADF that are involved"

"Four, we have a journalist that has linked terrorist actions to the general in Natal and a hit team that is operating with the full knowledge, or complicity of the general in the SADF."

"Five, there have been rumours of a third force in South Africa for a couple of years, and they appear to be more active now."

"Six, we know that there are training camps in the North of South Africa where the old commando forces are being trained."

"Surely all these facts add up to Don being right about everything, don't you think?"

"Well. We also know from our own Intel that the political murders are rampant in South Africa. There are many faction fights and even busloads of ANC and NFP supporters being mowed down by gunfire. This alone would suggest major instability." Mike said.

"So, what can we do now?" Ralph asked.

"We have to speak to the colonel, and also develop a plan of action to help Don." Allen said.

"I understand the first action but in what way can we help Don when the action is taking place now?" Ralph asked.

"Don, for all his lack of training, is a very resourceful man. I am convinced that he will escape to Mozambique, but that is where his problems will begin. Either sections of the SADF or the Mozambique forces will be hunting him down. He would not stand much chance against the forces arrayed against him." Allen said.

"Are you suggesting that we go and assist him?" Mike asked incredulously.

"Yes, but this time we get permission and travel with a full platoon." Allen said.

"Is it in the interest of her majesty's government to covertly deal with any subversive activity in South Africa? It would impact on trade and democracy's status in the world. It is too large an issue for the British not to act."

"Just supposing we did get permission, which I doubt, how the hell would we find him?" Mike asked.

Allen smiled and said, "That is the easy part, he has a cell phone with him, and all he needs to do is switch it on for twenty seconds every half hour, and we can locate him."

"If we can locate them so easily, so can the SADF and the Mozambique forces." Ralph said.

"Not really, we know the cell number that we are looking for and can set our scanners to detect the number. We can get an accurate location by the signal transmitted. The reporter had purchased a new sim card when she landed, and they would only be able to track her old South African number. They would get there in the end, but we would have a head start" Allen said.

"Actually, we can do better than that." Mike said. "GCHQ could zone in on the area and would pick up any transmission instantly. They could then feed that back to us whilst we were on our way. That still supposes that the boss would agree."

"You have both forgotten one thing." Ralph said. "We would need the cooperation of the Mozambique government. I hardly think that they would give their approval, do you?"

"We have been in many African countries in the past without permission and the respective governments never knew." Allen said.

"Very true, but this one would be difficult to conceal if we have contact with their forces." Mike said.

"We would have to wear unmarked clothing, and we would definitely not have protection of our government if caught." Ralph said.

"Since when did that bother you Ralph? I can recall many missions where that was the case." Mike said.

Ralph laughed and said, "Quite right. I must be getting old."

"Do you agree that we take this to the boss?" Allen asked.

They both nodded their agreement, and Mike said.

"We need to talk to Don now, can you call him?" Mike asked.

"I will try right now," Allen said.

Allen opened his phone and dialled the number that Don had given him. There was no response.

"No answer," Allen said.

"Then let us assume that he is on his way and possibly unable to answer." Ralph said. "I suggest that we go and see the boss right now. We may have to tell him our involvement in catching the poachers."

"He will hit the roof if we do, and we will be suspended, and probably have to face a court martial. We can bend the truth a bit and say we gave him advice only." Allen said.

"You know that he is a canny bastard and would not believe us for a minute." Mike said.

"What alternative do we have?" Allen asked.

"Let's go and see him and take our chances." Ralph said.

They left the bar and drove to the base. They parked outside the main building and asked to see the colonel.

They were ushered into the colonel's office, and they saluted.

"We have a problem that we would like to discuss with you sir." Allen said.

The colonel looked at the three men standing in front of him and could clearly see their discomfort. These men were probably the best in the regiment, and if they looked concerned then there had to be a serious problem.

He pointed to his table in the corner of the office and said.

"Sit down gentlemen and tell me your problem."

They moved to the table and waited for the boss to sit down before they lowered themselves in their seats.

"Now gentlemen what is of such concern?" He asked.

Allen started the explanation and went through the sequence of events that led up to the current situation. He passed the email to the boss.

Colonel John Masters read the email through and then placed it on the table in front of them.

"Are you telling me the whole story?" he asked.

Allen looked at his colleagues and said, "We have told you all that we know sir."

The colonel smiled and said, "I don't think so, but we can pursue that later. We have a situation that needs to be dealt with now. We have a British citizen embroiled in action that he did not create, and we have, it would appear at least, a planned military coup in South Africa. What you do not know is that we have suspected this was about to happen and have Intel that suggests that it is imminent. We have discussed this with the South African government but could not get them to react to our information. They have everything under control, or, so they think."

"You have brought a new dimension to the planned coup. It was never envisaged that the Zulu's would throw their lot in with the Afrikaners. This makes the situation even more volatile and concerns me deeply."

"We have an agent in the SADF, you all know him well. It is captain James Brooks. He is extremely well connected. You remember the captain?" Colonel Masters asked.

"I certainly do." Allen said. "He was part of the SADF that came over for training at Broadmoor. He was bloody good as well."

Ralph and Mike nodded assent.

"I would have found your story difficult to believe, but you even have the name of the General in your email. Captain Brooks is his adjutant."

"You have obviously thought this through, so what plans have you hatched?" The colonel asked.

"Don, the man that we know, has a cell phone with him. I have contacted him and told him to switch his phone on for twenty seconds on the hour. This will allow us to locate him. We propose to send in a platoon of our guys to get them out. With his information and the journalists account we can reveal the whole plot and the main players."

"And you expect me to agree to such a plan?" Colonel Masters asked.

"It is our best course of action," Allen said.

"And you believe that the government in Mozambique would welcome your presence in their country?" The colonel asked.

"We did not plan to notify them. We would get in and out so quickly that they would never notice our presence. We have done it many times before sir," Ralph said.

"Have you considered the repercussions if their forces make contact with you?"

"Yes sir, we have. We would not be wearing any insignia that would associate us with the British forces, and as you know, we never leave our people behind." Allen said.

"How many people would you need?" The colonel asked.

"Two groups sir." Allen responded.

"Have you decided which groups you would take?"

Yes sir, it would be our group to pick up Don and "C" group to clear a way for us to the border." Mike said.

"When you get to the border, then what?"

"We would move to a safe house in South Africa and debrief the personnel involved." Ralph said.

"Why not airlift them out before you get to the border?" the colonel asked.

"That would have to show the British government's involvement as they would have to be taken to a ship offshore or back to a base in Kenya. I am not sure that we could keep that undetected. Our method would mean that they would be safe in South Africa, and we could then be there unofficially."

"And what if you have contact with the forces in Mozambique." The colonel said.

"We are trained in evasion and would not try to fight our way out. This would only become necessary should we be ambushed. With "C" group clearing the way, we should be able to avoid detection."

"OK, set up your mission and brief sergeant Jones with "C" group. You will also have to bring Davis up to speed." The colonel said. "Now get on with it." He ordered.

The men rose, saluted and left.

Chapter 35

Justice Nkabo was met at Lenasia airport by the general's collection team. He was transported in a closed van to the meeting place in the Limpopo province.

Whilst being driven to the meeting, he thought about his options. If he could pull off the partition of South Africa, with Natal, as its own country then he would control the destiny of the Zulu's and not the dithering Chief Minister. He was getting old and way past his best. This would be a new country and the alliance between the three countries that were born out of the coup would need to cooperate to survive. Why stop at the borders of Natal? Perhaps he could squeeze some more territory out of the generals. He would play along and see what developed.

The real prize of course would be Gauteng with the powerhouse of Africa, Johannesburg, being the ultimate acquisition. The ANC could have the platinum mines and the coal in Limpopo, the Afrikaners could have the Cape and the Free State and the NFP would take the borders of Natal to include Gauteng. He would ask for more of course….

It was obvious that the Afrikaners did not consider the province of Gauteng their most precious asset. As usual they were going back to the good old days for the Boers, their birthplace, the Cape provinces.

The driver pulling to a stop wakened him from his reverie. The back doors were opened, and a man dressed in uniform said.

"Come this way please sir."

Justice Nkabo got out of the van and immediately tried to take in his surroundings. He had no time.

"Please follow me sir."

Justice Nkabo looked at the man and said, "I am coming."

The orderly led the minister to the anteroom where he was met by the NFP delegation.

"Fill me in with what has transpired so far." He immediately asked.

General Mkondo took him through the discussions and concluded,

"They will not release any more information until they have our signatures on a document that clearly implicates us and the NFP in the coup."

"What are they offering?" Justice Nkabo asked.

"They will disclose nothing until we sign that document."

"What does the document say?"

"They have not yet disclosed that."

"Then how can they ask us to sign something that we have not seen?"

"I told them that I did not have clearance to sign such a document, so there was no point in showing it to me."

"Well I have the authority, let's have a look at it."

General Mkondo rang the bell and the orderly knocked at the door.

"Come in." General Mkondo said.

The orderly entered the room, and the general said.

"Please tell the Generals that we are ready now."

"Yes sir."

The orderly went to the boardroom and knocked on the door.

"Come in." General Lauberschagne ordered.

"They are ready sir."

"Captain Brooks bring the delegation to the boardroom."

"Yes sir."

The generals took their positions round the table, but General Lauberschagne did not sit down. The NFP delegates filed in, and were greeted by general Lauberschagne.

"Minister Nkabo, please excuse me if I do not introduce all those present here. I am sure that you will understand."

"No problem general Lauberschagne, I think that I know all the people here anyway. We have met many times at various functions."

"We seem to have an impasse." General Lauberschagne said. "We want you to commit to our plans but your delegation wants a full briefing before doing so."

"I understand that you wish us to sign a document that clearly implicates the NFP in your plans. You wish us to sign this document when we have no idea what you propose. Would you really expect us to do that?" Justice Nkabo said.

"Then what would make you sign such a document?" General Lauberschagne asked.

"I think that we have shown that we are willing to commit just by our presence here. The problem that we have is that we do not know what you are proposing other than to overthrow the ANC. You could be using us as some pawn in your overall strategy, and this would obviously not be acceptable to my people. To prevent any misunderstanding I think that you should outline your plans such that we can have a broad understanding." Justice Nkabo responded.

"You realise the consequences of my group showing our plans and strategies, this would mean that you could not leave here until we have completed our mission." General Lauberschagne said.

"I think we clearly understand what you are saying. If we do not agree with your proposals, we will be held here until the coup is complete. Is that correct?" Justice Nkabo said.

"That is correct."

"Then what would stop us from agreeing with you and then exposing your plans the moment that we left here?"

"We would keep some of you as hostages. You have to realise that we are all risking our lives to try and save this country."

"We are also looking for a solution to our problem. We know that the ANC are active in Natal and are intimidating our members. There have been numerous murders associated with their actions. The only question that I would ask is does this fit in with our timeframe?"

"We know that you are intending to do a deal with the Korean industrialist, and we know that they are at this moment looking at your proposed site. We assume that you will make it lucrative enough to convince them to build their car plant. We do not need the detail. When do you believe that you will conclude the deal and take your first arms shipment?" General Lauberschagne asked.

"It will take a year to build the plant, but what we have offered is a site where they can, in the interim, assemble parts for their cars. They will be making their first shipment in two weeks time. They will mix with that shipment the small arms that we require and the ammunition. We would be ready in four to five weeks time. And you?" Justice Nkabo asked.

"It would take a similar amount of time to get all the troops together to secure the relevant targets. As you know, parliament breaks up in four weeks time for the summer recess. This would be when we would strike." General Lauberschagne said.

"That would mean that we could strike simultaneously, yet that would be very difficult to coordinate."

"We have all the best logistics people working on this. This would include the press releases and the management of the financial houses. There would be considerable resistance after it was known what had happened. We would fall back to our planned boundaries and control the situation there."

"If we work together then it could work. What would be the boundaries?" Justice Nkabo asked.

"If you agree to sign the document that clearly indicates that you will participate in this action then we will disclose our battle plans." General Lauberschagne said.

"Then I think that we have an agreement. We will sign your document, and we will bring our own logistic people to merge our plan with yours." Justice Nkabo said.

The relief in the room was palpable. The generals looked at each other and smiled. They knew now that the planned action was more than likely to be successful. The forces that they could now muster would be more than sufficient to seize control. They had control of the army, air force and the navy. There were some dissenters in the army, but they would be put under house arrest.

"Gentlemen," General Lauberschagne said. "Today is a great day in the history of South Africa; we can make this country great again. I suggest that we adjourn to the officer's mess and celebrate this momentous occasion."

They all stood up, and general Lauberschagne went to each NFP representative, and shook his hand. The other generals also stood up and shook the hands of each delegate. They moved off to the officer's mess.

Captain Brooks was waiting outside the room and could tell immediately when they appeared that agreement had been reached. He watched the men stroll down the corridor to the officer's mess as if they had just agreed a business deal. He felt sure that some of the people present saw it that way. He followed behind the group to the mess.

His thoughts were on how he could report what he had seen without arousing suspicion. General Lauberschagne interrupted his thoughts.

"You do not look pleased with the outcome of our meeting, Captain."

"Sorry sir, it was just that I was so preoccupied with the planning, and it seems almost unbelievable that we can actually get them on our side. I was thinking what a huge difference it makes."

"You're absolutely right captain. It makes a huge difference to only have to fight on one front, particularly when all the major barracks will be in our area, so much easier to control."

"I do not wish to talk out of place sir, but can we trust them?"

"Not entirely Brooks, but they have their own agenda and provided that the two coincide it will work out."

"I hope that you are right sir as the consequences would be dire if we failed."

"We will watch them carefully Brooks, and steer them in the right direction. I suppose that you are worried about your wife and family?"

"Yes sir I am. But I am bound by my duty."

"You are a senior officer in the army Brooks, you always do what you are told to do and ensure that your subordinates follow suite. That is the way it works. You cannot be held responsible for obeying a senior officer's instruction."

"Sir, I do not want you to think that I am doing this because I was told to do so. There was plenty of opportunity to opt out months ago. I believe in what we are doing and what we are doing is best for all the people in South Africa. I am not a mercenary."

"Well put Brooks; do you mind if I use those lines later?"

"I would be honoured sir."

They both walked towards the mess room. Inside the mess room, the group were bunched around the bar and drinks were being served. There was no joviality as both sides were wary of the other. They had split up with the generals on one side of the bar and the NFP delegates on the other.

"Gentlemen, please fill up your drinks as I propose a toast to South Africa and its entire people."

They all stood up, and general Lauberschagne said.

"South Africa."

All the delegates and generals raised their glasses and repeated the salute.

"Gentlemen, we will have some dinner and then we will get to work on the plans that we have to implement as time is of the essence." General Lauberschagne said.

The orderly came forward, and said.

"The dining room is this way." He pointed to the door opposite. "Please follow me."

Chapter 36

Colonel Masters was driven to Whitehall and was ushered into the Prime Minister's office.

"Do sit down," the Prime Minister said. "Now what is so urgent that I had to see you straight away? I was on my way to Chequers for the weekend."

"I will come straight to the point sir, we have Intel that a group of generals have planned a military coup in South Africa, they are also aligned with the NFP and hence the Zulu nation."

The Prime Minister sat down and called his secretary.

"Get me the head of MI6 James Banning and the joint chief of staff Sir Andrew Granville. Whatever they are doing tell them to get here immediately. Classify it as zone red. At the same time, I want a chronographer and set up the cabinet room and call the Home Secretary and the Foreign Affairs minister to the meeting. Oh, and organise coffee for two people, to my office now."

The Prime Minister looked closely at colonel Masters and said.

"Colonel, how secure is your information?"

"Sir, we have a mole at the highest level in South Africa, and he has been indicating that such an action was being planned. There are many senior military personnel involved including all the branches of the armed forces. They have a network of financial, business and police leaders acting with them."

"My God! How deep does this go?"

"It would appear to every level. We have one other problem as well."

"What is that?"

"We have a British citizen on the run in Mozambique with two South African Special Forces operatives that were caught poaching in Tanzania. They also have a female journalist that has all the information on the planned military coup. She went to see Scales that is the Brit, and got caught up in the action. It would appear that they are planning to escape using the game department's plane, as Scales is also a pilot. They were to land in Mozambique, and make their way to South Africa."

"Do we need their information?"

"Yes we do, they can connect the Zulu government to the conspiracy. Believe it or not, they were poaching to try and rearm the government forces that are taking a battering in Natal."

"Poaching? What would they achieve by that?"

"Rhino horn is big business, nearly as lucrative as drug dealing. The Asians will pay a lot of money for rhino horn."

"Trust me, Masters; I know what it costs to operate a military campaign. Poaching would not cover one day's operation."

"To re-equip the armed forces in Natal would not be that costly. They would be fighting a guerrilla war and not a conventional war."

"It still sounds implausible, what would they get for rhino horn?"

"They could raise a million dollars US, and to them, that would be a lot of guns."

There was a knock on the door and the Prime Minister said.

"Come in."

The tea lady entered the room with a coffee pot and some biscuits.

"Shall I pour sir?" she asked.

"Yes please. How do you take your coffee Masters?" he asked.

"Just black for me, sir."

The tea lady poured the coffee and left the room.

"Drink your coffee and no more detail until the rest arrive. What do you plan to do about the Brit and Co. on the run?"

"We will send in two groups, the first group to protect them, and the second group to clear a path for them to South Africa. They will be put in a safe house and then debriefed."

"Do I need to speak to the Mozambican government Masters?"

"We will not be detected so that will not be necessary."

"I hope that you are correct, if you are not, you know the drill."

"Yes I do sir."

They drank their coffee in silence until the Prime Minister's secretary came in and said.

"They are all assembled in the cabinet room Prime Minister."

"Follow me Masters," the Prime Minister said.

They moved to the cabinet room and sat around the table was the head of MI6 James Banning, the Joint Chief of staff Sir Andrew Granville,

Charles Pickering the foreign minister and John Brandt the foreign secretary. They all stood up as the Prime Minister entered.

"Good morning gentlemen, at least I was hoping it would be. Thank you for coming at such short notice. I want this meeting to be an exploratory meeting before we involve the cabinet and the full emergency committee members. I will not waste time. Colonel Masters please brief all present on your recent findings." The Prime Minister said.

Colonel Masters went through the sequence of events and brought them up to date on the current situation. He did not mention the mole that they have in the general's office.

"Colonel Masters, you have left out one vital piece of information, your mole." The Prime Minister said.

"Yes sir, I did, as the fewer people who know of the mole the better."

"They do not need his name merely the fact that he is in position and reliable."

The colonel looked around the table and said. "I can confirm the reported events and plans of the generals and the NFP via a mole that we have at the highest level in the general's office."

Head of MI6 asked, "How reliable is he?"

Colonel Masters merely responded by saying, "Very."

"Is he English, South African or African?" He asked.

"What is the relevance of your question?" The Prime Minister asked.

"I just wish to be satisfied with his credentials. We have heard rumours many times about planned military coups in South Africa, and yet they have never taken place." The head of MI6 James Banning said.

"I have just vouched for him myself." Colonel Masters said testily.

"That is good enough for me. So let's move on." The Prime Minister said.

"What about Scales and the journalist, why are they so important to us?" The foreign minister Charles Pickering asked.

"The reason that we want to get them back safely is that they have the information that clearly links the NFP to the coup. An ex Reccie, captain Khumalo, has all the detail. The journalist, Angela Murchison, has put it all together and has written affidavit's in her possession that links all the parties." Colonel Masters said.

"If we assume that the coup is imminent what do you suggest should be the next step, Charles?" The Prime Minister asked.

"We need at least some verification." The Foreign Minister said.

"Do we have anything more, colonel Masters?" the Prime Minister asked.

"Yes sir we do. From our mole, we have the names of the key generals; these are the Generals, Lauberschagne, Naude, Meyer, Van de Roodt and Van De Rey. There are three admirals of the fleet; they are Voight, Brannan and Pietersen. Commanders Jones, De Wet and De Breyn represent the air force. They also have people in position in the police force at senior levels, banking, industry and government. It is suggested that they have close to 45000 troops spread out across the country. These are mainly the Kommando groups that were formed during the apartheid years." Colonel Masters said.

"What about armaments?" The head of MI6 asked.

"They are well equipped as virtually all the armaments across the country are still in the white soldiers hands." Colonel Masters said.

"How long have you known this?" the Prime Minister asked.

"We had the first rumblings some two weeks ago, and this was only confirmed yesterday by our mole." Colonel Masters said.

"Who is involved from the NFP?" the head of MI6 asked.

"We do not know for sure as the only name that we have is a general Mkondo. That is why we need Scales, Murchison and Khumalo safely under our control." Colonel Masters said. "It would appear that the NFP are holding back. To them it is an ideal opportunity whichever way the coup goes."

"Explain yourself colonel." The Prime Minister said.

"The Zulu's have a history of being organized fighters and very brave in battle. If the coup were a success, the military would be hard pushed to control the whole country. The NFP would offer to hold back their forces for self-governance and the military commanders would then have a reduced area to control. If the coup failed, or even looked like failing, they would form the same alliance with the ANC with the same result. The ANC would have its back to the wall and would also want to reduce its exposure. So, whichever way it goes the NFP wins, hence their reluctance to come out into the open." Colonel Masters said.

"In either event it would be a testing relationship as, as soon as the ANC, or the military gained strength, they would turn upon the Zulu nation. As far as we are aware the NFP does not have the armaments to fend off a concerted attack." The Foreign Minister said.

"That was true until last week when the NFP did a deal with Soong Industries. They plan to build a car plant in Natal and part of the deal is supplying them with the armaments that they require." Colonel Masters said.

"What do you know about all this James?" The Prime Minister asked.

"We have been watching the Soong Industries group for a number of years. Chen Yoo Soong appeared out of nowhere and suddenly became a great industrialist. He is operating in so many different fields that it is difficult to keep up with him. He has formed subsidiaries under different names, and is known to deal in armaments in the Middle East, and across Africa. He is a very wealthy and influential man. He is totally ruthless, and demands total commitment of his staff. The only weakness in his armour is his son, Yamamata, who is currently one of the drivers with his racing team based in Essex. It is not known, at least by our department, that he was dealing in armaments, in South Africa. We knew about his plans to build a car plant, but did not know about the arms deal until now." The head of MI6 said.

"Well gentlemen we now have all the information in front of us. What do you propose?" The Prime Minister asked.

The Joint Chief of Staff, who had simply listened, said.

"Prime minister, the organization for this coup has been almost perfect. The forces are distributed across the country and include all the branches of the armed forces. That they have kept this under wraps for so long, is a remarkable achievement. The reason for this statement is to show that this is no ordinary African coup; it is planned to the nth degree and will be difficult to stop. We have to find a weakness in their plans."

"And how do you propose to do that?" The Prime Minister asked.

"We need to run the options through our strategic arm to find a solution that would not precipitate a coup. If they are so well organized, they will have a strategy to take out, or control, all the military bases, the television and radio stations, and all communication based technology. They will close off the airports and ports. That is one hell of a task for a country the size of South Africa. They would have to do all this simultaneously. They only have 45000 troops at their disposal. It is a logistical nightmare. Their borders would also need to be patrolled and manned, an almost impossible scenario."

"That is why they need the NFP." Colonel Masters said. "If they could fall back to the Cape and have Natal secure it would be possible. They would move all military aircraft to the Cape Province and destroy those that they could not move. The navy could blockade the ports and stop entry to shipping or any attempt from neighbouring countries to land troops."

"Charles, what should our reaction be?" The Prime Minister asked.

"The question is do we want to stop this coup? We know that the ANC have become more belligerent towards the UK and Europe. A new government would need our help to survive. The present government has been in contact with all the communist countries, asking for help, and supported all the despots in Africa, just look at Zimbabwe."

"Are you suggesting that we actually support the coup?" The Prime Minister asked incredulously.

"Do we do what is in the best interest for the UK or for South Africa? If we are honest, we do not need any of the minerals or other products, as we can easily obtain them elsewhere. I am taking a pragmatic view, Prime Minister."

"We have a history in that country." The prime minister said. "We cannot turn a blind eye to the proposed coup. For good or bad, the ANC is the elected government, and we did not spread democracy such that we could control what they do, we did it for freedom." The Prime Minister said.

"I was merely pointing out the options Prime Minister. We could also intervene to stop the coup. Informing the ANC of those involved and assisting their arrest can do this. If they take out the leadership, then the coup would either not take place or falter at the first hurdle. You have heard Sir Andrew raise the problem of logistics. We need to make it more difficult. It all depends on the time frame."

"The problem that I have with informing the ANC is that they are somewhat immature and would make a total cock up of the arrests. It needs to be coordinated properly, or they will precipitate the very action that we wish to avoid." Colonel Masters said.

"Then what do you propose?" The Prime Minister asked.

"Prime Minister, before we think about stopping the coup can we explore the possibilities of supporting the coup?" The Head of MI6 said.

"Out of the question, do not even think about it either directly or covertly. This government will not support any action of this nature." The Prime Minister said emphatically.

"Sir, they plan to split the country up into three separate and self governed units, similar to the mainland of the UK. The Afrikaners will take the Cape Provinces and the Free State, The Zulu's will take Natal, and the balance will be left in the hands of the ANC. That sounds like a very stable solution to me." Colonel Masters said.

"Gentlemen, you miss the point completely, it is not for us to decide on how a country is split up. If you want an example of what can go wrong, you do not have to look far. Just look at Yugoslavia. Would this be Bosnia and Serbia all over again? And what would the UN say? Please remove any such thoughts from your head or your planning. I will not allow it." The Prime Minister said.

"In that case sir, we have to get involved to control the ANC on how they react. As you quite rightly point out, Foreign Secretary, if they cock it up it will actually precipitate the coup. I believe that we have no more than three weeks to sort this out. The reason I say that is that their parliament breaks up for the summer recess in three weeks time. That would be the ideal time to plan a coup as most of the ANC government will be away on holiday or out of the country." Colonel Masters said.

"Then gentlemen, time is of the essence. I want a joint operations plan by ten am tomorrow such that the cabinet can review the plan. I will get my secretary to notify all the other cabinet members and Colonel Masters and James will present their plan. That is all, gentlemen." The Prime Minister said.

Chapter 37

Captain Khumalo set fire to the plane having doused it in aviation fuel. The fuel caught fire and crept up the body of the plane. Captain Khumalo made sure that it was burning freely and then turned to follow the tracks of Angela and Don.

He picked up a piece of brushwood and started to clear their tracks as he followed the spoor. He had travelled a hundred and fifty meters when there was a loud whoosh as the plane caught fire across its entire length and then erupted as the tanks exploded. He felt the heat from the fire as he turned to watch the plane burn.

He knew now that the local barracks would have seen the pall of smoke rising from the burning aircraft. They would have to move quickly to get away from the area as soon as possible. He had to be sure that he would erase their tracks successfully, or they would be easy to follow. Rushing the track erasure would leave traces of their survival. He calculated that the military commander would despatch a platoon to investigate the fire. They would also know by now that the occupants on the plane were escaping from Tanzania. They would be looking for them.

He worked his way slowly back to the Kopje erasing any sign of tracks at he went. It was a slow and tedious process, and he was constantly checking for sign of approach of any forces that may have been sent.

Don and Angela had heard the explosion, and saw the plume of smoke rising in the distance.

"Angela, we must stay down in case there are any government forces in the area. I will keep a lookout, but you stay where you are and wait for me."

Don moved to the edge of the Kopje but kept below the skyline. He had a panoramic view of the countryside and could see nothing moving. He returned to Angela and said.

"I can't see Khumalo"

"Do you think that he has dumped us?" She asked.

"I don't think so, he will be cleaning up our spoor, and that takes time."

Don kept watch and eventually saw captain Khumalo approaching the Kopje and said to Angela.

"Khumalo is coming back."

"Thank goodness." Angela said.

"I agree we need his skills now more than ever. The locals are bound to have seen the plume of smoke and will come to investigate. I hope that we have done the right thing."

Captain Khumalo climbed up the Kopje and met Don and Angela.

"I think that we had better move off before the Mozambican forces arrive. They will have seen the smoke and will come and investigate. We have about 2 hours before sunset, so we must move now."

"Do you know the way to the border?" Don asked.

"I do, but we need to find cover first and be able to hide as they may put out a spotter plane. We cannot be caught in the open. We will have to move at night."

"Khumalo, before we left our base I called my friend in the SAS. He has asked us to leave our cell phone on for twenty seconds on the hour every hour until they contact us."

"Are you saying that the SAS are coming to escort us?" Captain Khumalo asked.

"Yes that is correct."

"Mr. Scales, I can only assume from that information that you do not trust me."

"That is not the case Khumalo. I called him for advice before I spoke to you and he said that they would come out. I could not dissuade him."

"Is there anything else that you are not telling me?" Captain Khumalo asked.

"No, that is the truth."

"Then am I to be arrested again?" he asked.

"No, we need your information on the NFP involvement. They will not harm you."

Captain Khumalo looked at Angela and said, "Do you agree with what Don is saying?"

"I do, and I heard the conversation. If we are to protect you, and your family, then this is the only way." Angela said.

"You place me in a predicament, I can look after myself if I left you, but you most certainly cannot. I am putting myself at risk by allowing myself to be captured again. You may well believe that the SAS will not harm me, but, I know their methods, they trained me." Captain Khumalo said.

"Khumalo, what alternatives do you have?" Don asked.

"I can run and hide, and they would never catch me." Captain Khumalo said.

"They caught you last time." Don said.

"That was different. I was not expecting them, now I am." He said.

"Captain, if you go on your own it will not solve your problem. The NFP will draw you out by threatening your family. Doing it our way we can get you all to safety and once the plot is foiled, then you will be a free man." Angela said.

"What guarantees do I have?" Captain Khumalo asked.

"I will tell the SAS men that if they harm you then I will print the story in the Metropolitan. That would dissuade them as they would be exposed and condemned by all, not forgetting that they entered a foreign country without permission armed to the teeth. They would not take that chance." Angela said.

"Ok, let us find some cover, and we can discuss this further. I feel responsible for you, God knows why, and I do not want you to be caught by the armed forces of Mozambique. The longer we stay here the more dangerous it becomes." Captain Khumalo said.

They moved off keeping to the low acacia cover as much as possible. Captain Khumalo set the direction and then fell back to wipe out their tracks. He knew for certain that if the burning of the plane did not fool the Mozambican forces a skilled tracker would still find them. He had to make it more difficult such that it took them time to follow them. He also knew that once they had discovered the tracks they would follow them relentlessly.

They had to move as quickly as possible but also had to move with caution. He was concerned that whilst he was covering their tracks that they would walk into a platoon of the Mozambican soldiers. They were incapable of scouting forward and avoiding contact, and they would be exposed. He could not successfully scout to the front, and then return to erase their tracks. He judged that it was better to erase their spoor, and take a chance in front; as if they left their spoor they would be onto them very quickly.

They found shelter in an old cave.

"I will go back down the trail and check that we are not being followed. Do not be worried if I am gone for two hours as I must be certain." Captain Khumalo said.

"Do not light a fire." Captain Khumalo said. "They would spot the fire twenty kilometres away."

"I will not. I will switch on the phone though as instructed." Don said.

"I know that you will, and you are also concerned that I will not come back. I can assure you that I will."

"Thanks." Angela said.

Khumalo left them and moved at a steady jog back towards the aircraft. He took a different route that was parallel to their trek to the cave. His spoor would be confusing, as it would show that he had gone in the wrong direction. The trackers would be able to follow his spoor but in the wrong direction. On his return, he would erase his spoor as before.

"What time do you make it," Don asked Angela.

"I make it five forty five, but my watch is not that reliable".

"We could always put the phone on twice, once at the earlier time and repeat it one minute later. That way we cover all the alternatives." Angela said.

"How new is that phone?" Don asked.

"It was straight out of the box last week."

"Then the battery should hold out for well over forty eight hours." Don said.

"I would think so."

"We should move to the front of the cave, and, at six o clock, we will turn the phone on. If you will count down the twenty seconds with me then at least, I know that we are accurate." Don said.

"Is the correct time that important?" Angela asked.

"Yes." Don said. "That way they know that we have not been captured and forced to turn on the phone. Any time longer than specified will make them suspicious."

"Oh, I see." Angela said.

They moved out to the edge of the cave and waited for the time to reach six 'o clock on Don's phone.

"Are you ready?" Don asked.

"Yes."

Don switched on the phone, and they both counted for twenty seconds. There was no reaction on the phone.

They waited another minute then repeated the procedure.

There was no reaction on the phone.

"We have to wait another hour for Khumalo, what do you suggest that we do?" Don asked.

"I suppose that we should keep watch at least until the sun goes down." Angela said.

"That's right, shall we watch together or do you need some rest?" Don asked.

"No, I am fine, and we can watch the sun go down together." Angela said.

They moved together and Don put his arm around Angela. They both watched the trail and the setting of the sun. As always in Africa, it was remarkable how quickly the sun disappeared over the horizon. They could actually watch the sun moving behind the Kopje in the distance. It was a magnificent sunset. With the sky first turning amber, and then slowly the colours changed to brilliant red, as the sun disappeared below the horizon. The sun marked its passing by the distinct rays that quartered the sky in alternating red and amber.

They held each other and watched the panoramic view in front of them unfold. There was comfort in their togetherness that eased the tension. They kissed, and both turned to see the tip of the sun dip over the horizon. In seconds, it was dark. Night had arrived.

"What shall we do know?" Don asked.

Angela looked at him and could clearly see the desire in his eyes. She smiled and asked.

"Now Mr. Scales, what are you proposing?"

Don smiled and said.

"I was thinking more about moving inside, and finding something to eat."

"How long has Khumalo been gone for?" she asked.

"I would say for about half an hour or so, why?"

"He said he would be about two hours, did he not?" Angela asked.

"Yes he did." Don said.

She leant towards him and said provocatively,

"Now what could we do in one hour to give us both an appetite."

Don laughed, and said.

"My girl, you are incorrigible and insatiable. We got to know each other on the Kopje, did we not?"

"That was only an introduction. I want to really start to know you." Angela said. They moved back into the cave and both slowly stripped off. Don's excitement was more than evident, and Angela said,

"My, my, what have we here?"

Don looked at Angela naked and was so transfigured he could hardly move. She was beautiful. Her breasts were small, but pert, her tummy flat, and she had perfectly groomed pubic hair. He was both captivated and speechless.

Angela moved towards him and kissed him gently on the lips. She moved her hands over his body and felt his erection. He groaned with pleasure. He turned her around and put his penis between her buttocks and teased her breasts. It was her turn to groan.

They made love slowly and gently, their passions enhanced by their dangerous circumstances. They reached their climax together. They lost themselves in their togetherness. Afterwards, they lay side-by-side, and Don said.

"I think I love you."

"You had better be more positive than that you bloody Scotsman. I do not do this for everybody." Angela said.

"I know I love you." Don said.

"And I love you, but you do need to improve your technique." Angela said laughing.

"Are you complaining?" Don asked shyly.

"Yeah, it's over too bloody quick for my liking. Though, I must admit that I am equally to blame." Angela said.

They dressed and settled down to wait for captain Khumalo.

"What time is it?" Angela asked.

"It is six fifty five, we had better move to the cave mouth again as we need to use the cell phone again." Don said.

Chapter 38

The satellite that was directed over Mozambique, and was in its precise orbit, and ready to detect the cell phone signal. The satellite was linked to GHCQ in the UK and was on standby for the transmission. The SAS teams had already left and were over the Indian Ocean in an old transporter that could drop to 300 feet to avoid detection. The transporter was closing in on the Mozambique border. They would parachute out at five hundred feet above their target area. The transporter would then return to base.

The pilot of the transporter called Allen to the cockpit.

"We have just received confirmation of their position. They are on reference -23.392 north and 33.464 east. This puts them about two hundred kilometres east of the Kruger National Park, the border between South Africa and Mozambique. Our Flying time will be one hour and forty minutes. If they have not moved, I can drop you right on top of them."

"Brilliant." Allen said. He moved back into the bowels of the plane and said.

"We have made contact so check your equipment. We will be over the DZ in one hour forty."

The SAS teams were relaxed, and each checked the parachute of the other. Although the individual using it packed the parachutes, they were still checked by their team. There could be no mistakes. The two teams that would be operating in Mozambique had worked together several times before. They had become a unit that was dependable, and without any apparent weaknesses.

Each member of the team had their preferred weapons and the duties were allocated according to their skills, though if required, each member of the group was capable of any of the skills needed. They had their navigator, the marksman, the tracker and the radioman. The old days of massive back packs for radio communication had long gone for the SAS. They had little solar charged radios linked to the satellite, first developed in Japan and then improved at their specialist unit in Catterick. Though the teams could operate separately, if required, they operated best as a unit.

The pilot turned towards the coordinates and dropped to 300 feet. He would maintain this height to avoid detection by the Mozambican radar. They had done this many times in the past.

Chapter 39

Captain Khumalo, as good as his word, reappeared two hours after he had left them. He was not carrying good news.

"They found the plane, but it would appear that they did not believe that we had died in the crash. The reason that I say this, is because, they brought forward a tracker to search the area. He found our spoor." Captain Khumalo said.

"What do we do now?" Don asked.

"I can eliminate the tracker, and it would take a day or so for them to get another. I do not believe that the army group alone could follow our spoor. Yet, to safely take out the tracker, it would have to be a shot of at least 300 metres." Captain Khumalo said.

"Can you do that?" Don asked.

"Yes I can." He said.

"Which rifle do you need?" Don asked.

"At that range the 450 is useless. I would need the 375 rifle that Angela is carrying."

"Do we need to do this?" Angela asked.

Before captain Khumalo could answer. Don said.

"What time is it?"

"It is seven forty." Angela said.

"Do we have twenty minutes to wait here?" Don asked captain Khumalo.

"It would be wiser to move from here as they cannot track us in the dark and we should get as far away as possible. Why do you ask?" captain Khumalo asked.

"We have to turn on the cell phone at eight." Don said.

"You can turn it on whilst we are walking, they will still be able to track it. If we wait, the army group behind could catch us. I counted ten of them, but there could be more." Captain Khumalo said. "Have you tried the cell phone already?"

"Yes, but we did not get any response." Don said.

"Then we have to assume that they are not close, and the safe thing to do is move out. If they are tracking you now, they will follow the movement, and land close to us." Captain Khumalo said.

"Do you need to eat first?" Angela asked.

"No, I would rather get out of here as soon as possible. I can eat on the march. Collect your gear and we will clean up the cave before we leave." Captain Khumalo said.

They moved back into the cave and collected their rucksacks. They packed the bulk of their provisions in one pack on the instructions of captain Khumalo. He elected to carry the heaviest pack and Angela was not needed to carry a pack at all.

"We can move faster if you are not carrying anything." Captain Khumalo said to Angela.

"Angela, watch out for the time so that we do not forget to put the phone on." Don said.

"Will do." Angela said.

They moved off into the dark and captain Khumalo led the way. He was navigating by the stars and headed west, as close as he could determine. It was impossible to walk in a straight line as the terrain forced them to avoid Kopjes, and enable them to stick to the game trails.

Angela suddenly tapped Don on the shoulder and said. "It is nearly eight; we had better switch the phone on."

They stopped in a small clearing and switched on the phone. Almost immediately it bleeped with a message.

"Stay where you are as we are almost upon you. Do not move from this location. Respond at once."

Don tapped in a message. "We are in a clearing and are being followed by at least ten troopers. They are four or five kilometres behind us. We will wait for you." He pressed send and then turned and said. "They are close to us and have told us to stay where we are. I have advised them that there are some troopers behind us. I estimated that they are four to five kilometres behind us. Would you say that is about right, Khumalo?"

Before captain Khumalo could answer another message came though to the phone, "Leave your phone on now, our ETA is five minutes and thirty seconds."

"We must leave the phone on so that they can locate us precisely. They will be here in five minutes." Don said.

"Khumalo was my assessment correct about the troopers?" He asked again.

"Possibly further behind as they would have camped until daylight. They know our general direction and will put up a spotter plane tomorrow. The SAS group will probably parachute within a hundred meters of us, but their plane will probably be heard at the camp. The Mozambicans will not be expecting reinforcements so hopefully they will think that the plane is one of theirs. They should not be too concerned. It all depends on their commander." Captain Khumalo said.

Allen had received Don's sms and said. "They appear to have company. There are ten or so squadies behind them about 4 clicks back. We need to be precise, and the terrain is thick with trees. We will have to be careful when we land to make sure that none of the groups sustain an injury. I would suggest a slow descent."

They all nodded agreement. They had done this many times before and the parachutes that they had could almost be brought to a stop around one hundred feet. They would be able to select a landing site, and each would be in communication with the other.

"Check the direction finder Ralph, I want to be sure that it works before we disembark." Allen said.

Ralph had already set up the direction finder, and it was transmitting, as they flew towards their DZ. The signal was in colour and was silent. The closer they came to the target, the more the colour would intensify, and the range was given in meters.

"It is working OK, and the range is now 35000 meters. We need to get ready, as we are almost over the DZ." Ralph said.

The door hatch was removed, and a red light was glowing over the door. It would take at least six minutes before they were over the DZ. They had already discussed the disembarkation from the aircraft, and Ralph would go first, followed by Allen, as he would lead the force to Don's group. Ralph would be able to communicate via his headset, even as they were parachuting. It was standard procedure that they had enacted many times.

The light over the escape door changed to green and Ralph launched out of the aircraft. The rest followed quickly and opened their chutes as soon as they cleared the plane. Ralph was the lead jumper and now had to coordinate the teams landing.

"Allen, the targets are 200 meters to my right. Follow me in."

"Confirmed." Allen said.

He swung towards Ralph and glided down in a spiral to take the speed out of the descent. At 100 meters, he said. "I can see the clearing on my right, but it is too small to take us all. Group 1 follow me in, Group2 there is another clearing 200 meters to the left of our target. Acknowledge."

The groups acknowledged in order and split up to make their landing.

Allen led his group to the clearing and gently floated down. He touched down and immediately disengaged his chute. He had his Remington automatic ready and covered the drop for the rest of the group. They came in noiselessly and without incident.

Allen's group formed up and immediately took cover. They surveyed the site and confirmed through their headsets that all was clear. Group 2 leader came on his headset and said.

"All down safely and moving to your position."

Don had watched the men land and was amazed at how quickly they had disappeared. In less than ten seconds, there was positively no evidence of them being there. He made as if to move forward but captain Khumalo stopped him.

"They will find us." He whispered. "Do not move."

They waited in silence for what appeared to be an eternity. Nothing moved. No sound was made.

Allen suddenly appeared in front of them as if from nowhere, his Remington at the ready. "Stand still." He ordered.

Angela was petrified. She was frozen in position and could not move.

"Identify yourselves." Allen said.

"Allen it's me Don." Don said.

"Captain Khumalo."

Angela could barely speak but croaked. "Angela Murchison."

"Are you alone?" Allen asked.

"We are alone with a platoon of Mozambican forces some six clicks north of our position." Captain Khumalo reported.

"Group 1, report." Allen ordered.

"All clear boss."

Members 3 and 4 also confirmed.

"Group 2, all clear?" Allen asked.

"All clear, we are fifty meters away and checking the perimeter. No sign of any terr's."

"Regroup at the clearing with Group 2, with members 3 and 4 securing perimeter at 100 meters." Allen ordered.

Allen was all business and did not greet Don as he had anticipated. He was somewhat disappointed, but realised that Allen was here in his professional capacity, and he had not survived as long as he had, by letting his guard down.

"Come forward into the clearing." Allen said.

They moved out of the trees and into the clearing.

"You will understand if I do not introduce you to our group." Allen said to Don.

"I understand." Don said.

"Captain Khumalo, I need to speak with you. Please come this way." Allen said.

Captain Khumalo moved forward and followed Allen to the edge of the clearing.

"Captain, this is your territory, and you have obviously been trained in evasion. How were you planning to escape?" Allen asked.

"We planned to move during the night and get to the border on the east of the Kruger National Park. If that had been impossible, we would have moved into Swaziland, and crossed the border near Malelane. That would be a hard task for Don and Angela as this would be a further 350 K's to the south end of the Kruger Park and a further 100 K's to Malelane." Captain Khumalo said.

"Do you think that the couple with you are up to it?" Allen asked.

"If we cross into the Kruger Park Mopani, the ranger is, but not at the pace we would normally move at. I would suggest that he could cover no more than 40 Ks per night over the five days needed. The lady is an unknown quantity, and I suspect that she could only manage thirty Ks per night. If we had to take the long route, I am not sure that they could make it." Captain Khumalo said.

"You had no plans to leave them?" Allen asked.

"Honestly, I did. If they could not keep up, then I would leave them. At least at the beginning I thought that. The ranger changed my mind. He risked his life to save mine, and, in our game, that means more than self-preservation. I am sure that you know this." Captain Khumalo said.

"I do. Then you and I know that you could never reach the border, when the platoon behind you would be able to cover fifty Ks per day quite easily. What were your plans in that eventuality?" Allen asked.

I was to cover our tracks and get them as far as possible away from the platoon following. Then I would fall back and take out their tracker.

That would slow them down provided that we could cover our tracks effectively." Captain Khumalo said.

"I understand. That would buy you a day or so, and you could put more distance between you." Allen said.

"That was my plan." Captain Khumalo said.

"You realise that we cannot be seen in Mozambique or South Africa for that matter. If we engage the forces following us, there will be hell to pay. We need to evade capture without contact. We have detailed maps of the area, but there is nothing better than local knowledge of the terrain. We are all trained, but Don and the girl are not. We will need your assistance later I am sure, but, for now, we need to discuss the plan of action with the two groups." Allen said.

"I know this area well from all our excursions into Mozambique when the war was on. There are plantations close to the border where we would not be spotted. The problem is that they laid mines all over the place, and they have not been marked. The safest route to avoid the mines is direct to the Kruger Park. The problem there is that the cover is sparse, and detection would be at its most probable. We would be out in the open for long periods, and they are bound to put up a spotter plane or helicopter." Captain Khumalo said.

"I understand, please come and meet the groups, and we will discuss the options." Allen said.

Allen took captain Khumalo to join the groups. Angela was shivering even though the night was warm. These men were hard, and with their black military fatigues, they looked terrifying. She held Don tightly, and Don felt her shivering.

"Are you OK?" Don asked.

"I am petrified." Angela said.

"Remember Angela, they are on our side." Don said.

"I am more than thankful for that, I would hate them to be against us. They are so scary with their blackened faces and their efficiency. They move like predators." Angela said.

"They are predators." Don said. "They will get us home safely, but we are going to have to work hard to keep up with them. They are very fit, and a walk of 50 Ks is a stroll for them. Will you be able to cope?" Don asked.

"I will do my best." Angela said.

Allen introduced Captain Khumalo to the groups, and went through what the captain had said about the mines and the best route to take. They opened their maps and planned an escape route. They discussed at length their options with each member of the group having input. They concluded their plan, and Allen turned to captain Khumalo, and said.

"Do you have anything further to add?" Allen asked.

"I would just say do not underestimate the Mozambican forces. They are battle hardened and very fit. They are not as disciplined as other armies, but that only makes them less predictable. I have fought against them many times, and know that once they set out to achieve an objective they follow through relentlessly."

"We will keep that in mind captain." Allen said.

Allen turned to the group 2 leader and said. "Place your group as agreed, covering 4 kilometres ahead. My group will protect Don and the girl with the captain falling back to cover our rear with Mike. We will move due west to the Kruger Park, and we will travel at a rapid pace until we observe that either Don, or the girl cannot keep up. We want to do at least forty kilometres per night with breaks on the hour for five minutes."

The two groups agreed, and group 2 moved out.

"We will give them one hour, and then we will follow. We have our compass bearing that both groups will trace. We will only have radio contact on the hour or if an emergency occurs. Mike, captain, you can move back now. Keep about one kilometre apart and behind us. Captain, you take the right flank and Mike you take the left. That way we should form a box that they cannot penetrate without us knowing." Allen said.

The captain and Mike stood up and left the group heading back towards the platoon of soldiers.

Allen moved across to Don and Angela and sat opposite them. "We have made our plans, and we will be moving out in fifty minutes. This will be an arduous walk for you, but you must tell me if you are flagging. We would rather set an achievable pace than find that you are burnt out too soon. In any event, we plan to cross the border in five days time. If we can improve on that time then it will obviously be better. Do you have any questions?" Allen asked.

"No, I do not think so." Don said.

Allen looked at Angela and said. "I am sorry if we frightened you when we came in, but we never know what to expect, and we always take precautions. I can assure you that you are safe with us. We will get you home in one piece."

"Thank you, I must admit that when I saw you I was terrified. I am beginning to feel a little better now." Angela said.

"Rest now and we will let you know when we will move out. I will lead, with Angela following and Don behind. We have Ralph and Bennie, at the rear. Mike and captain Khumalo will be a kilometre back on our right and left flanks. Group 2 will be three kilometres ahead also covering our right and left flanks. We will not be taken by surprise. We have done this many times so just concentrate on using your energy efficiently. We move at a steady pace without speeding up, and we set the rhythm. Do not try to move faster as it will only disrupt your rhythm. You will be surprised at how many kilometres you will be able to cover if you move rhythmically." Allen said.

"I understand." Angela said.

"Good, we will call you when we are ready."

The group set off at the allotted time and moved down the trail. They moved at an easy lope that Angela found remarkably easy to maintain. She let her mind drift and got into a rhythm that was almost musical. She started to use a song in her head to keep the beat. Using it like a mantra. She was surprised when Allen called a halt. They had marched for one hour and the time had flown.

"We can take a five minute break now," he said.

They sat down and rested for the five minutes.

"It is time to move on." Allen said.

They repeated the pattern throughout the night without event. They had covered forty kilometres; they only had one hundred and sixty kilometres to complete.

Allen moved over to Don and Angela and asked.

"How are you both doing?"

"I am fine, the march was not that bad, and the terrain was flat. That made the march so much easier." Don said.

"And you?" Allen asked Angela.

"It was not as difficult as I thought, but I have trained for marathons, so I am reasonably fit." Angela said.

"Tonight we will leave earlier and cover a bit more distance. We have covered around forty K's already. Tonight we will do fifty K's. If you cannot manage then do not try to hide it, just let me know." Allen said.

"I will." Angela said.

"Good, we will find some cover now, and we will rest for the day. We will move out at dusk, so you will need to get some sleep. Do not worry about being attacked as the surrounding area is guarded. The outliers will be coming in shortly to report." Allen said.

Allen moved off, and found a copse that had excellent cover both from the sides and above. He called Don and Angela over and said.

"You get in there and use your backpack for a headrest. We will call you when it is time to leave. Have a drink and some food and then sleep as long as you can."

Don and Angela moved into the cover and checked the ground for unwanted insects. They lay together with their heads resting on Don's backpack. They were asleep in seconds. They were much more tired than they had supposed.

It seemed that they had only been asleep for a moment when Allen shook Don awake.

"Mike has just reported the platoon is on our trail some six kilometres back. We have to move out. It is three in the afternoon, and we will need to keep to the cover as much as possible." Allen said. "Drink some water now and get ready to move out in five minutes."

Don turned to look at Angela and could see that she was extremely frightened.

"Do not worry." Don said. "Allen and his men will protect us, with force if necessary."

"I must seem like a wimp to you, I am always frightened." Angela said.

"You and I both, but I just hide it better." Don said.

Chapter 40

They met in the cabinet room at ten sharp. "Well, gentlemen, what have you for us? As you can see all the cabinet is present, and we wait for your proposals. Colonel Masters, you will go first. The whole of the cabinet has been briefed so you do not have to repeat yesterdays briefing." The Prime Minister said.

Colonel Masters stood up and moved to the projector at the end of the table. He switched it on, and a white square appeared on the screen. He placed a laptop adjacent to the projector and connected to the input of the projector. He pressed enter on the laptop, and the first page came up on the screen.

"Prime Minister, gentlemen." Colonel Masters said. "We have produced a plan of action to cover three scenarios. These are." He pointed with his marker, and a red dot appeared next to the scenario marked.

(1) We do not interfere this would mean allowing events to take their natural course and then follow through after the attempted coup with actions to ensure stability.

"The next option will be a little more complex as can be seen." Colonel Masters said. Then colonel Masters moved to the second page.

(2) We advise the South African government of the planned coup and leave it to them to sort it out. Supplementary actions: -

(a) Monitor the response and ensure that British subjects are not maltreated

(b) Utilise our relationship to control the ANC

(c) Notify the UN of the possible coup and have aid standing by in the event of a serious conflict arising

(d) Move part of the Indian Ocean fleet to South African waters

(e) Enter into negotiations with the ANC government following the coup attempt

Colonel Masters then said. "We have one more option, and this is the preferred option, by the majority of the planners."

(3) We actively move in to try and control and defuse the situation. The ultimate goal would be to prevent the coup without bloodshed. We would achieve this by the following actions:

(a) We would use the Consulate staff to contact the key players

(b) The ANC would not be told all the Intel that we have and would be guided by our staff in MI6 and the SAS on how best to prevent the coup before it started.

(c) The planners would be quietly and efficiently arrested. This would remove the decision makers from the field and thus disrupt communications.

(d) The ANC would be kept under control at all times and only allowed to hold suspected participants as and when we direct.

(e) All ground forces would be brought back to barracks and controlled from there

(f) The air force would be grounded and pilots restricted to their barracks

(h) The navy would be brought back to port, and the Royal navy would be standing off shore at the selected ports, to prevent a break out.

Colonel Masters said, "This is just the bones of the options and there will be far more detail once an option has been chosen."

"Thank you." The Prime Minister said. "Foreign secretary, what do you think of these options and are there others that we could explore?"

"There is always a multiplicity of options, yet they are essentially a variation on the three put forward. I believe that the only viable option is option 3. You have made your position clear on doing nothing and picking up the pieces later, and option 2 in reality means the same thing."

The cabinet members discussed at length the proposals and the objectives. The meeting was in the second hour when the Prime Minister said.

"Are there any other comments?"

"Yes Prime Minister. How do we propose we control the ANC once they are aware of a coup? They are bound to have some suspicions and have probably gathered their own intelligence already. They would relish the opportunity to remove the white generals from office and the opportunity for them to seize control in Natal." John Brandt said.

"Colonel Masters, James, can you answer that question?" The prime minister asked.

Colonel Masters looked across the table to James Banning and said. "James, do you want to go first?"

"Certainly colonel," James Banning replied.

"We have run a number of scenarios through our computer and have selected the following. We will infiltrate the government of South Africa using our assets in South Africa. The key players will be monitored, and the latest communication systems will be used. This should prevent any surprises, as our technology will easily get past the South African governments jamming devices. We will be able to listen in to virtually all their conversations. Colonel Master's SAS team will be in South Africa and ready to assist our assets should it become necessary. We have also advised GCHQ that we will require satellite monitoring of both the SA government and the general's headquarters."

"Colonel Masters, do you have anything to add?" The Prime Minister asked.

"Yes sir, the two groups that we are using to escort the three fugitives are within one hundred and twenty kilometres of the border. They estimate that they will cross the border in two to three day's, dependant upon the need to evade both the Mozambican and then the South African forces. They will then proceed to Johannesburg, where we have a safe house, with the help of James Banning's assets."

"I do not need the finer detail of your plans, but I wish to be informed of any adverse developments, before they become a major issue." The Prime Minister said.

"That will be done sir." Colonel Masters said.

"Foreign Secretary, I wish you to be in control of this operation and liaise between me, the SAS and MI6." The Prime Minister said.

"I will meet daily with Colonel Masters and James throughout the operation." The foreign secretary said.

"Thank you gentlemen, then that concludes the meeting. I cannot stress enough how serious this planned coup is to the stability of Africa and the impact it could have on the rest of the world. This cannot be allowed to happen." The Prime Minister said.

Chapter 41

The generals and the NFP met the next morning, and general Lauberschagne opened the meeting by saying.

"Gentlemen, you have in front of you the document that we will all sign today. It does not completely outline the details of the proposal but is adequate to commit all the parties to the proposal." General Lauberschagne said.

The generals and the NFP delegates picked up the document and started to read the contents.

It is agreed that the country at present is going through turmoil that is a direct result of the ANC policies. This has gone on for far too long and needs to be addressed immediately. It is proposed, by the signatories, to take control of all government functions with a view to bring stability back to South Africa.

This will be done in the next parliament recess. The action will require all the armed forces that will be under the command of General Lauberschagne. This will include the air force and the navy.

It is intended that, with the help of the NFP, that this will be a bloodless coup. The territories will be broken up into three distinct governing countries. The NFP will govern from East London to Cosy Bay and the whole of Natal. The military representatives will fall back to the Cape provinces, but the Free State will also be under their control.

The territories north of the Cape Provinces will be under the control of the ANC. They will govern these territories without interference from the NFP or the armies of the alliance in the Cape Provinces.

In the event, of action against the alliance then the NFP will help the alliance and vice versa.

Signed

General Lauberschagne
General Meyer
General Naude
General De La Rey
General Beyer
Minister Justice Nkabo
General Mkondo

"General Lauberschagne, can we discuss the document and the border of the country that you propose to give to the ANC? We believe that Gauteng would be better placed in Natal." Justice Nkabo said.

"We believe that we have put forward the most acceptable solution for the country. If we try and take too much territory, then the ANC will have to fight to recover what they have lost. If there appears to be an acceptable deal, then they will, at least for a period, accept their lot." General Lauberschagne said.

"I understand what you are saying, but the ANC will not easily give up South Africa. In their minds, they liberated the country." Justice Nkabo said.

"Then you will appreciate that there has to be a region that would generate funds for their government." General Lauberschagne said.

"If we intend to take control of the government then why not govern the whole country with our alliance?" Justice Nkabo asked.

"If we were to do that then we would incur the wrath of the rest of the world. As it is there would be a period of difficulty but splitting up the country on tribal lines would be seen as a less of a problem." General Lauberschagne said.

"Do you believe that the ANC would accept such a situation?" General Mkondo asked.

"No, I do not. It may be more acceptable than taking the whole country as this would surely create a resistance of greater proportions." General Lauberschagne said.

"In any event, the country would initially be in control of the alliance and only after a period of time would the ANC be allowed to negotiate a settlement." General Naude said.

"Then you are suggesting that at that stage, we would negotiate the boundaries." Justice Nkabo said.

"I think that would be more practical." General Lauberschagne said.

"Then let us move on to how we propose to take over the country, without bloodshed, and what needs to be done in the next four months. It seems a daunting task, to say the least." Justice Nkabo said.

"The proposal is to move all military aircraft to the bases in Natal and the Cape provinces. The navy in the Cape and Natal will control the ports. The army bases will be in the general's hands and with the exception of the North West Province, they will be totally closed down." General Lauberschagne said.

"Do you have enough troops on the ground to do that?" General Mkondo asked.

"Not totally, this is why we are not touching the bases in the North West province. There are enough troops, with your help, to manage the rest of the country." General Lauberschagne said.

"What of the air force?" Justice Nkabo asked.

"All the fighter planes, transporters and helicopters, will be sent to the Cape with the exception of those squadrons in Natal. They will be left in your hands, and the closures will be coordinated."

"That would leave the police and the media as the only opposition, is that what you are aiming for?" General Mkondo asked.

"No, we will also shut down all broadcasters in both radio and television. We will even close down the cell phone companies until control is complete."

"How would you fund and feed the forces involved?" General Mkondo asked.

"We have stock piled sufficient food and equipment to last at least six weeks. I suggest that you do the same in Natal."

"There would be strikes at every factory throughout the country. How do you plan to manage that event?" Justice Nkabo said.

"We would announce a state of emergency and ensure that key installations are kept operating. This would be the power stations, hospitals, selected industries and communication networks." General Lauberschagne said.

"It sounds as though you will be thin on the ground to cover all these requirements. Where will you get all these resources?" General Mkondo asked.

"We have at our disposal a large number of process operators and engineers to adequately cover the assets that we need to maintain in operation. They are spread throughout the country and ready to do their part." General Lauberschagne said.

"How would you deal with the neighbouring countries and internationally?" Justice Nkabo asked.

"Prior to the action, we will create disturbances across the country that would lead to a state of emergency. We would then take control as a matter of preserving law and order as the situation would be out of control." General Lauberschagne said.

"You have plans to create these disturbances?" General Mkondo asked.

"Yes we do." General Lauberschagne said. "We will now sign the document committing ourselves to this action."

The document was passed around the table, and they signed against their name.

"Gentlemen, we will now go through the detail of the plan, and this will be presented by Major van der Rust. He will be able to answer all your questions with the help of my colleagues here. Our international specialist, Ruben De Kok, will go through the reactions of the countries both in Africa and the rest of the world. He has generated many scenarios and developed strategies to counter any event. When completed Mr. John Buys will take you through the financial systems, including the stock exchange, and the likely reaction to our takeover. He has also formulated plans to prevent the collapse of the country and analysed the countries that would still do business with the new regime. This has taken years of planning and will be the basis of the way forward from this date." General Lauberschagne said.

General Lauberschagne rang the bell and the orderly entered. "Tell Major van der Rust that we are ready for him now."

"Yes sir," the orderly said and left the room.

Chapter 42

They moved out at just after three in the afternoon. Allen set a fast pace and was worried that the girl would not sustain the pace. He was even more concerned with getting them to a safe hideout.

They covered ten kilometres and had a five-minute break. Allen went across to Angela and Don and said.

"Are you two OK?"

Don looked at Angela and said.

"We cannot keep up this pace much longer as Angela is almost exhausted. We have been running now for three days. How close is the platoon behind us?"

"They are about five Ks but closing on us. I do not want a confrontation, but it may be inevitable. If we have to fight our way out, we will. I would rather evade them than have contact. This will mean that we either slow them down, or we have to maintain the same pace as they are. Angela, can you keep this up for another hour?" he asked.

"I will do my best. I think another hour is about all that I am capable of." Angela said.

"The problem is if they have radioed in and given our direction. They would soon figure out where we intend to cross the border. The only advantage that we have is that they think there are only three in the group. They may well spread their forces a bit thinner if they think you are on your own. If we make contact, and there are any survivors, then they will know the real strength of our group and deploy accordingly. If we take them all out then, the military are bound to realize something has happened when they do not make radio contact. This would only buy us a day or so."

"But they would figure it out eventually and be even more determined to catch us regardless of the cost." Don said.

"Exactly, that is our dilemma. I calculate at the pace we are moving at, we would be over the border by late tomorrow afternoon. This would mean marching during the day and we would be exposed. If we take out the platoon behind us, they would almost certainly put up a spotter plane. They could flood the border ahead of us, and we would have to fight our way through. This would then alert the South African forces." Allen said.

"What do you propose to do?" asked Don.

"We have to push on until we reach the border. We will delay any action by the guys behind us until we get close to the border. We can take you through, and the rest of the group will hold back the guys following, for as long as possible. Once they break off they will never catch them." Allen said.

"Then we had better get going as I will only stiffen up waiting here." Angela said.

"I agree." Don said.

"Then we will move out now. I have contacted the SAS group behind, and they are now some 4 Ks back along the trail. I will set a reasonable pace and keep in touch with the group behind, measuring our progress. Follow me." Allen said.

They set off at a steady lope that would eat up the kilometres that they had to cover. Allen was checking every ten minutes on their progress. They were just maintaining the distance and would not be overtaken if they could keep going at the current pace.

"Group 1 leader; there is open country ahead for a couple of kilometres. We will have to take cover or risk being spotted." Group leader of unit 2 reported.

"Understood, we have two hours of light, and then we will be able to cross." Allen said.

"We will maintain watch here. I do not see any evidence of any army group in the area. We have checked for two kilometres to our left and right flank." Group 2 leader reported.

"Group 1 leader, this is number 2, the army group is speeding up and closing on us at a good speed. I estimate contact in one, to one and a half, hours."

"Group 2 leader, we have a situation here. We are about to be overrun by the platoon behind us. We will need your support in the event of contact." Allen said.

"Group 1 leader, we are returning now and will cover your position. When you pass we will then lay in wait for the enemy behind." Group 2 leader said.

"Ralph, Bennie. Fall back and cover our rear. Mike and Khumalo will join you soon. Group 2 will follow them. Meanwhile, we will head towards the border. If they make contact, then you must eliminate any threat. Understand?" Allen said.

"Understood." Mike said.

The platoon commander of the Mozambican forces knew that he was closing in on the fugitives. He had been given orders to dispose of them at the earliest opportunity. He had gambled on the direction they would take, and he had been right. He had sent forward his point man to give them the distance ahead and knew that contact was now imminent.

They had two flankers running adjacent to them at fifty meters on either side with the main group strung out behind. They would be difficult to ambush. He was still cautious, even though he knew that only one of the fugitives had any experience in the armed forces. He knew the Reccies from old and was not about to take any chances.

The only problem that he had was that they continually lost sight of the flankers due to the bush. They were running hard now, as their quarry was close.

Mike picked up the flanker on his side as Khumalo picked up the other. They signalled that they had spotted them and allowed the flankers to pass them. The platoon was allowed through.

"Ralph, two flankers heading your way, they are one hundred meters apart. The platoon is spread over another hundred meters from point to the back marker. We will cover the rear when you attack. Is group 2 with you yet?'

"Yes, Mike. They are set around the trail. We will allow the enemy to pass and then take them out. You should catch the rear guard on their way back."

Ralph and group 2 waited in the bush and could now see the flankers pushing through. They were immediately dispatched without a sound. The leading unit came running on and ran straight into the hail of fire. There was nowhere to escape. The rear sections of three squadies turned back and were quickly picked off by Khumalo and Mike. There were no survivors. It had taken less than a moment to decimate the platoon.

Allen heard the gunshots and this spurred him on to greater efforts. They did not rest until they had loped for another hour. Then Allen said.

"We will rest in this cover." Allen pointed to a thicket on their right. "The rest of the group will rejoin us shortly."

Angela and Don were too breathless to respond. They flopped down in the cover panting.

"Group 2 leader, all accounted for?" Allen asked.

"Yes, we back tracked three kilometres, but there was no follow up. Ralph, Mike, and Khumalo went on ahead. They will be back with you in twenty minutes."

"We will change positions with my group clearing ahead, and you follow up as our rearguard and flankers. We will cross the open ground after sunset."

"Understood."

Allen turned to Angela, and Don, and said.

"The immediate threat has been neutralised so you can rest for the next twenty minutes. We will then move on towards the border. We are now only eighty Ks away from our crossing point."

Don and Angela merely nodded, as they were still breathless from their exertions.

Allen moved away from the thicket and took cover to protect them both.

"These guys have just killed ten men, and they talk about it so nonchalantly." Angela said.

"That is what they do for a living. You must remember that they are also at risk. It is not easy for them, but they have to be professional about what they do." Don said.

Mike, Bennie and captain Khumalo arrived exactly as predicted. They reported to Allen their encounter and the fact that there were no survivors.

Allen moved over to Don and Angela and said.

"Time to move out, we will not have to run hard as we now have a little time to reach the border before the Mozambicans discover the missing platoon."

Don and Angela reluctantly rose from the ground and followed Allen down the track. Mike and Bennie had moved ahead, and Khumalo covered their rear. They ran at a steady pace for another hour. They were still one kilometre short of the open ground, and the light was beginning to disappear extremely quickly.

"Mike, are you across the clearing yet?" Allen enquired.

"Nearly there, we have checked the perimeter, nothing to report, its all clear." Mike said.

"As soon as it is dark we will cross the open ground and then head for the border as fast as we can." Allen said.

"How far is it now?" Angela asked.

"We will try and do thirty Ks tonight, and that will leave us about twenty Ks short. If we can achieve that, we will cross tomorrow. We will have a bus waiting for us in the Kruger Park. You could be home by tomorrow night, or at least in the safe house." Allen said. "Do not lose heart now, we are nearly there."

It was obvious to Allen that this had raised her spirits. She was more relaxed now that the end was in sight.

"You ran comrades?" Allen asked.

"Yes I did." Angela said. "Three times and I finished within the time limit each time."

"How did you feel when you were twenty Ks from the finish?" Allen asked.

"When you see that sign with twenty Ks to go, and you have already run seventy, you want to quit." Angela said.

"You didn't quit, though, did you?" Allen said.

"No, but each time I almost stopped." Angela said.

"The important thing is that you finished what you started." Allen said. "You are in that position now. All you have to do is tell your body that it has still got more reserves, and you will make it, as you did in the Comrades." Allen said.

"Yes, you go through the first pain barrier and then suddenly you get your second wind. It is the third and the fourth that get increasingly more difficult." Angela said.

"It is not the body that dictates what you do. It is your mind. When you believe that you can go no further it is amazing how much more you have left in you. I want you to use your mind to control your body and ignore the pain that you feel. Tomorrow, this will be just a bad memory." Allen said.

Don smiled and said.

"Allen, if you ever leave your beloved army, you could easily become a motivational speaker."

"How are you doing Don?" Allen asked.

"I am as stiff as a board, but still hanging in there." Don said.

"Good, that's the spirit." Allen said.

Allen called over captain Khumalo and said.

"You are still very fit considering how long it has been since you left the army."

"I am still in the army, and our exercise regime is as stiff as yours." He said proudly.

"No offence Khumalo. It takes a lot of physical training to keep as fit as you are." Allen said.

"You work in groups of four, whereas we work in groups of three. We could cover seventy-five kilometres in a day and repeat this as often as required. We trained with the Reccies, who trained with you guys in the UK. You never forget that training, and you keep going. It is all in the mind." Captain Khumalo said.

"Captain, you know the terrain around here. What is up ahead?" Allen asked.

"We have a tough decision to make. If we use the plantations for cover, we risk the possibility of stepping on land mines. The alternative is open savannah and then we can only cross at night." Captain Khumalo said.

"Is there no cover at all?" Allen asked.

"Not from an aerial reconnaissance."

"What about villages on the way?" Allen asked.

"Before the war, there were many villages, but Renamo and Freelimo forces, obliterated most of them." Captain Khumalo said.

"Yeah, that was a particularly brutal war." Allen said.

"That's Africa." Captain Khumalo said laconically.

"What is the distance of the savannah leading to the border?" Allen asked.

"It will be the last twenty Ks." He responded.

"That means we would be exposed for three to four hours." Allen said.

"That is about right considering the fitness levels of these two." Captain Khumalo said, pointing to Angela and Don. If we went at normal rate, they would never keep up. I would suggest that a reconnaissance group move ahead and lead us around the obvious ambush sites. I am sure that you do not want any further contact with the Mozambican, or the South African military." Captain Khumalo concluded.

"Yes, we have our group scouting in front now. They will stay four kilometres ahead and report any activity."

"If I may suggest something, I would split them in two groups at two kilometre intervals. They would then be able to cover the right and left flank at meaningful intervals as the Moz army are pretty damn efficient."

"Why do you say that, please explain?" Allen asked.

"They are bush fighters and can cover a lot of ground in the time it would take your men to cover four kilometres. Your men will have to be careful as they approach any possible ambush site, and this is bound to slow them down. The Moz army does not have to worry about an ambush and these guys can be out of sight but within striking distance. They will not use vehicles as the dust cloud would give them away." Captain Khumalo said.

"I understand and thank you for your advice. We will deploy accordingly."

Allen then contacted his group and said.

"We will reduce the forward cover to two kilometres. Please acknowledge.

"Understood and changing now." Ralph replied.

"OK, guys we can move out now." Allen said.

They moved at a steady pace that would cover five kilometres per hour. This was well within the reach of both Angela and Don. They marched on through the night in complete silence. Allen would allow them to rest five minutes in every hour and was constantly checking with both the rearguard and the scouts ahead. They met with no resistance.

To Don's surprise, the farther they walked, the fitter his body became. He had always been fit, but this was a new experience for him. The longer they marched the better he felt. He noticed the determined look on Angela's face and could see that she felt the same way. He found the strength to touch her and smile. She smiled back and was about to say something, but Don shook his head. Better to conserve their energy.

They made excellent time and were at the savannah strip before sunrise.

Allen, in front of the column, signalled for them to stop.

"This is the last piece of cover before the open savannah. We must wait here for the rest of the day and move out at dusk."

They bivouacked in a thicket and placed guards at the perimeter. The two groups including Khumalo had now formed into a single group, and sentry duty was meted out accordingly.

Allen called his group together and discussed the run for the border.

"We have to contact our pick up party. Bennie, can you bring the satellite phone please?"

Bennie brought the phone and waited for Allen's instructions. He dialled through to headquarters and sent their message in a compressed digital format that would be on the air for two seconds. This was acknowledged as received by their headquarters in Catterick.

"We will receive their instructions shortly." Allen said to the group. "We need to have an equipment check before we cross the border.'

They all ran their equipment check on ammunition, weapons and their personal radio connections. All were functioning as required and the ammunition levels were more than adequate.

"We will wait here for the sunset." Allen said.

He moved across to Angela and Don and said.

"We will spend the day here and cross the border tonight. Our back up crew will meet us at around seven thirty. Settle down, eat and drink what you can, and we will wake you at sunset."

They settled in the thicket of Mopani, and Angela and Don immediately fell asleep.

They moved off at dusk and the sky was clear and starlit. There was no moon, only pitch darkness. Allen set a fast pace. Don and Angela had recovered from the fatigue of the previous day and were now becoming hardened to the march. They kept the pace up until they were ten Ks short of the border. Allen called a halt and said.

"Take a rest now as we will be crossing over in around three hours. I will call you when we are ready to go."

"That's OK Allen we are both able to carry on." Don said.

"We need to check out the border fence and make sure that it is clear. You can rest now as it will be at least one hour before we have finished our reconnaissance." Allen said.

"Group 1 come in." Came over the comm's.

"Group 1 leader." Allen responded.

"We have a patrol of around twenty enemies coming in fast from the border side directly towards your position. They are well-armed and moving in groups of five. They are spread out over a distance of one kilometre. We will return to support."

"Understood, group 2 leader, we will rendezvous one kilometre east."

Allen called up Mike, Ralph, Bennie and captain Khumalo.

"We have a patrol of around twenty troopers coming towards us. They are set in groups of five and spread out over one kilometre. They are well armed and moving fast. They do not know our position, and they may pass us by, any comments?" Allen asked.

"We are about ten Ks from the border, and if we move ahead, and away from them, they will overrun our position, and not be able to locate us." Ralph said.

"I agree." Captain Khumalo said. "If we stay static they may just run into us. They have set their forces such that if one group makes contact, the others can move in rapidly and close us down. This was standard procedure in the bush wars. They may lose one group, but others will soon overpower us. If they think they have missed us, they will regroup and return. They will keep sweeping until they find us. It is also likely that they have back up, well hidden, to intercept us at the border."

"What would their normal compliment be on a mission like this?" Allen asked.

"It could be as many as fifty or as little as thirty. It will definitely be more than the patrol that we encountered yesterday." Captain Khumalo said.

"We cannot wait until daylight as we will be far easier to locate in good light. Our best chance is to move off now and risk the encounter." Ralph said.

"Although they are moving fast it will not be easy to detect them if they are experienced troops. They can move very quickly and virtually silently. We will need a point man on the south side and another on the north side." Captain Khumalo said.

"Any other comments?" Allen asked.

"We have about ten Ks to go. I would check the border and make sure that they are not waiting for us. They know the direction that we are headed and, with no variation, it is easy to predict where we will cross the border. We should consider moving south for ten Ks and then check again." Captain Khumalo said.

"I agree." Mike said. "If we keep moving in a straight line we are very predictable. I suggest that we send group two ten Ks south and get them to check the border along the way. This will delay our crossing but will still see us over the border well before dawn."

"If we do that then we reduce our force if we need to defend our position. We could easily evade the forces if we did not have the two non-combatants with us. They are not trained or capable of either fighting their way out or evading the troops ahead. We can only move at their speed." Allen said.

"Khumalo, how often do the SADF patrol the border with Mozambique these days?" Ralph asked.

"Not very often, we would be very unlucky to run into a border patrol. It would be much more likely to run into an anti-poaching patrol, and even that possibility is remote."

"Then if we took out the patrol ahead, it would be unlikely that the South Africans would respond?"

"Yes." Captain Khumalo said.

"Then why don't we drive straight through them using group two as a spearhead and we can follow up behind mopping up any resistance?" Ralph asked.

"Because then we would then put Don and Angela in the firing line and I think another contact would not go down well with the Boss." Allen said.

"Then the only option is to move up due south by ten Ks. We can use half of group two to forage ahead and clear the route, and we can then put out two points at one click intervals so that we can move quickly. This would protect our front and flanks with the balance of the group in protective formation around our group."

"I agree. We move in standard formation with two ahead covered by their support team of two. We then link with the balance of group 2, and head straight for the border using the same formation. It will take two hours longer but would be the safer option." Allen said.

The plan was agreed and communicated to group two. They would separate, and two SAS would check the border, and two SAS would be at point. They would move at speed.

Allen allowed the groups to set up their positions and when in place he gave the order to move out. Allen led, with Angela following, with Don bringing up the rear of the column. They were to stay close to Allen and move at a pace that he set.

They got the all clear from the point men and set out at a steady jog. They ran for six kilometres until the point man reported a patrol ahead. They stopped and took cover. The patrol passed without incident, and they moved on again. They reached their assembly point still four hours before dawn.

Allen contacted the two flankers that were checking the border. They had seen two patrols of ten soldiers, but had avoided them. The way was clear to the border.

"Hold your position on the border and wait for our arrival. We should be with you in one and a half hours." Allen said.

He received the affirmative.

"How are you holding up?" Allen asked Don and Angela.

"We will be fine." Don said.

The group of eleven was now much more confident of crossing the border without incident. They set up the same formation and set out to the border. They moved at a steady jog and were within two Ks when Ralph calling interrupted Allen.

"There is a patrol up front of around twenty soldiers. We will stop and let them pass. I will call you when they are through the area."

They took cover in a Mopani thicket, and Allen recalled the two point men, and posted them on their flanks. It took an hour for the patrol to clear the area.

"They are through." Ralph reported.

They moved rapidly to the border and reached the fence just as the dawn was breaking behind them. They regrouped at the border, and Mike quickly cut the fence, and they clambered through. Group 2 went first to check the area followed by Ralph, Mike, Bennie and Allen. Angela and Don followed with Khumalo bringing up the rear.

Suddenly a shot rang out, and Don fell to the ground, clutching his chest. Angela screamed and ran towards him. Allen rugby tackled her and brought her to the floor and covered her with his body. They were all extremely exposed.

Captain Khumalo turned and went back into the long grass and set up to cover their rear. He fired upon the patrol that was now firing from a position one hundred metres to their rear. The patrol was now running hard towards them.

Captain Khumalo picked off the leader with his first shot and then moved to the second runner. He took careful aim and the man screamed and pitched into the grass. Ralph, Mike and Bennie, slipped back through the Fence, and moved to support Captain Khumalo, firing as they ran. Ralph and Mike fired non-stop and then Bennie and captain Khumalo took over whilst they reloaded. The hail of fire was both accurate and effective. Five of the patrol went down at the first volley and the others dived into cover. The Group 2 leader then burst through the fence pinning down the patrol whilst captain Khumalo and Bennie moved forward, firing constantly. They then dropped to the ground to reload as Ralph and Mike took up the offensive position. The whole of group two then joined in, and they quickly mopped up the patrol.

Allen dragged Don into cover and could see blood oozing from his chest. He was in considerable pain. He ripped off his shirt, and was relieved to see that the bullet had crossed his chest without penetrating, and it was only a flesh wound. He removed his pack and dug out his first aid kit and quickly bound the wound. It would be painful, but not life threatening.

Angela was close to hysterics, and Allen said sharply.

"Angela, calm down, it is only a flesh wound. Come and sit with Don whilst I check on the others."

Angela moved across to Don who was laid on the grass and obviously in shock. She took hold of his hand and said.

"Don, you will be OK. Just lay still until they come back."

Allen moved cautiously through the fence and could see the two groups returning. Captain Khumalo was limping and had been shot in the leg. The bullet had passed through his right leg calf muscle and fortunately had not touched bone. He would be able to carry on.

They quickly moved through the fence and got into cover posting the sentries required. Allen checked on Don's wound and could see that the blood had stopped flowing but knew it would be painful for him to walk. He moved across to captain Khumalo and said.

"How is your leg, can you still walk?"

"I will be OK, just a flesh wound. I was lucky."

"We have to put some distance between us as they may follow us into South Africa. They will not be happy when they see what happened to their platoon."

"They will contact the SADF and report the incident, which will send a team out here to find out what happened and look for us." Captain Khumalo said.

"We are only ten Ks from our pick up point, and we should be OK. I have already called for collection, and they can move very quickly to our position. You will be transferred to a bus and then taken out of the Park as tourists." Allen said.

They moved off into the bush towards their pick up point. Don was in pain but could manage to walk at a steady pace. There was less danger now as they should soon be collected and they would head to the safe house in Johannesburg.

They received their call sign. "Cobra 1, this is Cobra 2, we are at the collection point." The voice said.

"Cobra 2 this is Cobra 1, ETA fifteen minutes." Allen said. "We have two casualties."

"Cobra 1, do you need an ambulance?"

"No, they will be OK until we reach the safe house."

They arrived at the collection point without incident. There were four Land cruisers waiting for them. MI6 had set up the vehicles to look like an expedition team to film wildlife in the Kruger National Park.

Don's wound was checked, and antibiotics applied. Although inflamed, it was not a serious injury. Captain Khumalo was treated and his leg bandaged. Their clothes now covered any signs of their injury. Their travel documents to get out of the park were well forged, and they crossed the border gate without incident. They had escaped, and would travel to Johannesburg and the safe house.

Chapter 43

Jay Ramasey looked at the DNA results and whistled out loud. He could not believe the name that he had in front of him. His assertion that the assassin was female had proven to be correct. He had to do some background checks before he took this information to his colleague, captain Andries Els.

He went down to the law courts in Durban and asked to see the administrator of the court. He then asked for the attendance record of attorney Annette Venter. The clerk was about to ask him why, but Ramasey said.

"This is a confidential matter, and I cannot discuss any of the reasons for my request. Please let me know when you have the detail that I requested."

He gave the clerk his card, left the courts, and went back to his office. He felt that he had finally cracked the case but proving it would be difficult. He had to decide if the suspect had been in the offices of Bailey and Bailey on the day that Molefe was shot.

He then drove to the offices of Bailey and Bailey and went up to the front desk. He saw the security officer at the desk and asked.

"Do you keep a register of visitors?"

"Yes, sergeant, why do you ask?" the security guard said.

"Police business, can you give me the register for Thursday, 15th May, this year?" he asked.

"Certainly." The security guard got up and moved to a cabinet and took out the ledger marked 'May'. He handed it over to the sergeant and said. "I would keep this in the office as we use this ledger for proof of visits of our clients."

"I will sign for the ledger and return the ledger if there is nothing that we require. Otherwise, it will be considered police evidence and will be locked in the evidence room." Jay Ramasey said.

Jay went back to his office and went through the pages referring to 15th May. He could find no evidence that Venter had been there. He checked throughout the ledger and Venter had, according to the ledger, not been to the offices of Bailey and Bailey any time in that month. He decided to go back to the offices.

He drove to the offices and went through the front door and saw the same security guard on duty.

"Does everyone who visits these offices sign the register?" He asked.

"Not if they are known attorneys and do not wish to be recorded." The security guard said. "This register is mainly for clients."

"So another attorney could enter the building, and you would not necessarily record their visit."

"That is correct."

"Thanks, I will be keeping the ledger for a couple of days."

"The boss will not be happy about that." The guard said.

"Then get him to call me." Jay Ramasey said.

He gave the guard his card and left the offices. He returned to his office and captain Els said.

"Jay you got a message from the clerk of the court, he says the information that you want is now available. What is this all about?"

Jay passed him the DNA results and watched the captain carefully. His response was astonishment, followed by disbelief.

"Are you trying to tell me that you suspect attorney Annette Venter is the assassin? Have you seen her, man?"

"I am checking out her movements on the days that the assassinations took place. If we can exclude her, then we know the hair was not a clue and can be discarded. Yet she is the right size and the hair is obviously hers." Jay Ramasey said.

"You cannot be serious, just look at her photo. She could hardly carry a rifle, let alone fire one. The assassin is a precision shot, and where would she have learnt how to shoot like that?" Els asked.

"I am not saying that she is the assassin. All that I am saying is that a strand of her hair was found at the scene. This is the only real lead that we have, and we must follow it up."

"Jay, get real. The probability of her being the assassin is remote. Do what you have to if you believe that it is necessary, but don't waste too much time."

Jay went back to his desk and called the clerk of the court. They talked briefly, and the information would be sent by fax to his office. Jay went to the fax machine and waited for the sheets, which came through almost immediately.

He took them back to his desk and then checked the dates of all the assassinations against her court appearances. On the dates in question, she was not in court. This did not prove her guilt, but neither did it prove her innocence. He would have to get a court order for her office diaries to be impounded. This would mean going to the commander who would also likely be doubtful that she was an assassin.

"Captain, I need a court order to impound Venter's diaries. We need to go to the commander immediately before tongues start wagging." Jay Ramasey said.

"Jay, you know what a stir that will make, and your evidence is meagre, to say the least. This is an attorney for Gods sake. The commander will not take chances without meaningful evidence. You will be wasting your time."

"We need to try."

"If you insist, but he will give you a hard time for certain."

They both went to the commander's office and asked to see him. His secretary went into the office and said.

"Commander, Captain Els and Sergeant Ramasey wish to see you."

The commander's heart missed a beat then he said.

"Send them in then."

Captain Els and sergeant Ramasey filed into the office and stood in front of the commander's desk.

Commander Pieter Verkramp looked at both men and said.

"Sit down and tell me what is so important that you need to disturb me."

"Jay thinks that we have a lead on the assassin." Captain Els said.

"Oh really, then enlighten me, sergeant." Commander Verkramp said.

Sergeant Jay Ramasey went through the investigation of Annette Venter and why it was conceivable that she could be the assassin. He then asked for a court order for the impounding of her office diaries.

"Do you agree with Ramasey?" Commander Verkramp asked captain Els.

"No sir I do not."

"Tell me why."

"The evidence is not conclusive. To link an attorney of her standing to the assassin is just not credible. The only evidence is the hair on the clothes in the bin. That, in its self, is not sufficient evidence to raid the offices of Venter and Marriot." Captain Els said.

"I agree." The commander said.

"Commander, finding the hair is extremely significant. According to the office ledger, kept by the security guards, there were no recorded visits for attorney Venter either that day or any day prior to the event. The cleaners that operate in that building clean out the rubbish bags every evening when the staff has left. The hair could only have been dropped in the bin on that particular day." Jay Ramasey said.

"Every visitor to the building is recorded?" The commander asked.

"Not always. Sometimes visiting attorneys do not wish to be seen in consultation if they are trying to strike a deal on a case." Jay Ramasey said.

"Then you cannot in all honesty say that she was not there on business." The commander said.

"Not without the diaries." Jay said.

"Do you really expect me to pitch up at a senior law firm and ask them for their diaries on the evidence that I have at hand?" The commander asked.

"Yes sir." Jay said.

"Then you are mistaken. I will not embarrass the police force with this nonsense. I suggest that you move on and put more effort into finding the real assassin. Your hypothesis is outrageous. You may leave and do not bother me again until you have real evidence." The commander dismissed them.

They left the commanders office in silence and returned to their office.

"I bloody well told you so Jay. He would never buy that story."

"I will keep looking." Jay replied.

The commander left his office and went to the first public phone he could find. He called his controller, gave his call sign, and said.

"It would appear that the officers investigating the assassinations have put an identity together. I don't believe it, but I should warn you they are investigating an attorney, Annette Venter."

"OK. Call me back in one hour using the phone number thirty four." The voice replied.

The controller relayed the message to captain Brooks who informed General Lauberschagne.

"Get her picked up and under cover in a safe house. She must stay at the house until further notice." He ordered.

Chapter 44

The British Consul, Sir Gordon Parsons, was due to meet the President of South Africa at eleven thirty at the Union Buildings in Pretoria. There had already been a long consultation with the Foreign Minister on the events in South Africa, and the strategy proposed to resolve the intended coup without bloodshed.

Sir Gordon Parsons had agreed with the strategy and was about to present the first part to the President. He had to convince the President to take consultation with the British Government on what action to take. This would be no easy task.

He was ushered into the president's office, and the president got up from his seat to move towards him. They met in the middle of the office and shook hands.

"Mr. President, it was good of you to see me at such short notice. I know that you are a busy man." Sir Gordon said.

"How can I help you, Sir Gordon?" The President asked.

"I have come to help you." Sir Gordon said.

"How so?" asked the President, guiding Sir Gordon to the table and chairs in the corner of his office.

"We have detailed information of a planned coup that is about to take place in South Africa." Sir Gordon said.

The President laughed and said.

"We hear about these plans every day. There is always some right wing movement that believes that it could succeed. Yet we always stop them before anything serious happens."

"This time it is quite different and much more of a threat, I assure you." Sir Gordon said.

"Please explain why."

"We have infiltrated this group at the highest level and know their capabilities. If it was just some radical outfit, with insurrection in mind we would have told you immediately, and left it to you to sort them out. In this case, we believe that a coordinated action is needed to prevent any serious threat to your government." Sir Gordon said.

"If you are truly concerned, then give my government the information you have, and we will resolve our own problems." The President said.

"The difficulty with that is that we have used some of our assets to infiltrate these groups, and you would not know who they are, and you would put them in danger. We believe with the help of these assets we can prevent any coup. We still need to preserve their cover." Sir Gordon said.

"You are telling me that your spies are operating under cover, in South Africa, and that I should use your assets that are illegally deployed, to prevent a coup in my own country?"

"Yes I am." Sir Gordon said.

"You British have never lost your arrogance. What makes you assume that we do not know of these groups that are planning a coup?" The President asked.

"We believe that you do know some of the people concerned, but not the extent of the conspiracy. If the situation is not handled efficiently, and, with due care, you may well precipitate the action, that we all want to avoid." Sir Gordon said.

"Then what are you proposing, Sir Gordon?"

"I propose to bring in the head of MI6, Gordon Banning, and let him liaise with your cabinet and intelligence agencies to mop up the main players and disrupt their communications."

The President gave Sir Gordon a long hard look, and asked.

"How long has this been going on for?"

"Our assets infiltrated the key groups the moment it came to light that a coup was planned. That was nine months ago."

"You have kept quiet all this time, and now you want me to trust you in your offer of help. Why did you not come to us at the beginning with the information?"

"That is because we did not know the extent of the conspiracy and wanted to come to you and your government with all the facts. Otherwise, we may have just driven the insurgents underground before we knew all their identities." Sir Gordon said.

"Alright, I will arrange a meeting with our intelligence agency and the cabinet. We will listen to your proposals and then decide on our course of action." The president said emphasising the word "our".

"That would be fine." Sir Gordon said.

"I will arrange a meeting at two-o-clock and would you please have your representatives here by then." The President said.

"We will be there." Sir Gordon said.

The meeting was held in the cabinet room of the Union Buildings. The representatives of the British Government and MI6 were sat at the end of the large boardroom table.

"Sir Gordon, I have briefed my cabinet, and they are eager to hear your proposals. Before you start, I will also advise you that our own head of intelligence is here. He has advised me that they know much of what you are suggesting, and does not entirely agree, with your assessment. We have our own assets deployed, and they are not reporting the perpetrators of this so called coup, to be as extensive as you believe." The president said. "He believes that this matter can easily be handled in house without your assistance."

"That is your decision Mr. President. We are offering to help, but should you not want our assistance, we will remove our assets to safety and allow you to take your own course of action." Sir Gordon said.

"I suggest that you provide us all your information and we will take it from there." The President said.

"I am afraid we cannot do that as I would be exposing our people in the process. We can remove our assets in the next twenty four hours should you not require our assistance." Sir Gordon said.

"Mr. President." Gordon Banning said. "We are not suggesting that your government and security services are not capable of handling this situation. We are merely saying that together we would solve this problem quickly and efficiently."

"Thank you Mr. Banning, but we believe that another country being involved in our internal affairs is out of the question. It is actually interference." The President said.

"Then why did you agree to the meeting?" Sir Gordon asked.

"We wish to include your intelligence with our own such that we can plan a way forward. When I say we, I mean, the South African Government." The president said.

"Then I am afraid that we cannot help you. We cannot put our own people at risk as I have already pointed out." Sir Gordon said.

The meeting was at an impasse, with neither side wishing to relent. The debate around the disclosure of information went on for more than one hour. Each time that they came close to a resolution, a cabinet member, would object to a course of action. They eventually decided to take a twenty-minute break and then reconvene.

The British contingent adjourned to one room whilst the South African Government adjourned to another. They drank tea or coffee while they waited for the resumption of the meeting.

They resumed after their break, and the President said.

"Sir Gordon, we need your information, but the stumbling block is your need to be involved thereafter. If we can solve that problem, we can move forward."

"We need to be involved as you do not know the extent of the conspiracy. If you were to arrest ten percent of the conspirators, then you would precipitate the coup. This is a well-organised group of people. They extend to all levels of society and are more than capable of pulling off this coup even with ten percent of their leaders missing. You would be walking straight into a trap. They would use the arrests as propaganda and even more people would join them." Sir Gordon said.

"Let me put on record that the South African Government is thoroughly disgusted with the British Governments duplicity in this matter." The President said.

"Your objection is noted Mr. President and will be communicated to my Government. That still does not solve the problem." Sir Gordon said.

"Then how do you propose to assist?" The president asked.

"If we have agreement that we are to be involved then we can move forward. Do we have an agreement?" Sir Gordon asked.

The President looked around his cabinet and asked.

"Do we have an agreement?"

They all nodded assent.

"We have an agreement." The President said.

"Then I suggest that we leave the detail to Mr. Banning, and we will call in colonel Masters of our Special Forces to meet with your intelligence and local forces. I would suggest that this discussion is only performed with the most trusted of your colleagues as this conspiracy runs very deep into your armed forces and political partners."

"I agree, Sir Gordon. We will have daily meetings in the cabinet room to discuss progress and ensure cooperation at all levels. We thank you for bringing this to our attention." The President said.

Chapter 45

It was a sunny day with the prospect of rain later. Angela looked across at Don resting by the pool. He was relaxed, but the scar across his chest was still evident. They had been lucky; they had survived and were now contemplating their future.

They had been interrogated for days, and without the British Government intervention, God knows what would have happened. Don was released before Angela but refused to leave until she was also free. The press were sniffing an extraordinary story, but they would learn nothing.

The British Consulate had placed them in the safe house prior to them being flown out to England. It was no longer safe for them in South Africa. That they had fallen in love with each other was more than obvious. They were confident they would be happy in their new life together.

She looked across at Don and felt her arousal. She blushed at her thoughts. Good God, she thought, the seasoned journalist blushing at dirty thoughts, who would have believed it.

"Don," she said, "Do you fancy some hanky panky?"

Don looked up and smiled.

"Are you trying to put me back in hospital?"

"I suppose if you are not man enough I will have to go without."

Don leaped from the chair and swiftly moved across to her. He scooped her up in his arms and headed for the bedroom. They were stopped in their tracks by the television and the news being presented.

It was reported today, that a plane crashed in the Northern Province. The plane was a military personnel carrier and all the occupants were killed. General Lauberschagne, General Naude and three other senior officers were killed in the crash. The government is investigating why five senior staff where flying on the same plane.

In other news Petrus Khumalo has been appointed as the liaison officer for the new party of Natal. This new party has taken over from the old NFP and believes it will take a stronger presence in Natal and will make the ANC difficulties at the next election."

They looked at each other, and Don said.

"It has started; I knew the cleanout would come but not so quickly. There must be a lot of worried people out there."

They had both lost their appetites for sex, and they sat on the settee. They both were glued to the television as the anchorman went through Petrus Khumalo's recent rise to prominence and his background in the armed forces. Khumalo smiled back at the camera and looked the consummate politician.

Don laughed, and said.

"If only they knew what we know. Good luck to the man, he is a good man and with him around there may well be hope for their new party."

"He saved our lives and nearly lost his own. I agree he will do well. We must keep in touch with him as I believe he has a lot of potential."

"Once a journalist, always a journalist, you guys are a breed apart."

She smiled provocatively and raised her breasts and said.

"Talking about breeding; where were we headed for?"

"You, my girl, are utterly impossible. You are wanton, brazen, but I love you so much it is actually painful."

"I think I know how to relieve the pain," she said laughing.

"There you go again, is that all you think about?"

"When I am around you, yes!"

Yet before, they could indulge themselves the news again interrupted their intimacy:

The final story of the news today concerns a repeat of an interview that was held with P.W. Botha, the past President of South Africa. He talked at length of the folly of the ANC and the aggrieved Afrikaners. He said that they would not tolerate the ANC interfering with their history and their culture. He concluded with finality.

"Beware the sleeping Tiger."

The End.

Lightning Source UK Ltd.
Milton Keynes UK
178021UK00002B/34/P